ARK BABY

ARK BABY

LIZ JENSEN

THE OVERLOOK PRESS
WOODSTOCK & NEW YORK

First published in the United States in 1998 by
The Overlook Press, Peter Mayer Publishers, Inc.
Lewis Hollow Road
Woodstock, New York 12498

Library of Congress Cataloging-in-Publications Data

Jensen , Liz.
Ark baby/Liz Jensen.
p. cm.
I. Title.
PS3560. E592A85 1998 98-14740
813'.54—DC21   CIP

Manufactured in the United States of America

ISBN 0-87951-833-2

1 3 5 7 9 8 6 4 2

FOR MICHEL

Natural selection is daily and hourly scrutinising, throughout the world, every variation, even the slightest; rejecting that which is bad, preserving and adding up all that is good . . . we see nothing of these slow changes in progress, until the hand of time has marked the long lapse of ages, and then so imperfect is our view into long lost geological ages, that we only see that forms of life are now different from what they once were.

Charles Darwin, *Origin of Species*, 1859

Forgive, O Lord, my little jokes on Thee,
And I'll forgive Thy great big one on me.

'Forgive, O Lord', Robert Frost, 1962

PROLOGUE

In the beginning, the ocean. Huge. Ink-dark beneath a black sky. The sunlight chinking through: bright, dangerous. Beneath the bunching clouds, rain slashes the waves, walls of glass that crash in brutal shards against the *Ark's* hull. The vessel is a speck on the face of the deep. A toy of wood and string.

The air rumbles.

Inside his padded leather cabin in the *Ark*, the Human awakes lurching in the gathering storm. Flings out an arm, grasps the hip-flask, glugs at blood-red claret. Then splutters and curses. His language: the Queen's English.

'Buggeration.'

Something's wrong below deck. The Human can sense it. Listen: from deep in the sarcophagus of the *Ark*, come screeches, yowls, grunts; whistles, growls, barks; snarls, baying, primal hoots. The Human fumbles in his breast pocket and peers at his greasy fob-watch. It's four o'clock. This racket is the usual feral cacophony of feeding time – but the beasts have already devoured their hay and slop. And Higgins, Steed and Bowker administered them their phials of laudanum an hour ago. The creatures should be comatose, drugged into quiet. They've slept through storms before.

Yes: something is awry.

Sniffing the air, the Human begins to sense the creatures' panic. He can smell their fear, too. And then, suddenly, his own, prickling from his armpits into his ruffed shirt.

He mutters a word to himself. The word is 'mutiny'. As if

1

he has been waiting for this moment. As if he has known it would come.

A sudden wave jolts the ship, and the Human's hip-flask falls to the floor with a tinny clang, bounces and skids under the bunk.

The Human jangles the alarm bell for Higgins and the crew. The men know the drill. As the clomp of running feet fills the gangways, the Human notices how the animals' smell has changed. Mingling with the odour of his own sudden fear, it permeates the whole vessel, insinuating its way through cracks in the wood and snaking into his nostrils. It is sweet and violent. Urgent and metallic. Fresh blood.

The noises from below grow louder and more ominous. Baying, growling, yapping, squawking. And the shrill scream of a woman.

The Human pulls on his thigh-high boots. Reaches for a metal-and-glass syringe. Charges it carefully with praxin. Screws on a sturdy needle. Sways to his feet. And descends with a clatter to the hull.

As insurrection explodes below deck, outside, the storm breaks with a murderous thud.

A month later, when the Travelling Fair of Danger and Delight was encamped in Riverside Fields, the Frozen Woman arrived at the Greenwich Workhouse with her cloak turned to ice, a rigid tent. Beneath it, the skirt of her ballerina's tutu stuck out horizontally from her hips. It was 5 December 1844 and the air was so cold that ravens were dropping dead from the trees like wasted fruit, thwopping into the snowdrifts in tiny, efficient acts of self-burial. She was a little stick of a woman, an icicle herself.

'Where have you come from?' asked Sister Benedicta, aghast.

'The ocean. I swam. Then got caught in a fishing net. The others drowned,' she croaked.

That was all she could say. Her tutu had to be cracked off her. The nuns plonked her naked in a metal tub of lukewarm water, averting their eyes. But Sister Benedicta could not help taking a peek.

'Call the midwife, somebody,' she gasped, as the peek became a wide-eyed stare. 'She's in the advanced stages of a delicate condition!'

'She opened and closed like a pair of nutcrackers,' the midwife reported afterwards. 'It just wasn't natural,' she added, expressing her astonishment at the Frozen Woman's pelvic control – due in part to her double-jointedness – and the unusual ease of the birth. She'd just squatted down and out he came. As if to echo her anxiety, a sickly wail and a stream of vomit emerged from the baby's mouth.

Word soon spread through the Workhouse that the Frozen Woman's offspring was the child of the Devil. Inspecting the newborn infant, and consulting his Bible, the Principal, a man of girth and gravitas, made the same assessment. Ponderously informing the new mother that he ran a Christian establishment, he then had two man-servants throw her out into the winter night. What the Frozen Woman called over her shoulder to the Principal as she left came as further proof, they all agreed, of her Satanic connections.

'See you in Hell, you fat bastard!' she yelled, as she picked her way through the snow towards the twinkling lights of the Travelling Fair of Danger and Delight, the swaddled baby stuffed under her arm askew like a parcel. She was wearing only the torn remains of her tutu, and a pair of thin ballet shoes on her small feet.

The next day the Travelling Fair of Danger and Delight decamped and headed north.

The Frozen Woman was not seen in Greenwich again.

CHAPTER 1

2005: IN WHICH A ROGUE MALE ESCAPES FROM THE HERD

Boundless hope; that was what flooded my heart as I pressed my foot on the accelerator of my spanking new car, and headed north towards my spanking new life.

Boundless hope, and the bright motorway up ahead. I slipped in a CD and flooded the car with Elvis: 'Blue Suede Shoes'. I sang along. A few pints inside me, and I'll do you a good impression of the King.

> *Ah you c'n burnah mah hous-ah, stealah mah car,*
> *Drinkah mah wiskha fromman ol froojar . . .*

He died the day I was born. 16 August 1977. Like a phoenix, he was just waiting for me to come along, I reckon. Knowing he could hand over. But unfortunately I'm not much of a singer, which is why I'm a vet.

Snakes shed their skin at least once a year. You find their faded, papery husks caught on bracken, gorse, or heather long after the creature inside has slipped away. I'd sloughed off my old Vauxhall at the Motormart and emerged in a sleek little Audi Nuance. A bit of whoosh, a bit of poke. That's me sorted.

On the map, Thunder Spit just looked like a scramble of broken veins two centimetres above Hunchburgh, but driving out of London I was already building up a clear mental image of my destination, based on nostalgic memories of camping holidays on the seashore in the 1980s: glorious summers of seagulls pecking at ice-cream cones, we boys ritually burying Dad in sand and fag-ends while Mum sat cooped in the tent, drinking thermosed vodka and listening to the Weather; the smell of chicken nuggets, sun-cream, popcorn, piss. Who said there was no such thing as society?

How was I to know, as the North Circular receded in my driving mirror, and the M1 hove into view, that my future was about to be hijacked by someone else's past?

> *But uh-uh, honey, lay off of my shoes, er don't you,*
> *Ah steppon mah blue suede shoezah . . .*

And how could anyone have predicted, as I slid back the sun-roof and inhaled the smell of freedom, that the Victorian legacy unearthed in the attic of the Old Parsonage would change the course of human evolution?

> *You c'n doanythin-ah-ba-lay offamah blue suedah . . .*

And how could –

No. Switch off Elvis. *Begin at the beginning, go on until you come to the end, and then stop.*

All right then.

The beginning wasn't actually the day I revved up the car, but the previous month, when Giselle, the catalyst for my upheaval, arrived in my surgery for her appointment with death. What's that saying, 'Never work with animals or children'? I did both.

It was only October, but the sun was sinking earlier every day over Tooting Bec, and Christmas had already muzaked its way into the shops. Giselle was one of my afternoon clients; a moody-looking, low-slung macaque monkey. She was wearing a pink dress, with the obligatory nappy beneath, and was clasping the hand of a bloke in a cable-knit sweater. It's something of a commonplace in the veterinary profession that the owners

5

resemble the pets and vice versa, so Mr Mann's appearance was a surprise. That he was male, for starters; since the Fertility Crisis, primate owners were 92 per cent female, according to *Pets Today*, to which my surgery was a reluctant subscriber. Plus there was nothing low-slung about him at all; on the contrary, he was quite high-stepping and angular. More of a dog type, I'd have said: red setter, bordering on the whippet. He probably owned one once upon a time, back in the old days.

The monkey was sucking her thumb.

In the last couple of years, since the National Egg Bank closed its waiting list to women over thirty, I'd been seeing ten or twelve macaques a week. Plus chimps, spider monkeys, orang-utans, even the occasional gibbon or baboon; the usual specimens that doting pseudo-mums brought in, freshly shampooed, complaining of bowel blockage and needing a psychiatrist. The real fanatics would shave them, and openly breast-feed in the waiting-room. It made my flesh crawl.

Sure enough, it quickly emerged that Giselle wasn't Mr Mann's at all, but belonged to his wife, who was away on a business trip. When I inspected the monkey, I remembered the wife clearly: brawny but petite, fanatical-looking, clumpy heels. That figured.

'No need to examine her,' Mr Mann announced bluntly, lifting the macaque on to my op table. 'I want her put down.'

Giselle's hairy legs, poking out absurdly from her pink dress, dangled over the side, and she swung her feet experimentally. She was wearing ankle socks and a pair of the expensive elasticated trainers that were all the rage in primate fashion.

'Humanely,' Mr Mann added, as though it were an afterthought. As though there might be a messy, non-humane option, involving torture, and available for a lower fee.

As I went to the cupboard and selected the usual carbo-glycerate of praxin concoction, I wondered idly what his reasons were. She was a good specimen; probably about three or four years old. The Fertility Crisis dated back to the Millennium, so none was over five. When I turned back with the loaded syringe, I saw that Giselle had now swung her feet back up on to the table, and rucked her dress up to expose her muscular tummy, which she was grooming busily. So much for instinct, I thought.

Holly was standing by with the paper towels and the self-sealing incinerator bag, trying to stop the tears. She liked animals. Primates especially. She was a temp.

'Nope,' said Mann. 'No particular reason. Just, as I said, the wife's away.'

'You mean, if she were here you wouldn't be asking me to do this?'

'Got it in one, mate.' He stood there, expecting me to join in the joke. He was smirking, as though betrayal were a clever new idea that he'd developed and patented, and he was just waiting for the dividends. He began to stroke Giselle clumsily on the head, and she paused from her grooming to look up at him with the surprise and gratitude that only females can muster in these situations. Then she handed him a flea.

'I can't do it,' I said. 'Not if you're not legally the owner. Did you bring the licence?'

I should have asked him all this before, of course. As her name suggests, Holly can be a bit prickly. She gulped a bit, and I noticed her eyes hardening up in the way they'd taken to doing when she reckoned 'human rights' were involved, but she kept quiet, thank Christ. I didn't want her thinking she had some kind of moral hold just because we'd crumpled her duvet together a few times. It had been a busy morning, and she knew it: there'd been a massive cat-fight in Sainsbury's car-park the previous night and I'd already seen to six of the injured and had to deal with their owners, too. The waiting-room reeked of cat-spray. A cockatoo, an innocent psittacosis booster case, passed out in shock when the squalling started, and I'd had a dud batch of spider-monkey flu vaccine, and bugger me if the surgery wasn't out of nitrate capsules. I put my head round the door; I was going to ask those with baskets to wait outside, but just then an obese, growling mastiff with testicular cysts

7

came in, which solved the caterwauling problem but gave rise to others, namely an IOU from the owner, and a pool of piss on the lino.

'Licence?' Mann was saying. 'Didn't know I had to bring it.'

'New regulations,' I told him. 'Since the Fertility Crisis.'

'Don't know where she keeps it.' He said this accusingly, as though I should have telepathically intercepted his thoughts and phoned to warn him about the paperwork before he left home.

'Primates, dogs and horses have licences,' I told him. There was a silence, during which he sucked in his cheeks and rocked to and fro on his heels a bit, so I elaborated. 'Cats, no.'

Mann then said pointlessly, 'Well, I don't have a cat. I've got a monkey, though.'

'So I see,' I said, and winked at Holly. Giselle, crouched docilely on the operating table, emitted an odour. Holly blushed.

'No,' Mann was saying. 'I mean I've got *another* monkey. *My* monkey. Used to belong to my sister but she –'

He stopped. He didn't need to say it. The post-*fin-de-siècle malaise*, they called it. No babies, no future. Did she do it dramatically, I wondered, from a cliff-top? Or quietly at home, with chemicals?

'We live in terrible times,' I said, shaking my head. I wasn't kidding; we did.

'Ritchie's a macaque, too,' Mann was saying. 'Not a pedigree, like Giselle here, but –'

I always practise faces in the mirror after I've brushed my teeth. So now I tried out quizzical on Mr Mann. Like I didn't know what he was getting at.

'Well, couldn't I just bring *his* licence, instead? Wouldn't that do?' He was asking me like a boy asking his teacher. 'They don't get on, see.' And now his tone was becoming dangerously confessional. 'Her and him. Giselle and Ritchie. They fight, see. Ever since my sister – well, ever since Ritchie's been living with us, he's been disturbed. Bereaved, like. And he tries having a go at Giselle here – mounting her, sortathing, wanting sex, like – but she don't want it. She's neutered, see. So she's like frigid.'

8

I remembered neutering her now. Mrs Mann had been insistent that Giselle had never been with a male, and that there was no risk of her already being impregnated.

'She's virgin territory, I assure you,' she'd said smugly.

But of course when I operated, I'd found twin foetuses clinging to her uterus. I always charged extra for that.

'Ritchie's just a frisky lad,' Mann was pleading. 'What he needs is a playmate, not some stuck-up little thing that's always going to spurn him.'

There was a desperate look in his doggy eyes: he needed a chocolate drop, a pat on the head, a rubber bone to chew on, a stamp of approval for the churning cauldron of petty emotions that functioned as his intellect.

I remembered Mrs Mann's expression when she'd come to collect Giselle after the operation; the delicate little jaw set firm, the victorious smile nudging at her mouth as she wrote the cheque. I told her about the foetuses.

'Not such virgin territory after all, you see,' I'd said. 'Your Giselle here isn't as innocent as she looks.'

Mrs Mann adjusted her face.

'Well, I came to you in the nick of time, then,' she said finally, with a brisk smile. It struck me, her decisiveness, the cool way she took it. (The way the mastiff man had behaved over the cysts this morning, it was like his own bollock I was planning to cut open.)

'She's too young to be a mother,' she'd added brightly. I'd heard that one before. It was a fairly standard remark, uttered by women who bought themselves a baby-substitute, then got jealous when little Miss Primate became a teenager and got knocked up. 'Giselle couldn't possibly cope,' she said. 'She comes from a very sensitive pedigree, you know.'

I remember snorting, and exchanging a glance with Holly. Someone out there – probably the same bloke who designed the elasticated trainers – was whacking up a fortune with this pedigree scam. But there was no point telling Mrs Mann that the monkey family-tree business was a load of shite;

she had that appalling look of conviction on her face that people have when they've been nourished from birth on pure gibberish.

Mr Mann was still looking at me expectantly. So was Giselle. 'Well? Will you do it?'

I didn't reply. I pretended I hadn't heard.

'I'll pay you an extra five hundred Euros.'

Holly looked at me.

'Cash,' he said, interpreting my lack of response correctly. There was no shame in his voice, and no shame in mine when I answered.

'A thousand, and I'll do it.' It seemed a risk worth taking. 'But mind you find that licence and destroy it as soon as you get home. I won't be answerable.'

I shook the clammy hand he offered me, and he gave me the Euros then and there. Giselle watched as he counted it out; she mimicked his hand movements, and moved her lips like he did, as though she were counting it, too.

It was all there.

'Right, Giselle, I'd like you to roll up your sleeve now for me, will you, darling?' I murmured. She complied obediently.

Mann turned his face away while I found the vein on her hairy little arm. It was his right, I suppose. After all, he'd just paid me a thousand yo-yos not to do the honours himself. Holly turned away, too.

Giselle didn't. She watched closely, interested in the procedure.

'See?' I said, squeezing the syringe. 'It doesn't hurt. Night-night, then, baby.'

She nodded, as though she understood the transaction. She even flashed me a toothy smile. Then went out like a light, the little pink frock crumpling beneath her as she sagged, then horizontalised. Her tail twitched briefly, then hung limp.

Mann made a choking noise.

'Too late for regrets, mate,' I told him. His face had faded to a chalky white. He mumbled something I couldn't make out, then

10

stumbled out of the surgery faster than you could say verbal contract.

Afterwards, Holly bagged up the stiffening but still-warm Giselle, and said she was handing in her notice.

'What you did was wrong,' she snivelled, 'destroying that lovely little girl, and the guy wasn't even the legal owner. What'll you do when she comes in? The wife?'

I was annoyed. Holly didn't normally question me. But she was new, I had to keep reminding myself.

'Look, she wasn't a *girl*,' I said, nudging at the body-bag. 'She was a sodding macaque monkey.'

This stuff was old, old hat to me. I explained to Holly how, having been in the veterinary business now for ten years, five of them since the Fertility Crisis and the quadrupling of domestic animal ownership that it had engendered, I was used to the charade-playing of pet-keepers.

'The psychology of pet-ownership has undergone a sea-change, since the Fertility Crisis,' I told her, quoting verbatim from an editorial I'd skimmed in *Pets Today*. Holly nodded impatiently; she'd clearly read the same article. 'Certain animals have almost literally become children to certain people. Especially the primates.'

Anyone could have told you that.

'Mr Mann was defending his nephew-substitute against his stepdaughter-substitute,' I analysed for her. 'He's following his own human instinct to protect the nearest he's got to his own genes. His sister's offspring, or offspring substitute, is closer to him, genetically speaking, than his wife's child-substitute that she bought before they met. It's all imaginary, so it's bollocks, but it means a lot to their subconsciouses.'

'OK, Mr Super-Intelligent Psychologist,' goaded Holly, still upset. 'But how's Mrs Mann – or should I say her *subconscious* – going to react?'

I outlined the forthcoming scenario to her simply: how in the next few days Mrs Mann would come in on a weekday morning surgery with her husband's dead sister's monkey, Ritchie, to exact revenge. How she would instruct me to destroy him, and probably offer me some extra money to forget about the licence. How she'd of course be bitter with me over the Giselle thing, but would have the sense to bite her tongue if she wanted Ritchie to join Giselle up there in Great Bananaland.

'And you'd murder Ritchie, too?' Holly spat out the histrionic word 'murder' with the unaccustomed venom of the recently innocent. 'You'd really do it?'

I took her by her plump little shoulders and kissed her very long and very hard, the way my temps always seemed to like it. Holly was a sweet thing. I found the puritanical taste of her toothpaste, combined with her naivety, arousing, and Sigmund stirred in my boxer shorts. It was the end of the day, and the last clients had shuffled out of the waiting-room. I was tempted to have Holly then and there, but she wrenched herself away. Her face was still half-angry, but half-admiring, too. I could see that she was as ready for sex as Sigmund and I were, but Ritchie and Giselle were preying on her mind.

'You'd really do it, wouldn't you?' she repeated. Her brain seemed to have stuck in a groove.

'There's no point in lying,' I said. A whopper in itself, of course. There's *always* a point. 'Yes, I would.' But honesty wasn't going to budge her. So I added, with sudden inspiration, 'Don't you see? I'm actually assisting in the mercy killing – the *euthanasia* – of something much bigger.'

That got her thinking.

'Like what?' she asked. She didn't get it, but she wanted to. 'Like what, exactly, Bobby?'

'Like a failing marriage, Holly,' I said. Sigmund was straining at the leash. 'Like a marriage in the throes of death.'

She understood then, because she didn't resist as I undressed her and laid her naked on the operating table. Very slowly, I parted her legs and began to lick between them. I felt the origami folds of her flesh thicken; she didn't move.

But I was wrong about Mrs Mann. I was wrong about Holly, too.

The phone rang in the kitchen at home the next morning. I'd just finished defrosting half a dozen sausages in the microwave, and was opening a tin of sliced mushrooms. I picked up the phone, still clasping the tin by the tin-opener, and holding three eggs in my other hand. Not a good idea, because what the woman said made me drop one of them.

'I'm lodging a formal complaint.' Splat, on the lino. I sat down heavily on a chair, and nursed the mushroom-tin in my lap.

'Who is this?' I asked, to buy a bit of time, though of course I knew. I remembered those hard little eyes of hers: what I'd taken for sexual repression was clearly something more dangerous. 'How did you get my private number?' I wondered about my pulse-rate. It was probably way up around the hundred-and-forty mark.

'From your assistant. Holly, isn't it? Lovely girl. You don't deserve her.'

'No,' I said. *Holly?* I felt my heart squeeze up and bang against my rib-cage, like a fist. 'I *don't* deserve her.'

'What you don't understand,' said Mrs Mann, 'is that Giselle –'

I knew what was coming. I was a killer. I had murdered her baby-substitute in cold blood.

'Giselle was a *person*,' she said. She'd been crying, I realised, and was now struggling to keep her voice level.

'Mrs Mann –' I began.

'Yes?'

'Mrs Mann, I –' (This could develop into something absurd, I realised. It was also, at the same time, quite serious. So now I'm going to put down my remaining eggs, and my tin of mushrooms, very gently, on the floor, and put into action that phrase women hate. Here goes.) '*I can explain.*'

'Go on, then,' she challenged. Her voice still had that deranged crack in it, a fault-line that could suddenly become a chasm. 'Explain.'

'Your husband told me –' I started. But she didn't play by the rules: she butted in.

'I know what happened. He paid you off. You're – you're just

13

a cheap contract killer! *A thousand Euros*? Is that all a child's life is worth to you, Mr Sullivan?'

She used the word 'child' without a trace of irony.

'Mrs Mann,' I said gently, thinking: Those yo-yos are going towards my spanking new Audi Nuance, missis, so don't knock it! And then I said her name again, even more gently. 'Mrs Mann. As far as I was concerned, it was a perfectly standard procedure. I put down at least five primates every working day.'

This was a wild exaggeration, I'll admit. It was one a month, max. As I spoke, I was beginning to wonder if I could tell her that Giselle had been terminally ill. That when I'd inspected her, I'd found inoperable bowel disorder, of the kind monkeys are prone to when they've been fed the wrong diet. That Holly, being a temp, had misunderstood. It might get me off the hook. She might even be grateful. But too late: Mrs Mann's crazed voice was veering up at me again.

'I'm going to fight you all the way,' she said.

Some instinct made me glance over at the doormat in the hallway. I peered at the single white rectangle that lay on it. The envelope was addressed to me in Holly's schoolgirly handwriting. That did it. I'd been caught in a pincer movement.

'Bugger off,' I told the Mann woman, and slammed down the phone.

Holly's letter was hand-delivered and brief. She was leaving 'for ethical reasons', and 'would not hesitate' to give evidence against me in an inquiry.

It was that phrase, 'would not hesitate' that pissed me off the most.

I lit the gas-ring and cleaned up the mess. As I stabbed away at the sausages sizzling gently in the frying pan, I thought about Giselle, and the excruciating Manns, and the silly Holly, and the statement that she would make on Mrs Mann's complaint form. It was generally true, I realised, that, apart from the fleeting exoticism of a sick tarantula or a truly challenging road-accident case like the paralysed collie whose hind legs I'd replaced with little wheels the previous year, my life had become a banal treadmill of feline vaccinations, mauled rabbits, cracked terrapin shells and primate psychiatry. But the Giselle incident was excitement of a kind I didn't need.

And then, watching the little flecks of sausage-fat hitting the tiling behind the hob, where they congealed opaquely, a sudden, simple and quite mind-blowingly compelling thought came to me. Primates were a metropolitan thing, largely.

So quit the jungle.

Leave them all behind. Holly, and the Manns, and the apes and the monkeys. I could let the surgery to some starry-eyed newcomer, and be gone within the week. A change of scene. Some outdoor stuff. Cows, sheep, geese; the kind of animals that paid their keep, and were brutish, messy and unappealing enough to keep human sentimentality at bay. A place with farms, by the sea. Slurry lagoons. The seaside. Burying Dad in sand and fag-ends. Pissing into the waves. The smell of popcorn. Sex on the beach. Crabs.

I felt light-hearted and light-headed. As I turned the sausages in the frying pan, I noticed that I had begun to whistle a tune: 'It's Now or Never'. Telling, that. And I hadn't whistled in weeks. Elation was whirling through me like a snort of ether. Then I prodded at the sausages. Yum, yum! My mouth waters just thinking about them. They were prime pork, flecked with dark-green spots of sage. I inhaled, and my heart soared. They smelt of freedom.

Boundless hope, and the bright motorway up ahead. As my car whooshed northwards to Thunder Spit, I was filled to giddiness with the knowledge that the future was mine.

CHAPTER 2

IN WHICH A MISTAKEN
PIGLET HOVERS NEAR
DEATH

They sed it wuz not POSSIBEL, the Frozen Woman wrote years later, with her splattery peacock quill. *But I PROOVD it WUZ, tho I never SETTE OUT to do so, as I hav no lernin of SYENSE, and at that TYME I had not herd of Mister DARWYNNE'S beleefs.*

The onion-skin parchment on which she laboriously penned her garbled testimony (in blood? In mud? In a hideous mixture of the two?) is now cracked and split with age, and the text itself is smeared with Parson Phelps' snotty tears, which were to flow and flow in the Sanatorium, before dissolving into the sudden, insane laughter of pure joy.

All I REKOGNYZED, she wrote, *wuz that I had ikkstreemlie BAD LUK in LUVVE.*

She could say *that* again.

It is perhaps necessary to state, at a time when fiction is rife, that the account of my life that I deliver here is punctiliously reported, and scrupulously faithful to both truth and fact. That stated, shall I begin?

Picture first Thunder Spit: a peninsula in the shape of a herring, its tail nailed to the mainland, head straining out to sea. A God-fearing, wave-slapped place, an outcrop of harsh winds and cowering, gnarled trees and shrubs that hug the land like devilish suckers. Follow the promontory: follow the line of the herring's back and find the dorsal fin, a beach of grey bleached sand and grey bleached rock. Look back across the

16

fish's belly, past the flat shimmer of the River Flid, and see the grey slate roofs of the town like a mesh of scales. Further west, see the Church of St Nicholas, a spike its skull. The smell of salt, and thyme, and rock, and seaweed, and rotting fish. Sea-water washing and sloshing at you from north and south. There are floods each year, when the tide spills too far.

Thunder Spit; this was home, the home I still wear inside me like an extra ventricle, pounding away: Thunder Spit; a village famed for its annual bare-handed Thistle-Pulling Contest, for which a special field is set aside; a village where men have always been raised to seek out discomfort, and to thrive on it, striving to maintain the rigorous hair-shirt mentality of their forefathers. My foster-father, a moon-faced, passionate man who encouraged this approach to hardship, always used to say, 'Coddle yourself, Tobias, and you slip away from God.' On Fridays, he would stuff marbles into his shoes: he believed in paying penance whether you owed it or not. But my foster-mother, who suffered from bunions, and who would have liked to coddle herself and slip away from God once in a while, perhaps into a little brushed cotton, made a rigid horizontal of her lips and said nothing. That was her way.

Thunder Spit, home of the herring gull, the kittiwake, the storm petrel, the guillemot, the Lord Chief Justice sheep, the Hildamore cow, the famous Thunder Spit tortoiseshell cat, a variety of dogs, and three hundred and twenty-three of God's human citizens.

Soon to be three hundred and twenty-four.

This is how the story goes: I heard it often enough. The white light, the piglet, the doctor, the infection, the gift-from-Heaven nonsense. The story changes, with the appearance of the umbilical cord, but that's for later. The happy part first: my famous arrival in the Year of Our Lord 1845, as recounted by the God-fearing gent who was to become my father, for better and for worse, and despite himself.

Parson Phelps was well aware – sometimes most painfully so – that miracles did not often come to Northumberland, much less

17

to Thunder Spit. Quasi-occult dabblings involving tea-leaves and chicken-droppings, accusations of witchcraft against Mrs Boggs' idiot cousin Joan, moral transgressions of the adulterous variety, calves with two heads, yes. But miracles, never, if he was honest with himself. (And when was he not?) The biggest excitement for months had been the Travelling Fair of Danger and Delight, which rolled out of Judlow yesterday, leaving the usual hot and silly mess of yearning in its wake. Parson Phelps had preached against it, as he did every year, and all the more fervently when he had heard that this year's exhibits included a Man-Eating Wart-hog, a Ten-Foot Woman, and a Latvian hermaphrodite with a fan of ostrich plumes poking out of its exposed anus. The Fair, with its spangle-maned horses and Mechanical Millipede and dizzying bravura, always left the villagers goggle-eyed and addle-brained. Last year, a Judlow lad, drunk on exotic decadence, had sailed away on a Chinese skiff, and was now living among the heathens of Xiang, doing fancy basketwork and *tai chi*. The Fair always gave rise to a desire among the young to cast off their scratchy hessian, to popinjay themselves in silk and taffeta, to escape and see the world. Even though, as the Parson repeatedly told them, bellowing from his honest and unadorned wooden pulpit until he grew hoarse, all of God's kingdom was before them, here beneath the vast flat open sky which is God's window, and the salt ocean which is the residue of his tears, water which is both cruel and angry and beautiful and full of the triumphant sardine, the Lord's own fish. Search no further than your own doorstep to find magic! It is already here, all about us, in God's creation!

Slosh, slosh, went the grey North Sea as the Parson hell-fired and brimstoned his message to the fisherfolk.

Oh yes? thought the young men, their hands sore from thistle-pulling and scraping out lobster pots. Is that a fact? mused the young women, wiping their bloodied hands on rough aprons after a hard morning's work, gutting fish and singing, cracked and tuneless, the rhythmic ballads of drudgery that were passed down from mother to daughter in these parts: 'Hey-a-Minnie,'

18

'Bobby Shafto', 'The Crab's Lament'. Their lives were hard and thankless. No wonder they craved fairgrounds. Who in their right mind would say no to a toffee apple?

It was the day after the Travelling Fair of Danger and Delight left Judlow that I arrived in the church.

'No coincidence,' went the village whisper.

St Nicholas is the patron saint of fishermen, which is what most Thunder Spitters were. The Cleggs with their rolling seaman's walk, the squint-eyed Lumpeys, the silent Peat-Hoves, the literal-minded Balls, the crabby Barks, the Morpitons with their tendency to exaggerate the size of every fish, the stubborn Tobashes: these were all net-heavers and lobster-pot-wielders down the generations, and proud to be so. The church that bears the saint's name is constructed of sea-flint, with a black slate roof. Its darkness makes it a perpetual silhouette, even in bright sunshine, when the slates become a sheet of mirror and God's home lurks beneath. Inside, as a rule, a somewhat gloomy darkness reigns within its thick stone walls, but today the rules are broken, for on this particular and momentous morning, as the Parson enters his cherished domain, he is suddenly aware of a cloud of glittering light, a ball of luminescence, an unaccustomed and dangerous brightness which comes whirling at him so hard that he feels his heart might be in spasm. In such a mischievous manner, he knows, does the great queller and provoker, God, sometimes see fit to manifest Himself.

It was this vision of white, Heavenly light, tinged with pink, he reported to his wife Mrs Phelps afterwards, that convinced him there was something special about me, even after I had bitten him and the whole episode had turned to vinegar.

At first he just saw the light (hallelujah!); then he saw the feathers. They gathered in a mighty white cloud, billowing in transcendental swirls, refracting the shafts of sunlight that came in through the wide-open door. Humbled by the glory, and afflicted by a weak left knee, Parson Phelps backed his be-cassocked rump cautiously into a pew and watched the feathers float down, recognising a message from God when he saw one.

As the import of what he was witnessing became embedded in his consciousness, the Parson, humbled and amazed, sank down from the pew to the lower level of the floor, where on his knees he now began to pray in a most fervent and passionate manner. And as he prayed, more feathers flew, and more and more and more, *like unto a whirlwind*, he thought, and although he knew that there was something miraculous going on, he now began to grow increasingly aware that there was also something plain odd, so he begged the Lord to forgive him for interrupting his own prayer, but might he just hurry over and inspect what kerfuffle was taking place in the vicinity of the altar? For he had begun to hear the strangest little grunts that came as though from a young swine.

And sure enough, through the flying feathers, the Parson could now make out something small and reddish-pink at the epicentre of the movement. Yes: a piglet, or perhaps a goat, attacking a goose-down pillow. So much for God-given messages. So much for miracles. He suddenly felt somewhat disappointed and not a little foolish for having wasted the Lord's time, not to mention his own, with a prayer of thanks, when there was nothing to be thankful for, and he would now be better employed, God help him, summoning Mrs Phelps for a dustpan and brush, and Farmer Harcourt to catch the piglet, left there no doubt by some naughty village boys, pleasure-seeking pranksters for whose idle hands the Devil had found work.

But now the feathers were flying more wildly, and the noises becoming more acute, like a furious squealing snowstorm doing battle with its own self.

Alarmed and dismayed, Parson Phelps resolved to catch the creature with his bare hands. He had seen Farmer Harcourt do it, with a sudden grabbing movement, plunging down, and bagging the beast for market. He could then throw it out, and let it trot away. No; that lacked a sense of charity towards its owner. Tether it, then, from the birch tree, until Farmer Harcourt came to fetch it. Or, more Christian still, incapacitate it by swaddling it in the altar-cloth, and carry it over to the farm himself. Yes;

this, surely, was the option the Lord was most likely to favour, containing as it did elements of consideration to both man and beast, not to mention a level of inconvenience to himself that would elicit a merry glow of innocent satisfaction later.

'So be it, young swine!' he boomed aloud. 'Parson Phelps is a-coming to get you!'

The piglet was still ripping at the pillow, so the Parson decided to take advantage of the creature's violent preoccupation to swipe downwards with both hands, the feathers flying. Choking on them, he managed to grab the beast. Its flesh was hot. Parson Phelps, blinded by feathers, spat and choked. He breathed a scatter of fuzz-fringed plumes in through his nose and sneezed explosively, the hot little animal wedged against his knee and still squirming in his hands.

'Ouch!' A sharp pain ripped its way up the Parson's leg. The creature had bitten him, suddenly and hard, on the shin. He dropped it and kicked at it; it landed on the devoured pillowcase with a noise that went *thwonk!*, and lay there twitching. And now the Parson felt a wetness on his cassock. He looked down, and saw blood.

Blood that came pouring from the piglet.

A piglet that was not a piglet.

It was, by God and by merciful Christ in Heaven, who gave His life for us that we may be saved, and by the Holy Ghost, and by the saints also, the following thing: a human baby, armed with a full set of sharp milk-teeth.

A miracle after all. (Have you guessed, gentle reader?)

It was Tobias Phelps!

Me!

That not-quite-nativity scene in the church is what I call the mistaken-piglet episode. Like the Morpiton family, from whom they had both individually descended five generations back, the Parson and his wife were prone to exaggeration, so how accurate their representation is, I cannot say, although I convey the spirit of their reports as faithfully as I am able, I do assure you.

21

Near death comes next.

This section of the story unfolds as follows: my bloody wound, consisting of a lacerated lower back, was so terrible that the Parson and his wife feared that by morning I would be dead. But being blessed by God (though in a later, more cynical version this changed to 'cursed by the Devil') I made it through the night, sweating furiously, and as hot as a cooking pot. Dr Baldicoot arrived in a cloud of seaweed pipe-smoke and inspected my wound, and took note of my other physical oddities, and shook his head, but he refrained from voicing his thoughts in front of the Parson, knowing they would be interpreted as a slap in God's almighty face. What Dr Baldicoot thought was that it would be kinder to let me die. Was this what God called fairness? Who, or what, could have been the cause of my ghastly mutilation? And what mother could have abandoned a baby with such an injury? In a cold church?

As I look back in time, I find that I harbour no resentment of the good Dr Baldicoot within my heart. He knew the odds were grievously stacked against my survival. I have since consulted Professor K.G. Hornblast's weighty tome, *The Rudiments of Spinal Injury*, which states categorically that a wound of this nature affecting the lower vertebrae means that the victim, in the rare event of his recovery from inevitable infection, will never walk straight. Not that my gait would ever have been normal in any case. There exists another weighty volume, *Congenital Abnormalities below the Knee*, which discusses, *inter alia*, deformities of the foot. Club feet, flat-footedness, the hereditary long toes of the egg-scavenging cliff-climbers of the Orkney Islands, et cetera. My flat feet, and the somewhat thumb-like big toe, emerging at a right-angle, which made them resemble nothing so much as a pair of squashed and rather hairy hands, fitted into several of these categories, though none exactly. But as J.M. Bellowes, its author, points out, 'The variations are as many and varied as *Homo sapiens* himself.' (So where does *that* leave us?)

Dr Baldicoot was a simple country doctor, with little room in his bulging bag of instruments for books, weighty or otherwise. So he puffed on his pipe, administered a large dose of morphine, and shook his head. Apart from the formalities of greeting and parting, he remained taciturn. As the room filled with Dr Baldicoot's noxious seaweed smoke, Parson Phelps' heart filled with anger. He had not read *The Rudiments of Spinal Injury* either, but he had read the thoughts that boiled beneath the doctor's silence. He diagnosed pessimism, born of lack of faith.

'I shall cure him myself,' he stormed, breaking Dr Baldicoot's pungent silence. It was a Friday, and the marbles were afflicting him.

Dr Baldicoot, in turn, had also divined the Parson's mind: arrogance, born of ignorance. He knocked his pipe out into the fireplace, bade my parents goodbye, and stepped out of the Parsonage into an east wind, which blew his cloak up into a great dark bubble. As the wind-buffeted doctor wobbled off into the night, Parson Phelps sat down heavily to take the weight off his bad knee at last, and took his wife's hand. He said, 'God has given us a chance.'

They were both forty-six. A baby at last. A foundling babe whose own mother has attacked it and thrown it from the nest like a vicious herring gull, thought the Parson, stroking my cheek, which was covered with a soft down of rust-red baby-hair. As he was fond of remarking, herring gulls can be the worst parents in the world, after humans. He resolved in that moment, he told me later, to be the best father a boy ever had, and Mrs Phelps made a similar vow concerning motherhood. This solemn promise undertaken, she made the sign of the cross with her blunt, practical finger, and took out her needle and thread, and a roll of hessian. I would be needing nappies.

Years later, when my foster-mother was delirious and dying, I discovered why she and Parson Phelps had no children of their own. It was due to a private incompetence of the Parson's male object and related accoutrements, dating back to a childhood incident. He had discovered a live snake – an adder – in his knickerbockers, and had been obliged to strangle it with his bare hands. The trauma had tragic consequences, for as he passed through adolescence and into adulthood, every time his object stirred, Parson Phelps saw the adder in his mind's eye and was forced, despite himself, to remember its strangulation – the effect of which was to quell whatever tentative excitement had occurred well before any occasion between himself and Mrs Phelps could be risen to.

'And that's a true fact, Tobias,' she breathed to me hoarsely on her deathbed. 'That killjoy creature had a lot to answer for, in our bedroom.'

Had they not been so desperate for a child, would they have taken me in? I cannot tell you, but they were good people, and until the moment of my father's great madness, they did not wish me ill.

But I digress.

Back, instead, to the thrust of my memoir, which has begun, in the traditional manner, with the story of my coming into the world, insofar as I am able to convey it. Yes, Ladies and Gentlemen, I was a foundling. But a fortunate one; Parson and Mrs Phelps took me into their home, the Parsonage, Thunder Spit, near Judlow, Northumbria, England. There was nothing to be done about my mis-shapen feet, so they applied clean bandages to the wound at the base of my spine and prayed for a week. My foster-father, like a champion player of the bagpipes, did not lack stamina when it came to communicating with the Lord. Together, my adoptive parents removed my bandages, applied seaweed and dandelion poultices that the Parson made with his own hands, sealed them with oatmeal mash, and prayed some more. Within six weeks, their prayers were answered. The skin began to heal over the wound, creating a bulbous and jaunty scar over the coccyx.

Now, on his knees, Parson Phelps forgave the adder its treachery and thanked the Lord: 'This is Thy mission for us, O mighty one, for we had given up hope, but now Thou hast sent us a baby, though I mistook it for a piglet, which as Thou canst imagine, is easily done when the creature is surrounded by cushion-feathers, to raise in Thine honour, Lord, and in Thy worship, here in Thunder Spit, home of St Nicholas's Church, and home also of three hundred and twenty-three, nay now three hundred and twenty-four, human souls. Not to mention beasts of the sea, such as the mackerel, and the octopus, and the whale, and last but by no means least, Lord, the sardine, Thine own fish. And the birds of the sky, among them the cormorant and the noble kittiwake and at the risk thereuntofore of losing the thread of my prayer, Lord, I, that is to say me and Mrs Phelps my dear wife, even though our marriage is not strictly speaking consummated in Thine eyes, on account of the ignoble adder incident, we thank Thee most profoundly for the unexpected but most welcome addition to our family. Praise be!'

So, Edward Phelps, thought Mrs Phelps. This foundling creature is the least you can give me, being such a dolt in bed. She said nothing, but merely smiled at her husband in that half-weak, half-heroic way she had, and sighed in queasy gratitude. Surely, any child is better than no child when one is nearing the change, she acknowledged, as she pursed her lips and changed my scratchy nappies. My stool didn't seem normal to her, appearing greenish and a smidgeon cowpatty; Mrs Phelps wasn't accustomed to children, but she was a willing servant of the Lord, and when she investigated the soilings more closely, she knew what needed to be done. She bundled me in a cloth so that I wouldn't wriggle, and gamely nestled my little thin-lipped mouth and squashed-up nose against her floppy dug, and let me suck. If ever there was a consummate example of the triumph of blind faith over human physiology and reason, it was this. For three days, nothing came, and Mrs Phelps' forty-six-year-old nipples were sore and cracked, despite the camomile cream she applied day and night. But then, suddenly, just as she was about to give up, another miracle: full-cream human milk sprang from her bosom and I began to gorge myself and thrive and grow a head of fiery red hair, thick and coarse as a donkey's. So my parents lurched down on their knees on the embroidered pew-cushion placed on the stone floor for just such spontaneous exultations, and praised the Lord, even after I had nearly bitten off my mother's nipple.

That's the story.

Like Jesus, and many other small boys whose parents dote on them, I grew up being told that I was 'a gift from Heaven'.

Later, this changed to 'a curse from Hell'.

What is a man, I wondered then, but a conglomeration of skin and skeleton, his giblets and his kidneys trapped inside? And what is this thing, his brain, but a mere giant overgrown walnut in a case of bone? What is his heart, but a mere organ?

As for his soul –

CHAPTER 3

CUISINE ZOOLOGIQUE

In London, it is a chill February. The year is still 1845, but it is a very different 1845 from the simple churning of Nature's seasons that constitutes the twelve-month in the tiny nowhere of Thunder Spit, where Tobias Phelps has just arrived. This is a metropolitan, sophisticated, and worldly 1845, an 1845 of monumental historic changes and fierce political and social debate, an 1845 of philanthropy and commerce, Empire and oysters, multiple petticoats, child chimney-sweeps, grocery deliveries and boiled breast of mutton with caper sauce. A bright, shining 1845, full of hope and grandeur, with not a little debauchery and grime at the edges, a year in which we are now crossing the capital in an imaginary Montgolfier balloon, gazing queasily down at the lumpy grey quilt of London spread below. There's St Paul's Cathedral, a great blackened dome, peeking out through the lurking cloud of chimney-smoke. And there's the Thames, twisted like a cobra with appendicitis, and Tower Bridge, and the Houses of Parliament, both fortressy and cake-like, and the great thrust of Big Ben.

Oi, can anyone steer this thing?

If so, float west now, and guide our craft over elegant Belgravia, and here pause a moment to admire the crescent curves of white-painted brick and the shiny black doors, the forbidding doorsteps and the potted boxwoods of the exclusive cul-de-sac called Madagascar Street. And hover here a moment, by the third-floor window of number fourteen, to observe a pair of two-legged mammals in their natural habitat, the home, a

27

nest that is also a den that is also a warren that is also a lair, a repository for food, a rearing site and a thinking parlour. What a strange creature is man! Strange, too, that unlike many mammals, the human animal has no particular mating season. All the luckier, then, that we have arrived here on what will turn out to be a momentous day.

Peer through the ground-floor window first and observe Dr Ivanhoe Scrapie, taxidermist, in his workshop, engaged in the complex process of stretching the skin of a Chilean bear over a plaster cast he has made of the carcass in the ridiculous, sentimental position chosen by the Queen. The creature is to stand upright, Victoria has commanded, with its paws together, as though at prayer. In keeping with all animals destined for her Royal Highness's Animal Kingdom Collection, its genitalia must be excised completely; as a double measure of prudery, the creature will also, later, be clad in custom-sewn breeches. Furthermore, as per usual, the Monarch has commanded Scrapie to endow the beast with eyes that are 'blue, a sort of eggshell blue, such as you gave our other royal mammals'. But, she had specified, 'somewhat larger than the normal for a bear of this kind, which should, we feel, be gazing Heaven-ward as though in holy contemplation'. The idea being to transform the bear into a sort of noble, brutish creature of piety, fit to join the growing ranks of beasts in her whimsical bestiary: a whole Arkful of stuffed and de-sexed mammals, absurdly clothed, and in the posture of religious maniacs. As though, Scrapie is fond of remarking, Buckingham Palace were not such a vessel itself.

'Buggeration and damnation,' he mutters now, through a mouthful of pins, then lifts one foot off the floor and raises a haunch, to facilitate the emission of a thunderous fart, which echoes through the workshop and out into the hall, as he bellows, 'To Her Majesty Queen Victoria, Royal Hippopotamus and bane of my life!'

Meanwhile upstairs in the drawing room, Mrs Charlotte Scrapie, wife, mother, and celebrated medium, has sprinkled lavender-water in an attempt to drown the stench of that noble medicine, laudanum, which fuels the engine of her psychic thoughts. Observe, through the chintz, this: that her daily dose has had its narcotic effect. That despite an unappetising luncheon, cooked by Mrs Jiggers, there is something aphrodisiac in the air. That suddenly Mrs Scrapie's husband, finally bored by the silence and wire and sawdust of his workshop and fed up with the increasingly ludicrous demands of the Monarch concerning her Animal Kingdom Collection, tired of the jars of camphor and the little trays of glass eyes and the rows of pegs and steel pins, and the sheaves of notes and the skins and the little rubber noses that are the tools of his trade, is ascending the stairs.

For there is only one thing to do when you are in this sort of mood, in Dr Scrapie's experience. Impose the needs of your reproductive organ upon your wife, Charlotte Scrapie, affectionately – and sometimes not so affectionately – known as the Laudanum Empress. Whether or not she is drugged.

And there is only one way to respond to such a mood on the part of Dr Scrapie, if you are his wife, and in a laudanum daze: succumb.

There is nothing shameful in a little voyeurism. So adjust your balloon until the basket is level with this sash window here, and peer through the curtains of the drawing room. And witness the following things: a *chaise-longue*, a tumbler of whisky, a glimpse of curved breast, and a stiffened male object. Catch sight of a whalebone corset being cast to the ground like the chrysalis of a metamorphosing grub. See what might or might not be two semi-clad human bodies groping for balance upon the *chaise-longue*. The windowpane having now – infuriatingly – steamed up, press your ear to the glass and hear instead a series of noises: a whispered cajoling, a languid rejection, a thick-voiced insistence, an acquiescent sigh, a jostle of petticoats, an unclipping of braces, a fumbling and a slapping, a grunting and panting, a squeaking and a moaning, an increasingly rapid rhythmic thudding, a lion's roar, a little moan, a big, heavy sigh.

A quiet couple of minutes. After which, the mission of his male object accomplished, Dr Ivanhoe Scrapie returns to his workshop, to do battle with a Highland stork, while his wife, surrounded by a cloud of psychic particles which shape and re-shape ghostly images of the Great Beyond, sinks back into the shadowy dreamland of her addiction.

Then, as your balloon floats upwards into the night, imagine, in the light of the full moon that is emerging through the London clouds, a period of hormonal risk beneath the Scrapie corsetry. A meeting of sperm and egg deep inside the Scrapie anatomy. A fertilisation within the confines of a Scrapie fallopian tube. And then –

Abracadabra! An embryo! An embryo which –

But no! Quick, let loose more hot air, I beg you, into your Montgolfier, and chuck out a sandbag! Let us leave the embryo Violet Scrapie there, going about her homunculoid business, and fly rapidly to London docks, where her future guru, the man who is to shape her – quite literally – into the majestic woman she will become – awaits us on board a ship named *HMS Beagle*.

A beagle, as we all know, is a breed of hunting dog. An odd name for a ship.

You'll need binoculars at this point. The docks are far, far below; night has given way to morning and the bevy of vessels crammed into the dockside is tinged with an orange glow – among them Captain FitzRoy's ten-gunned three-masted *Beagle*. She is berthed there next to the *Paradigm* (cargo: linen, peacock feathers, liquorice, candle-wax, nuts, bolts, and Brazil nuts). The *Beagle* is a serious, non-profit-making vessel, a vessel that, until several years ago, contained a small group of respectable scientists doing a difficult and painstaking job, but more recently, has housed only the melancholic captain and his brooding whims. Yes; all the scientists, Mr Darwin included, have long since departed to their personal residences and taken their bulky microscopes and notebooks with them. The heyday of the *Beagle* is past, and she has set sail only a few times since then, for survey work in the North Sea. Now, today, Captain

FitzRoy has wandered off, mad and alone, leaving only his crew on board. The sea was rough during their most recent trip, and the seamen are laid low from sickness, bad food and exhaustion. The *Beagle* has a mixed crew, mostly English, but with a few Spaniards. And a Belgian. Let the English and the Spaniards stew in their own juice: it's the Belgian who's our man. Land your balloon on the dockside, alight from the basket, and meet Monsieur Jacques-Yves Cabillaud, a seasickness-sufferer who this morning, having cooked breakfast porridge for twenty men and received no thanks for his pains, has thrown down his oat-choked ladle and declared, '*Ça suffit.*'

A proud man. An ambitious man. A man about to do a bunk. These are the facts that are known about Jacques-Yves Cabillaud's past:

1. That his father sent him to sea during the Belgian potato blight, forcing him to leave behind a sweetheart named Saskia whom he feared he would not see again. (He was right there; she married his cousin Gustave, a baker, whose croissants won prizes).

2. That the young Jacques-Yves became first a cabin-boy on a whaler in the North Sea, and then a cook on board a French merchant ship.

3. That in Cape Town, he answered an advertisement for a chef on a zoological research vessel, the *Beagle*, and was taken on.

4. That when the *Beagle* sailed all the way to the Galápagos and then to Tahiti, Cabillaud was both so seasick and so lovesick that he never even bothered to look out of a porthole.

5. That the only thing that relieved his physical and mental torment was the occasional request, from Mr Charles Darwin, to concoct recipes for the various exotic meats the scientist brought on board from his shore visits.

6. That this made a change from the usual seaweed-and-biscuit diet Cabillaud was forced to serve up, and once

31

the seas were calm, despite his melancholy state he became increasingly excited by the possibilities of what he termed '*Cuisine Zoologique*'. Emu, iguana, finch, snake – some of the ugliest and humblest of God's creatures, he realised, could, with the appropriate garnishes, be a culinary delight.

7. That this was a hypothesis that he went on to prove with great aplomb, to the delight of the not-yet-famous Mr Charles Darwin, who personally gave his compliments to the chef on several occasions.

8. That as a result of his experimentation, and the compliments he has received, Jacques-Yves Cabillaud discovered within his bosom the seed of a great ambition.

Now, finally, staring out at London docks, bereft of his beloved Darwin these six years, and left only with the crazed FitzRoy, he is grimly considering his future. Surely the knowledge he has gained of the skinning of lizards, the grilling of ostrich meat, the handling of rodent liver and the braising technique required for giant turtle cannot – *must not* – be wasted?

Certainement pas! With this in mind, he shoulders his knapsack and heads for the Zoological Gardens. So let us land our imaginary Montgolfier, tether it to this handily situated monkey-puzzle tree, don our walking shoes, and follow him on foot.

The city into which the absconding Cabillaud queasily stumbled from aboard the *Beagle* was a metropolis reeking of parsnips, cabbages, coffee-stalls, the putrefying flesh of poisoned rats, freshly cut flowers, rotten herrings, oysters, and smoke from charcoal burners. Down alleyways, in open sewers, excrement wound its way towards the Thames and thence to the sea, while in the sky, as ever, a thick pall of smoke hung low like a throttling blanket. God knows how Cabillaud managed to leave the *Beagle* unnoticed on his wobbly legs. Nor how this small, intrepid, stubble-jowled man came to stagger halfway across the capital, jostled by an unruly

March wind, and enter the elephant enclosure in the Zoological Gardens. And above all to remain there, unnoticed, for a week, nursing a fever and eating only swill, straw and mouse-droppings. Or how it was that the chief zoo-keeper, Mr Gardillie, rather than tipping him back on to the streets, took a perverse liking to him and, once Cabillaud had explained that his *Beagle* experience had accustomed him to wildlife, offered him a job shovelling elephant shit. Cabillaud, who took a long view of things and possessed a formidably stoical side, accepted the job with the humility required, retreated to the enclosure of Mona the elephant, bided his time, hatched his plans, and shovelled. And lo and behold! After three weeks of negotiating with elephant turds the size of the moon, the kind of opportunity he had been hoping for – as a first step on the glittering pathway of his dreams – arrived on a plate. On a plate, in the form of an irascible-looking man who one morning entered Mona's enclosure without so much as a by-your-leave, and set up a step-ladder.

The surly gentleman, who is none other than the bipedal mammal we spied earlier from the Montgolfier, mating with his drugged female in Madagascar Street, ignored the Belgian completely. But Cabillaud scrutinised the taxidermist closely. He had already heard much about Dr Ivanhoe Scrapie from the head keeper. Scrapie was one of several taxidermists who often came by the Zoological Gardens, like a vulture in search of carrion. News of Mona's stomach upset, which was keeping Cabillaud busy round the clock, must have spread to the museum, where Dr Scrapie was not only chief taxidermist, but in charge of Her Majesty's own personal bestiary of stuffed animals. Which the Monarch was anxious to enlarge in proportion to her growing Empire. Mr Gardillie had told Cabillaud about her proposed Animal Kingdom Collection, which would contain a stuffed example of every living creature in the world, clad in human clothes and depicting pious scenes. Impressive. And now, here, was the man who was by all accounts charged with stuffing the things; all fifteen thousand or so of them. No wonder he looked haggard and distracted. (The Animal Kingdom Project was indeed to blame, but only partly; there was also the fact that the Laudanum Empress was wearing her pregnancy badly, and even at this early stage, arising sixteen times a night to empty her bladder.) Cabillaud, his mind racing with possibilities, leaned on his giant shovel, and observed Scrapie with interest, as the tall thin man reached the pinnacle of the step-ladder, and raised a lamp to Mona's ear. She flapped it like a gigantic wing, irritated, and Scrapie wobbled precariously.

'Monsieur,' announced Cabillaud, who had by now decided upon his plan of attack. Scrapie slowly looked down, annoyed at the interruption. Then, realising the social stature of the man who had addressed him, he took out his magnifying glass and peered through it at the human insect on the floor.

'I sweep out elephant's piss, I clear away *merde* all day,' Cabillaud informed him by way of self-introduction. 'And all night, also, now, because ze creature is *malade*.'

Scrapie polished his magnifying glass on a hanky.

'Zis,' Cabillaud elaborated, indicating the shovel and the sloppy lagoon of *ca-ca* that Mona's breakfast had engendered, 'is not my natural position on ze ladder of nature, Monsieur.'

Scrapie, tottering on his own ladder, leaned forward to peer closer at the elephant-keeper. He could see nothing much: just a black-and-white blur, and some facial hair in close-up. Cabillaud continued, 'I am not slave of elephant creature, I am *artiste*. Give me to spend one day in your kitchen, Monsieur. I zen will show you what is in true fact *la gastronomie*.'

Mona, swinging her trunk, shifted silently and ominously on her umbrella-stand feet, and Scrapie, sensing danger, disengaged himself jerkily from the step-ladder and re-arranged himself on to the straw next to Cabillaud. This time he drew up close, applied the magnifying glass to Cabillaud's face and inspected the man again: he noted five days of stubble, a torn and infected ear-lobe from which an earring had clearly been forcibly ripped, a foul odour, and a huge brown eye, larger than a cow's. An overseas specimen, he concluded. Nothing rare. Probably

European in origin. Satisfied with his diagnosis of both species and genus, Dr Scrapie pocketed his magnifying glass.

'Well?' he said.

Cabillaud recognised an order when he heard one. His life-story, as relayed to the taxidermist, necessitated holding the shit-shovel between his knees, clamped as in a vice, so that the hands were free to gesticulate their accompaniment to the tale. Cabillaud described how he was destined for great culinary fame (a reaching on high of the right hand), but had mistakenly ended up on board the *Beagle* (here Scrapie pricked up his ears), a terrible vessel (a thwack of spittle aimed at the water-butt), full of Englishmen (a turning-down of the corners of the mouth), on which since leaving the Galápagos, apart from his experiments in *Cuisine Zoologique* (Scrapie looked puzzled; he had no French), all he had been required to cook was porridge, pickled herring, and seaweed (more phlegm). Dishes containing, sometimes, when the sea was rough – *Dieu me pardonne!* – his own seasick vomit.

'Seaweed soup, seaweed fishcakes, fried seaweed, mashed seaweed. I make seaweed *gratin* one time, because some cheese falls off another ship, I fish out, I make *gratin*, zey send it back, say no good. You English, you would take the choice to eat human *ordure* if it had lumps in it unchewable *suffisamment* to your taste of like.'

It was a challenge. Hands on hips. *Fini. Voilà.*

'I'll consider the matter,' said Scrapie, eyeing up Mona once more, and estimating her weight to be approximately two tons. As every taxidermist can tell you, it's not the stuffing so much as the skinning and the construction of the armature that are problematic in such cases. Not to mention the space constraint imposed by one's workshop. Scrapie's conclusion: Forget it, Your Majesty. She's overly gigantical; discussion over.

Mona shifts uneasily, as if telepathically interpreting Scrapie's train of thought, which is now moving on (she sighs a big windy sigh of relief) to the subject of the Monarch, who lurks permanently at the back of the taxidermist's brain like a constant nagging headache. Bloody woman! Scrapie is thinking. Bloody, bloody woman! Look at her, with her pink-splotched map of the world and her Animal Kingdom nonsense! Only a woman as rich and unhinged and as grandiose as she is would come up with such an idea. And only a man like Horace Trapp could have the audacity to persuade her that he could actually bring a thousand foreign species home intact, in a single vessel. A royal Ark! What hubris!

'Bloody woman!' says Scrapie aloud.

'*Comment?*'

'The Queen. I told her not to. I said it was a bad idea. More than bad. Noah did it, but that was in the Bible.'

'Ah,' murmurs Cabillaud, doing his best to look sympathetic, and wondering how he is to steer the conversation around towards his own goals. He is also preoccupied with a parallel train of thought: Would the acidic tang of a gooseberry *coulis* go well with the succulence of raccoon?

'Everyone knows that Trapp is nothing but a fool,' Scrapie is saying. 'A dangerous fool.' Blast him, thinks Scrapie, his exhausted brain churning with rage. The man has a whole history of entrepreneurial disaster behind him. Not to mention the slavery business. It was well known that the only reason he'd been forced to quit trading in humans was because a whole ship-load had died on him for want of food. Bloody hell! What possessed the Hippo to put her faith in such a man? What wild promises did he make her? (I must have some sleep. Sixteen times in a single night! And she had drunk no liquid!)

'A dangerous fool,' echoes Cabillaud, not having a clue what Scrapie has been mumbling so angrily about, but hoping to please. 'I too have heard zis same thing. Dangerous, and a little bit deranged also, zis man Tropp.'

'Trapp,' Scrapie corrects him wearily, patting Mona on the big leather wall of her thigh. 'Horace Trapp.'

'Yes,' rejoins Cabillaud with enthusiasm. 'That's iz name! Trapp! Complete madman! Complete *idiot!*'

Scrapie remains lost in thought. It is now two years since

Trapp and his entourage set sail for Africa, and needless to say, nothing has been heard since. Just as well, maybe, the taxidermist reflects. For it is he, Scrapie, who will be in charge of stuffing the creatures on their return. As if he doesn't have his hands full already. (The Laudanum Empress is no help to him. Pregnancy sends her into a nine-month trance, broken only by her nocturnal sorties to the Crapper.) Meanwhile, Horace Trapp appears to have taken the royal money and run.

'And that's no surprise,' says Scrapie.

'No, no it is surely not,' agrees Cabillaud. 'Not one bit surprise at all, I sink.'

'Bugger the Queen!' concludes Scrapie.

'And bugger Trapp, also!' says Cabillaud with gusto. 'Bugger him utterly, zis madman who I hate with all my heart and my very soul also! And ze Queen also who is nothing but a big, big, big, big, big –'

'Hippopotamus,' finishes Scrapie.

Mona snorts through her trunk in agreement, and begins to work her way through a bale of hay.

Then Cabillaud, emboldened by his own vehemence on a subject about which he knows nothing, ventures; '*Vous acceptez, donc, ma proposition, Monsieur?*'

Scrapie takes out his magnifying glass again and stares the man in the eye. Yes: they appear to speak the same language.

'I'll give you three days in my kitchen.' And he turns to leave.

'Thank you, sir,' whispers Cabillaud, barely able to contain his joy. His heart is all set to leap out of his very chest! 'You will not *regrettez*!'

Scrapie folds his step-ladder and swings himself over the gate. 'Three days.'

Cabillaud and Mona watch him as he makes his way down the gravel path past the monkey enclosure, a tall, lanky figure with a rolling walk.

Then they see him turn. Cabillaud blanches. Can the man have changed his mind?

The taxidermist is cupping his hand over his mouth to yell something.

'Any objections to cooking unusual meats?' comes his voice, faintly, over the chattering of chimps. 'The casualties of the Zoological Gardens have a tendency to come my way. Waste not, want not!'

Mon Dieu!

'No objections at all, sir! My very own delight!'

He is grinning so widely, he realises, that his jaws hurt. When was he last so happy? He kisses Mona on her trunk, which she curls around him affectionately. Then like the lady she is, she lifts her keeper clear of the ground and high into the air like a little toy, and gratefully opens her bowels.

The dusty old peacock feather bobbed in the gaslight as the Frozen Woman scratched away with its quill on a sheet of onion-skin parchment.

My first mistake, she wrote, *woz to BELEEV that wen a man sez he has a DREEM, that DREEM is to be TRUSTID and must command RISPECT. It is NOT. The things He spoke of were*:

1. *Distant CUNTRIES were I wud be a QUEEN.*
2. *Fame and RICHIS.*
3. *A new kind of WURLD to be made, wer nobody haz to WURK.*

He twurld his MUSTARSH, and I beleeved him.

She paused, and fingered the nib of her quill, then bent her head again, and continued her laborious scratching. *Wel, He wuz gud to me wen we furst met, I was dansin at the Kings Arms, nites, then. E see me an He wont me, that's wot E sed.*

E sed, you do the SPLITS like that for me?

Posh talking. Munny in iz vois, I thinks. He stands me on the table.

38

Now do the SPLITS, E sez.
No, I sez. Cant. Legs gone. So SKARED I cud piss.
He just sits ther, twurls His Mustarsh. Waitin.
HORIS, wuz is furst name. Then comes the TRAPP.

CHAPTER 4

2005: IN WHICH THE
ROGUE MALE EFFECTS
METAMORPHOSIS

The Nuance was in her element on the motorway. She purred with oil like a randy lioness, and before I knew it, I'd covered a hundred and fifty kilometres, and had entered a transcendental travel limbo. There's nothing like having A behind you, and B ahead.

> *Lovah me tender, lovah me trewah* [I sang.]
> *All my dreams fulfiyul*
> *For my darlin, I love yewah ...*

Nah.

I turned on the radio. It was one of those programmes where grown-ups get paid for indulging in opinionated argy-bargy. They were talking about the Fertility Crisis again.

'My feeling is that we reached an evolutionary cul-de-sac,' pontificated an earnest woman. I imagined her: reading specs, dangly earrings, a Ph.D., halitosis, a brooch. 'We'd gone as far as we possibly could, in terms of sophistication, civilisation, humanity –'

Then a bloke, a religious type, cut in. No-no-no-no-no. Sorry, sorry. Ha-ha. Lovely idea, Susan, blah-blah, he was saying, but with all due respect, the facts couldn't be plainer. I pictured him, too: dog-collar, dentures, sensible Y-fronts, dumpy wife at home trying to tune in but not being able to find the right wavelength. The Crisis happened, he was saying, because the Lord had become angry with the world, just as He had done once before. He'd sent the Flood then – he quoted something here – bla-de-blah – and *unleashed mighty waters*, et cetera, so that only the meek should inherit, bah blah, and it was all our own doing.

'If I could just cut in here –' the Ph.D. brooch woman began, but he was on a roll.

'– *Not* because we were so sophisticated, civilised, morally advanced, and humane as a species, but the very OPPOSITE. We didn't honour what He had done for us. We, here in Britain. This once great nation.'

'Susan? Would you like to come in here?' said the radio man. He was just a voice.

'Yes. Well, what we experienced was hardly a flood,' the earnest woman remonstrated. 'You can't possibly call it a real flood! It was no more than a few inches!'

She was right there, I thought. The hallelujah types liked to call it a deluge, because of what happened after, but it was hardly what you'd call a big deal. New Year's Eve, 1999 – very apocalyptic, of course. They all seized on that. But it was just a bad shower, maybe; no more. 'A noxious squall,' the Met Office called it at the time. The surgery got swamped, but it was nothing that a couple of *Sunday Timeses* couldn't mop up, in the end.

'Now come on. You can't deny that it changed our lives,' said the radio man. 'Flood, heavy shower, call it what you will, things haven't been the same since.'

'Nobody's claiming they *have* been,' said another man. He had that reasoned, slightly chewing voice that scientists use when they're on the radio. 'I'd be the *last* person to say that the sudden infertility of the human egg in Britain isn't a national catastrophe. As for whether the flooding on the night of the Millennium was the cause of it –'

'But Professor Hawkins,' butted in the woman. 'I don't frankly *care* about the cause of the problem. I care about the *solution*. We've got to remember that if it weren't for the National Egg Bank, the British would already be headed for complete extinction. All *I'm* saying is –'

41

'Should we really be that pessimistic?' said the radio man. 'After all, the Government's telling us that in fact it's only a matter of time till the fertility curve swings up again. And in the meantime, we've got the stored eggs to tide us over, so –'

'But there are nowhere near enough pre-Millennial eggs in storage to deal with the queues!' The women was getting quite shrill. 'Look at the evidence. There hasn't been a single natural conception since New Year's Day 2000! Five years of sterility! I say release ALL the eggs now, and get the girls pregnant as soon as possible, and –'

'Big mistake,' said the religious man. 'Look, if God had *wanted* us to store human eggs, he'd have *designed* us to store them. It's this very type of scientific intervention we were being punished for in the first place.'

'*Punished*!' squawked the woman. 'You think –'

'Yes, *punished*. You don't like that word, do you. It's not very liberal-friendly, I'm afraid.'

'Well, you can't deny it's incredibly *value-laden*.'

'I can't, and I won't. I say, *What's wrong with values?* And if I may make another point, I don't call two inches of rainfall 'just a shower'. I call it a flood.'

'So you're saying God just wants us all to fizzle out, then, does he? You lot are quite happy to witness our decline? It's all right for you. You've had your children, haven't you? Boys, I'll bet. If you had girls, you *certainly* wouldn't be taking that line. When I see my daughter taking hormones so she can breast-feed an orang-utan, my heart breaks. If you take away the human eggs that were put in storage before the Millennium, you're killing their only hope of becoming mothers. Not to mention the future of Britain as a nation.'

'*God* knows what He is doing,' the dog-collar man said complacently. 'I'm confident that He'll offer us some hope, if we show humility. Can't you see it? This is a *test*! *A challenge for us all!* We will arise from the ashes of our impurity, as Christ arose on the third day!'

But it wasn't going to be like that, and he knew it. Everyone knew it. I remembered the sequence of events, when the Fertility Blip officially became no longer a blip, but a crisis. First, when it became clear that male sperm were not affected, only female eggs, there'd been a whole spate of hastily arranged marriages to foreign imports. The women arrived here, fine, amid much domestic resentment, but within a couple of months, it became clear the new pregnancies weren't going to materialise. Nature had played its wild card; their eggs seemed to have died as soon as they passed Customs. The whole country was an egg-killing zone. A nation of ovarian doom. The quickie divorces followed, and the Sperm Drain began. The tourist industry collapsed completely, and overnight, we became a third-world leper colony. Europe poured millions of Euros into fertility research, but was desperate to get shot of us.

'How can anyone be resurrected, when half the men have left?' snapped the woman. She was becoming quite strident. 'Even the frozen eggs in the Egg Bank are only 50 per cent viable. I suspect it's less. When did you last see a baby?' she accused. They were getting rarer than hen's teeth. It was like the Lottery used to be; anyone who benefited from the Egg Bank had to go into hiding. 'Unless something's done soon about the Sperm Drain,' the woman was saying, 'there'll be no men left!'

True. A lot of blokes were leaving, now that it was clear the country was blighted. There was nothing wrong with British sperm, after all. Or foreign eggs. Emigration restrictions for men were on the cards; there was a rumour that, come next year, you wouldn't be able to leave unless you could prove you'd fathered a genuine *Homo Britannicus* before the Crisis.

And that there'd be Loyalty Bonuses for men who stayed.

Was it the prospect of that, that stopped me going abroad? Not really. The fact was, I didn't give a monkey's about the future.

Carpe diem, I say. Seize the day. Grab it by the throat and rattle its bollocks.

Before I left London, I phoned the Veterinary Society to inform them of my change of name by deed poll. I spoke to a Mr Jenks. I told him I needed confidentiality. Should anyone, such as a woman called Holly Noakes, or Mrs Patricia Mann, for example, try to contact me by the name Bobby Sullivan, he was to inform them that I was no longer on their books. I could hear the sound of a Jenks eyebrow being raised.

'There was a sort of vendetta against me,' I explained.

'A vendetta?' Jenks asked.

Oh Christ, I realised. He's interested now. I've used a foreign word. He wants details.

'A client with a grudge,' I said, going for a spot of honesty. Busking it. I pictured Mrs Mann with a little silver revolver pointed at me over Giselle's body-bag. 'A dead-monkey scenario. Husband gets me to put the animal down, licence in order, all legal and above-board, wife comes along, threatens me. Bad marriage, baby-substitute, the old story. You feel more like a shrink sometimes.'

'A common complaint,' Jenks sympathised. When I assured him that I was completely in the clear, and (stroke of genius, this) that I was taking out a legal injunction against the deranged pet-owner concerned, he became even more understanding. 'There's a lot of it about,' he confided. 'We had a member shot with a crossbow last year, over a bushbaby. Claims and counter-claims, insurance hoo-ha and now the Court of Appeal. It's the anthropomorphism,' he mused. 'Gets people carried away.'

There were several possibilities, Mr Jenks explained, clicking away at the vacancy file on his computer. A Saudi Arabian zoo, for instance, if I was interested in sunshine, but there was a strict no-women-no-booze clause which wasn't everyone's *cup of tea*, as it were. 'Not many reproductive possibilities there, I'm afraid,' he said. 'Most men opt for Holland or the Far East.'

'Anything closer to home?' I asked. 'I'm not bothered about reproduction, myself.' This was true. Unlike Elvis, I'd never felt the urge to pass on my genes. No rock-a-hula baby for me.

'Well, there's a locum going up north,' he said. 'A suburb of

44

Judlow called Thunder Spit. By the sea. Famous for a breed of sheep called the Lord Chief Justice.'

'Sounds interesting,' I lied. But the idea of the coast appealed. I thought of those camping holidays, with sun-cream and popcorn.

'I'll put in an application, then,' I told him.

'An excellent choice of name, if I may say so,' said Jenks, when I spelled out my new identity for the records. I was pleased with his reaction.

'You'll be hearing from us soon, Mr de Savile,' Jenks said. 'Or may I be among the first to call you Buck?'

'It's a tragedy,' the brooch woman was saying, as my windscreen wipers swished me past Axelhaunch, Fibber's Wash, Blaggerfield. Viking names. I'd heard a couple of blokes speaking Danish once; they sounded like clogged drains.

'But to go back to the central point, as long as we have our stored eggs, then we have hope, surely?' put in the radio man. He was paid to make sure people didn't get too depressed. A difficult job. As the discussion took its usual apocalyptic course, the earring-and-brooch woman's voice grew ever more quivery with emotion, and the hallelujah man with the Y-fronts and dentures became more and more triumphant, and the reasonable professor sounded more and more like a herbivore chewing old cud, and I thought: Desperate times. And desperate women. Hence the primates. No self-respecting woman over thirty could afford to be without her cute little companion. That's what it said in an old copy of *Cosmopolitan* in the surgery waiting-room, anyway. I had a sudden clear picture of Giselle, the doomed macaque, handing Mr Mann a flea.

Desperate times, but a bonanza for vets.

My involvement with animals began with blood, meat, and a gizzard stone.

I am six. Unexpectedly, I visit the butcher's shop with my mother.

'Why not the supermarket, Mum?' They had a popcorn machine, and photo booth where you could have your picture taken with the Terminator.

'Because he's organic.'

She walks fast, dragging me by the wrist, to buy lamb cutlets for her actressy dinner party, at which she plans to call them *côtelettes d'agneau*. The year is 1983, and the shop is one of those expensive old-fashioned London butcher's you rarely came across, even back then. (You see extinction everywhere, when you look for it.)

Meat hangs from hooks and languishes in little bloody trays; crimson sawdust confettis the floor. I gob in it and rake it about with my toe as I stand in the queue next to Mum. Then suddenly the butcher is heaving down towards me, holding something out in his palm. It's a stone. I take it. It feels smooth and slightly oily.

'From a chicken's gizzard,' says the butcher. 'For you, mate. Freebie!'

I clasp it tight. In my innocence, I recognise I belong here.

'When I grow up, *I* want to be organic,' I say as we leave the shop.

'Oh Bobsy-Wobsy, how horrible,' says Mum, popping the plastic bag of bloody *côtelettes* into her shopping net. 'Meat's so grisly, darling.'

'I like that. I like grisly.'

'Well, be a surgeon, then,' says Mum. 'You can open up people's bodies, and take out the bits with cancer and sew them up again.'

'I don't want to cut up people.' I am fingering the gizzard stone in my pocket. And there, by the Norwich Union Building Society, the enormity of it stops me in my tracks.

'I want to cut up animals.'

There's nothing abnormal in this.

When I was twelve, I built a rat-trap, and then one for squirrels, because in those days the Council, which still deemed them urban vermin, gave you 50p for every tail you brought in. I

46

dismantled the bodies the way my friends dismantled toy cars or aeroplanes. I kept a plastic box of animal bits in the far corner of the fridge, and another in the freezer. Mum never really noticed. As long as her ice and lemon were within reach, she paid no heed. Mum rested a lot, 'Because actresses just bloody do,' and because of her migraine sessions. It was left to Dad to see us boys through. He raised us efficiently, and he raised us to be men.

At fifteen, I was spotty and sweaty, with limbs that seemed roughly modelled out of plasticine and a penis likewise. All were embarrassing and unmanageable. It was this version of myself that began work as the organic butcher's assistant. My mother hated the idea, and went off for one of her migraines. She was having them daily by this time. Dad was seeing another woman, Jilly, who wore tight-fitting jodhpurs and was married to a fox-faced man who skulked in the City all week. Fact: Jilly caused Mum's migraines. Dad's version: Jilly had 'come into his life' (he said it like she was Jesus) because Mum was always drunk.

But when I started work at Mr Harper's, Mum made it clear that today's migraine extravaganza was for me.

'You'll chop off a finger!' she screeched through the door. 'Or worse! You could lose a whole arm in those electric slicers!'

But this did nothing to put me off. In fact, the idea that I'd be working with lethal instruments increased the thrill. I pictured feeding my right index finger into the greedy blade, and saw it emerge in wafer-thin strips of pink flesh with a central spot of pellucid white bone. From behind the door, the familiar whiff of Amontillado sherry and the sound of heartbreak. Like all Mum's noises, it had a thespian ring to it: Mrs Sullivan, stage left, falls to floor, clasps magnificent bosom, dies in sorrow. Exit spotty teenage son running, head in hands.

Things evolved from there, and before I knew it, I was at vet school.

The radio discussion had degenerated into a phone-in: a woman from Cleethorpes was wanting to know why it was *Britain* that had been affected by the Crisis.

'It's so unfair!' she wailed. 'Why not the whole of Europe? After all the kow-towing we've done to Brussels!'

The brooch-woman gave a piggy snort.

'Well, the infertility is certainly very *regionalised*,' said the radio man, covering for her. 'Do you have an explanation, Professor Hawkins?'

'Well, if you look at it globally,' he droned, 'it's perhaps unfortunate that it should have just hit our archipelago of islands, but in evo*luti*onary terms, it's not unusual for a disaster to be contained in this way.' He paused, chewing on his words. 'Islands are well known for housing species that aren't found elsewhere in the world. But by the same token, their populations are *also* prone to be wiped out in accidents such as this. Be they caused by rainfall, triggering a genetic malfunction, or something else which we don't yet understand. The end result, of course, being –'

I switched off the radio. *Extinction.* I'm fed up with that word, I thought. Let's put on our blue suede shoes and dance like we did in the good old days, before I was born! I have twenty-nine virtual Elvis concerts on tape.

I peer through the windscreen: outside, the land is as flat and bare as a splat of emulsion, and the few trees seem to be cringing from something. As I drive past the hypermarkets, car-phone warehouses, carpet wholesalers, discount shoe shops, DIY stores and bungalows that herald the outskirts of town, a sign enlarges ahead of me. WELCOME TO THUNDER SPIT.

Which is the cue for the butterfly that is Buck de Savile, emerged from the caterpillar that was Bobby Sullivan, to press his foot harder on the accelerator and speed into town.

Yo! *Homo Britannicus* is dying, but the son of Elvis is going to live!

CHAPTER 5

FATHER OF THE MAN

Dr Baldicoot said I would die, but I lived. The Parson and his wife christened me Tobias, and I formally took their surname, Phelps. A solid name, evoking oakwood and rainy autumns and English brawn, passed down through many a generation in Thunder Spit.

But I was not as sturdy as the name I bore. Unlike the Phelpses who had gone before, whose graveyard epitaphs spoke of long, industrious and healthy lives, I was small and sickly; they said that all the energy of my babyhood seemed to be put into growing more hair. My head was a great thick tangled clot, and I had copious body hair from an early age, which promised great manliness, my father said wistfully.

Others took a different view.

'His real parents must've been infidels,' I heard Mrs Tobash say once, as she and Mrs Fletcher gutted fish at the harbour market. 'There's nothing Christian about body hair.'

My hair was rust-red.

'Another sign of evil,' asserted Mrs Fletcher, throwing some mackerel innards down for the tortoiseshell cats to gobble. 'He's crawling with fleas, too, they say.' This much was true. 'I reckon he's witches' spawn.'

'And *I* reckon he's from the Fair,' said Mrs Tobash. 'He's a misbegot. One of them freaks. He'll never be a man.'

I ran and hid in my mother's skirts.

I will be frank with you, reader: I grew up with a distinct sense that all was not well.

Proud though I am now of my eloquence and literacy (if you will forgive me a moment of self-praise), it may come as a surprise to you that in childhood my lack of speech was the cause of great anxiety to my foster-parents. It was clear to them that I was not unintelligent (indeed, I was quite the opposite, although it is perhaps immodest to mention it) but it was evident that some inexplicable blockage was preventing me from uttering a single sound other than a squeak or a grunt, which bore no relation to the human language. In the opinion of the good Dr Baldicoot, the matter was related to my general sickliness at birth, and the trauma caused by my unfortunate mutilation.

'For who knows,' he argued, puffing on his vile-smelling pipe, 'what effect such an attack may have had upon the psyche?'

My father had a more theological explanation for my silence.

'"*I speak in the tongues of men and of angels*,"' he would quote from the Bible, comforting his worried wife. 'He is an angel. These grunts are angelic discourse.'

My foster-mother, who had the task of dressing me every morning and knew with intimacy the extent of my physical oddities, including my singularly un-angelic hairiness, was not so sure.

'Speak to me, Tobias,' she would wail. 'In God's own English, I pray!'

It was not, in fact, until my fifth year that words finally emerged from my mouth. I remember the occasion well, for it was my official birthday. My true date of birth being unknown (a common problem with foundlings), we celebrated the event on the anniversary of my parents' wedding. See them there, at the big kitchen table, every knot of whose oak surface I know with intimacy, their hands clasped; it is the thirtieth year of their marriage. My father moon-faced, earnest, his bushy brows turning to grey; she quiet and unassuming, like a friendly potato or a lardy bun. And see their smiles of parental pride as they gaze lovingly at the child sitting opposite them, the linen napkin

50

tucked beneath his chin, a fried sardine before him on his plate. I am their darling, their joy.

'Happy birthday, Tobias! May the Lord bless you and keep you!' booms Parson Phelps.

I smile. In my lap, I finger the wheels of a toy train they have given me. It is made of wood, carved by the cobbler, Mr Hewitt.

'Eat up,' whispers my mother, her eyes bright with excitement, her mouth trembling with delight. 'And then you shall have your surprise!'

Dutifully, I pick some more at my sardine, and leave the spine on the side of my plate.

'Now shut your eyes,' whispers Mrs Phelps, 'and make a wish!'

I close them, and (my imagination being limited, and the hair-shirt mentality of Thunder Spit prompting luxurious urges in me even at this early age) I pray for a magnificent cake.

It has already been established that miracles did not often come to Thunder Spit. So when two came into the Phelps household within the space of five years, there was joy to be had indeed, and a feeling of extra-special blessedness. There is no physical explanation for what happened (although the good Dr Baldicoot did his best to come up with a diagram of a larynx that had been blocked and then suddenly unplugged, due to a sudden stimulation of the psyche, thus confirming his theory) but – for what it is worth – it is my belief that at that same moment that I was wishing for a cake, my mother was making a wish of her own. How else to explain what next transpired? In her neat and careful script, my mother wrote down in her diary that night:

> The sequence of events, as Parson Phelps and I recall it, was thus:
> Firstly, the child opened his eyes, and saw the cake.
> Secondly, he blew out the candles, one by one.
> And thirdly, clear as a choirboy, Dear Lord be thanked, the CHILD SPOKE!

At the bottom of the page, in writing that was a mere scrawl, and jittered with emotion, she had added: *Fourthly: I shall die a happy woman!*

My first words – 'Words we will cherish for ever,' declared my delighted father – came suddenly, unbidden, from my mouth.

'What a delicious-looking cake,' I said. 'Please, dear Mother, would you kindly be so good as to cut me a slice?'

A child prodigy! And so polite with it!

'Manners maketh man,' choked my father, then joined my mother in weeping with joy. As I helped myself to another slice, I smiled at the pleasure I had given them, and watched them hauling out the prayer-cushion and flinging themselves on the floor to thank God. Their prayers were so long and passionate that I managed to polish off the whole cake before they got to their feet again.

From that day, I never squeaked or grunted again, and so proud were my parents of my newly acquired talent that they encouraged me to read long passages of the Bible aloud, and to memorise tongue-twisters: *Peter Piper picked a peck of pickled pepper, Miss Mosh mashes some mish-mash, Betty Botter bought some butter*, and the like. My ability to surmount difficult verbal challenges such as these has been much remarked upon throughout my life, and remains a source of pride. Needless to say, soon my father was training me to read aloud long passages from the Bible in church, and the congregation marvelled at my sudden precociousness.

But in a community as small as ours, I was still the foundling boy, the outsider. People stared at me and jeered when I ventured into town. (They said redheads smell different, but if you're one yourself, how can you tell? And even then, what can you do about it?) The villagers accused me of frightening the sheep and the cows in particular, and I was banned from Harcourt's farm because of the havoc I once wreaked in his paddock when I accompanied my mother to buy eggs. The whole flock of poultry refused to lay for another two weeks. I was also the cause, according to the farmer, of his favourite horse throwing a nervous fit. Dogs growled at me, too. My unfortunate effect on the animal population of Thunder Spit soon earned me a bad name, and some villagers began to mutter biliously about an 'evil eye'.

This enraged my father. I was the Lord's own chosen child, and my love of God and the Scriptures was proof of it; how could anyone who had heard my readings in the church – to a packed and admiring gathering of Christian brethren – think otherwise? How could a boy who sang hymns so eagerly and with such a clear and angelic voice be anything other than special to the Lord? But after the epileptic-horse incident, I avoided Harcourt's farm, and walked a lonely path to school, where the creatures would catch no whiff of me. My trips to the cobbler were the source of deep shame, and I always kept my socks on to hide the unnatural shape of my feet. Mr Hewitt's shop was poky and dank, and it stank of badly cured leather, a smell I have come to associate with death and fear. Here he made me special shoes, with leather and bark soles. They looked like fishing boats. Over the years, perhaps to counteract my natural inclination to crawl somewhat crab-wise rather than to walk, and to disguise the oddity of my gait, I began to tread slightly on tiptoe.

In the village, they called me Tobias Trotter.

At every school, there is an unattractive boy who lurks in a corner of the playground, fiddle-faddling with a stick or a stone, who is unruly, who sometimes reverts to scrambling on all fours, who has no great talent to compensate for his oddity. In Thunder Spit, that boy was me.

And yet do not pity me, gentle reader, for I was not unhappy; far from it. My parents loved me, and my memories of those early childhood days are golden, because I had the sea, and its astonishing contents. It was a huge toy-box to me, and every day it spewed forth a new miracle. See me there, on the grey beach, a speck of humanity beneath the great unrolled carpets of sky and ocean, sitting on a sand-dune with my bare toes dug in deep and my soul unlocked, watching.

The sky turn from coral pink to pale gold, the clouds flattened against the sea, the pearl waves rolling into green. The rocks grey, cold, shimmering with sea-salt like sacred dust. There, alone, I would stare into rockpools; for hours, I gazed in deep, watching the vague clutchings of sea anemones and the swirl of jellyfish and the little light-explosions made by shoals of baby herring. Plunging my arm in deep, I captured crabs, miniature lobsters, crayfish, shrimps, mussels, cockles, quillsnappers, aquatic and semi-aquatic feats of engineering that wear their skeleton on the outside like armour. Searching tenaciously, I found bigger and better rockpools, bigger and better crabs; picking them apart, I found inside a maze of inter-connecting meat-chambers, like Parson Phelps' church organ decked with knuckles of calcium, yet the divisions as smooth and papery as the internal walls of a Japanese samurai's abode. 'God's doodlings', my father called them, inspecting what I brought home in my tin bucket. His belief was that molluscs and other sea-creatures were drawn from the margins of the Lord's great sketchbook, in which the masterpiece was man.

He certainly broke His nib the day he drew me, I thought, as I looked wistfully at my reflection in the rockpool. The squashed-up face, too crammed with features for its size, with thin lips and round, dark eyes like two raisins shoved deep into a burnt cake.

But, 'Beauty is in the eye of the beholder,' my mother always said, and I came to believe her.

To most Thunder Spitters there were two types of Nature: the Nature man could vanquish, and the Nature that vanquished him. The Nature we conquered had long been domesticated for us, by previous generations of Thunder Spitters: our famous cats, that were black-and-red-patched like cows, with a distinctive stripe down the nose, and always fled when I entered the room. Or the skinny sheep who scattered at my approach, or the cows whose milk I was alleged to curdle, or the dogs that so loathed me: mostly sheepdogs, collies and whippets which inter-bred like the families here, the Peat-Hoves, the Balls, the Cleggses:

54

long lines of intermarriage and gravestones to match. But the other Nature always remained: wild Nature, the Nature we couldn't guard against; the Nature that was always erupting and rattling around us. The swarms of stinging jellyfish, the Portuguese men-o'-war that could kill you or, as in the case of Robbie Tobash, lose you the use of an arm; the floods and the winds that knocked over our boats like paper hats, the giant octopuses that grabbed men overboard in the night, the potato blight and the centipedes and lice and silverfish in the sacks of corn, and the fleas that attacked us, and the parasites we bore within.

My mother had a theory that I was inhabited by a particularly tenacious tapeworm, which had been my lodger since babyhood. She claimed this sordid stowaway was the cause of my sphincter trouble, and she spent much of her time thinking up new ways to purge me of it.

'This'll do for you, you evil creature,' mother would murmur, her plain potato features wincing in concentration as she forced the foul concoctions down my gullet. She christened my tapeworm Mildred. The name was also – 'By pure coincidence,' she said – that of a woman my father had once been sweet on in his bachelor days. But try as she might, my mother could never abolish my invisible passenger. Or the fleas, or the bats, or the toe-fungus that haunted us all.

Yes, Nature infested us, and we fought it off. But it came back. We fought it off again and it came back again. It was like the fizzing waves on the shoreline, leaving a lacework of foam and history that clung to our lives.

'Father, how exactly, how *exactly*, did God make this?' I remember asking Parson Phelps one day. I was brandishing a mermaid's purse at him, a black dogfish egg with twirling strands protruding extravagantly from its four corners.

'By His holy craftsmanship,' the Parson explained patiently. I pictured God in a sort of workshop, like that of Mr Hewitt the cobbler, puzzling over the engineering. 'And what is more, he created all this, and more, in a mere day. The fourth day.

Remember, Tobias? Remember your scriptures? What did God do, Tobias, on the fourth day, that is so apt to your question? God said let *what* bring forth *what?*'

I had scriptures coming out of my ears.

'God said, "*Let the waters bring forth abundantly the moving creature that hath life, and let fowl fly above the earth in the open firmament of Heaven,*" Father.'

'Well remembered, Tobias. A sound memory is a blessing.'

'But, Father, did he really make it all out of nothing?'

It just didn't make sense.

'He made it out of the void, Tobias. "*For the earth was waste and void –*"'

'"*And darkness was upon on the face of the deep,*"' I finished. I was mesmerised by the beauty of it.

Like him – like all of us – I believed the words of the Bible implicitly, just as I believed Herman's *Crustacea*. Neither book had ever given me any cause for doubt. God was as real to me as my tapeworm, Mildred. Both were invisible, but housed within. Both made their presence felt in a hundred small ways.

'"*And the spirit of God moved upon the waters. And God said let there be light,*"' intoned the Parson. I loved his big voice. It boomed with righteousness.

'"*And there was light,*"' I replied.

When you live near the sea, all this is obvious. As I discovered later, it's in towns and cities that your soul is caught unawares.

'And,' continued the Parson, but in his other voice, his less appealing, thinner, somewhat nagging voice, 'returning to your dogfish detritus, not to mention your crab collection and your cuttlefish and your sea-beetle and your dead cormorant, which your mother spied on Wednesday in your chest of drawers and threw out, Tobias, because it was smelling foul, what else did God do on the fourth day? He created the great sea-monsters, Tobias, and every living creature that moveth, which the waters brought forth abundantly, after their kinds, and every winged fowl after its kind – and what did God see, Tobias? What did he then see, son?'

56

'He saw that it was good, Father,' I replied, picking at a sea-urchin spine that had lodged painfully beneath my thumbnail.

'Precisely. Which is more than can be said of your smashed limpets, and also your lobster shell, which I found lurking in the vestry, when tracking down the source of a vile odour. I saw then, and smelt, that it was *not* good. Not good at all. No more carcasses in our house, son, or in God's.'

'No, Father. I promise.'

'Good boy.'

'Father.'

'Yes?'

'What is this?' I thrust my stone at him. There were many such stones on the beach, and I had never understood them. This was a wonderful specimen, its dark whorl with radial stripes reminiscent of a shell.

'That,' said Parson Phelps, stopping in his tracks, 'is one of God's jokes.'

'God makes jokes?' I questioned, aghast.

'Yes. Some big, and some small. On scientists.' My Father hated scientists. They were responsible, he often claimed in his sermons, for much of the world's confusion. They were a scourge, and ranked as low in his estimation as rude children and fallen women. 'Your stone is called a fossil,' he continued, 'and God planted them in the earth to muddle a certain breed of scientist known as a geologist. He knew exactly what He was doing.'

'A geologist? What is he?'

'A man who dares to question the truth of Genesis,' my father replied. 'These fossils are red herrings, planted by God, to trick geologists into believing they are right. And thereby wasting their time on a grand scale.' He laughed, sharing God's joke. 'Do not forget, son, that he is a *jealous* God!'

My father seemed to find this most mightily amusing, and chuckled at God's holy sense of humour, but I was merely confused. I believed passionately in the Lord, but His fossil joke and other holy eccentricities led me to question His divine purpose on more than one occasion. Another question vexed me, too.

'Father.'

'Yes, son?'

'Who made God?'

Well? Is that such a foolish question? What *were* his origins?

My father had the answer, though. 'God is self-made,' he said finally. 'Like a self-made man. But God.'

'I see, Father,' I said. But I lied, for I did not, and it remains to me a puzzle.

After I dun the SPLITS for Him, the woman wrote, *Trapp claps his hands, cals me to His tabel to drink WINE.*

He was hansom enuf. Big MUSTARSH, with wax tips, keeps TWURLIN and TWURLIN away at it. Sumthin about Him. Dont no wot till later.

I likes you, He sez. You hav nacherel GRASE, animal GRASE. I has wot? I arsks.

Exept wen you speeks, He sez. So I kept my mouth shut mostly arfter that remarke. HE was in business, He says, but He doesnt say wot.

He takes me home. I dont object to THAT, wot with my lodgings at Mrs Peersons, the BICH. The hous is big and shabby but posh, no mistake. Grand PIANNA in the drorin room, big chairs, big PIKCHERS on the worls. Pikcher of him, Trapp, standing on top of NELSONS COLUM in TRAFALGA SKWER. He sez its Him, anyway, THE FACT IZ the man is too smorl to see and He is SPITTIN on the crowds below. Thats wot E sez, but thats too smorl to see as wel.

I enjoyed that IMENSELY, He sez. An EXELENT evenin that wuz. See that PIANNA, He sez. I wonts you to stand on top of it an DARNS for me.

So He plays the PIANNA, and I darnsis, and He has teers in his eys after, I SWER IT. That was a good nite, that furst nite with Trapp, but it didnt stay good.

UNFORCHENATLY FOR ME.
My next mistake woz to moov in with Him as a servant,
but to liv with Him as a wyfe, and thus to lern all about
SLAVERIE.

CHAPTER 6

HEADS WILL ROLL

As Tobias Phelps pursues his lonely childhood in Thunder Spit, let us now catapult ourselves back in time to observe the beginnings of a parallel childhood: that of Miss Violet Scrapie. The normal gestation period for *Homo sapiens* is nine months, and it is now November 1845, forty weeks to the day since we bore voyeuristic witness to the scene of marital union enacted by Dr Ivanhoe and Mrs Scrapie behind the chintz curtains of Madagascar Street, Belgravia.

Time for some screaming!

'AAAGH!'

That is the Laudanum Empress, in the early stages of child-birth.

And some cursing!

'Buggeration and damnation!'

That is Dr Ivanhoe Scrapie, reacting to this piece of ill-considered timing on his wife's part; he is battling with an awkwardly lopsided yak which refuses to conform to the structural requirements demanded by the armature. He is loath to leave his workshop to hang around outside the bedroom door; he will stay here, he decides, and fiddle with the armature, and smoke a cigar, as is traditional. Damn the whole business, he thinks, surveying the yak. He has approximately seven other children, if his memory serves him. Aren't they all more or less grown-up by now? He thinks so. Many have surely departed abroad, or have married, or both. And now – just as the Queen's Animal Kingdom Collection is weighing him down with work (eighty-one animals completed; fifteen thousand-ish to go) another wretched child!

The screams are getting louder. Scrapie hears the midwife calling for more water. He hears Cabillaud shouting *merde*. He puffs at his cigar.

'AAAGH!'

The Laudanum Empress again. Unlike other mammals, who bear their offspring in silence, *Homo sapiens* has a tendency to scream in agony. This is due to bad design on the part of God. He wished to give man a large brain, but forgot to give woman a proportionately structured pelvis.

'*Merde alors!*'

That is Jacques-Yves Cabillaud.

Symbiosis describes a relationship in the natural world by which two creatures very different in nature and characteristics come to a mutual accord of assistance. This is the status that the two human animals, Jacques-Yves Cabillaud and his employer, Dr Ivanhoe Scrapie, have quickly reached in Madagascar Street. At the heart of the exchange is the use of the carcasses of other, non-human animals – largely mammals, but embracing also bird-life, reptiles and fish – and the motto, beloved of Nature itself, *Waste not want not*. And thus it is that while Dr Scrapie puffs on his cigar and adjusts his lopsided yak in the taxidermy workshop upstairs, Monsieur Cabillaud, in the basement kitchen, has been preparing a hearty yak-meat stew, which he is now forced to leave on the back burner, while he heats vast quantities of water for the midwife attending Mrs Scrapie in the throes of childbirth.

Merde encore!

He fills another kettle. But it must be said that, apart from today's interruption, Cabillaud is pleased – more than pleased, with his lot. His instincts on the day Scrapie walked into the elephant Mona's enclosure had all been sound, and now, the initial territorial disputes with Mrs Jiggers sorted out (a common occurrence when one animal low in the pecking order is ousted by another who presumes to be slightly higher), Cabillaud has assumed his role as dominant male in the Madagascar Street kitchen, and by pure force of his culinary talent, has revolutionised the Scrapie diet.

Doing his best to ignore the sounds of childbirth which can still be heard, faintly, from the Scrapie bedroom two floors above him, Cabillaud settles the kettle on the hob and pokes at the simmering yak stew.

Mais oui, he reflects, he has the world at his feet, *quand même*! He had arrived at the Scrapies' home in Madagascar Street armed with a dead wallaby from the zoo, and that very evening, had furnished Dr and Mrs Scrapie with their first decently cooked meal. Decently cooked? May he presume to say that it was in fact unparalleled? The meat was neither burnt, nor stone-cold, nor tough – the three idiosyncrasies that had been the hallmarks of Mrs Jiggers' cooking. Cabillaud had been declared a genius (a fact he was already aware of), and Mrs Jiggers relegated to housekeeping duties. Because how, having tasted *wallaby aux dix-neuf oranges*, could the Scrapies ever look back?

'*Mais bien sûr que non*,' murmurs Cabillaud, fishing out a ladleful of stew-juice and sniffing something to which the adjectives *majestueux* and *formidable* might well (though it is not for him to say) apply.

'AAAGH!'

That is Mrs Scrapie once again. How did she come to be in this sorry mess? And is she now about to pass to the Other Side? She remembers nothing of the episode that triggered her condition. Phantoms whirl in a miasma about her head, and in the middle distance, her cloud of psychic particles shimmers ominously. As Mrs Jiggers trickles more laudanum-water into her mouth by means of a sponge, the Empress sees the cloud's inner recesses writhing into strange shapes. Is that a piglet among all those flying feathers? Is that a child sitting on a beach? Surely that's a swarm of seagulls, over there! And is that a fossil? And surely *that* is a sardine?

What does all this mean?

She wails again, as her ravaged womb contracts once more. As the pain lunges through her and appears to rip her very soul apart, the particles swirl and re-form. From a high corner above her bed, she observes herself sprawled horizontally, her legs aloft, Mrs Jiggers mopping at her brow, the midwife prodding at her nether regions. And as the particles shimmer, the future dances before her: she sees a monkey in a short pinafore dress, and a man with a syringe; a gleaming motorised vehicle shooting along a huge wide road; an immensely fat woman dressed as a meringue, a pair of identical female twins, an odd-looking man in extraordinary shoes hopping on a doorstep – *her* doorstep – Her Majesty the Queen wielding a scimitar and splitting in half the belly of a –

'AAAGH!'

The doorbell clangs. Two minutes later, the door of Scrapie's workshop is suddenly flung open by a flushed Mrs Jiggers, whose apron is falling off and whose hairpins are dangling skew-whiff across one eye.

'Boy or girl?' asks Scrapie, laying down his skinning-knife.

'Neither, sir. She's still in labour. But there's a messenger arrived from the Palace, sir! Says he's the Queen's equerry! He awaits you downstairs!'

With some reluctance, Scrapie stubs out his cigar. Mrs Jiggers wipes her hands on her apron and dances about nervously. It's not every day there's this much activity in the house. Or such news arriving! The good woman cannot contain herself.

'He's come to tell you, sir, that Horace Trapp's *Ark* has landed at the docks!'

Scrapie groans. Two years and five months behind schedule! The nerve of the man!

'Oh, and I'll be needing more water, sir,' Mrs Jiggers frets as she pants her way along the hallway, Scrapie striding purposefully in her wake. 'It won't be long now.'

'Cabillaud will see to it. What else does he say, this equerry?'

'Oh. Just one thing,' says Mrs Jiggers, stopping in her tracks and turning to look down with excitement at her employer. She wipes her hands feverishly on her starched apron, and bites her lip, scared and thrilled in equal measure. She has not felt this way since the Travelling Fair of Danger and Delight passed through London last March, and she rode on the Mechanical Millipede.

'Well?' barks Scrapie.

'He says that Horace Trapp is missing, sir. And that all the animals are dead!'

And she gathers up her skirts and rushes out.

Our imaginary Montgolfier awaits us; let us therefore abandon the Laudanum Empress to her ghastly screaming (which will continue for several more hours) and follow Scrapie, Cabillaud, and the equerry to the docks, to witness the scene of devastation that is Trapp's *Ark*. The Hippo's equerry, a man of a certain femininity and nervous energy, has been voluble on the subject of Trapp, as they made their way, post-haste by hansom cab, to the docks.

Rumour had it, he said, that Trapp had fled.

Rumour had it, the equerry claimed, that Trapp had abandoned the *Ark* in order to marry a foreign princess.

Rumour had it, the equerry counter-claimed, that Trapp had drowned.

Rumour had it, the equerry mused, that Trapp had gone back into the slavery business, and was working out of Georgia.

Rumour had it, too, that –

'Shut up,' said Scrapie tersely, descending from the halted hansom cab. 'Just show me the bloody ship.'

Silently, the nervous equerry leads Scrapie and Cabillaud to the *Ark*. The balloon goes like the wind. Before we know it, we too have arrived.

The *Ark* is berthed next to *HMS Barcelona*, and is in comparison a sorry sight indeed. A huge hole gapes in its hull, its sails are torn and bedraggled. It lolls in its berth, its belly ragged as an old husk.

'Jesus Christ on a penny-farthing!' exclaims Scrapie, who has quickly scurried on board and is now heaving open the door of the cavernous beamed hull. He is hit full-force by an atrocious stink. The *Ark* is a former galley ship, a slave-trader, and the first things the taxidermist can make out in the gloom are the rows of manacles chained to the wooden planking of the walls.

Now, pinching their noses, Scrapie and Cabillaud peer through the darkness, attempting to decipher what they can. Cabillaud, who after his miserable seafaring experience is less than keen on ships, lurches out on to the gang-plank to inhale fresh air. Dr Scrapie, who is made of sterner stuff, notes that the smell of putrefaction means that many of the specimens – in the unlikely event that they are not completely ruined – are beyond taxidermic hope. The rest must be frozen immediately. The equerry hovers in a corner, shifting nervously from foot to foot. This place gives him the creeps, and he doesn't mind who knows it.

Cabillaud now returns from the quarter-deck, staggering, and grabs Scrapie's arm. As they accustom their eyes to the darkness, both men blanch, for neither has ever before witnessed such a terrible scene of destruction. Every door of every cage, large and small, has been opened. The carcasses are strewn everywhere. Fur, feathers, reptilian skin, broken bones, staring eyes. Huddled, stiff little shapes. Wings awry. Dry crusts of maroon-coloured blood.

'*Merde!*' yells Cabillaud suddenly. He has tripped on something, which now rolls slowly across the planking to land at Scrapie's feet. A rotten old coconut, by the look of it, its hair long and matted, and stinking to high Heaven. Scrapie is about to kick it away, but something stops him. Instead, he squats, holding his nose, to inspect the object at his feet.

'My God,' he murmurs. 'It is a head!'

It is indeed a head. The head of a human. Months old. Reeking.

Despite its rottenness, Scrapie recognises the moustache. And the excellent teeth.

'God Almighty,' he whispers. His voice is hoarse, a mere croak.

This head is Horace Trapp's.

Scrapie has long prided himself on his lack of squeamishness, but his normally cast-iron belly now turns to gelatine, and he lunges forward, grappling with the door, to escape. Outside on the deck, Cabillaud and the equerry, who have swiftly followed him, both vomit copiously over the side of the *Ark*, and Scrapie tries to calm his frayed nerves by reciting to himself a smorgasbord of logarithms. Finally, he pulls himself together.

First things first.

'Tell the Queen,' he orders the equerry, 'that Trapp has been murdered. And that as far as the Animal Kingdom Project is concerned, I shall be needing a ton of Arctic ice shipped over immediately. Immediately is in fact an understatement. I need ice NOW. I will commandeer her supply until my own arrives. Understood? There is no time to lose. We have work to do.'

That, too, was an understatement.

The project Scrapie was about to embark on would take him twenty years.

'AAAGH!' comes a faint cry from the bedroom. The Montgolfier has whisked us back to Madagascar Street.

In the nick of time!

Welcome, Miss Violet Scrapie! Welcome to the world!

As the Laudanum Empress sinks back on the pillow and retreats into the comfort of her psychic particles, the newborn Violet yells lustily for the milk that is her birthright.

The other Scrapie children had the small bones and delicate features of the Laudanum Empress, a famous belle. The four sisters were beautiful. The two brothers were handsome.

But now, into this collection of valuable Society china, charged the big-boned Violet.

Crash, thump, disaster. What had gone wrong? There was no rhyme or reason to it, as far as Dr Scrapie could tell, when he returned, badly shaken, from the débâcle that was Trapp's *Ark* and inspected his newborn infant. It was a bad day altogether.

First, all the Animal Kingdom nonsense, then Trapp's severed head rolling about like a pustular football, and then another bloody girl. Skeletally, the child was definitely bovine. So much so that the Empress, for whom the act of union had been just a vague interruption of her normal psychic trance, wondered whether she could perhaps have been impregnated by a visitor from the Other Side, and she surreptitiously inspected the *chaise-longue* for signs of ectoplasm. Meanwhile odd visions still swirled among her cloud of psychic particles, and she remained puzzled by their import.

Time passed, and the baby grew, and grew, and grew, a great greedy cuckoo in the Scrapie nest. Neither of her parents was sure when it was that Violet decided to up sticks and descend into the basement kitchen, to live with Cabillaud. Was she perhaps three or four? Or maybe as young as two? Both were too preoccupied with their own doings to pay the girl much attention, that much is certain, and it was a good month before they noticed her absence, prompted by hints and mutterings from Mrs Jiggers, who did not approve of the new arrangement. It was wrong for a child born to be a lady, a member of the upper classes, to descend to the level of servants. It upset the natural order of things. Being uneducated, Mrs Jiggers had not heard of the word *hierarchy*. But it is the word she would have used, to explain what it was that was being overturned, in her humble view.

But no one listened to her. Least of all Violet herself. It was Cabillaud to whom she was drawn, as though by magnetism. And to his domain, the kitchen.

So while Tobias Phelps spent his boyhood years climbing trees and digging his unusual toes in the sand of the beach, Violet Scrapie spent her childhood on the floor of the kitchen in Madagascar Street, playing with pots and pans, and gobbling up whatever tasty morsel the Belgian chef Cabillaud threw her way. For he had soon spotted the child's unseemly preoccupation with ingestion, and her vocation as a gastronome.

Nature or nurture? Who cares!

'*Ouvre la bouche, ferme les yeux, ma petite chérie!*' Cabillaud would order, and the child Violet would duly comply, her cherub's mouth agape, like a baby seal waiting to receive a herring from its mother. When she opened her eyes, she would have to guess what delicacy Cabillaud had popped through her parted lips.

What better training for a fine palate?

How many children have the good fortune to be able to distinguish, by the age of five, between fifteen different types of poultry? A whole genus of rodents? A hundred different herbs and spices? And how many children can claim to have access, via the carcasses in the ice house at the bottom of the garden, to a whole arkful of frozen meat, including such exotic rarities as the smooth savannah rhinoceros, the Mediterranean spotted turtle, the lesser quaggar, the two-headed Goan snake, the black-footed rabbit, Humboldt's penguin, Rufous Tinamon, the Surinam toad, and the Gentleman Monkey?

Answer: not many!

Time passed, and Violet cooked and cooked and cooked. And ate, ate, ate.

By the age of ten, she was fast turning into a human pyramid, a heavy wedge that moved about the house from kitchen to dining room, from dining room to kitchen, sweating like a great cheese on castors, a stack of cookery books a permanent fixture under her arm. The Empress was at her wits' end, and repaired with increasing frequency to the comfort of the Ouija board and the seance.

'The girl's a mystery!' she confided in the spirits. 'She reads a cookery book the way she eats a plate of cake. Blink and it's over!'

The spirits shrugged their shoulders.

Could Violet perhaps be shipped off to somewhere like Australia? the Empress wondered.

Crash! The breaking of a mixing bowl.

Sloop! the licking of a sauced finger.

Yum yum. *C'est bon.*

'Or might New Zealand be further, as the crow flies?'

The spirits shrugged again. 'Wait and see,' they said.

'Fat lot of good *you* are,' muttered the Laudanum Empress, crumpling up a page of automatic writing and hurling it into the fire.

She bought Violet her first corset at the age of eleven. The child was popping out all over the place; her body had to be put under control. One day she actually fainted from constriction in the street, and collapsed on to a grocer's cart, knocking a thousand carrots off a precarious pile. With considerable difficulty but even more exasperation, the Empress took her by the scruff, and they stumbled through the sea of rolling orange veg, the grocer's boy yelling, the Empress flinging a sovereign behind her as you might throw salt over your left shoulder to ward off evil.

To Harrod's, pronto!

'Bring us the biggest corset you have,' ordered the Empress, 'and be ready to add gussets.' And she made a thin, tight line of her perfect mouth.

'A relative?' asked the assistant, as Violet disappeared to try on the hosiery.

'No,' responded the Empress quickly, checking the mirror, where a fine figure of a woman – a creature of remarkable beauty, in fact, to whom the word 'paragon' could be applied without exaggeration – greeted her gaze. 'Just a child I happen to know.'

From the changing room, the sound of huffing and puffing, and the distinct odour of adolescent perspiration.

'I despair of you,' hissed the Laudanum Empress later, as they sat before a plate of cinnamon muffins in the tea shop downstairs. What could a mother do with such a child? Having felt lately the call of the Other Side, she knew she was not much longer for this world. Could she perhaps have some influence in death, which she had so signally failed to have in life? It was worth trying.

'You'll be the death of me, Vile,' she warned, stirring sugar into her tea with an angry clatter.

There's nothing wrong with *me*, thought Violet, as she crammed another muffin into her face.

Even then she had a sense of purpose – that rare sense of purpose that comes to children who instinctively know part of their destiny. She didn't play with dolls. Or hoops. Or marbles, bats or balls. She watched Cabillaud, studied the recipes of Mrs Beeton and Miss Eliza Acton, and hatched grown-up plans.

CHAPTER 7

IN WHICH THE ROGUE MALE
ATTEMPTS INTEGRATION IN
THE STONED CROW

Thunder Spit relished its heritage, both ancient and modern: its ancient chalk soil, its spanking new community centre, its fame among amateur botanists for its wide variety of sedges ('the sedge capital of England', according to the *Outdoorsman*), its proximity to the Gannymede power station, its sugar-beet and parsnip polyculture, its history of unprecedented cowardice during the plague of 1665, its tortoiseshell cats, its two petrol stations, its River Flid, winner of the Pollution Challenge Award of 1997, its mobile video-hire service, its post-modern vicar, its intolerance of New Age travellers, its prehistoric fossil heritage, its electronic speed-sensitive road-signs which flashed the words SLOW DOWN, YOU ARE GOING TOO FAST at vehicles that drove through the high street at over 50 k.p.h., its Great Flood of 1858, its early and wholehearted commitment to agricultural phosphates.

All this I learned from Norman Ball, my first Thunder Spitter. I met him in the Stoned Crow. I arrived at 6 p.m., and thought: First stop, a beer. I gave the Nuance a little pat on the arse. She'd done well. I parked her round the back of the pub, near the quay. Across the car-park I saw a driving-test centre and a billboard advertising Lucozade, both dwarfed by sky. Too much sky, I thought, as I locked the car – chk! – with the remote-control doo-da. So much sky, compared to land and buildings, that it seemed to be pressing down on you. Agoraphobia is probably quite similar to claustrophobia that way. I looked across to where I reckoned the sea should have been, but there was a huge

71

concrete barrier in the way, covered in strangely hopeful-looking graffiti:

DON'T DRINK AND DRIVE – TAKE CRACK AND FLY
ROSE AND BLANCHE ARE SLAGS
URBAN CHAOS

Forget the geography, I told myself, as I pushed open the swing door of the pub. Concentrate on the social life.

So it was through the cheery cigarette fug of the Stoned Crow that I caught my first real glimpse of the town that was to be my new home. The pub windows had that thick Olde Worlde glass, but through a more transparent section I could see the black, gloomy silhouette of a church spire, and a row of bollards. I watched a woman in a sou'wester being dragged by a border collie across the high street. The lead she was holding had a handle like a giant trigger. The dog was wearing a bright coat with a spaceship design; the sort of thing a boy of six might have specified if his granny had offered to knit him an exciting woolly. Bloody hell, people and their pets, I thought. At least I'll be dealing with farm animals here. I remembered Mr Jenks at the Veterinary Society saying something about Lord Chief Justice sheep. What the hell were they? I downed my beer, and was just telling myself to go and buy another, when I saw a fat man at the bar waving at me.

'A stranger in our midst!' he called across. 'What's the betting you're the new vet?'

He was coming towards me now with two pints of bitter, foam frothing down the sides of the glasses and on to the red-patterned carpet, walking carefully, like he was giving his own blubber a piggy-back. He planted the pints on little flannel mats, then eased himself down next to me. The red velour stool shuddered.

'Welcome to Thunder Spit, mate. You're among friends.'

'It's an honour to be here,' I said, though what I'd seen of Thunder Spit had yet to enthral me. 'I'm a big fan of the countryside. Used to come up this way on camping holidays as a kid. Plant flags on sandcastles. Cool stuff.'

We shook hands.

'Buck de Savile,' I said. I was pleased to notice that he looked impressed.

He told me that Norman Ball was the name. 'Good journey? Saw you drive up while I was in the little boys' room, pointing Percy at the porcelain. Noticed your Audi.' He gave me a thumbs-up sign. 'Nice one. Nuance, if memory serves?'

'Yup. Turbo.'

Despite the burp smell, you couldn't help warming to a man who'd buy you a beer and could appreciate the thrill of a shiny red chassis. Norman told me he was in insurance, and that, for his sins, he commuted to Hunchburgh. As well as being an active member of the village council, he was a keen DIY-er.

'A fanatic, you could say. I'm a dab hand with a router, though I say it myself. So need any advice, just give me a tinkle.' Something about the way he spoke made me feel that I knew him already, but I couldn't put my finger on what it was. 'So, young Buck,' said Norman. 'To what do we owe the pleasure?'

I had known this question would pop up at some point, and I'd formulated a few Giselle-free replies on the journey up, while trying out some of my new faces. Knowing the veterinary complaints procedure well, I reckoned I had at least six months' leeway *vis-à-vis* Mrs Mann. If not more. According to my enquiries, most complaints were dropped as soon as the pet-owner acquired a new baby-substitute. Boundless hope.

'I got fed up with pets,' I told Norman. 'They were too –'

'Tame?' Norman guffawed. I couldn't help laughing, too.

'After the wild stuff then?' Norman asked. 'I'll give you wild stuff. My wife Abbie was clearing out the loft, doing a big old spring-clean-and-chucking-out job, cos the planning permission came through to refurbish. It's a listed building, the Old Parsonage, so we had a helluva wait. Anyway, what do we find up there?'

I realised he was waiting for an answer, and racked my brains.

'Some of that vintage Japanese pornography?'

'Not even close, mate.'

'A skeleton in a cupboard?'

'Hey. Getting warmer. A collection of stuffed animals, as a matter of fact.'

My heart sank: I knew what was coming next.

'Heirloom of Abbie's, bless her heart,' Norman is saying. 'Dates back to the nineteenth century sometime. Reckons there must've been a taxidermist in the family, way back. She says they're a dust-trap, wants the whole lot binned. Fancy a squizzerooney?'

You come across this in all jobs, I suppose. You're a lawyer, and they ask if you've ever had to defend someone you knew was guilty. You're a dustman, and they enquire whether you've ever come across a wad of banknotes in a rubbish bin. You're a doctor, and people want you to look at their piles. You're a vet, and they demand an inspection of Great-Aunt Ethel's stuffed menagerie.

'It'd be a pleasure,' I said, groaning inwardly. 'I did a bit of taxidermy myself at vet school. It's quite an art. Not one I ever mastered myself, I'm afraid, though,' I told him, remembering a succession of botched squirrels and rabbits with wire sticking out in unhelpful places. We were taught by an ex-con, who said it was his way of putting something back into the community. 'It's the ears,' I added. 'They're a bugger. So what've you got? Any interesting specimens?'

'Most of them birds and small mammals, by the looks. Oh, and an ostrich. Blue eyes, rather human. And they're all wearing old-fashioned frocks and breeches and stuff, like something out of a kinky costume drama. There's a monkey, too. Wearing pantaloons.'

I had a sudden picture of Giselle in her pink frock and her nappy, stiffening with rigor mortis on my operating table, and felt a chill creep over me.

'You all right, mate?' he asked. 'You look like you've seen a ghost.'

'I'm fine,' I mumbled.

'Talking of ghosts,' he said, 'we've got one back at the Old Parsonage. Victorian lady. Quite a beauty. She'd be fanciable, I reckon, if she had a bit more flesh on her. The Laudanum Empress, she calls herself. Wears a lot of petticoats. Abbie reckons she popped out of the same wardrobe she found the animals in. She's been wreaking havoc with our telly.'

That was another post-Millennial thing. I'd read about it. Supernatural sightings had gone up by 300 per cent. This, I thought, does not bode well.

'Fancy some nibbles?' Norman's asking. 'Pork sushi? Cheese Loons?'

And he's wheeling his bulgy bottom across to the bar.

What did Norman and I discuss that night, before the momentous newsflash?

The usual things: how United were doing, my virtual Elvis collection, the new freak strain of ulcerative arthritis in Spain, the pros and cons of the new Windows software, the fact that it was quite a year for aphids but you could zap them with that new eco-chemical, the latest on the Fertility Crisis. It made Norman glad he wasn't my age. He had two grown-up girls, he said, his 'Gruesome Twosome'. Rose and Blanche. The names somehow rang a bell.

'We've had twins in the family since way back when,' Norman is saying. 'My side of the family, that. My mother was a Tobash.'

He might as well have told me she was a Martian, for all it meant to me.

It was that evening, from Norman, that I learned that Thunder Spit, population fifteen thousand, had once been a herring-shaped peninsula, but a land-reclamation scheme back in the late 1980s had knocked sense into its impractical geography, rendering it more a suburb of Judlow than a separate town.

'Some folk were against it being rationalised,' said Norman.

75

'But not me. Include me out, I said. Me and the hard core on the Council stuck to our guns. It put paid to the barmy one-way system for a start.' He had a weak bladder; as he wobbled off for yet another 'Jimmy Riddle', he called over his shoulder: 'Show me a man who says he isn't proud of being a Thunder Spitter, Buck, and I'll show you a liar!'

While he was gone, I wrote a mental list:

1. Sort out the surgery.
2. Check out the farmers.
3. Get laid.

Norman returns with two more beers, slosh, slosh, and another fistful of plastic-wrapped snacks. He plonks the lot on the table, and beer-foam whudders down the sides of our glasses.

'Cheers.' He slurps a big mooshful of bitter.

And then, as though intercepting item number three on my list: 'Women. I love 'em to bits, but do I understand them? The hell I do!' There is a pause, as I nod and he ruminates. 'Woman's a mysterious creature,' he pronounces finally. 'And we're entranced by her mystery, aren't we, Buck, as men?' I try out one of my new agreeing faces. 'I saw a documentary about it,' he continues. 'It's all to do with the DNA business.'

Here we go, I thought. Another spouter of gobshite putting in his ha'p'orth on the subject. There's nothing worse than a scientific ignoramus with a biological theory. They pick them up like verrucae. Norman's telling me it's all in the genes.

'DNA's simplicity itself, Buck. I reckon that, in a nutshell, it's all about history having to replicate itself. Enigma variations on a theme, type-of-thing. Bit of this, bit of that, chuck it all in the melting-pot. You've heard about these new pig-heart transplants. Their DNA's been doctored so's we don't reject them. Amazing, eh? And Jessie Harcourt, she's got a llama's pancreas. You know what I reckon about this Fertility Crisis,' he said. 'I reckon our time's up. That's the bottom line. Look at the

76

dinosaurs. They died out, didn't they? Same thing's happening to *Homo Britannicus*.' He paused to burp. 'We've evolved as far as we can, mate.'

That's what the woman on the radio had said, too.

As a child, I used to try to imagine how the earth looked when it all began, those millions of years ago. The whole planet was just a wilderness of mares' tails and dinosaurs and stagnant pools, back then. And the wind wasn't so much wind, as a load of blue steam whirling about. I used to dream about earthquakes splitting the crust of the earth, like a failed soufflé of my mum's, or eczema. I'd read those science-fiction comics. They'd show artists' impressions of lower life-forms squabbling for supremacy. They were always bulbous, with little eyes on stalks, and they'd be submerged in a kind of churning primordial gloop. I had a vision of time speeded up, and dwarfy creatures with fins – not animals, but not plants either, a kind of horrible in-between thing – wriggling and twisting. Eating one another and being eaten.

'I once watched a praying mantis eating a beetle,' I told Norman. 'Its jaws crunched from the side. They're like mechanised clamps, an insect's jaws.' I demonstrated with my thumb and index finger, making pinching motions at Norman's nose, and he shrank back in mock-fear, laughing. 'The beetle put up quite a fight,' I said. 'It was still trying to defend itself when it only had one leg left, hanging by a thread.' It had really impressed me. Things like that do, when you're six. Then you forget about them, until suddenly they snap into your head one evening, years later, in a pub, after a few lagers. 'Kicking and struggling to the very last. In the end, all that was left was a back foot, waving.'

Norman was looking at me sideways.

'Well, that's us, isn't it?' I continued, remembering why I'd thought about the mantis. 'We're that foot, waving. We're being eaten alive. Swallowed up by time.'

He nodded slowly. 'Point there, Buck. Bit of a philosopher, then, are you?'

To counteract this flattering but way-off-the-mark impression, I did him one of my brooding Elvis looks, and he guffawed.

It was my dad who told me about evolution, or rather his idea of it. I don't suppose that either of us realised, then, how important it would become.

Even before the gizzard stone and, later, my Saturday job at Harper's, I'd had a passion for skeletal biology, fuelled by the discoveries I made in the back garden, a long, narrow sliver of land subsiding towards the canal, black as Coke, which flowed sluggishly in a diagonal across the south of the borough. Both garden and canal were flanked by thin privet hedges and dust-filled urban weeds – bastard forms of dandelion, burdock, teasels, and rosebay willowherb which had mutated to outwit the weedkiller my father used to attack them. Every September, around the time the school term started, the cotton-wool tufts of willowherb drifted aimlessly on gusts of wind and settled on the lawn like lint, stirring up that strange feeling of melancholy that accompanies the changes of season in a city. At weekends, while my brothers helped our father fight weeds or prune hydrangeas or tackle rhubarb, I'd pick my way over the upturned earth, avoiding the lumps of half-buried cat-shit, to exhume the more ancient detritus of nature: snail-shells, cow's teeth, old sparrow-skulls, a dog's femur as drilled and pocked as a hard sponge. By the canal I found dried beetles, dead dragonflies, stiffened birds, and once, three-quarters of a fox. I became obsessed with this jetsam of calcium, and the audacity of its design.

'Daddy, how did they make this?' I ask, thrusting part of a shrew up at him.

My father's spade is an extension of his foot, a submerged stilt. He's digging a trench for beets. 'Make what?'

'This bone. Look, it's teeny-weeny. Look, Dad.'

'It made itself, Bobby. The shrew grew in its mummy's tummy.'

'But who made the mummy shrew?'

'The mummy shrew's mum and dad.'

'So, Dad, who made the first ever shrew, then?'

'Evolution. It developed from another type of creature.' Dad heaves his weight down on the spade, makes an '*Eurkah*' noise, wipes sweat from his upper lip, stands back, and looks love-hatingly on his tiny, fenced kingdom. The beet-trench has thrown up a negative of itself: a long bulbous spine of earth.

'What kind of creature, Dad?'

'The elephant, I believe. Now help me with this root.'

'And the elephant?'

'From the pig.'

'And the pig?' I'm enjoying this; it's like that game where you keep asking *why* until they give you some money for sweets.

Dad sighs. 'There were little fishy things. They crawled out of the water and lost their fins and learned to breathe and eventually became pigs.'

'And the fishy things? Where did they come from?'

'From the sea.'

'But how did they get in the sea, Dad, in the first place?'

'They grew from plants. Plants that –' He looks uneasily about, checking that no neighbours are in earshot, perhaps sensing that he is on shaky ground. He lowers his voice slightly, just in case. 'Plants that developed from tiny underwater mushrooms.'

'And the mushrooms?'

Dad looks up at the sky and frowns. A pigeon whizzes past, as though on a mission. 'There was a big bang in space, and they burst out of nowhere.'

Even at the age of seven, I suspected that this was bollocks.

Norman's still talking about DNA. I haven't really been listening.

'Anyway, this documentary I saw, on BBC 2 – no, I tell a lie, it was Channel Four – there was a bloke saying the mystery of woman is actually just a mystery of DNA. And once we've unravelled the conundrum, the women's eggie things'll get back to normal, and they'll start getting pregnant again, and we'll be laughing. But in the meantime –'

Here he threw up his hands and made a face, and I made a face, too, and laughed.

'Crying, more like,' I joked, picturing Holly and Mrs Mann huddled together over the complaint form, with a little urn containing Giselle's ashes stood next to them on a plinth.

'Anyway, *chez moi*,' says Norman, 'for mysterious, read infuriating. Take my Abbie: illogical is putting it mildly. She tries to set the video to record the Lottery, right, but she wants to watch something else while it's on. So what does Madame do? I call her Madame sometimes, Buck,' he confided, 'cos she's a French teacher. Well, French and home economics, actually, *pardonnez-moi, Monsieur*. Anyway, she records the thing she's *watching*, then acts all surprised when she discovers she hasn't recorded the *other* thing. And d'you know what she says to me? "Stupid machine," she says, and I quote: "I thought it could record two programmes at once, but all I've got is a blank tape." Woman's the eighth wonder of the world, I reckon. Mind you, joking apart,' says Norman (''Scuse I') belching, 'I'll give credit where credit's due. My two gals – Tweedles Dum and Dee, I call 'em, my daughters – they've never had any problems with technology. If there's one thing they've learned from yours truly, it's how to use an instruction manual.'

As I was to discover for myself, some weeks later, when they expertly demonstrated to me the workings of their vibrator.

I was in the middle of my Elvis impression – 'Jailhouse Rock', as I recall – when the barman shouted at me.

'Hey, you! Shut up over there! Shut up!'

Norman and I whirled round on our stools; so fast, in my case, that I had to grab hold of the table to stop myself spiralling into lift-off. When I regained my bearings, I saw that everyone in the pub had suddenly congregated around the television above the bar, and was gawping intently at the screen.

'Newsflash!' mouthed the barman through cupped hands,

and turned up the volume so that the television was blaring at full pitch.

The whole screen was filled with a scene of devastation. Dust falling. Firemen at work with hoses, shooting water and foam at the twisted metal-and-concrete armature of a multi-storey building in flames. A reporter in a hard hat and gas-mask picking his way through the smoking debris.

'This is all that remains of the National Egg Bank tonight, after it was blown up by a massive Semtex bomb,' he said. Even through the gas-mask, you could tell he was almost in tears.

We all gawped at the screen.

The reporter couldn't go on. After some more shots of fire-fighting and smoking detritus, all he could manage, through a muffled sob, was, 'Back to the studio.'

Where a tougher news nut took over. 'Britain's hopes for the future were dashed tonight,' the newscaster said, 'when a huge explosion ripped through the National Egg Bank. The building – and its contents – were completely destroyed. No organisation has claimed responsibility for the attack, but religious fundamentalists are suspected of being behind tonight's blast.'

The pub went completely silent as the news continued. There was now not a single British egg left in the world.

We watched, Superglued to our seats, to the very end of the extended news programme. Then the barman stood up and flicked off the TV. Still no one said anything. But the implications of what had happened must have sunk in to all of us at about the same time, because suddenly, as though choreographed, we all reached for our beers and downed the remains in one.

Then Norman spoke. 'Looks like that's the end of Albion, then, folks.'

Which was as good a cue as any to get rat-arsed.

CHAPTER 8

IN WHICH
DISEASE STRIKES

I did the splits agen the next nite, the woman wrote, *even tho sumthin about Him makes me scared enuf to piss. Him on the table an He kissis me an wen He stops I feel lik Im in luv but still scared.*

Wot els can you do, He asks me.

Revers crab, I sez. Scorpion. Headstand. Handstand. Human notte.

Bed, He sez. You is cumin to bed wiv me now.

Only after that I find out Hes rich.

It was on the beach that I looked up from a rockpool one morning and saw a boy. He was a stocky little figure, standing on the shoreline in the distance. He was wearing a strange knobbled head-dress, which I was curious to inspect more closely. When I approached, holding a crab in one hand like a gift but also, just in case, like a weapon, I saw a tough, confident face, topped by a huge lump of seaweed. Sandhoppers were shooting out of it hysterically in all directions.

'This is my warrior's helmet,' said the boy. He had a stone in his hand, which he threw and caught, threw and caught. I was frightened he might throw it at me: I was an easy target in the village. Only the week before, a four-year-old girl, Jessie Tobash, had called me Prune-face.

'I can see a little wentletrap in it,' I said, in a conciliatory way. Thanks to Herman's *Crustacea*, I knew the name of everything, from abalone to Nilsson pipefish, from dog cockle to sand-smelt.

From this distance the boy's helmet looked like the sort of hat Mrs Simpson wore to church, all precarious-looking and featuring cornucopias of foodstuffs and flowers made of felt: more a market scene than a piece of headgear. I recognised him now, from the playground at school. He was Tommy Boggs, the blacksmith's son. The Boggses were a rough, threatening family. They had loud voices and they shouted unstintingly, as if it was their job, and the father, Matthew Boggs, was often drunk: not quiet-drunk, like the fishermen, or happy-drunk, like Farmer Harcourt, or even tipsy-tottery drunk like Mrs Sequin, but wild and angry drunk like no one else. The Boggses were heathens, too, according to my father. I never once saw them in church, not even at Christmas or Easter. Their aunt read the future in tea-leaves, a sure sign, my father said, of spiritual wantonness.

As Tommy approached, I dug my toes into the sand to hide them. But he was looking at me questioningly.

'I collect crustacea,' I blurted, by way of conversation, hoping that words might defend me from him in case he saw fit to attack me. But the boy said nothing; he simply stood there in his seaweed get-up and stared, a human fortress. I felt the opposite – vulnerable without my shoes, like a hermit crab that's left the shelter of its shell.

Still the boy said nothing. He neither threatened me, nor shrank away.

In fact, he smiled.

And then, because I must have felt, suddenly, that I could trust this boy, and because I was lonely enough, despite my self-sufficiency, to feel the need of a young friend my own age, I did a desperate and unprecedented and foolishly brave thing: without warning, I withdrew my toes from the sand, and showed him the sad deformity of my feet.

'There,' I said. My soul was at that moment laid barer than it had ever been, and inside I quailed at the risk I had taken with this boy whom I did not know, and partly feared. What had possessed me? To this day, I am not sure, though I like to believe it was an inner instinct that guided me.

Tommy gazed down at my feet. Sea-water was lapping at them, leaving little bubbles that popped and died. He noted my flat-footedness, and the way my hairy toes sat all wrong.

'I can't run fast,' I told him. 'But I can beat my mother in any race, because of her bunions.' Still he said nothing, so I went on: 'And on Fridays I can beat my father, too, because of the marbles in his shoes.'

Tommy looked puzzled, but interested. He was clearly unacquainted with the Parson's weekly idiosyncrasy. He was still staring at my feet.

'I like them,' he said finally. 'They don't look too foolish to me. In fact, I would say they are magnificent.'

My heart somersaulted in joy, and I felt the tears sting in my eyes.

'But please tell no one,' I whispered.

'Our secret, then,' he said.

From that moment, Tommy and I were friends. Apart from the secret we now shared, we had other things in common: Tommy also had fleas, and an aggravating tapeworm, he told me. His was called Benedicta, but she mostly kept herself to herself.

My own tapeworm, Mildred, was a cruel mistress, however. Knowing her likes and dislikes to some extent, I did my best to appease her. Fortunately I shared her love of fruits, fungi and sweet berries – and it was Tommy who taught me where to find them. Sugar was unknown in Thunder Spit, though Tommy assured me that the streets of London were paved with hundreds of minuscule sugar-cubes like Roman mosaics, depicting the glories of Empire. But there were fruits aplenty. We went searching in the early mornings, before school, the cows staring at us as they always did with that resigned look they cast on humans, then trundling away, mucus trailing from their noses, when they caught a whiff of me. In summer, there were raspberries, and in autumn, we'd trawl the hedgerows and copses for hazelnuts or cram our mouths with wild strawberries.

Tommy and I became firm friends. When it rained, or during

84

the winter months when only a crazed fool would step on to the frozen beach, choked with salt and ice and lashed by a screeching wind, I used to visit Tommy and we would play together at the back of Mr Boggs' forge, where the furnace kept us warm. We'd spit on the dirt floor, full of iron filings, and rake the resulting grey-flecked mess about, while watching Tommy's huge muscular father bashing at red-hot steel as if it had done him some terrible wrong.

'That'll be me one day,' said Tommy, with that careless certainty of his, that was as part of him as his shadow.

Later, it was Tommy who taught me how to spill my seed, and I soon became expert at it, though I knew it to be wrong, because the Lord had said so, and my father had reinforced this message with another, more immediate threat; that the profane activity would blind me. Every time I indulged in my foul habit, I pictured my vision blurring until all I could see were little pinpricks of light in the firmament, but this never happened. In fact, the opposite; I always had the impression that my eyesight was clearer afterwards, as though a blockage had been removed.

Looking back, I can try to see myself as they saw me.

A boy with a need to ask questions.

A boy with a low-slung walk, a love of cliff-climbing, and a coarse thatch of red hair, always in his eyes.

A boy always small for his age, but surprisingly strong and agile, and with a natural love, said Parson Phelps, of the blessings of the physical world. (Also a natural love of throwing tantrums and playing practical jokes, such as placing a dead hedgehog on the seat of the Parson's chair at Sunday school. For this misdemeanour he was forced to administer three blows of the cane, to set an example to the other children.)

A boy who puzzles and infuriates his adoring parents with his need to show off by climbing dangerous rocks.

A boy who has become a little unruly.

And then, suddenly, a boy whose mother has developed an alarming cough.

A boy who, terrified by this cough, and hoping to take some of God's punishment on to himself, has now, at the age of thirteen, taken to extreme naughtiness.

The ship was a whaler *en route* to Hunchburgh, dragging an entire whale skeleton destined for Queen Victoria's wardrobe. I can still see it: the huge vessel lolling slowly out on the ebb tide, dragging the great bobbing stinking creature behind her as she drifts with the tide. And I can still recall the scene the next morning, and the ensuing cries and screams when the whole village realised what had happened: that Tommy Boggs and I, having stolen a file from Mr Boggs' forge, had cut the vessel loose from its moorings. By the time the sailors aboard ship worked out what had happened, and scolded the night watch for falling asleep, they were a league out at sea. It took a whole day to manoeuvre the ship back.

When you grab something, such as the attention of a whole village, you pay for it later. They put us in the village stocks and pelted us with wodges of goose-dung. And then, when the sun went down and we were released, our fathers came to collect us; Mr Boggs angry, and brandishing the metal bottom-whisk, Parson Phelps sorrowful, ashamed, and preoccupied with distressing events at home concerning the cough.

And now it is his turn to punish. I have been called a naughty jackanapes, and sent to my room, and locked in, but I feel safe, my world condensed to the span of this one room. And now I am here, eating stale bread and with only a drop of water left in my pottery bowl, unsure of why it came upon me to perform this act of naughtiness, and wondering whether the recent upheavals in the house – upheavals I have done my best to ignore – could have provoked me into an odd kind of madness.

For the sound of the cough has been getting worse.

If I close my ears and my eyes, time will stand still, and I will be safe.

My room is an attic they have arranged for me at the top of the Parsonage. There's a criss-cross of low beams, ideal for gymnastics, a writing desk, bed, a chair, and a simple rag rug, woven by Mrs Phelps in my favourite colours, mauve and green. And on the wall a picture I love: of Noah and his animals of the Ark. Noah stands on the deck, with his three sons and his nagging wife, and below him is spread the hierarchy of creatures, from mighty elephant down to humble ant. Looking down on them all from the top right-hand corner is the face of an elderly gent whose white beard dissolves into the grey storm-clouds of the Great Flood. Behind his head, a silver Heaven gleams. This is God, who has made us all. I am snuggled into my goose-down quilt, looking at the picture. A sea-beetle has crawled across its canvas surface, and is making its way inexorably towards God's Roman nose.

At last, I hear the rattle of the key in the door, and my father enters, pale-faced. Silently, I pray that he has simply come to punish me some more. But I know in my heart as I look at his drawn features and the set of his eyes that, next to what lurks downstairs, my misdemeanour with Tommy will pale into insignificance.

If I shut my ears and my eyes.

'Your mother is unwell,' he blurts out. 'I should have told you before, but I could not. I hoped that if I ignored it –'

I say nothing.

'Tobias! Did you hear me?'

Then I speak. 'So according to this picture, man's place is between God and the animals.' What I am thinking is that I would like to bring some warmth to his cold face. I notice on the Ark picture that the sea-beetle is now attempting to tunnel its way up God's left nostril, but to no avail. 'Why is that?'

'Why is a big question,' says the Parson, smiling stiffly. 'And it has a big answer. It's because we have souls, and the animals do not.'

'What does a soul look like, Father?' (Downstairs: cough, cough.)

'Well, some are bright and shining, if they are righteous, and others are blackened and shrivelled, if their owners have committed foul acts.' (Cough, cough.)

'If you cut up a man's body, would you see his soul?'

'Yes, son, you most assuredly would. It is situated above his heart, where it forms a translucent canopy.'

Later in life, when I had cause to reflect upon the nature of the human soul, I would wonder how Parson Phelps, who was not a stupid man, came to dream up such lunatic twaddle.

Then, from the floor below, the terrible sound comes again. I will remember it for ever. This time it is too loud to ignore. Loud and brutal.

'That is nothing like her usual cough,' I venture.

And he takes me to his breast and holds me tight.

That night I dreamed I was aboard a vessel that was like a whale inside. I was Jonah but a son of Noah, too. My job was to feed the caged beasts that surrounded me – tigers and hippopotami and giant wingless birds – but I could not for I too was caged, and manacled like a slave.

My foster-mother was always good to me. I remember her bent over the stone sink, scaling fish, the plainness of her face, the redness of her hands, rough from heavy work. Or forcing down my throat a new purgative she'd invented to oust our mutual enemy, Mildred. Or standing by the stove, frying barley flip-cakes for my tea. Or at the scrubbed-pine table stripping the perfumed seeds off sprigs of lavender, to stuff into little bags and put in my underwear drawer. The trouble she took to make a fine man of me, knowing how much harder I would have to struggle in life than my contemporaries! She must have known, deep in her soul, as she watched me clambering up the huge oak tree outside the door, my crazy shoes slipping on the bark, that I would one day have dire need of those little civilising touches that make a God-fearing gentleman.

I suspected it myself, too.

My mother's cough could no longer be hidden; we lived with it every day. We saw it doubling her up. Tearfully, one day, she informed me that she had become possessed by a Thing.

88

'If only I could cough the Thing out,' she said, 'I feel I should recover, Tobias. It is crushing me from within.'

But the Thing stayed put, and grew; every day her breathing became shallower, and her suffering racked the whole house.

At night, I lay in bed watching the sea-salt twinkling on my collection of shells, listening to the cawing of sea-birds above my attic room, and my mother's wild cough coming up from below. It mocked us all. It was like a demon's laugh. I prayed, but a little pang at the base of my spine told me that prayers were no use.

Mother took a whole summer to die; I measured out her wasting in the progress of the vegetable plot which grew lusher and more abundant every day, as though it were a parasite siphoning off her vitality and growing fat on it. And I was a conspirator in this process: for two months I tended the vegetable patch with a fury and an intensity that startled me. I was surely searching for something other than earth, but I never did discover exactly what. We moved my mother's bed to the window, so that she could see me working. The sight of it pleased her, but I felt she was watching me digging her grave.

I was thirteen, that age of reckless physical sprouting and transcendental uncertainty, which provided me with a new cross to bear: a permanent uncouth urge in my loins, which I did my utmost to quell. I worked harder and harder, hoping to exhaust myself thus. As Mrs Phelps drank thin soup, and spluttered into a handkerchief, I planted potatoes, and grew crimson radishes whose furious sting punished the mouth, bulging Cinderella pumpkins, skinny haricot beans, and purple-veined, crinkle-leafed cabbages. While her mind wandered back repeatedly to the goose farm of her girlhood, and to the incompetence of the Parson's male object (it was from her delirious ravings that I caught my first inkling of the human mating process), I killed slugs with sea-salt collected from rockpools, and planted garlic to keep the snails at bay. Autumn came, and as Mrs Phelps lay skeletally dying in her bed, I harvested a bumper crop of sprouts, and carrots as thick as a bull's horn, and an ornamental gourd, knobbled and useless, stippled pale and dark green.

One day she waved her hand at me, summoning me to her bedside. When she spoke, her words were wheezed out like air from a stiff pair of bellows, and her inhalations were winded gasps of pain. I put my ear close to her mouth.

'I love that gourd,' she croaked. 'It is a freakish vegetable, without obvious purpose, but it has its place in our garden. God knew what he was doing when he made the gourd.'

There was a pause, as she breathed in and out a few more times, raspingly. I wished I could breathe for her. But all I could do was watch.

'That gourd, in its oddity, and freakishness, reminds me of you,' she said finally. If this was supposed to be a compliment, it was sadly misjudged, I thought. Oddity? Purposelessness? Freakishness? A gourd? I'd have preferred her to use her precious breath on something a little kinder.

She fell asleep again. It was midnight when she woke up, or seemed to, and sat rigid and suddenly attentive. Then she said, 'Listen to me carefully, Tobias. I have some requests I must make of you before I go to Heaven.'

'Yes, Mother,' I whispered. 'Tell me what you want. And I will do it.'

'Firstly,' she breathed, 'I want you to plant that gourd upon my grave so that I can take the memory of you with me where I go.'

'I will, Mother.' I would have agreed to anything, at any level of absurdity, to make her happy.

'And Tobias,' she croaked. I put my ear to her lips again, to hear. 'I would have liked to purge Mildred,' she mustered. 'Perhaps I tried too hard. When I am gone, do all you can to coax her out, Tobias.'

'I will, Mother. I swear.'

'And Tobias.'

'Yes, Mother?'

'Remember that God does not like a man to be naked.

90

Keep your body covered at all times, son. For the sake of modesty.'

'Yes, Mother. It goes without saying.' It had always been an unspoken rule in the Parsonage that one should always keep as much clothing on as possible, even when washing. I had never so much as glimpsed myself naked, and would not think of doing so.

'And there is something else,' my mother croaked. 'We do not know where you came from,' she whispered. 'But promise me that you will never visit the Travelling Fair of Danger and Delight.'

The Fair came once a year, and though I had always been forbidden to go, I had longed one day to taste its illicit pleasures. My mother's mention of the Fair – and of my unknown origins – puzzled me. Had my parents not always told me that, unlike other children, who were brought by storks or found beneath gooseberry bushes, I had been left at the altar of St Nicholas's Church by none other than God himself? This was the first time I had thought otherwise, and then and there, a seed of curiosity was planted deep within me.

'Promise me,' my mother repeated.

'I promise,' I told her. *We do not know where you came from.*

'Good boy,' she said, and fell back into a painful twitching doze.

'She wants to be buried beneath a gourd,' I reported to my father the next morning. He had been cleaning his shoes at the kitchen table, waxing them with great care with black wax polish, and buffing them, bashing the brush against the leather in the same particular motion and rhythm that he always used. Now it was his turn to look surprised and pained. I remember him standing there, a buckled shoe in one hand, the little black brush in the other, the smell of black shoe-polish, vinegary and burnt.

'And holding the Bible, of course,' I added quickly. The lie seemed to help.

The next day my mother coughed suddenly, and very hard, and the Thing that had been tormenting her shot out of her mouth and on to the white sheet. We stared. My father groaned.

'What is this?' she mouthed faintly, picking up between thumb and forefinger a purple-black object, leather-like and riddled with holes. She held it aloft. 'Look, dear Edward, dear Tobias, I have coughed up my own soul and it is all shrivelled with sin, and as black as night! Forgive me, O Lord!'

Two minutes later she was dead.

The Parson and I did not believe the Thing could be her soul. It was too solid, and it stank. So when the doctor told us it was a cruelly diseased lung, we were enormously relieved.

'For if that poor good woman contained an ounce of evil,' sobbed the Parson, grinding his teeth in sorrow, 'then I contain three thousand tons.'

And I five thousand, I wailed inwardly, thinking of the pleasurable but unholy habit Tommy Boggs had taught me in the privacy of the sand-dunes, and at which I now had considerable and shameful expertise. There was no more talk of translucent canopies after that. We buried my mother in the cemetery beneath a huge mackerel sky, the sea-salt mingling with our tears, the sand-grass prickling our ankles, the kittiwakes squalling, the sea roaring wide as a whale's yawn. The next summer, a gourd plant was to appear on the grave, but the gourds were not of the same variety as the knobbled green one I had planted. These fruits were orange, with a frilled rim, and yellow stains; Parson Phelps said he found them miraculous but disturbing, a sign that God's plan for Nature had veered off course.

As indeed it had.

CHAPTER 9

THE SCRAPIE DINOSAUR

'There will be two world wars,' murmurs the Laudanum Empress, yawning over her untouched cup and saucer. It is the heyday of her psychic particles. 'As a result, a million skulls will be strewn all over France.' She pauses, squinting sideways. 'But on the more positive side, there will be something known as long-life milk.'

Since the birth of her bovine daughter Violet, the particles have not ceased to swarm about her head like a cloud of angry mosquitoes, and the slightest peripheral glance on her part can conjure up a dizzying maelstrom of flotsam from the future. Even Dr Scrapie, a strict non-believer in hocus-pocus, has recognised the presence of the famous particles.

'Pardon?' he says irritably. He hates being interrupted while reading the paper, and this morning he has been engrossed in several articles of interest. A more experimentally inclined scientist might have been inspired to harness the Empress's particles to his research, but Dr Scrapie's imagination is sadly limited. Of what concern is the future to him, he argues, when the present is proving so problematic? The Scrapies are taking breakfast with their daughter Violet. Time has passed, as it does; the child is now sprouting two majestic bosoms.

'There will be heat-seeking missiles, and split-crotch panties,' says the Empress. 'Not to mention a substance called Play-Doh.'

Scrapie grunts, and shuffles his newspaper. She's talking balderdash again. Violet butters some more toast, pours green

Gunpowder tea into bone china, swirls in milk, applies her spectacles and skims an article on a page her father has discarded about how slavery on the American plantations is a cruel and inhuman thing, and must be stopped. She bites into a beef mushroom. All men were born equal, the writer argues. Then a sliced tomato, somewhat underdone for her taste. Rich and poor, Negro and white man. But we must beware of taking things too far. This butter is rancid! Women, for example, might anticipate sharing these equal rights. But if we accept that, as some strident females in our midst are urging, what next? Children? Dogs? Macaws? Woodlice?

'There will be gambling machines called one-armed bandits,' says the Laudanum Empress. 'And artists will display their own excrement in galleries.'

'Pass the marmalade, will you, please?' says Violet, sipping more tea, as she glances at her mother, all madness and beauty and draped shawls and shimmering particles and glistening jet beads.

'Marmalade,' murmurs the Empress. Her heavy-lidded eyes have turned inward again, speaking silent volumes: *Daughter – bother me not, for I am not at home.* Aerial buzzings, automatic writing, Ouija boards, phantom scraps, whisperings and groans from the past and the future; these have been the stuff of Mother's life for as long as Violet can remember. How much is drug-induced, how much the result of insanity, and how much real, Violet has never fathomed; all she knows is that Mother is very much elsewhere, and always will be. Returning to her article on human rights, Violet fails to notice the dish of marmalade levitating itself. Or making slow but efficient progress across the table in her direction, as per her request.

'Do you know,' whispers the Laudanum Empress softly, 'that there will still be beggars on the streets of London in two hundred years' time? Progress is a dangerous myth, I can assure you. If my particles are to be believed, the world is moving not forwards, but backwards. I see men and women dancing and cavorting in the open air half-naked, like savages.

I see a vehicle called the Audi Nuance. I see the entire nation fizzling into extinction!'

'Come along now, Mother,' says Violet briskly, patting the Empress's arm and adjusting her shawl like an invalid's. 'You are getting hysterical again.'

'Hysteria is in the eye of the beholder. Your orange conserve has arrived.'

'Thanks, Mother,' says Violet, as the dish settles itself on the table before her.

The Empress sighs. We see only what we wish to see.

Dr Scrapie shuffles his newspaper. There is an article in it about old maids. Distressed spinsters. Their financial cost to the family. Their social status. Their general undesirability. As he observes his daughter Violet consuming her usual gargantuan breakfast, a terrible note of doom strikes within the heart of Dr Ivanhoe Scrapie, and shudders there for several minutes.

'According to this newspaper article, a girl like Violet will never marry,' he announces bleakly.

'I don't trust the word *never*,' declares Mrs Scrapie. 'Especially in print. My spirits say that Violet's actually in with a chance.'

'No,' says Scrapie firmly. 'Impossible. Never in a thousand years. Just look at her. She'll never marry because she's *completely unmarriageable!*'

'Good,' thinks Violet, dusting toast-crumbs from her two newish breasts. 'That's one thing Father and I *can* agree on.'

Violet is opposed to marriage – or rather, to the act of union it legitimises. It was only last week that she witnessed Jacques-Yves Cabillaud coitally occupied in the chopping room with Maisie, the scullery maid from next door. She shudders as the scene revisits her: Maisie is crouched on the chopping-table, her skirt over her head, an apple in her mouth like a stuck pig. Cabillaud rocks behind her, as if he is steering a boat, his face wild and throttled.

'Water will cost more than wine,' the Empress is droning.

'And there will be a Millennial flood that rains down poison!'

Violet sighs, as the Empress's wretched particles spew forth their usual crazed concoctions, relayed by the channel of her vocal cords. 'A cobweb of misinformation and gossip will buzz all over the world like an aura,' she continues, 'but it will be corrupted by a giant lunatic headache, and sink into mist.'

'She'll never marry because she is a dinosaur,' says Ivanhoe Scrapie, ignoring his wife and expanding angrily on his old-maid theme, fuelled by the spinster article in *The Times*. 'Look, Charlotte. Observe the quantities. She eats as much as a bloody dinosaur.'

Mrs Scrapie jerks out of her trance of future particles and gives a faint smile of acknowledgement.

'Did that man over there say something?' she questions vaguely. Her voice is slurred. Scrapie rustles his newspaper angrily; there's another article here that's getting his goat, concerning a newly recycled zoological rumour that's doing the rounds. Meanwhile Violet remains silent: it's impolite to speak with your mouth full. Besides, she agrees with her father. She *is* like a dinosaur, in that she is developing a thick skin.

'It's what's inside that matters, Father,' she grunts, finally, wiping her mouth on a napkin and patting her satisfied stomach. Her celebration of the alimentary canal, aided and abetted by Cabillaud, has given her a wisdom beyond her years.

A wisdom, and a certain kind of odd grace.

Don't laugh: despite the uncooked-pastry aspect of her face, and her somewhat buck teeth, which render her not a *traditional* beauty, she has grace, and there's no explaining it. You either do or you don't. All sorts of things can be embedded in fat. Grace is one of them.

Violet, under the auspices of Jacques-Yves Cabillaud, has been continuing to expand her childish girth. At two she had already been pronounced a heffalump; by seven, she was the size and shape of a barrel. And now –

'Why do her very expensive dresses always manage to look

like an old rug thrown over a milking cow?' the Empress murmurs, sipping her laudanum.

But yet – deep down, deep, deep within, there is grace.

'I said a *dinosaur*,' repeats Dr Scrapie, returning to the subject of spinsters and society.

'Yes, dear,' murmurs the Empress, whose particles are now receiving some unusual signals from the ghostly and unappetising future, concerning freeze-dried coffee granules. 'A dinosaur. That's what you said.'

Dinosaurs were the talk of the town; the terrible lizard had the educated world a-jitter with excitement. Bones of these lumbering and monstrous creatures had recently been discovered in the chalk soil of Lyme Regis, and fossilised dragons had been unearthed in China. A new and frightening light was being shed on the makings and doings of the earth. Minds boggled. Dr Scrapie had attended a banquet in Crystal Palace, inside a concrete replica of the iguanodon, where afterwards, in a japonica bush, he had come across a set of false teeth stuck in a meringue. The incident had marked him. Meanwhile a Czech monk called Gregor Mendel had made some alarming discoveries about reproduction in peas, which might or might not disprove the existence of God, and there were rumours that Darwin's *Beagle* voyage, on which his own chef Cabillaud claimed to have been a crew-member, had gathered enough zoological information to challenge the Creation story itself! Furthermore, in this morning's *Times*, Dr Scrapie has just read that Lamarck's Theory – that it is possible for a child to inherit characteristics acquired during its parents' lifetime, such as a liking for mulligatawny soup, or an ability to play scales upon the pianoforte – is once again being resurrected, and that as a result (oh foolish clowns!) London is now rife with allegations that, as of tomorrow, if a man lost an eye, his son would be born a cyclops like the porcupine in the Zoological Museum's Abnormality Annexe.

'Tosh!' Scrapie now yells, having finished the article, and flinging down *The Times*. 'I stuffed that porcupine myself! Its

97

father was completely normal, and I have the paperwork to prove it! It's all a pack of bloody lies!'

'That's where you are wrong,' says the Empress languidly. 'There's something in the air. I can feel it wafting past me.'

Violet, future distressed spinster, butters yet more toast with a practised hand.

'But these gaps in the fossil record,' muses Scrapie. 'There's no explaining them. It's not enough for Darwin to say that they will be *filled* one day, that the geologists of the future will *find the missing pieces*. We want to know the answers *now*, dammit!'

'They will never find them,' says the Empress suddenly, and sharply. 'The gaps will remain just that, Ivanhoe: gaps. I've seen it. They are evidence of sudden, rapid changes. Transformations. There is . . .' but here she trails off.

Scrapie lights a noxious Havana cigar, and the Empress sinks back into her cloud of particles, which is now exhibiting the collapse of the worldwide Web.

'A bloody dinosaur,' repeats Scrapie, his glance once again scaling the human Himalaya that is his youngest child and twiddling his pencil over a diagram he is working on. He is having a table made out of fossilised dinosaur turds, sliced through and arranged in a mosaic pattern.

I am the child of mad people, reflects Violet Scrapie, scribbling a note of the ingredients for this evening's dinner on the tablecloth.

'Tell me about the Gentleman Monkey, Father,' she says. 'Cabillaud and I are planning to stew its flesh tonight. With coriander and a rather unusual shrimp sauce.'

Over the years, thanks to the imaginative genius of Jacques-Yves Cabillaud, the willingness of Violet, and the ready availability of exotic animal carcasses, the Scrapie diet has grown ever more refined, audacious and splendid. Violet has learned how to baste and pickle and stuff and jelly and devil, and to make forty-five different kinds of pastry. She has also thrown herself wholeheartedly into the waste-not-want-not philosophy of *Cuisine Zoologique*. By the time the second shipment of Arctic ice arrived for the ice house, she and Cabillaud had prepared material for the first three chapters of Cabillaud's book, *Cuisine Zoologique: une philosophie de la viande*. Cabillaud would cast his mind back to Brussels and remember dishes he had seen through the windows of restaurants, or smelt wafting from beneath the doors of imaginary châteaux, castles of air. Reminiscing and imagining, he would describe and then re-formulate, and together with his young assistant, concoct recipes that grew increasingly unusual. Cabillaud was particularly inventive when it came to sauces – so much so, Mrs Scrapie had the nerve to complain in one of her more practical moments, that one was never sure what kind of meat or fish one was actually eating, so drowning was it in an artful mix of flavours. By now he and Violet had invented successful recipes for a variety of creatures salvaged from Trapp's *Ark*. They had eaten zebra and boa constrictor and walrus, experimented with mongoose and emu and Goan lizard, partaken of tiger, and conjured up budgerigar mousse *à la Grécque*. And tonight they are planning to cook another primate carcass – the umpteenth casualty of the Trapp *Ark* débâcle. It is in the chopping room at this very moment, defrosting after its years of residency in the bosom of the Arctic iceberg.

Violet sips more tea. 'I said the Gentleman Monkey, Father.'

'Oh him. Yes. Fascinating creature,' replies Scrapie, pleased that his daughter is finally taking an interest. 'Quite strikingly human in appearance. Almost shocking. I'm working on him today. The Hippo wants him as a bloody towel-holder for the ladies' powder room in the banqueting suite, so I've done an armature with an elbow bent crooked, so they can hang the towels off that.'

'But I thought it was part of the Animal Kingdom Collection,' objects Violet. 'Aren't they all supposed to be stuffed in positions of prayer?'

'Mostly, yes. But she's taken a liking to the primates. She doesn't want them in the Museum, she says. She wants them dressed more like servants, helping out at the Palace. You know.'

Violet nods. She gets the idea. She finds it mildly unsettling – like the article in the newspaper – but cannot identify why.

'He's animal number three thousand and eight, if I recall,' Scrapie is sighing. 'You can come and have a look if you like. He's not finished, but it'll give you some idea. Good specimen. The last in the world, apparently. From a Moroccan menagerie, originally, according to the paperwork, such as it is. Trapp got about all right. Do you realise, he followed the same course as the *Beagle* in that old slave tub of his?'

'He went all the way to Australia?'

'He most certainly did. No wonder it took him so long. He went bloody well everywhere. South America, the Galápagos, Mauritius, Tasmania, North Africa, South Africa – bloody lunatic. If that man was ever a naturalist, then I'm a pink-footed goose.'

'How exactly did he die, Father?' asks Violet.

The chef, Cabillaud, has told her the story of the human head a thousand times. How, on the day of her birth, he had boarded Trapp's *Ark* with Scrapie to examine the damage, and stumbled over a rolling, rotting thing that had once been attached to a human body. How Scrapie had squatted down and stared into what remained of its face, and recognised Trapp. How he and the equerry had both rushed out on deck to be sick, while Violet's father had remained level-headed and iron-stomached enough to report Trapp's murder to the Royal Hippopotamus in the same breath as ordering a ton of Arctic ice.

'Nobody knows,' returns Scrapie darkly, recalling the same scene. Trapp's bruised and broken face, caked with blood and filth, a ghastly ball of gristle with a human brain within, is an image that he, too, has found it hard to dispel over the years.

'They never found the rest of him,' he said finally. 'And the crew had all disappeared. Higgins, Steed, and Bowker; they were gone, too. Along with the lifeboats. They say there was a woman, too. A ballerina. Quite a mystery.'

For a moment Scrapie sits there silently, brooding on the doomed expedition. Then he snaps out of his dark reverie. 'Come up to the workshop after lunch and I'll introduce you to the monkey.'

Violet stifles a burp. 'Thank you, Father.' It is important to know what one is eating.

'And people will one day have mechanical hearts implanted by a surgeon operating through a keyhole,' warns the Empress, reaching for her medicine bottle with a fluttering hand. Dr Scrapie rolls his eyes Heavenward.

Trapp wuz givin me a job, the woman wrote. *I wuz His mistris and His dancer. Big house, and He giv me munnie. Gents cumin and goin. I DANCIS for them wen E sez. I dont see nufin at first, cos most of the dors is LOKD, but I herd stuff at nite. Screems, LARFIN, Trapp and gents havin there way wiv girls. I lys in bed and I crys one nite. Trapp cums in. He is the wors for DRINK. But insted of hitin me He sez He LUVS me, and taks me in His arms. Dont no wy, but my will is gon. Ther is somthin you must do for me, He sez. Wot, I say. E shows me a big emptie CAGE.*

CHAPTER 10

IN WHICH THE
ROGUE MALE SEARCHES
FOR A MATE

The first client at my new surgery was a bloke called Sequin, who thought his border collie might be gay. It didn't bode well, I thought. Overnight, people seemed to have become more morose, introverted, and prone to obsession. The whole country was succumbing to a kind of mourning process after the bomb at the Egg Bank. No one could seem to see the wood for the trees.

'I prescribe a holiday for Chum-Boy, Mr Sequin,' I said. 'Get him out and about a bit. Take him to a national park and play fetch. It might do *you* some good as well.' He skulked off, looking doubtful.

I'd stayed in the Stoned Crow the first week, then set up shop in the surgery of my predecessor on Crawpy Street. The house was attached: a small cottage overlooking the River Flid. Norman Ball told me that a few years back, the Flid had won the Pollution Challenge Award (north-east section), but looking at it now, you got the sense that it was no longer a contender. From time to time, Norman warned me, it would bear a batch of foamy-scummed fish, which he referred to as 'eels flottantes'. There was a chemical factory at Fishforth, fifty miles upstream, specialising in detergents. Sometimes the water frothed violet, like something in an extravagant technicolour cartoon. It didn't really matter any more, how much we screwed up the earth, I thought. Or at least our part of it. The rest of Europe will probably use the whole island as a nuclear dumping ground, once we're gone. And who can blame them? Strange, but the fertility thing hadn't bothered me till now. In fact, I'd felt quite cavalier about it.

I didn't any more. I felt strangely coshed. I kept thinking: I wish I'd been born in the good old days. I wish I'd been alive before Elvis died. I wish I could've seen him perform on stage, just once, in the flesh. I'd have been one of those fans that tried to catch some of the sweat that flew off him, to keep in a little bottle. Try capturing *that* virtually. I wish –

Oh well. As Norman said: life must go on. What would Elvis have done? He'd have rocked around the clock, that's what.

But no matter how loud I played my virtual concerts, I couldn't quite get in the mood.

I reckon urban man must have evolved lungs that needed a certain degree of environmental contamination: I experienced positive withdrawal symptoms during my first week in Thunder Spit, and felt quite nostalgic when I caught a whiff of exhaust. The air, as well as being cleaner than in Tooting Bec, was a couple of degrees colder, and it took my nose a while to detect any smells at all. But when I did, they were pleasant enough: wood-smoke, fresh tarmac, the salt wind. I still hadn't actually clapped eyes on the sea. The concrete barrier that hid it had been erected, Norman told me, in the 1980s, when they'd done the rationalisation project. Before the land reclamation, Thunder Spit had been prone to flooding: back in the nineteenth century, the water had sometimes come in as far as the church. He said if I looked hard, I'd see the water-line at the back of the pulpit, but I said I'd take his word for it. I'm not into history. After I'd made the first round of phone calls and goodwill visits to a few local farmers – Ron Harcourt, Billy Clegg, Charlie Peat-Hove – I felt I had the measure of the place. It was turning out to be an easy locum. I'd heard rumours about my predecessor; phoney BSE certifications and kickbacks, among other things. He couldn't be a hard act to follow. If the cuddly stuff – domestic pets like Giselle – had represented a form of chaos, then farm livestock represented the opposite: here were working creatures with a pre-determined lifespan who paid their keep by ending up as leather or meat, and producing milk and eggs in their lifetime; functional beings you could respect, not the slaves-cum-mental-health workers that urban domestic pets had become, sad breeds of prostitute for the lonely and confused human. From now on the budgie-neutering would be restricted to the population of one town. As bad luck would have it, I had to perform an operation on an Indonesian iguana belonging to a little girl – the daughter of some Healthplan bigwig called Baldicoot – on day two, but I put out word in the pub that Buck de Savile was more into the rugged outdoor stuff. It fitted his image, I reckoned. And sure enough, when I visited the farm of the silent Johnny Peat-Hove, I found that I liked pigs. Visiting the squint-eyed Mr Lumpey over at Hawthorn Farm, I discovered I liked the Lord Chief Justice sheep, too – even though, disappointingly, their only difference from ordinary sheep turned out to be a diminished brain capacity and a tendency to fight. I saw to Mrs Harcourt's addle-brained chickens, which kept drinking from the slurry lagoon and poisoning themselves, and prescribed Narcomorph – a mild hallucinogen with healing properties – for Mrs Clegg's disturbed foal.

Despite my overall *Weltschmerz* – this was the big buzz word to describe the current national mood since the Egg Bank exploded – I felt pleased with myself on a practical level. Within a week, I'd crossed the first two items off the mental list I'd written that first night in the Stoned Crow. Only one remained.

It was in the unromantic setting of the hypermarket in Judlow that I first clapped eyes on the girls. When I first saw Rose, or was it Blanche, I remembered item number three: get laid. Then I spotted the other one, and invented a new item. Number four: get laid again.

I was near the checkout, where a huge sign flapped: BUY THE SAUSAGE AND ONION LATTICE PIE, GET THE COLE-SLAW FREE! I was conscious of dithering about which queue to join, aware that there was a petite, attractive, rusty-haired girl on each. They stirred a strange feeling of recognition in me, though I couldn't have put my finger on who or what it was they reminded me of.

You see, I didn't notice, at first, that the girls were identical, and that they were actually reminding me of *each other*. To my eye, all checkout girls, frankly, are much of a muchness, insofar as women tend to break down into a few basic but useful categories: young and attractive, old and attractive, young and unattractive, mother-type (drunk: avoid!), Holly-type (betraying: avoid!), available, unavailable, et cetera. These categories could all be subsumed into two broader sets, if you were in a hurry: the shaggable and the unshaggable. These two, despite their rather charmless orange-and-white chequered uniforms, were eminently shaggable, so here I was, torn between two checkouts. The shopper nudging at my back with a chariot of wire decided me, and I veered towards Blanche with my mesh basket of essentials: margarine, razor blades, frozen dinners, cans of lager, crisps, ice-cream, socks – a basket which I reckon should have yelled out Buck de Savile's eligible bachelorhood without him having to say a word.

I strewed my consumer items on the conveyor belt with manly assurance. But reaction came there none. Blanche didn't even look up. So feebly, I tried to make conversation ('Wanted to buy that pie, you know, the sausage and onion lattice one, but couldn't find the coleslaw'), but she ignored me. Like her sister, she was in a round-eyed trance. As I was paying, I had another stab at it ('Do you take Visa, darling?'), but she barely reacted to my presence. When I'd finished loading my carrier bag, I turned to have another look at Blanche, and saw she had switched checkouts. She'd been on number nineteen. Now she was on number twenty. Except that when I looked at nineteen, I saw her again. I looked carefully again at both of them. Scrutinised them thoroughly. No, not double vision, I suddenly realised. Identical twins!

It was then that I remembered something. Norman had twin girls, didn't he? Double Trouble, he called them. Or the

Gruesome Twosome, or Two Peas in a Pod, or Tweedles Dum and Dee.

I stood there with my two shopping bags, just staring first at one, and then the other. They still didn't notice me. The hypermarket was busy, and I was impressed with the deftness of their movements as they weighed plastic bags of fruit on their electronic scales, whisked the bar-codes over the infra-red, and dealt with credit cards and loyalty vouchers. It intrigued me, the way their hands could be so busy when you could tell that their minds were blank.

On the way home, I couldn't stop thinking about them. And that night they must have crept into my dreams, because by the following morning, they were under my skin, like an itch.

As Buck de Savile, formerly Bobby Sullivan, spiritual son of Elvis, busies himself with his veterinary tasks and worries away at his desire, the two young women who are causing his pleasurable discomfort are now sitting on bar-stools in the Pig and Whistle in Hunchburgh. Rose and Blanche Ball, conceived of a single bifurcated egg and born on Midsummer's Day, 1985, more or less simultaneously by Caesarean section to Abbie Ball, née Boggs, home economics and French teacher, are enjoying a glass of Liebfraumilch, which their personal tutor Dr Bugrov has told them means 'the breast-milk of spinster virgins'.

'Cheers,' says Rose.

'Here's to the end of the world as we know it,' adds Blanche grimly. The *Weltschmertz* thing has hit them both hard; like all girls their age, their names have been on the Egg Bank waiting list since the beginning. Norman and Abbie hadn't wasted a moment getting them enrolled. Fat lot of good *that's* turned out to be. Oh well. They've earned a hundred Euros this morning.

'I'm a lucky man,' smiles Dr Bugrov, with the smile of a man who knows about cash well spent.

'And we're lucky girls,' says Rose, smiling sweetly at the balding professor, while her sister takes advantage of his back being turned on her to waggle two fingers at her throat in a being-sick gesture. Rose sniggers.

In the beginning, the man who is now their genealogy teacher had been a bit of a long shot, a lonely old git they'd taken pity on in the cinema queue because it had been a day or two since they'd had any excitement in their lives. Dr Bugrov – 'Call me Sergei,' he'd insisted, but they couldn't – had proved a disappointment, and not worth the gamble, until he came up with an unexpected proposal, in the form of cash. A hundred Euros to do it regularly; say, once a week? They didn't dislike him. His accent was quite sexy if you shut your eyes. And he'd been intelligent and practical enough to recognise straight off that they weren't going to do it again for free. After a few sessions, he had offered to throw in genealogy, too, as a bonus.

'Like a Loyalty voucher?' asked Rose as they lay in bed doing special studies.

'Like two Loyalty vouchers, my dears,' Bugrov had smiled, squeezing Blanche's tit. 'I'm in charge of a module.'

The whole enterprise had seemed like a reasonable idea, since they were always short of money, and Dad had been saying he may be sticking his neck out here, gals, but wasn't it time they got themselves some gainful employment, instead of forever scrounging off the state? What's more, Dr Bugrov led them to believe that genealogy could lead to financial self-sufficiency – wealth, even. Now that the whole of the British race was headed for extinction, everyone was looking backwards, rather than forwards, he told them. Ever since the bomb at the Egg Bank had hammered the last nail in the coffin of the British, the whole nation had gone ape-shit. Everybody was in shock. The crisis lines were jammed solid, the worldwide Web was overloaded, all flights out of the country were fully booked.

A side-product of this madness, Bugrov predicted, was that there would suddenly be millions of gullible Americans wanting to trace their roots, before those roots completely shrivelled. Enter the twins.

'You could set up a service,' Dr Bugrov advised them. 'Once

you have your diploma. You offer to trace their families. You produce a brochure. Three hundred Euros per generation for the first three generations, then four hundred Euros per generation after that. Anything they don't like, history of madness, criminality, sex changes – you offer to doctor it for a surcharge.'

They had liked the idea of a weekly 'grant packet' from Dr Bugrov, who was indeed connected, in some tangential way, to Hunchburgh University's Department of Human Sciences. He was fifty, and he always smoked a pipe of Three Nuns after sex. Like many of the men captivated by Rose and Blanche, he was excited by the idea of two women catering to his sexual whims simultaneously. And intrigued by the way that when one of them climaxed, the other would, too, as though by proxy. It was telepathy, they explained. Everything was interchangeable, with them. Plus they had a strong natural urge. 'We're animals,' they purred sexily. And then spoilt it by sniggering. But Dr Bugrov wasn't complaining. Like many before him, he would lie back and close his eyes and feel their hands creeping over him – Rose's right, Blanche's left – and imagine it was just one woman doing all this to him, an octopus-woman who could kiss him on the mouth and suck him off at the same time. Sometimes he didn't even want to do it, but just lie there and stroke their four bored tits and reminisce about academic politics, departmental meetings he had attended, and witty ripostes he claimed he had made to deans of this or that institute of higher learning in Britain or America – ripostes so heavily overwrought that it was clear even to Rose and Blanche that they were only remarks he wished he had made, dreamed up years later when nursing the ancient wounds of missed opportunity.

They'd wash the Three Nuns out of their hair afterwards, and spend the grant money on the usual things: depilatory creams, leg-waxes, or electrolysis.

Heigh ho. They knew all about unwanted heredity, thank you very much. Witness the hair problem that they battled with on a daily basis, and the toe thing they had. Thank God for those new elasticated trainers that were all the rage for pets. Shoes had been quite a headache, till then.

'More Liebfraumilch, my dears?' offers Bugrov. He pronounces it elaborately, stressing the *ch* ending.

'We wouldn't say no,' says Rose.

'In fact we'd say yes,' asserts Blanche.

They are twenty years old, and they have the world at their slightly deformed feet, and they know it. Nobody can take that away from them.

'And some soya balls,' adds Rose.

'Here's a pink one,' the obstetric surgeon had said when the girls were born, holding up a screaming female baby by the ankle with his left hand. At which point, according to family legend, Abbie murmured in French, 'Rose.'

'And here,' announced the surgeon, wielding a second baby in his right hand, 'is a white one.'

'Blanche,' croaked Abbie, and fainted, thinking the baby was dead, because she was so pale and uttered no sound. And from that day, it was always Rose who spoke first of the two.

Blanche didn't stay white and Rose didn't stay pink: the colours melded until they were both equal parts peaches and cream beneath a down of coarse body hair that was to be the cross they bore through life, requiring leg-waxes once a week and extensive electrolysis. Blanche and Rose, beloved twin daughters of Abbie and Norman Ball, citizens of Thunder Spit, England and the world. Marital status: single, but looking! Blanche and Rose, who grew from rock-climbing tomboys into nubile teenagers, who were attractive in a wild, buck-toothed, unclassical sort of way, who had, after leaving school and maturing physically, been to secretarial college and who now worked Saturdays on adjoining checkout tills in the hypermart in Judlow, who kept their socks on during sex so that no one should see their embarrassing feet, who were identical except that Rose always spoke first and was right-handed, while Blanche always spoke second and was left-handed; and who now, in the Pig and Whistle, are watching the elderly Dr Bugrov ordering more Liebfraumilch and soya balls from the bar.

'Oh, and some calorie-free peanuts, please!' Rose yells across.

'Boring old fart,' mutters Rose, as Bugrov returns bearing brimming glasses of spinster virgins' breast-milk, and crackling half a dozen packets of nuts, and plonks himself between the girls. He is basking in pleasure. And who wouldn't be, with beauty to the right, more beauty to the left, a morning of sexual gratification behind him, and more just like it ahead if he can only get to the cash machine?

'Here, look, there's going to be a reward,' says Rose. She has chosen her CD track from the juke-box terminal at their table and is now flicking through the Internet news pages. 'Five million Euros for the first British pregnancy!'

'What?' says Blanche, grabbing the mouse. 'That'll get things moving again,' she predicts, scanning through.

'How d'you prove it's British, and not foreign?' asks Rose.

Blanche reads some more. 'Cos it has to be born in Britain. Look, read the details,' she says, handing over the mouse. 'Nothing's born in this country any more. Look at Harcourt's Filipina. He paid a fortune to have her sent over, and she hasn't produced doodly squat.'

'It's a blasted heath, this nation,' muses Dr Bugrov, pulling out his reading glasses and peering at the news on the screen. 'Your culture has died and now you are dying, too. Money is not going to fix it.'

Rose darts him a sharp look. 'It fixes some things, though, doesn't it, Dr Bugrov?'

A pause, as Dr Bugrov pretends to be more deaf than he is, and fights to open a packet of peanuts.

'We need a new bloke,' murmurs Blanche, reading her sister's mind. Dr Bugrov looks up. There is no disguising the pained look on his face.

'Some young blood,' agrees Rose pointedly, just loud enough for him to hear.

Time, perhaps, to cash in those Loyalty vouchers?
The twins look at each other.
Yes. A new man.
Now where on God's earth are they going to find *that*?

CHAPTER 11

THE FLOOD

'Now, Tobias. What can a squid do?'

'Shoot ink to a trajectory of fifteen feet, Father.'

'Describe an isosceles triangle.'

'Two sides the same length, one not.'

It is a December evening, and I am studying at home, at the kitchen table, with my father. My education had been haphazard since the age of ten, at which age the local school washed its hands of children. The other boys began work on the fishing boats then, or on their fathers' farms, or in Tommy's case, at the forge, but I remained at home, at the mercy of my Father's well-intentioned but scatter-gun pedagogical techniques. We would do mathematical puzzles, and he would order me to memorise maps of the world and parts of the Bible, and I read daily from Hanker's *World History*, which ended in 1666 with the Great Fire of London.

'Has the mystery of the *Marie Celeste* ever been solved?'

'No, Father.' I look out of the window: the sky is suddenly turning black.

'Pay attention, Tobias. Can you name the parts of a flower?'

'Petals-fruit-stamen-pollen-stalk.'

'What did Donne say?'

'"No man is an island."'

'Good boy,' said my father, himself now glancing worriedly out at the yellow pall which hung over the sea. 'That colour bodes ill,' he announced. 'Now clean your quill and put away the ink. Class dismissed.'

112

An hour later the River Flid gurgled ominously, there was a restlessness among the cows, and Farmer Harcourt found the milk had curdled to cheese in their udders. The goats, bleating in their panicky way, and craving shelter, made lunatic compasses of their tethering-posts. The sheep huddled in groups, scattered across the land like fallen clouds. The women herded the beasts off the promontory, and into fields in Judlow belonging to relatives of the Peat-Hoves and the Morpitons.

'Close all the windows,' commanded my father. 'And then go and spread a horse-rug on your mother's grave.'

I went about this and other duties; by mid-afternoon, a threatening mass of foggy air, gun-grey, had congealed on the horizon, the wind had grown heavy and dank, and the herring gulls became self-destructive and reckless and infanticidal, tearing their own nests from the cliff-face and sending the eggs hurtling down to smash on the grey rocks below, streaking them with yellow. After the gulls' display of panic-induced violence, it was apparent that this year, God's wrath was going to be mighty indeed. The sky stayed black. When the clocks said it was night – though no stars appeared and only a thin rind of moon hung in the blackness – the villagers loaded themselves and their belongings on to boats, and sailed to Judlow.

But Parson Phelps and I stayed, along with a scattering of men – Bark men, Hayter men, Balls and Tobashes – who were determined to defend their homes, come what may.

'We are remaining here,' Parson Phelps said, 'because it is God's will.'

And the Lord's word, as usual, was final.

'But –' I faltered.

'God objects to the word *but*, with a great intensity,' Parson Phelps warned. He was intimate with God's opinions about vocabulary, as they were uncannily congruent with his own. 'We shall not abandon the church!' He thundered this at me as though I were Satan trying to drag him bodily away. The wind was banging at the windowpanes of the Parsonage, like the Devil himself knocking.

113

'But God can surely fend for himself,' I argued. 'He is omni-present and omnipotent, and everlasting, Father – but we are mortal! We cannot even swim! The church is just a building! It's *people* that matter!' My tapeworm Mildred appeared to agree with me on this issue, for she was giving me holy hell as I spoke and turning my bowels to water.

'There are other people staying, too,' my father replied. 'They are my parishioners. My flock. How can I leave them?'

'Because they all own boats, and we do not!' I answered. But he turned his deaf ear on me, and when I pursued it further, he cast me aside and pointed in the direction of the harbour, where the fishing boats were being loaded with passengers anxious to leave.

'So go, then!' he shouted, so that my ears hurt. 'Leave your father to the mercy of God, and to the flood-water that riseth!' But I couldn't leave him, mutinous sphincter or no.

Outside, the lightning cracked and the thunder rolled in a sky of a dingy and malicious purple hue. But it was only when the rising sea-water began to insinuate itself beneath the oak door of the Parsonage that we wrapped ourselves in oilskins and left our home; I with a sinking feeling of dread, my father swept along by the frightening tidal wave of his own faith. Carrying an ember from the dying fire with us in a puffball, we stumbled past the wind-whipped trees and through the flattened bracken to the church. Here we made our camp; first by the altar, where fourteen years earlier the Parson had mistaken me for a piglet, and then, as the water rose, to the pulpit. We watched as the waves sloshed beneath the door and swished up the aisle. I remember the sight of Parson Phelps, as he stood in the pulpit like Canute, his hand willing the flood to abate. But despite the force of his will and his character, it did not, and the level of the water continued to creep ever upward. We stayed there all day and all night, drinking from a hip-flask of rum and eating raw the stray sardines that slapped on to the pulpit. At first, my father would only allow us to burn two candles at a time.

'One for light, and one for heat,' he explained solemnly.

114

On the second day, it was just one. By evening, the last candle guttered and died, and we just had a thin impression of daylight though the stained-glass window by day, and by night, the ghostly, fungal phosphorescence of plankton in the nave.

It was here, over the course of those three days and three nights that my father chose to tell me about the world. Sometimes I would ask a question. But mostly, he just talked. It was cold enough to freeze a toad, and mostly dark, and looking back, I realise that it was his passion for life, combined with the rum, that kept both our hearts from stopping. Every article that he had read in *The Times* over the past quarter of a century was now being hauled up from the vast archive of his memory and filtered through the prism of his faith until it formed clear shafts of light by which I might see God's truth; I remember that I listened gratefully and attentively, and that for the three days that we were to live in the besieged church, my father kept us both alive with alcohol and with the earnest and fortifying bagpipes of his informed discourse, while I made paper boats from the pages of a collapsed hymn-book and sent them bobbing across the water in search of land and safety.

As the waves slapped at our ankles in the pulpit, he told me about the Monarchy and the hierarchies of the Kingdom in which we lived, starting at the top with Her Majesty and working down the ladder through dukes and archdeacons and Sir Thises and Sir Thats, as laid down through the ages, down to humble us, Parson Phelps and Master Phelps his son. As we heard the wind screaming around the church spire, and the rusty weather-vane spinning wildly on its axis, he spoke about a man, Cromwell, who in history had once attempted to overthrow the Monarchy. An ugly man with warts on his face, and a wart for a heart, said my father. He told me, too, as we rescued an exhausted cormorant, about the heinous slave trade in America, and the slave-traders who had pillaged Africa for its manhood and shipped the poor savages half-dying to labour in the sugar plantations so that vainglorious trollops in London

115

could sweeten their cakes, as if honest honey from the noble bee wasn't good enough for them. And as dawn broke on the second day, about happier things: the invention of the hot-air balloon by a Frenchman, Montgolfier, and about the conquest of the Empire, and the conversion of millions of native savages who, were it not for Queen Victoria, would still be hopping around worshipping baboons and practising cannibalism. That night he told me about Galileo and his charting of the planetary system, which had once been seen as heretical, but was now an accepted truth. He named the Planets for me, and though we couldn't see the stars through the stained-glass window, he described them to me, and even now, when I look at the constellations, I remember his words. ('Three fingers to the right of the Plough . . . a little southerly from the North Star . . . draw a diagonal line directly left of the Milky Way and you will discover . . .') He waited till dark to inform me, in a vigorous but incomprehensible way, with many praise-thees and therefores, about the reproductive process, as enacted by a type of Highland cattle not seen in this part of the world. He made no mention of the human equivalent, and I dared not ask. Nor did he mention the adder in his knickerbockers which had prevented him from pleasuring his wife – but he reminded me, in the anonymity of darkness, of the brimstone and hellfire that would come raining down on me and strike me blind if I were to practise the deadly vice of onanism. On the third dawn he told me the history of the sea-storm in 1822 in which three boats capsized, killing fifteen fishermen from two families in one fell swoop, and of how Mrs Firth's idiot cousin Joan came to live with her, having been hounded out of Judlow accused of being a witch, after she had vomited on the floor and the regurgitated stew created a puddle in the shape of a five-legged sea-monster, complete with horns.

Then he told me, not for the first time, that no man was an island. It was a favourite theme of his.

'"No man is an island, entire of itself!"' he thundered.

'– self, elf, elf, elf!' his voice echoed in the dark rafters.

(Ironically enough, during this evocation of Donne's topological conceit, we were now actually marooned on the very geographical feature in question. Though we did not know it, the peninsula had been cut off from the mainland, turning our speck of land into a small and threatened oval, like the back of an engulfed spoon.)

'Every man is a piece of the continent, a part of the main!'

'– main-ain-ain-ain!' the church replied.

It was at that moment that the pulpit broke, and we fell into the water.

I recall little of what immediately preceded my holy vision: only that I saw a jellyfish wobble past me, its trailing skirt a-jingle with tiny bubbles. That a herring collided with my nose. That a crab pinched my finger. That for a moment my floundering sent me bobbing up to the surface, where my father floated serenely, turning slowly in a whirlpool, his cassock expanded around him like a big bubble of faith.

That he announced, 'Have courage! The Lord has seen fit to challenge us, Tobias, and we shall rise to His command!' And that then, instead of rising, I sank like a stone beneath the surface.

And here, deep in the freezing waters of the flood, I met an Angel.

It is said that a dying man sees his life pass before him in the form of a small morality play, so that when he reaches St Peter's Gate, he may humbly accept whatever direction the saint commands him to follow. This thought only came to me much later, as an explanation for what I experienced while I drowned.

The Angel before me is beautiful, and I love her instantly.

She is dressed like a ballerina, in a white garment with a skirt of stiff fabric sticking out horizontally from her waist, and white stockings on her small legs. Her wings must be folded behind her, or perhaps they are transparent as gossamer, for I do not see them. Her face is pale, and in her dark hair she wears a band of gold. A stream of silver bubbles pours from her mouth.

Sunlight is streaming in on us from somewhere high above. The Angel smiles at me. In the background, I hear people laughing and cheering. I am in a golden cot, with bars. A huge bristle-haired animal is on the other side. Its snout is soft, its eyes are ochre-orange, the irises vertical slits. I hear a high, grating song in my head, like a distant echo of something long gone.

> Rock-a-bye-baby, on the tree top,
> When the wind blows, the cradle will rock . . .

'O Lord do not take him from me, I beg you!' a man's voice is crying. It is far away, as distant as the moon. 'Hold on!' yells Parson Phelps, louder this time. My Angel trembles, like a reflection in a pool. Then something grabs me and yanks me upwards with a wrenching pain. I break the surface and scream, and the water takes me again, this time to Hell, where I see –

Other things. A cage. Teeth. Blood. The Angel, screaming. Broken glass.

And worse.

My father was slapping my face, hard. The water sloshed about us.

'Now wake, Tobias! Wake up!' And he slapped me again. 'Wake-up-up-up-up!' echoed the church. The vision of Hell disappeared in a flash, and only the swirling waters remained.

'You are delirious with hunger and exhaustion,' my father said at last.

'I saw a vision of a Holy Angel,' I spluttered.

But I had seen Hell, too.

When the Flood finally drew back, and the sea was calm, the church was strewn with seaweed and oysters and clams, I was weak from too much knowledge on an empty stomach,

118

and shaken by my visions. Parson Phelps had lost his voice completely by now. He could only croak his praises and his heartfelt thanks to the Lord in a ragged manner. We staggered up the aisle, gathering fish in the collection bucket, fighting off the gulls that swarmed in, and headed for the Parsonage.

We were met with a shock. The whole exterior of the house, from top to bottom, was covered in giant barnacles, which clung on with an awesome force. (I had never seen such huge specimens; later Tommy and I would lever them off with crowbars.)

My father laughed shakily. 'God has cracked a joke,' he explained. 'For his own almighty pleasure!'

And God had more pranks up His sleeve, because when my father opened the Parsonage door, a huge wall of sea-water came hurtling out, knocking him sideways. He lay there as it flooded over him and spent itself in the sodden earth. Then he stood up, and laughed, and said, 'Praise be, for the Lord is in good humour!'

Ever the optimist. Personally, I did not think much of God's sense of humour. Then or later.

That morning, as the villagers came rowing and sailing back, there was a sky as capricious as oil, conjuring itself back and forth from light to dark under a wedge of lemon sun. The heavy salt-bearing wind still racketed in from the east, and in the harbour, the masts and sails of the returned fishing boats danced and glimmered in a chaotic mirage. That's how I remembered Thunder Spit, after I left it. Strewn about in pieces like a smashed glass bowl, after the storm. Later, in the city, when I was lost, if I put my whelk to my ear, I could hear it, smell it, taste it. Wind and fish, fish and wind, salt and spike-grass and gulls.

Home sweet home!

Sweet, but sour, too. The Parsonage never fully recovered from the Flood, and the first of the jokes that God was to play on us. Most of the house was ravaged, and was to remain so for several years; from then on, when we needed to salt our food, we just scraped a kitchen flag-stone with a penknife. In the meantime, sea-life rotted in corners, and for months the larder was a rockpool, containing a variety of living creatures, including a blue starfish, an array of clams, and four lobsters. We spent the rest of the year trying to repair the damage, and every fine day we would haul out our furniture and belongings in an attempt to dry them out.

Look: there's the sofa steaming in the warmth of a spring morning.

And listen: crrrkkk! That's the sound of the mahogany dresser splitting suddenly, and gaping soggily apart to reveal a lumpy mass of disintegrating jellyfish on its floor.

Don't inhale: hold your nose! Pffffwah!

'God moves in a mysterious way,' boomed my father, the eternal looker-on-the-bright-side, as he chopped up the useless furniture wood, 'His wonders to perform!'

If my father was distraught at the damage the sea had inflicted upon my mother's grave (the blanket he had bade me lay upon it had been carried off by the waters), he hid it well. The waves had churned up the earth, and all the shrubs and plants we had so carefully tended were destroyed. Or so we thought, until the following autumn, when the gourd plant appeared.

'Praise be, for the life that sprouteth from Thine earth!' he shouted, when I told him that I had identified a gourd shoot among the nettles and sand-grass.

He must have felt vindicated after all for his meek acceptance of the damage at the time. We cared for the plant as I will warrant you no plant has ever been cared for before or since, including those in Her Majesty's own greenhouses. My father would collect horse-dung from Harcourt's farm, a mile away, every day, including Marble Friday, and drip pure spring-water into its roots from a glass pipette he received by courier from a medical supply shop in Hunchburgh, to mimic God's rain falling drop by drop. And I must confess that there were some startling results to be had from this method. It's a well-known fact that gourds hate a salty climate, and do not normally thrive north of London. They are a Mediterranean quasi-fruit, quasi-vegetable, and they crave the sun, which was always in short supply in Thunder Spit, but the plant, nourished by manure and goodwill, thrived in an almost obscene way, and when its yellow flowers fell, ten fruits began to swell. And what gourds they turned out to be.

It was only years later that I heard about the monk Gregor Mendel, and his experiments with peas. By selective breeding, Mendel could create green peas from yellow, and tall from short. Within a mere two generations, he showed that a species of plant can abandon the inheritance of its forefathers, and create a new legacy all its own. Our gourds must have decided to take such a step – alone. For on inspection, it could be seen that they bore little or no relation to the original green-striped gourd my mother had so admired. They were whorled in orange and yellow, with bulbous protuberances and a distinctly hairy leaf.

– *this big emptie CAGE.*

Get in there, He sez.

Wot for, I sez, steppin in. Ther is a BUKKIT on the floor, and a sort of bed, like a litel shelfe. There is a bole of WATER, that is all.

To see if it is the rite SIZE, He sez.

The rite size for WOT, I sez.

The rite size for you and SUMWUN ELS.

He loks the door and puts the kee in His pockit.

Good gerl, He sez. We will be leevin next week, so get acustomd, ay.

I forls to the flor and I crys and crys and crys.

Wot a stupid cow, ay? Wot a stupid –

CHAPTER 12

THE EMPRESS TAKES
HER LEAVE

'Phew! Oomph! Whuuur! Huh!'

The primate carcass now chopped and its flesh marinating gently in the coriander-and-lemon preparation, Violet Scrapie is huffing and puffing her way up the stairs to the workshop, where her father is smoking a cigar.

'You need to get some exercise,' he tells her as she flops in, panting. The child is bearing far too much weight. Completely overloaded. Her skin will overstretch itself. Her internal organs will be squashed. Her armature will give way. 'A bit of walking. That'll do the trick.'

'Yes, Father,' says Violet dutifully, peering through the fug of cigar-smoke at a small, humanoid creature perched on the table. 'Is that the Monkey?'

'Most of him, yes. One arm and a pair of buttocks missing for now. Made a mistake with the cutting. Bloody annoying. Had to re-do it. And the tail's a bugger. Take a look.'

Violet manoeuvres her bulk around the table, and surveys the half-finished creature, some of whose skin hangs loose, falling away from the sawdust-sprinkled wire of the armature. The animal is bigger than she expected from the bits of carcass Cabillaud had chopped earlier. There hadn't been much in the way of meat, once you'd eliminated the bones and gristle. Its tail rises behind it like a question mark.

'A handsome beast,' she comments. 'There's something very *noble* about him, considering he's just an animal. You can actually begin to see why he's called a Gentleman.'

'Yes,' agrees Scrapie. 'Intelligent, too, by all accounts. Shame they're extinct. They were a very under-researched species, unfortunately. A type of ape, according to some, but the tail sets them apart. And then they died out, so there's bugger all way of finding out more.'

'Definitely handsome,' repeats Violet, musingly, stroking the creature's hairy arm.

'He will be, when he's finished. Such a waste. Not a mark on him, though. Still haven't fathomed how he died.'

This was true. Of all the creatures Scrapie had chosen from the remains of the *Ark* menagerie that day, the Gentleman Monkey had been the only one without any traces of violence on his body. Odd, that. As though he'd died of something else altogether.

Violet glances down and sees a pair of blue glass eyes on the table.

'The Hippo still wants them all to have blue eyes?'

'She does indeed, God blast her.'

'And the –?' Violet blushes; the subject is rather intimate.

'Yes. That, too. No genitalia of any kind. And then the pantaloons on top, to discourage the curious. Bloody woman.'

Every time he thinks about the Monarch, Scrapie becomes enraged. He twiddles with the glass eyes, doing his best to calm himself, and then observes his youngest child once more. She really is enormously fat. Almost a young woman, and as distressed a spinster as you could ever wish to meet! Will he be stuck with her for life?

'What you need,' Scrapie tells Violet with sudden inspiration, 'is a dog.'

Later that afternoon, his mind still preoccupied with the distressed-spinster issue, Scrapie left the house and returned with a corgi pup, spared from a vivisector's laboratory by his charm.

'Here,' he says now, shoving a wooden box at his daughter, with a snuffling thing inside.

'Thank you, Father,' she replies dutifully, wiping her hands on her bloody apron and peering down into the wooden box.

She has no interest in pets. A small puppy looks back up at her with large brown swelling eyes.

'Hello, dog,' she says doubtfully, calculating the creature's weight with a practised eye.

'What are you going to call him?' enquires Scrapie. There is an edge of annoyance in his voice. As far as he can recall, the creature is the only gift he has ever presented to his daughter. She might at least attempt a little gratitude.

'Suet,' she replies vaguely. What is actually on her mind is a recipe for Alsatian, of which suet is a major ingredient.

Scrapie sighs in exasperation, and returns to his workshop to do battle with the monkey towel-holder.

The newly christened Suet whimpers in his box.

'We'll need to fatten you up a bit, eh?' murmurs Violet, lifting the creature out. There is even less of him than she had thought; he can't weigh more than two pounds. She and Cabillaud have developed a marvellous canine repertoire. Dog (in case you have not partaken of it, gentle reader) tastes similar to fox, which is in turn not unlike rat, though with more of a venison twang.

And nothing at all like Gentleman Monkey, as the Scrapie family discovers that night when they take their first taste of the extinct, de-frosted primate. The flavour is strong and slightly musky – though by no means offensively so. The flesh, they agree, is tender, almost veal-like in consistency. Of the parts of the carcass Cabillaud and Violet have removed from the ice house and chopped, the thigh and rump were certainly the best cuts, followed closely by the ribs.

'Excellent!' pronounced Dr Scrapie.

'Delicious. I haven't enjoyed flesh so much for a long time,' agreed the Laudanum Empress.

But under the table, the puppy Suet whimpered.

'He must be hungry,' murmured Violet, retrieving the last remaining scraps of the braised primate from her mother's plate and chucking them on the floor. But instead of snapping them up, as any normal dog might have done, the ungrateful Suet merely growled suspiciously at the meat.

'Oh well,' said Violet. 'Suit yourself, stupid.'
But Suet's canine instinct turned out to be astute.

It was the following day that gastric illness struck the Scrapie household. Violet and Dr Scrapie were doubled up with acute diarrhoea, and Cabillaud took to his bed. On the *chaise-longue* in the drawing room, the Empress's psychic particles dispersed, and the shadow of death took their place.

'I see a town called Thunder Spit,' the Empress muttered feebly, her eyelids flickering. 'I see a jar on a shelf. I see a gourd plant, and a rockpool, and a ballerina and a –' The Empress never finished her sentence.

She had officially crossed to the Other Side.

Cuisine Zoologique had claimed its first victim.

CHAPTER 13

GONE TODAY,
HERE TOMORROW

'Food poisoning?' asks Abbie Ball, aghast, when the Victorian phantom has finished recounting the circumstances of her death. As a home-economics teacher, Abbie is more aware than most of the dangers of unhygienically prepared food. 'Most likely to have been salmonella, I expect. Or E coli. Well, I suppose you didn't have fridges and clingfilm in your day. Things can't have been as developed then as they are now, Mrs Scrapie.'

The phantom sighs. This silly woman, Abbie Ball, in whose home she has recently had the misfortune – thanks to something called a 'loft conversion' – to find herself, appears to be convinced that the world has improved in the hundred and fifty years since her death – although a quick glance at the year 2005 is enough to inform one that this is far from so. Why, the whole British race is becoming extinct, according to the electronic spirits inhabiting the crystal box in the living room. Only last week, the news spirit told her that religious fanatics had destroyed something called the National Egg Bank – making a disaster out of a crisis. Can this really be called progress?

'Actually, it wasn't the flesh that was poisonous,' she tells Abbie, adjusting her petticoats and sipping at the glass of Pepto-Bismol that is her one physical indulgence in these godforsaken times. 'It was the praxin the creature had been injected with before death. My husband did an analysis of the remaining meat. Suet was right not to touch it.'

'Suet?'

'My daughter's dog.'

'The stuffed corgi in the attic? Is that him?

'Well observed, Mrs Ball,' murmurs the Empress.

'Oh do call me Abbie.'

'I'd rather not, if you don't mind. Now please excuse me for a moment; I do believe *The Young and the Restless* is showing on your crystal box.' And she floats off into the living room. Seconds later, the signature tune of her favourite soap opera blares out.

Abbie winces. 'I wish she'd keep the sound down,' she mutters.

When, a month ago, Abbie Ball had first spotted the Victorian wardrobe up in the attic, she had assumed that it contained the outdated camping equipment of her late parents, Iris and Herman Boggs, who had been tragically killed in a Swiss avalanche ten years previously. The huge second Empire *meuble* towered over her, two metres high and almost as wide. It was made of a darkly polished walnut, lovingly adorned with cherubs, bulging of thigh and cheek, bearing fruit and trumpets and little scrolls tied with ribbons. Abbie had not been keen to re-awaken memories of her beloved parents, but her domestic urge to clear up the loft overcame her hesitation, and she prised open the wardrobe's vast door, which creaked and wheezed with age, and leaked from its ancient hinges the bitter dust of woodworm. Imagine her surprise when, instead of finding the poignant items she had anticipated, to wit, a chemical loo, aluminium pots and pans, folding camp beds and a portable gas cooker, she had instead unearthed a collection of stuffed mammals, ranging in size from small (a guinea-pig) to large (an entire ostrich), an ancient cookery book, an old painting of Noah's Ark, a fossil, a scientific treatise about evolution, and a curious flask in the form of a crucifix, smelling faintly of rum.

'Norman!' she had wailed.

Her husband came heaving breathily up the stairs and followed the direction of her accusing finger. 'Look at all this junk!'

'Blimey,' said Norman, sitting down heavily on an old laundry basket. You could have knocked him down, he said, with a proverbial feather.

'What d'you reckon, love?' he asked Abbie. 'Worth a call to the Antiques Hotline?'

Neither of them spotted the phantom till later. The ghost – dressed in myriad petticoats – took a day to materialise, and then another day to declare herself fully.

'My name is Mrs Charlotte Scrapie,' she had announced, wafting into the room one Sunday teatime. 'Although my family knew me as the Laudanum Empress, because of my unfortunate enthralment to a certain opiate. Is there a chemist's shop in the vicinity? I feel the need of some pink medicine.'

And with that by way of introduction, she had allowed herself to solidify sufficiently, as a presence, to polish off four of Abbie's barley flip-cakes. Her attention then turned to the execrable dress sense of her hosts, which she criticised in no uncertain terms.

'What's this?' she had accused, snapping at Abbie's elasticated waistband. 'And what are those?' she groaned, pointing at Norman's giant frog slippers. 'In my day we stuck to whalebone.'

By the following morning she had solidified completely, installed herself on the settee in the living room, and promptly substituted her laudanum dependence with an addiction to Pepto-Bismol and television.

As uninvited guests go, she was something of a pain, but there was no getting rid of her.

'She's one of those *après-fin-de-siècle* phenomena whatsits,' pronounced Norman, after reading an article in the *Sunday Express*. '"*A tangible symptom of the Zeitgeist*", in boffin-speak. They reckon there's more and more of them about, with the Extinction Crisis. People looking backwards, rather than forwards. Going a bit doo-lally over history.'

Abbie made a face. 'Well *I* certainly didn't invite her here,' she said firmly. 'As far as I'm concerned, she can get straight back in that old wardrobe and stay there. All she does is criticise.'

'I heard that,' the Empress called through from the living room. 'And by the way, your upholsterer should be shot.'

The Balls had mentioned the Old Parsonage's new inhabitant

casually to the Vicar at the Twitchers' Association AGM, but they were disappointed; he said he was only interested in her as an artefact of their joint psyche. Later, in the pub, Norman had discovered that the Vicar had said exactly the same thing, *vis-à-vis* the Peat-Hoves' poltergeist, and the Morpitons' haunted barn. 'These sodding marriage-guidance counsellors,' he grumbled. 'They've got a one-track mind.'

So for lack of a means of exorcising her, the Laudanum Empress had, in the last month, become a fixture at the Old Parsonage. Apart from costing the Balls a small fortune in Pepto-Bismol, she made no real demands, Norman finally conceded, and reached the conclusion that they should be grateful for small mercies. Every cloud has a silver lining, after all.

'And every silver lining has a stinking great cloud,' muttered the Empress, who wasn't keen on her side of the deal, either, but didn't share Norman's natural optimism. She would *gladly* go back in the wardrobe, if only they'd finish emptying it of stuffed animals, and would supply her with a portable crystal box.

Today Norman and Abbie are occupied with their Saturday jobs: he Black-and-Deckering at an intransigent piece of skirting in the upstairs toodle-oo; she preparing her weekly TV rehearsal. The Empress is still in the living room, engrossed in a soap opera. She'll get square eyes if she doesn't watch out. Meanwhile Rob Morpiton's huge red setter has found its way into the garden of the Old Parsonage. Sensing the presence of the supernatural, it has now begun to bark frantically.

'Sodding dog,' mumbles Norman, fiddling with his drill-bit. 'If that hound does a *mea culpa* on my lawn, I'm phoning Ron to come round with a pooper-scooper pronto. There's a limit to goodwill, and it's just been reached.'

But as well as inciting Norman's anger, the red setter has also prompted animal connections in Norman's brain, because after a couple of minutes, he remembers something, and wheezily plods his way down to the kitchen.

'Getting to know the new vet,' he tells Abbie. 'He's become quite a regular at the Crow. In fact, as regards my hangover the morning after the explosion at the Egg Bank, I can confidently tell you that the finger of blame points at him.'

'Hope he's handsome,' Abbie remarks. 'That'll be a nice treat for the girls.'

'How about a nice treat for me?' Norman ogles at her, forgetting Buck de Savile's rendition of a string of Elvis Presley hits, his drunken monologue about a macaque monkey called Giselle and an insane woman called Mrs Mann, and the workings of the veterinary complaints procedure, and remembering instead how, last night, after the pub, beneath Abbie's nightie – brushed cotton in winter, plain in summer – her White Cliffs of Dover had allowed themselves to be attacked by his eager earth-moving equipment. Norman's *jeu de mots* concerning earth movements was in tribute to Ernest Hemingway's famous *oeuvre*, *For Whom the Bell Tolls*, in which the leading lady says, after having it away, 'The earth moved.' Sometimes, as a variation on the same linguistic theme, he would ask afterwards, 'Did I toll your bell all right for you, then, love?' Abbie would always smile and say, 'Yes thanks, Norman,' and pull the nightie back down over her bony knees. She wasn't bothered about not having her bell properly tolled: she always used the time to think up a new dessert recipe. Last night had been a gratifying experience for both of them; Norman's earth-moving equipment had scraped through its MOT again, and Abbie had dreamed up a new way with profiteroles.

'What?' says Abbie, oblivious to Norman's sexual reverie.

'What d'you mean, what?'

'You said something.'

'Did I?'

'Yes. About the vet.'

'Oh,' remembers Norman. 'Nice bloke. He says he'll look at the junk in the loft for us.' He reaches for the biscuit tin. 'He says he might have a book on taxidermy antiques. Reckons if they're vintage, and a professional taxidermy job, they could well be worth something. Expect it depends on how they're mounted.' He chuckles, and wiggles his eyebrows up and down. 'As 'twere!' he adds, popping a barley flip-cake into his mouth.

'I'd better have another look,' sighs Abbie. 'And give them all a good dust. How many are there, d'you reckon?'

'Well, there's the famous ostrich, for starters,' says Norman through a mouthful of flip-cake. 'Plus a wombatty-looking job, a big monkey, and what looks like a badger. Oh, and a dog. He's got a whatchermacallit on his collar with SUET engraved on it.'

'That name rings a bell,' says Abbie, taking out her notepad and adding DUST CREATURES to her list in her neat script. 'I think the Empress said it was her daughter's dog.'

'The girls've enrolled on another course at the university,' Abbie says, when Norman returns from chasing the red setter off the lawn. She checks the percolator. 'Special studies, they call it.'

'What's that, when it's at home?'

'Something modern, by the sound.'

'So they're going intellectual on us again,' smiles Norman, twirling a three-centimetre screw between finger and thumb. 'Bless their cotton socks.'

As Norman returns to his DIY, picture his wife Abbie now a million miles away in her kitchen, reading, as she does every day, from the Recipe for Happiness. The recipe, writ large on a poster featuring cherubs with cooking pots, is dear to her heart; its homely kitchen philosophy has served her well:

Take one ounce of goodwill, and mix with a measure of frankness. Add a pinch of lovingkindness and stir in well with humour, the spice of life. Sprinkle generously with open-mindedness and courtesy. Add sympathy and optimism to the melting-pot, and apply warmth until a merry glow is achieved. Serve with a dash of glee and garnish with hope. Note: this is a dish for sharing, and is very more-ish!

It never fails to make her smile, and to put her in the mood for the task ahead. For which observe her now, checking her utensils for the morning's full dress rehearsal of minestrone *suivi par* artichokes Riviera, *ensuite* potted pears *avec* cinnamon custard. Some people have things in their blood: she has food in hers. She'll be trying out another of those Victorian veggie recipes later, from *The Fleshless Cook* by Violet Scrapie. The Laudanum Empress says they'll be disgusting because they're her daughter's recipes, but what sort of taste does a self-confessed drug-addict have?

Pots, pans, knives, casserole, whisk, scissors, sieve, garlic-crusher, colanders, baking tin, all present and correct, standing by Worktop A ready for Camera One. And soup ingredients to the ready: pre-prepared stock, vermicelli, seasonings, peas, beans, carrots, Parmesan, white wine. The artichokes Riviera and potted pears ingredients are to stay in the fridge until after the commercial break. Camera Two, as always, she pictures perched several centimetres above the microwave, for the wider shot. Quite a flattering angle; she's checked it from a step-ladder, narrowing her eyes and picturing the on-screen effect. It's absurd, but despite her years of cooking experience, she still feels a little nervous.

Yes; nervous. The big day is right around the corner. She can feel it in her bones.

The scenario for the big day is as follows: an independent television producer's car breaks down on the A210, and because his mobile phone is also on the blink, he walks to Thunder Spit where he smells a wonderful smell coming from the Old Parsonage. He rings the doorbell, and Abbie answers its chimes, her apron still on. The television producer, whose name is Oscar or perhaps Jack, wonders if he can use her phone to call the AA, as his mobile isn't charged up. While they are waiting for the AA man to arrive, Abbie offers Oscar or Jack a cup of freshly brewed coffee and some of her home-made Apfelkuchen, and he is so bowled over by the Apfelkuchen, and the elegance and poise and *je-ne-sais-quoi* of Abbie Ball herself, that he enquires whether she has ever considered working as a television presenter, and would she do him the great honour of accompanying him to the studio for a screen test?

132

After that, the rest will be history.

But now, today, is pre-history, and Abbie stands framed for the opening shot of her rehearsal.

'Hello. Now it's easy to get into a bit of a tizz when you're thinking minestrone,' she begins. 'But just remember that the secret of success is to take it one step at a time.'

Minestrone is a good metaphor for Abbie's life, she reflects, as she runs through the list of ingredients for the benefit of the imaginary viewer at home: full of bits and pieces of interesting things, swirling about in the family pot. Like genes passed down through the ages, some items will crop up more frequently, and others sink to the bottom. One night, she, Norman and the Empress had all watched a programme called *Death of a Nation*; the extinction of the British was all down to DNA, apparently. Bad thoughts, good thoughts. Traits from Norman's side, traits from her own side. Look at Rose and Blanche: the red hair; that's definitely a Boggs characteristic. But their manual dexterity; that's surely Norman's side of the family? The Tobash feet, poor dears, and the over-developed coccyx – though they haven't got it as badly as Granny had, and that was in the days when they wouldn't operate so readily if it didn't affect your gait. The excess body hair: guilty again, as charged: that's the Tobash side, but the cosmetics industry has come up trumps there. I came off quite lightly myself, but thank God for hot wax! The trouble with so many ingredients in the gene pool, in the pot of thoughts and memories, is that there are always a few that you find less appetising than others, and some which are so downright appalling that you force yourself to gulp them down without looking too hard.

'Now a cook's best friend is her chopping board,' says Abbie gaily, smiling at the imaginary Camera Two. 'And as you can see, I use the traditional wooden kind, though if you're thinking kitchen hygiene, the plastic variety is best, to be honest. Nice sharp knife' (she holds it up to the imaginary Camera One and lets it glisten in the light) 'and you're ready to go.'

The Laudanum Empress, her soap opera finished, has been

133

watching Abbie, transfixed. Noting the woman's passion, her exhausting single-mindedness, and her slightly buck teeth. And thinking.

'You remind me of my daughter,' she says suddenly. Abbie looks up in shock at the opaque phantom perched on the draining-board. 'Could you by any chance be related?'

Outside, the sky is a jovial cobalt blue, and the trees are punchbags for a wild, irrational wind. While Abbie has been rehearsing, Rose and Blanche have travelled back from Hunchburgh by bullet train, and are now stomping purposefully up Crawpy Street in their elasticated trainers, past the giant Lucozade billboard, up a little alley decorated with dog-shit and old Coke cans, and squeezing their way through a rusty turnstile, past a big FOR SALE sign, into the graveyard of St Nicholas's Church. A cluster of teenagers – the twins recognise Clinton Tobash, Cameron Mulvey, and Jade Yarble, regular truants from Abbie's home-economics class, among them – sit on a gravestone smoking and kicking at the long grass and nettles. Nearby, an ancient Lord Chief Justice sheep nuzzles about the gravestones like a self-operated Hoover, the mobile nozzle of her lips wiggling to reach the most succulent dandelions: the new ecclesiastical administration, to establish its green credentials, had insisted on not buying a new church lawnmower, but had instead persuaded Ron Harcourt to contract out one of his flock to graze. Rose and Blanche pat the sheep. Then nod at the kids, remembering their own tendency to come here when skiving off school. History repeats itself, they think, as they pick their way past the crumbling gravestones.

'Look,' said Rose, pointing to a grave from which sprouted a mass of indecently sprawling vegetation with yellow flowers.

'Eugh,' said Blanche. 'Creepy.'

'It's a gourd plant.' A long-haired, ineffectual-looking man stepped out from behind a gravestone. 'I looked it up. It's famous for its adaptability. Repeats itself every four generations. Green one year, yellow the next, then orange, then mauve, then back

134

to green. Amazing, eh? The Lord moves in a mysterious way. I'm Josh – remember?'

'Hi, Josh,' said the girls.

They did remember. He helped organise things like the Thistle Festival. They'd seen him at the Yard of Ale Contest, and he and Dad had taken turns to MC the Karaoke nights at the community centre. And wasn't he the bloke who did that embarrassing cabaret thing for the Birdspotters' Association? Yes: the Vicar.

'We wanted to look at some old church records, for our genealogy module,' said Rose, stepping carefully over the tendrils of the gourd plant. At the base of each yellow flower, an odd-looking purplish fruit was beginning to swell.

'See who married who, in Mum's family,' added Blanche. 'And then put it in a diagram. Family trees are all the rage in the States. We're going to set up a business.'

'Do a sort of trace-your-roots service,' Blanche elaborated.

'Yeah, charge a fortune,' suggested Rose.

'Uh-huh? Well, follow me,' said Josh. They stepped into the gloom, where after a moment the mournful shapes of some dingy pews began to loom into view. A bucket of whitewash stood on the floor in the middle of the aisle. 'I'm trying to get rid of the water-mark,' explained Josh. 'It dates back to the Great Flood of 1858, but now we're selling up, the estate agent wants it looking marketable.'

'Selling soon, then?'

'Hoping to. We've had a few nibbles from a McDonald's franchise. It makes financial sense; we can't compete with the satellite services. I'm off to the States, myself.'

So, think the twins. Another wanker exports himself.

'You'd better get a move on,' said Rose, 'before the Emigration Restriction.'

'The clergy are exempt. I'm doing an ecclesiastical MA in Louisiana, home of the water-melon.'

'So where's the marriage register?'

'Over here,' said Josh. Then, suddenly inspired: 'Ten Euros, and it's yours.'

135

Rose and Blanche exchanged a glance.

'Let's have a look, then,' said Rose.

They wandered into the registry and inspected the book. It was old, thick and faded, its pages oddly bulbous.

'Another victim of the Flood,' commented Josh. 'Nowadays we put it all on disc, of course, and send it to the Office for National Statistics.'

The girls leafed through the tattered pages. The ink had run on many of them, rendering them illegible. 'It's a bit shop-soiled,' complained Rose.

'That's history for you,' said Josh with a smile. 'Take it or leave it.' He was looking forward to his three-year creation-studies course.

'Five Euros, and you're on,' said Rose.

They settled for seven Euros fifty.

All right if I invite him to a barbie, then?' asks Norman, popping his head round the kitchen door.

'Invite who?' asks Abbie.

'The new vet. Buck, he's called. Buck de Savile.'

'Ooh, a Frenchman?' enquires Abbie hopefully, putting away her imaginary TV equipment. She'll be able to flex her subjunctives.

'Seemed as English as beef to me,' says Norman.

'Oh well. We'll soon find out. Tell him the Saturday after next,' says Abbie.

'Tell who the Saturday after next?' call Rose and Blanche, slamming the front door behind them. 'No one boring, we hope.'

'Ah, the return of Double Trouble,' comments Norman.

'The new vet,' says Abbie. 'Nice man, according to your father.'

The twins exchange a glance of amused contempt.

'Age?' they ask together.

'Oh, youngish to middle-ish. Told me he was born the day Elvis Presley died, so work it out for yourselves. Drives an Audi Nuance. You can't say fairer.'

Rose and Blanche exchange another look; this one more optimistic.

'Any more ideas about earning your keep, you two?' Norman is asking. 'Sorry to raise the subject, but there's been a lot of hoo-ha about the pensions issue, since the Egg Bank. The P-word, they're calling it. Your mother and I aren't the only parents racking their brains about how you're going to cope financially when we're six feet under.'

'We're planning to get pregnant,' announces Rose. 'That's *our* P-word!'

Norman and Abbie exchange a God-help-us glance; they've also heard about the Reward on the news.

'Along with twenty million other bounty-hunters!' sighs Norman, in frustration. This Reward thing is a big mistake by the Government, he and Abbie have agreed. All it's going to do is raise hopes, start off a national rutting fever, spread a lot of venereal disease, and break young hearts.

'Have you tried thinking of anything on a *practical* level?' sighs Abbie. 'Just in case you *don't* manage to become the first British girls since the Millennium to get pregnant by natural means?'

'Yes, as a matter of fact,' says Rose. 'We're going to research the Ball family tree.'

She and her sister dump their handbags and a crumpled carrier bag on the hall table. Keys, cigarette packets and chewing gum spill out.

'It's part of our genealogy module,' says Blanche.

'Module?' asks Norman. 'As in space module?'

'That's education jargon for you,' says Abbie.

'Dr Bugrov reckons that with the British becoming extinct, the family-tree market is going to be the next big money-generating thing. We're going to get into it. We've got to start off by making a sort of chart, showing the Ball family's ancestry.'

'Get the Empress to help you,' suggests Abbie. 'She reckons her daughter might be a great-great-great something or other of ours. *She* was a famous cook, in her day.' The twins groan in unison.

'No thanks,' says Rose.

137

'In any case,' adds Blanche, 'oral testimony isn't allowed.'

'Certainly not phantom oral testimony,' adds Rose drily.

'Yeah,' agrees Blanche. 'It's all got to be in writing. Empirical, it's called.'

'We've got hold of the Thunder Spit marriage register,' says Rose, pulling it out of a crumpled carrier bag and waving it at her parents.

'We'll be using that,' says Blanche.

'To make a chart,' continues Rose. 'Showing who's related to who.'

'Whom,' corrects Abbie, scooping the girls' belongings back into their handbags. 'It's not who,' she says. 'It's whom.'

'For whom the bell tolls,' says Norman, winking at Abbie.

'Pardon?' say the twins together.

'Ernest Hemingway,' says Norman, slapping Abbie on the bum. 'She's a thoroughbred, your mum. Ask not for whom the bell tolls, it tolls for her.'

The twins groan in unison and do their puke-face.

'Now on to matters serious,' announces Norman, aligning his belly over his belt and rocking on his shoes. 'Have any of you three gorgeouses nicked my strimmer? Because in case it has slipped your collective memories, it's the Thistle Festival next week. And there's no peace for the wicked!'

138

CHAPTER 14

THE ORIGIN OF SPECIES

There is no peace, Parson Phelps always maintained, for he who is pure in heart. 1859 was the year that Charles Darwin's book, *Origin of Species*, was published, and it was a date which also marked the decline into melancholy and madness of many a theologian – including Parson Phelps.

He and I laughed at first. The idea that we were descended from monkeys and apes was not new, Parson Phelps informed me, but this was the first time it had been voiced with such apparent authority. It was only when he realised the extent to which otherwise sane people were actually taking the scientist's beliefs seriously, that my foster-father's outrage began in earnest. He was not alone in deciding that the ungodly book was the last straw in a long and uncivilised barrage of assault upon the Lord's word by his great bugbear, that unseemly vehicle of destruction, science. The whole Christian world – or that part of it that Parson Phelps and I represented, i.e. the humble common clergy of the land – was still weary and frustrated from all the geology battles over fossils, but we rose up against it, stones in a great wall of faith that united us all.

These were heady days in the Church, and every day, including Marble Friday, my Father walked to Judlow to purchase the *Thunderer* and keep abreast of developments in the Great Debate. But he was no passive participant. His sermons at that time took on a force and a passion I had never seen before, and it was thanks to his stormy sermons from the pulpit that Charles Darwin – hitherto a complete stranger to all Thunder Spitters –

became such an object of public contempt in the village that he replaced Guy Fawkes in effigy on Bonfire Night. Shortly after its publication, Parson Phelps appeared in the church brandishing a copy of the infamous book, and during the service ripped out and tore page after page. If the congregation had been permitted to cheer in God's house, they would have done, but instead they smiled and allowed their faces simply to shine encouragingly in support of Parson Phelps as the pages went fluttering to the floor.

'This is my message to all heretics,' warned my father. 'That he who dareth to challenge the word of God, as evidenced in the words of Genesis, may be treated as a worshipper of the Devil himself, and punished accordingly!'

The congregation had come to adore such scenes – but afterwards Dr Baldicoot looked worried, and shook his head.

'I fear he may have a brain tumour,' he confided to me. 'He is taking this evolution debate too seriously.'

I disagreed. I knew my father, after all. He was simply a man of deep conviction, and I loved him for it. Besides, I knew him to be right, and shared his beliefs most passionately myself. Of all the books of the Bible, that of Genesis was the one that I had always held most dear to my heart, and I felt its truth deeply. The Earth had been without form, and void, and darkness had been upon the face of the deep! And then man appeared! For me, there was simply no denying it, and science could hang.

'I believe that time will show you, Dr Baldicoot, that it is Mr Darwin – and certain sections of society – who have a malfunction of the brain,' I said. 'Five years hence, I do assure you, this ridiculous craze will have died away, and the crisis we are living through will appear as nothing more than a season of ill-judgement and fashionable whimsy.'

Dr Baldicoot shrugged and poked at his abominable pipe, and said we would see what we could see, and I smiled to myself, proud of my father's stand. For the controversy over the *Origin of Species* united our small family of two most happily, and some of my fondest memories of him, before madness struck,

140

date from that year, when together we spent many hours poring over Darwin's profane tome, by the light of the candle in the kitchen, the flag-stoned floor twinkling with salt. And as we read, our concern about his heresies grew.

For was Mr Darwin not making three uniquely dangerous propositions?

1. God's word in the Book of Genesis was a lie.
2. All life – including human life – developed by a gradual and haphazard process of evolution, from basic, humble life-forms such as the sardine, and that man himself was by implication but a glorified baboon.
3. That – *quid erat demonstrandum* – our faith and my father's life's work was as nought.

It was the third item on this list that was soon to plant the seed of madness in Parson Phelps' poor brain. Had I only heeded the words of Dr Baldicoot, and pulled my father back from the edge of the abyss! But I had not known he was standing there, and I with him. I had thought we were safe.

But the world had begun to tilt.

There is a fallacy among city dwellers that goes as follows: there are four seasons in a year. Yet as anyone who lives outside a city knows, there are not four seasons in the year, but twelve. Each of the main seasons, spring, summer, autumn and winter, is divided into three distinct sections: the beginning, the middle, and the end, stretches of time in which certain preordained natural miracles occur, such as the forsythia blooms, the razor-bill mates, the beech-leaf falls, or the bat hibernates. I explain this to demonstrate how regulated our lives were in Thunder Spit; how governed by the wheel of the calendar. It was early autumn, for example, when my mother died. It was mid-autumn the following year, when the Flood came and I experienced my disturbing visions and the gourd plant sprouted. And it was early winter – November – when the first frosts were biting, that the Travelling Fair of Danger and Delight came to Judlow. And it was there, in a single minute of a single hour of a single day, that a portcullis slammed down behind me, marking the close of that season of my life called childhood.

My age: fifteen. It is a Sunday afternoon, and for my own subversive reasons, I have just told my unsuspecting father a triple untruth: that despite the winter chill, I wish to go to the schoolhouse to meditate, and conjugate Latin verbs, and read the Bible. Far from arousing his suspicions, Parson Phelps' reaction to my elaborate lie is one of surprise and pleasure. He ruffles my coarse thatch of hair with his hand.

'I admire your dedication, Tobias,' he says. He is gutting sardines to make a pie. 'It does a credit to the upbringing your mother gave you.'

I bite my lip at his mention of my mother. 'We do not know where you came from, Tobias,' she had whispered to me on her deathbed, ravaged by the cough, eaten alive by the Thing, and clasping her precious gourd to her breast. 'But promise me that you will never visit the Travelling Fair of Danger and Delight.'

Which was precisely what I was about to do. For why would a mother make a child swear to such a thing, if the Fair did not house a secret? Conscious of my imminent betrayal of her deathbed wishes, I hang my head. But Parson Phelps misinterprets the gesture.

'And modest, too,' he says fondly, making the sign of the cross first over me, and then the sardines. Yet as I gulp back my shame, my spine tingles with the anticipation of the illicit.

It is only natural, is it not, for a child to be curious about his origins?

It was only this morning that my father had delivered his annual sermon – to a crowded congregation – about the evils of triviality, to coincide with the arrival of the Fair, an event which came a close second to the great enemy, science, as a target for his personal wrath. The church-going families of Thunder Spit – the Tobashes, the Peat-Hoves, the Balls, the Mulveys, the Barks, the Hayters, the Harcourts, the Cleggs and Mrs Sequin had all listened attentively, as my father, preaching at full volume, his breath leaving him in chilled puffs and mingling with the sunlight that streamed through the stained glass, held forth with passion. Tommy and I, somewhat less attentive than the others, sat crushed in a back pew; we had been to the far end of the Spit to collect conkers from the gnarled little horse-chestnut tree, which had produced a bumper crop, and our pockets were full to bursting.

A certain Godless event was taking place in Judlow, my father was telling his flock. An event which marked – in God's eyes – a low point to an otherwise wholesome year of toil. An event which should be avoided in much the same way as one might avoid a venomous snake.

The congregation nodded sagely.

'The magic is here, in Nature and in our hearts,' Parson Phelps had warned solemnly. 'We have no need for man-made entertainment; it is all around us, God-given, for which we thank Him.'

I had heard it all before: about how birdsong is God's way of making music for us, and lobsters are for our nourishment but also for our entertainment because of the way they change colour in boiling water, and wave their claws at us. About how God thought of Man first, when He created the animals, sending camels to live in the desert where they can function with precious little water and so be of use to the desiccated bedouin, and keeping lions in the jungle, well out of our way. Why, my father argued, should anybody need to look at a painting, when he can gaze at the wing of a butterfly? Et cetera: he never mentioned the Fair by name, but he took care to damn it with his every word.

'He has never been to it,' Tommy muttered to me, as we shuffled about under our pew, retrieving the rolling conkers that had spilled from our bulging pockets. 'So how does he know?'

For my own part, to house such a thought in my own bosom would have been heretical; I was only just now beginning to question my father's omniscience, and every time I did so, I

143

felt guilty and ashamed. But as I returned to my hard seat and polished my largest conker with my handkerchief and listened to the continuation and climax of Parson Phelps' righteous drone, I realised that my father's sermonising only increased my desire to venture into the forbidden land of the Travelling Fair, whose very toffee apples spelt moral depravity.

And so it came to pass that on that same afternoon, despite God's most specific wishes on the subject, Tommy and I set out for Judlow, a town that boasted nine shops, a pub, a mayor, a Sir Eustace and Lady Antonia Yarble living at the Big House, a slaughterhouse, and a newfangled closed sewer system, that sent the town's waste trickling into the sea. I had not visited Judlow more than ten times in my life, and on each occasion it had felt like venturing abroad. (The thought of going to Hunchburgh, where my father had studied theology, was even more daring, like voyaging through Parson Phelps' vision of space to the constellations. From Hunchburgh, I imagined, one could look down on the world like the Man in the Moon.) But although the excitement of our adventure gave me additional energy, my gait hindered me, and it soon became abundantly apparent that I could never keep pace with Tommy for the full three miles of our journey.

'Hop on my shoulders,' he suggested, when we had left the village behind us. 'Else we'll never make it before dusk.'

How I loved this! My unorthodox transport, coupled with the guilty pleasure of transgression, charged the atmosphere of the day with a tingling light. Swaying up there on Tommy's shoulders, I could see for miles: the sparkling sea, the whirling ridges of cloud, the distant hum of the town – all filled my blood with the sharp, unrivalled thrill of freedom. At the edge of the promontory, the hawthorn and the bracken stopped, and other shrubs began. Mainland shrubs.

'I can smell it!' I yelled. 'I can smell the Fair!'

Here Tommy set me down, and we sniffed the air. Sure enough, we caught the scent of animals and rotting straw and burnt sugar. As the wind gusted towards us, it bore with it, too, the faint sounds of screaming and laughter.

Ten minutes later, we entered the swirling, chattering crowds, and I immediately lost sight of Tommy. I began to panic, leaping up to catch a glimpse of my friend over the heads of the milling strangers, but the next thing I knew, there he was, back at my side, thrusting a famous Danger and Delight toffee apple under my nose. He had stolen two. The toffee apple contained real sugar, he told me, harvested by manacled slaves in cruel overseas plantations. It was the best thing I had ever tasted. The Ten-Foot Woman swung past us, smoking a clay pipe and showering everybody with confetti, and I giggled with joy. Walking arm in arm with Tommy, licking my toffee apple and surveying the scene, I soon realised that there were faces here from my father's congregation. Tommy spotted them, too.

'Look! There's Johnny Clegg at the coconut shy!'

'And Ron Tobash! Over there! He's guessing the weight of that pumpkin!'

We saw others, too: Mr Mulvey scolding his son Johnny, and Farmer Harcourt and his family braying with laughter as they descended the helter-skelter, and Mrs Sequin arguing with an urchin who she claimed had stolen her purse. Seeing all these citizens of Thunder Spit enjoying themselves thus, it seemed that my father's sermon had had the opposite effect to that intended. I felt ashamed on his behalf, and, conscious of my own betrayal, pulled my hat low over my brow.

'Let's look at the Two-Headed Snake,' I suggested to Tommy, eager to remain incognito. We paid a farthing each, and the one-eyed man in charge of the Snake whipped back a curtain to reveal a glass case with a tangled rope-like creature coiled within.

'It's two snakes bound together,' Tommy pronounced, after inspecting the reptile closely, 'with some kind of glue.'

'Time's up,' snapped the man, and whipped the curtain back. Disappointed in the fraud, we headed for the world-famous Mechanical Millipede, an iron and wood construction which was so big that, had it been transported into the church at Thunder Spit, it would have obliterated the altar and spilled out into the nave and the vestry. We rode on this contraption three times, so that Tommy could understand its engineering, which, he informed me, wriggling out from underneath it later, involved a system of interlocking cog-wheels and a steam-powered piston accelerator mechanism, designed by a genius.

'Oi, Tobias, come here!'

Tommy was now hopping about at the edge of a big crowd standing around a pen that contained a piebald horse. I joined him: I stood on tiptoe, and Tommy peered through the elbow of the man in front of him. A red-faced gent was yelling questions at the horse, and the creature was answering by stamping its front hooves on the earth.

It was fed sugar lumps as reward for its intelligence.

'It's incredible!' said Tommy, commenting on its arithmetic abilities.

But I wasn't so sure. 'It's a trick,' I told him. 'No animal is that clever.'

We wandered off.

According to my recollection of that day, it was when we visited the Man-Eating Wart-hog that the nervousness began to engulf me – a nervousness so strong and so sudden as to have an odour all its own. There was a high enclosure of sticks, which we entered. And there the creature was, slumped in a filthy cage, licking its hairy accoutrements next to a pile of fetid meat-chunks. He looked up, and although I had the time to note, in a rational manner, that he resembled in many ways the illustration I had previously seen of such an animal in *Hanker's World*, its eyes unnerved me immediately. They were a colour midway between orange and ochre, with vertical irises, like narrow doors into another world. The smell that emanated from him made me shudder. It was the raucous odour of captivity and rotting meat, which though hitherto alien, seemed suddenly as familiar to me as the scent of wax candles in the church. As

Tommy and I approached, toffee apples still in our hands, the creature, a pig-like animal covered with hideous carbuncles, stared at me, sniffed, and gave a sudden, low grunt of hatred.

I was by now well accustomed to animals reacting disfavourably to my presence, but the reaction of the Wart-hog – perhaps because I knew him to be a man-eating beast – unnerved me. My nervousness deepened, and I felt faint, as though at the periphery of my vision, beyond my control and my comprehension, something invisible and dangerous swarmed. I caught my breath, and grabbed Tommy's arm.

'It's all right,' he said. 'He's only a big piggy-wig. Eh, porky?' And he laughed.

My head spun. As the Wart-hog's ugly bristle-covered snout and tusks rammed up close to my face, and his unblinking orange-ochre eyes stared me out, I shuddered. Then, as the creature grunted ominously again, I felt my hackles rise in a sudden, unaccountable fear. Why did this hideous, grunting creature seem suddenly familiar to me in a way I could neither fathom nor describe?

Puzzled and shamed by my now raging sense of anxiety, I tugged my eyes away from the Wart-hog's gaze, and turned to leave. Tommy was already walking out, oblivious to my discomfort. 'Come along,' he said. 'There's a show starting in the Tent of Miracles.'

We do not know where you came from, she had said. I regretted coming here, and I wanted nothing more than to go home, but I dared not tell Tommy this. As we turned our backs on the creature in his cage, and headed towards the tent, the nervousness came with me, and I could not shake it off.

By the time we arrived at the Tent of Miracles we had no money left, of the shilling Tommy had stolen from his father, risking the metal bottom-whisk. When the guard's back was turned, we slipped inside; Tommy out of curiosity, and I out of the feeling that here, away from the Wart-hog's orange-ochre eyes, I might find shelter.

Foolish hope.

Inside the darkened tent, a crowd stood around a small podium, staring at the creature upon it. It was her face that you saw first: it was alarmingly beautiful, and ageless, and wild. Her hair shot upwards, scraped into a tight knot that sat balanced upon her head like a ball. At first, her head seemed simply to float there, in boxed suspension, white against the darkness of the sheeted backdrop, but as our eyes grew accustomed to the gloom, I realised that the dark frame that housed her face in fact consisted of her own black-clad legs and feet. From her neck, an oval locket hung down, trembling and catching the light, flashing it around the room. Tommy and I drew a breath and looked at one another. No wonder Parson Phelps had preached against this place from the safety of his pulpit. There was an aura of disgrace about the little ballerina, but pride, too, and a feral quality which increased my nervousness enormously. Tommy, too, was jiggling at his conkers in a disturbed fashion. We stared at the spectacle of the little figure, her legs arched up from behind her, her back bent like a scorpion's. We stared at her for a long time. Then slowly, as the tent filled up, she began to loosen the grip of her shins and feet, and move slowly, slowly, and with great precision, to unwind herself. It was absurd, and frightening, but also gracious and miraculous, like watching a camel successfully passing itself through the eye of a needle.

As she emerged slowly from her scorpion position, we saw that she was of diminutive stature. Her whole torso, like her legs and feet, was clad in the tight-fitting black of an unbroken silhouette, except for the stiff little skirt which stuck out horizontally from the waist. Something physical and visceral stirred within me, twisting my guts.

'Mildred is punishing me,' I told Tommy. 'Let's go.'

'No. I'm staying,' said Tommy firmly. 'Look, she's tying herself in another knot!'

And sure enough, she is on her belly again, balancing a tray on each foot. On the trays are tiny glasses of Madeira sherry. It seems you can pay twopence to come and take a glass, and drink it, then put it back on the tray. 'Sherry comes from Spain,' whispers Tommy. 'It makes you drunk just to sniff it.' I try to refrain from breathing at all; God forbid that Parson Phelps should discover me intoxicated! Now, still balancing her tray and a dozen little glasses, and still bunched in her uncomfortable knot, the woman has launched into song. I strain to listen over the babble of voices. There is a tune to it, of sorts, but no words, and for some reason I find her singing unspeakably unsettling and poignant. She has a small, cracked voice, and the clatter of notes that emerges sounds oddly familiar, though I cannot place them.

Maybe it was that lonely, wordless singing. Or maybe it was what happened afterwards. Either way, unaccountably, I found myself suddenly in tears, a curious, nagging sensation of sorrow mixed with happiness tugging at my innards and infuriating Mildred.

She had stopped, suddenly, mid-note. At first I thought she had merely missed a beat, and would resume her song, but it was as though she had lost interest in her own performance, and simply switched herself off, for there was a jagged hush. A few murmurs began to swell among the small crowd, and Tommy shifted from foot to foot.

'Get on with it then,' he muttered.

I drew in a sudden breath, and swayed on my feet. She was looking at me! Staring into my eyes! I could swear it!

It was when she flung her tray to the ground that I began to shake uncontrollably. It felt as though I were drowning all over again. I wasn't alone in my fear, for I heard several women scream as she hurled the tray. It flew high into the air as though slowed down by an invisible hand. Then it reached the height of its arc and with a brutal suddenness, went crashing to the floor. There were more screams and gasps as the sherry glasses smashed, tinkling and sending up a spray of golden droplets that smelt sweet and harsh and forbidden.

'Oh dear God!' I murmur.

Now she is unwinding herself, but in a hurried fashion, pulling at the knot of her own body with impatience. Her limbs free, she's sniffing the air, ignoring the crowd who are beginning to shuffle about nervously, and to hurl little balls of paper and gumdrops in her direction.

It is then, in the space of a single second that seems to last an hour, that I am drowning once again. I am dashed back into the flood-water of St Nicholas's Church, and the memory returns to me as vividly as a blow to my stomach.

My Angel is near. I am in a cot with golden bars, and I can hear the sound of a woman's voice singing a lullaby. *Rock-a-bye baby on the tree top . . .*

A bristle-skinned animal with orange-ochre eyes guards me.

Then I hear Father's voice calling me through the flood-water, begging me to return. I remember bobbing to the surface, and seeing the Parson's cassock balloon about him in a bubble of righteousness. I sink again, and this time visit Hell.

My Angel has disappeared, and my golden cot has become a rusty cage. I am lying in a pool of blood. And I hear a scream, high and shrill, that plays up and down my spine like fingernails screeching across a blackboard.

Yes: I remember this.

And as I do so, my heart begins to thump horribly, banging at my ribs like a caged beast desperate to escape. The Contortionist is pointing at me. On her face is anger, and pride, and wildness, and beauty, and desperation, all in one. Tommy clutches my hand.

Time freezes.

And remains frozen.

It is indeed fortunate that I am in many ways my father's child. For there, stuck in frozen time, I find a mood of sudden calm growing within me, and I feel the presence of Parson Phelps as solidly as if he were there in the flesh. And there, as I stare at the woman staring back at me, the full force of my faith tells me in a sane and measured fashion that there is nothing here that I know. The face, the ballet shoes, the little tutu whose skirt sticks out horizontally: nothing about the Contortionist is familiar to me in any way. Nothing, I realise, could in fact be

150

further from my world, and the calm and ordered life of Thunder Spit: that I can swear with my hand on my heart. A heart which, although it is still thumping within me madly, witnesses no swirl of recognition, feels no stirring of memory, and experiences no instinctive rush of hatred or of love. None. Nothing.

Just a desire to run away and return to my father, and the church, and God, and all the safety and security of home.

'Come along, Tommy!' I croak. I have grabbed his arm so hard that he yelps in pain. 'Let's go!'

So from that place of horror and depravity, gumdrops flying around us, the smell of sherry in our nostrils, the memory of a tuneless, wordless ballad ringing in our ears, we flee.

– *stuk ther. Nothin to do. NOTHIN, ever.*

Then I waks up one day and am SUMWER ELS. Dark. I ratles the CAGE. I screems and screems. Wer am I, I screems.

London Doks. This woz a SLAVE SHIPPE, says Trapp. I used to keep slaves in it. Afrika, and Gorgia. Gorgia, and Afrika. To-in and fro-in, like that. NOW it is sumthin els. Much mor CUMFTERBLE, He sez. Lots mor roome! It is an ARKE. And he is gon, larfin.

Ther is a man cald Higgins, feeds me, changis my BUCKIT. Wen do we sail, I arsks. Wer to.

He dusnt no, or says not.

But He tels me their is a LIST, and wen we hav got everythin on the LIST, we can cum home agen.

Wot kind of things is on this List, I sez.

Animals, He sez. The animals went in two by two, HURRA!

A few lines are obliterated here. But further down the page, the writing continues:

– *so they brings me FOOD, and water. Empties my buckit of piss and shit. Then TRAPP cums bak. Cumfterble? He arsks. Barsterd.*

We will go to DISTANT CUNTRIES wer you will be QUEEN, He sed, that nite wen we met, wen I was DANSIN at the kings Arms. Long Ago.

151

Let me out of this CAGE, I sez. I am screemin and cryin. Wot is this for, I sez. Wy cant you treet me like a lady.

Becos you is an ANIMAL now, He sez.

I am an animal alrite, I sez, I am a COW, I sez, I am a stupid COW. He stil has a hold of me. Dont no wy. I luvs Him stil, even wen He shuttes the dor of the CAGE and leevs me in the darke agen.

Its WOT YOU WONTS, He sez. Wimin DREEM of this.

I opens my mouth to speek but ther is no words ther for wot I feel. And not a thing in the WURLD that I can do. Becos by now the ARK is aflote.

CHAPTER 15

LONG LIVE DEATH

Which guests to invite and which to shun, what type of frilled smocking would best suit the bridesmaids, whether there will be enough champagne to go round, how the in-laws will get on: from as young as three, a normal healthy young girl will spend a fair proportion of her time, in the company of her favourite doll, agonising over the details of her hypothetical future wedding. Mrs Charlotte Scrapie being neither normal, nor healthy, nor a young girl, and in addition being already married, and indeed also dead, had long been concerned with a ceremony of the more gloomy variety, involving not white lace, but black. The happy hours she had spent preparing for this day! Earth to earth, ashes to ashes, dust to dust! Ding-dong, loud and long and tragic may the bells toll! A time to live, a time to die, a time to love, a time to hate, a time to bawl your eyes out and blow long and hard into a big black hanky!

'It was a marvellous funeral,' bragged the Laudanum Empress to Abbie Ball, a hundred and fifty years later. 'Far be it from me to boast, but it was certainly one of the most moving occasions I have ever attended.'

In accordance with her wishes, set out in detail in a document of some twenty-five pages, the ceremony was a grandiose affair, involving acres of pungent waxen lilies, hymn after tear-inducing hymn, black confetti, white faces, a fawning tribute to the deceased penned by the Empress herself and read by a hunch-backed vicar, and much booming organ music. Many of the Empress's grateful former clients – from both sides of the Great

153

Divide – sat in rigid and respectful attendance. In the front row of the church, Violet Scrapie, clad in mourning garb, dabbed at her eyes as the coffin was borne in, heaped with a mountain of lilies topped with the Empress's favourite old fox-fur.

'I'll let you into a secret, Vile,' murmured the dry-eyed Scrapie, sitting next to her. 'I gave her that fox because I botched it. It was unstuffable. Too many bullet-holes.'

Suet, reprieved from his fate as a dinner of the future, wheezed at Violet's feet. For him at least, something positive had emerged from the calamity: from now on, the kitchen would be needing an official food-taster. Neither Scrapie nor Violet noticed the presence of the psychic particles hovering above their heads. It was an extraordinarily moving service, Mrs Scrapie felt, allowing her own ghostly bosom to shudder and a single human tear to roll down her pale cheek as she listened to the hunchbacked vicar's heartfelt eulogy. 'Mrs Charlotte Scrapie, adored by all who knew her – gone, but still with us!' The tear fell upon the nose of the dog Suet with a plop. Crouching low with fear, he licked it off and whimpered.

'Farewell, Mrs Charlotte Scrapie!' intoned the vicar. 'May you rest in peace!

Rest in peace? Fat chance!

It is a well-known fact that grief can set all manner of other emotions shooting off in odd directions. The result of Mrs Scrapie's untimely death by food poisoning was to cause a deep doubt to hatch within the breast of Violet Scrapie. The week after the funeral, Monsieur Cabillaud, in an effort to relieve the child's troubled spirits and take her mind off her bereavement, urged her to resume her hitherto tireless work on his great tome *Cuisine Zoologique: une philosophie de la viande*, but she refused outright.

'I'm having nothing more to do with the wretched book!' shouted the blubbering Violet, distraught. 'I have poisoned my own mother!'

Cabillaud had the common sense to button his lip, but at the back of his mind lurked rebellion. Should his life's work grind to a halt, just because of a single, isolated misadventure? Should *Cuisine Zoologique* fail, just because a lone recipe within it had proved (in one case only) fatal?

There is a saying that goes: Too many cooks spoil the broth. Did too many, in the Scrapie household, now mean two? Was the Scrapie kitchen, spacious though it was, large enough to contain two consciences as afflicted as those of Violet Scrapie and Jacques-Yves Cabillaud? Both were volatile. Grief hung over them like a pall.

A philosopher such as Confucius might have said, 'We witness before us here an imbalance of yin and yang.'

But a young woman such as Violet Scrapie said instead, 'This is unbearable. I'm going out. Find your lead, Suet, and follow me!'

Cabillaud, kicking the stove, said, '*Merde!*'

Was it the ghostly presence of the Laudanum Empress and her cloud of psychic particles that steered Violet and the faithful Suet in the direction of Oxford Street that day?

Or was it simply fate that caused them to barge past the stalls selling roast-chestnuts, past the organ-grinders and the charlatans and the hansom cabs, and clatter straight, slap-bang, into a placard on which the following words were printed: MEAT IS MURDER?

The placard was attached to a man. The man in question – now cast in the role of victim, picked himself up off the pavement, and patiently awaited the apology he deserved. He was accustomed to abuse from strangers, but being a Christian, he also made a point of always hoping, most fervently, for the best.

'I am most terribly sorry,' said Miss Violet Scrapie. She said it with simplicity and grace. The man noted that, despite her quite monstrous size, she had a pretty, sad face, and was wearing mourning garb. So feeling suddenly sorry for her despite the shock she had caused him, he smiled at her, and began to speak.

'Your apology is – OUCH!'

He yelped in pain. He had been assaulted a second time.

Violet never knew what it was that came over Suet. So far his canine instincts had been proved utterly sound – witness his refusal to eat the braised primate that caused the death of the Laudanum Empress – but surely this was utterly out of character? It was not in his nature to hurt a fly. It will take more than another gracious apology to fix this, Violet thought, as she whipped out her black lace handkerchief – still sodden with funeral tears from a week ago, that's how much she had cried – and began dabbing at the wound on the man's curiously skinny leg.

'Suet's never attacked a human before,' Violet mustered. 'I don't know what's got into him. He's gone after rats, but . . .' Her voice trailed off in confusion. 'Look, can I escort you anywhere?' she offered the bleeding man.

'As a matter of fact you can,' he told her, mopping furiously at his shin. 'You can be good enough to help me stagger to a meeting I am about to hold in the public chambers.'

'What's happening there?' asked Violet, picking up the MEAT IS MURDER placard and propping it against a railing.

'A meeting of the Vegetarian Society,' he replied. 'Let me introduce myself. My name is Henry Salt, and I would like to invite you, miss, and your dog, to be my guests.'

'I am Violet Scrapie,' she said, proffering her hand. 'And this is Suet.' She kicked the creature lightly, and he hung his head. Going to the man's wretched meeting was the least she could do, she supposed, as she half-carried the limping Mr Salt to the public meeting hall, the reluctant Suet pitter-pattering along in their wake. The hall was dusty, and as Violet seated herself, it was filling up with an odd selection of people, all spectacularly thin. Violet shuddered, grateful for her own padding on these hard little chairs.

'Silence, please!' called Mr Salt, standing before them with his hands in a supplicating gesture. 'I would like to welcome a newcomer to our gathering! Please allow me to introduce Miss Violet Scrapie!'

There were murmurs of acknowledgement from the crowd, and a woman next to Violet, who looked like a bony fish, piped up, 'Pleased to meet, you, miss, I'm sure!'

Mr Salt's speech was a lengthy one, during which he exhibited himself to be most passionate about his fellow beings. More particularly those with feathers, fur and scales. Violet, who had seen the carcass of many a fellow being, and cooked and eaten not a few of the more exotic ones, thanks to *Cuisine Zoologique*, listened with irritation to his evangelistic discourse. It was clear to her, glancing briefly round the half-empty hall, that Mr Salt was preaching to the converted. His argument was contorted, wordy and earnest, but boiled down – reduced, as you might reduce a stock – its central argument was simple: men are hypocrites.

'Look at us,' he stormed, 'cherishing our pets, and treating them like humans,' here he cast a glance at Suet, who retreated further beneath Violet's chair, 'and then destroying a whole class of animal for our ghoulish consumption.' Suet began to wheeze unhappily. Violet, meanwhile, recalled her father's work on the Animal Kingdom Collection, and the Royal Hippo's insistence that the stuffed beasts be clothed in breeches and the like, and conceded that Mr Salt had something of a point here. 'Anthropomorphism makes cannibals of us all,' he continued. 'The only solution is to abandon our lust for the carcass, and eat herbs of the field!'

Now here, they parted company.

'We are the most complex and highly developed creatures on earth,' he proclaimed. 'Yet despite our thousands of years of civilisation, we pander to our primitive urge to feed on flesh. Is this the pinnacle of humanity, to breed creatures in order that they may be killed for our consumption? Are we no more than uncivilised fatteners of calves?'

As Mr Salt delineated the rights of God's beasts, and the holiness of St Francis of Assisi, and the inhumanity of man, a guilty tear rolled down Suet's cheek, but Violet's mouth remained set in refusal. After Mr Salt's speech had ended, there

157

was much applause from the group of undernourished-looking people, and the bony-fish woman next to Violet rose to her feet, reached beneath her chair, and whisked a linen cloth off a platter. Violet began to concentrate, sniffing the air as the thin woman sidled round with the platter, bearing lumpy vegetarian pies. Violet took a single bite, then spat.

'That's disgusting,' she said.

'Any chance you might be interested in becoming a member?' asked the thin woman, apparently undeterred. 'Vegetarianism is excellent for the figure.'

'No chance at all,' said Miss Scrapie, suddenly peckish and feeling the urgent desire for a pork chop. Dragging the distressed Suet behind her, she swept her huge bulk out of the hall, and headed for the butcher's.

Again: was it the ghostly presence of the Laudanum Empress and her cloud of psychic particles, or was it fate, that gave her this desire for a chop? Or was it simple, straightforward human greed?

Whatever the cause, Violet Scrapie finds herself, minutes later, peering through the window of Mr Samuel's shop, where a plaster statuette of a pig, whose chubby, cheeky face displays no irony, proffers a platter of chops, sausages and bacon rashers. Violet enters, dragging Suet behind her. But – what idiocy has entered the creature's foolish brain? He's whimpering! What's going on?

'Shut up, you silly dog,' Violet hisses, and kicks him again. He squeals on the blood-stained sawdust. In the crowded butcher's shop, upside-down poultry hangs from hooks, exuding that seductive and atrocious smell of death, so familiar to Violet from an early age, when she played on the floor of Cabillaud's chopping room. The butcher, like Cabillaud on his chopping days, wears a murderous apron and Violet notices how his fat fingers, mottled with blood and cold, are indistinguishable from the chipolatas he holds bunched for wrapping in paper for his customer. It's as though he has wrapped his own severed hand.

'Lovely piece of meat, there, madam,' he murmurs, handing it over to the woman in a little bloody parcel.

The invisible ghost of the Laudanum Empress hovers above Violet as she gazes about her, taking in the scene – so similar to the chopping room back home, but suddenly so alien. What's come over her, all of a sudden?

Suet squeals again, and whimpers, pulling on his lead to get out. 'Herbs of the field . . . cannibals of us all . . .' These are Mr Salt's words. Why are they coming back to her now? Why here? Still rooted to the floor, Violet gawps as the butcher now serves his next customer, a little coughing man, with a rack of lamb; watches as he wields the chopper, slamming it down with a crunch, brutally cleaving the gristle and holding up half a rib-cage for the man's inspection. She turns, and sees dead pigs hanging gaped open like small pianos, alongside calves' heads, mutton thighs, trays of kidneys in puddles of ink-dark blood, slobbery white brains and strips of tripe, thick and pale as undercarpet.

'Good afternoon, miss,' says the butcher, addressing Violet, who has suddenly reached the front of the queue. He offers his bloody hands. 'How can I help you?'

She stares for a while at the butcher. 'You can't,' she says bluntly. Something is choking her. 'There's too much blood.'

'Begging your pardon, miss?'

Silence. Then a strangulated gulp. Suet, flooded with a sudden audacity, seizes the moment and tugging on his lead, drags Violet Scrapie forcibly from the shop.

Violet Scrapie has since argued that it was indeed that chance meeting with Mr Salt in the street, and the eye-opening visit to the butcher's shop that was the first step on her road to Damascus. For that afternoon, sweaty and disturbed after her adventure, Violet returned home to find that, despite herself, the words of Mr Salt were still ringing in her head. 'Anthropomorphism makes cannibals of us all,' he had proclaimed. 'If we truly believe that animals have souls, then we

159

should refrain from eating our brothers! And if they do not have souls, then why, I pray, does the elephant shed tears and the mother leopard lay down her life to save her cub?'

Violet heaved her way up the stairs in Madagascar Street, with Suet anxiously scampering in her wake. She flung open the door of her father's workshop and gazed upon the scene before her. Her father lay slumped over his work table, fast asleep and snoring gently. An eviscerated squirrel dangled on a hook above his head, and in front of him, pinned to the wall, was a diagram of a jaguar's skeleton and musculature. Suet drew in a sharp breath; it was his first foray into this chamber of horrors, and doggy memories swirled in his brain: long-forgotten inhumanities performed upon him at the laboratory as a pup came floating into his consciousness, and he shuddered and whimpered. Violet, sensing his unease, took a step back, and stumbled over a jawbone. A crocodile lay belly-up, slit open on Scrapie's stuffing table, its flesh and a wobble of unspeakable viscera gleaming in a pile beside it. Violet recalled Cabillaud's blood-stained chopping room, and felt, for the first time in her life, a pang of remorse.

Those dishes they had prepared together had indeed been a delight – but a price had been paid, in the form of lives. Animals' lives – and now that of a human. What's more, her own mother! Could there not be some other way? She stroked Suet, deep in thought. Mr Salt's words began to haunt her. Imaginary tastes turned to ashes in her mouth. And imaginary smells – smells that had once made her mouth water – now began to make her retch.

She descended to the basement kitchen, from whence the odour of walrus tripe was wafting ominously.

'There is a problem,' Violet announced.

Cabillaud looked up from his cooking pot. 'Ah, *chérie*. You have returned. I am making ze mustard sauce with ze peppercorns, and a little tiny hint of sweetness, in ze form of my own rosehip *compote*.' Cabillaud had not yet noticed Violet's stony and tear-besmirched countenance. 'This walrus, he has need of lifting a little from his unhappy heaviness of taste.'

'I said a problem.'

The chef looked up, saw the finality on the face of his protégée, and read some of her thoughts, for was she not an open book to him? Was she not his own little Violette, whom he had personally perched on his weighing machine a million times, and to whom he had fed the best morsels of everything! His own little Violette, whom he had single-handedly educated in the pleasures of the palate!

'Meat is murder,' she announced.

His own little Violette, now turning against him? *Mon Dieu!* How could she?

'But ze human being is a carnivore!' countered Cabillaud. 'Ze animals, is not ze peoples! Zey have no human rights, *chérie!*'

One thing has a terrible tendency to lead to another – and sure enough, this sudden, bitter exchange proved to be but the *hors d'oeuvre* to a whole menu of conflict, whose main course was the marinated and long-simmered substance of Violet's grief, accompanied by an ethical dispute on animal rights featuring *mille-feuille* and crushed garlic and coriander, leading into a rich, repercussive meringue and sherry trifle of a debate on personal morality, an argument with scalloped icing and raspberries, a confrontation of furiously clashing flavours, multiple toxins, and flagrant disjunctions of taste. Tears were shed on both sides. A pan was thrown. Knees were got down upon. Belgian beseechings were to be heard. Pages from *Cuisine Zoologique* were spat upon and shredded out of pique. And finally, sobbing but victorious, the mistress of the house, the loyal dog Suet at her side, dismissed her former guru. Violet Scrapie. No longer a girl, but a woman. And what a woman.

As Violet Scrapie experiences her coming of age in the basement kitchen, a banging rhythmical noise is emanating from the taxidermist's workshop on the ground floor. *Thump, thump, thump.* It is the sound of flesh on wood. Fist on table, to be more precise. It's a busy life, being dead, reflects the Laudanum Empress; satisfied with Violet's progress, she drifts upstairs clutching her phantom petticoats to discover Dr Ivanhoe Scrapie in a state of utmost distress.

'Why, why, why?' he wails, his voice catching. As she passes through the closed door of his workshop, the Empress pats her hair and adjusts her ghostly face. She is briefly touched by his display of emotion, but also somewhat piqued; could the man not have tried a little harder to summon up such feelings while she was alive? But her sympathy is short-lived; it soon becomes apparent that the emotion we are witnessing here is neither grief nor remorse over the death of Mrs Scrapie; it is that green-eyed monster, professional jealousy.

'Bastard!' he moans, thumping harder on the table. 'Damned, bloody man!'

When the findings of the great scientist Charles Darwin had been published yesterday, Dr Scrapie's reaction, after he had stayed up all night reading the scholarly work, had been even more extreme than that which we are now witnessing. They had involved his forehead, and a marble mantelpiece. Human blood had been shed.

And why not? For he had been an idiot, a buffoon, an intellectual amoeba!

'Thirty years in zoology – *how could I not have seen it*?' he growls. 'It's so *obvious*! Any child who has visited a bloody *farm* could have spotted it!'

The hideous fact at the epicentre of Scrapie's misery is this: Darwin's *Origin of Species*, charting and explaining the great ladder of Nature, has made the sum of his own life's hitherto not inconsiderable achievements look suddenly so unambiguously lightweight that they almost fly into the air of their own accord. His historically successful stuffing of an earthworm, the publication of his paper *On the Epidermis of the Chameleon*, his appointment as Taxidermist Royal, his work on the Animal Kingdom Collection and the defunct specimens of Trapp's *Ark*, his discoveries about the rhino's hip-joint: all are as nothing compared to Darwin's spectacular triumph! Dr Ivanhoe Scrapie will now be consigned for ever to the dustbin of history! The grotesque injustice of it leaves him winded. His whole career blotted out by another's fame! It is all so monstrously galling!

He slumps over the table and breathes heavily, his chest shuddering, as though it houses a volcano instead of a heart. A volcano now on the verge of a most dangerous eruption. Oh, God! If only *he*, during his long career, had made a discovery of similar note! If only *he* had ventured forth on the *Beagle*, journeyed to the Galápagos, and, when drunk on ship's rum (how bloody well else?) imagined a stretch of time over which scales became feathers, fins mutated into legs, legs metamorphosed into wings, and swim bladders fashioned stomachs of themselves, all through the vagaries of chance. Instead, he had stayed here in London all these years, working for Her Majesty's absurd Animal Kingdom Collection, and faffing about with the carcasses of Trapp's *Ark*. In short, spending years of his life cleaning up another man's mess, to feed the whimsy of a crazed monarch, and a woman to boot! Why? Why? Why?

'Bloody book!' he yells, now flinging the tome to the floor in frustration, rage and pique.

'It's *obvious* that human beings are primates! I always *knew* we were! It's *obvious* that we evolved from monkeys and apes! So why didn't *I* come out and say so? Instead of messing about stuffing the buggers and putting breeches on them?'

'Calm down, Ivanhoe,' soothes the Empress, floating away from the shelter of the moose antlers to hover opaquely above him. 'I foresee that this kind of violent emotion will be the death of you.'

'*Charlotte*?' he murmurs. 'Charlotte? Is that you?'

'You will blow a gasket in your heart,' predicts the Laudanum Empress.

'A gasket in my heart?' he breathes. He must be hyperventilating, he concludes. Dreaming. Overworked. Something.

'If you think Mr Darwin's revelation is shocking, let me inform you, my dear Ivanhoe, that there is far worse to come! Don't say you haven't been warned!'

163

'Worse to come? What? Charlotte, what are you talking about? Are you there?'

But she's gone. Vanished. Skedaddled. That's the trouble with ghosts.

CHAPTER 16

THE FEEDING
RITUAL

It was a time of national panic. The Fertility Crisis was now officially a disaster, and the Sperm Drain became so intense that the Government decided to launch the Loyalty Bonus Scheme immediately. Overnight, I found myself eligible for an extra hundred yo-yos a week. In the meantime, the Pregnancy Reward had been announced. There's nothing like greed, is there? Five million yo-yos aren't to be sneezed at. The plus side of it all, of course, was that Britain was a lad's paradise. I was in with a chance now, I reckoned. A bloke could have any girl he wanted.

Or girls.

The Saturday of the barbecue came. Norman and his wife Abbie were in their element there on the patio, he fussing with charcoal pellets and firelighters and wind direction, she all flushed with mother-hen excitement at the prospect of a new palate to tempt at her elegant pale-green plastic flexi-table.

'Meet the harem,' said Norman proudly. 'This is Abbie' (I shook her flour-covered hand) 'and these are Tweedles Dum and Dee.'

'Buck de Savile,' I said. The girls looked at each other and giggled. There was a glamorous but rather eccentric-looking woman in white petticoats hovering about in the doorway; I caught a whiff of mothballs.

'And who's this?' I asked.

'Oh, she's just our ghost,' said Norman. 'The skeleton from the cupboard. I told you we'd been invaded by Victoriana. She came with the stuffed animals. Don't mind her.'

I laughed. 'Nice one, Norman! I hear they're all the rage!'

The eccentric woman made a sour face, and slunk back indoors.

'Nice cuts of pork you've got there,' I said, eyeing something marinaded. Those teenage Saturdays working at the butcher's hadn't been entirely wasted.

'Oh, call me Abbie,' said the head of the harem. 'Much friendlier. The pork's organic, because you never know, do you? I'm a bit of an ingredients nut.'

'She likes food that'll respect her in the morning,' put in Rose, reaching through the window for a pot of dip, then joining her sister to confederate next to a concrete urn. They kept looking in my direction, and I couldn't help wondering if I was the topic of their whispered conversation. Rose and Blanche were both wearing dresses, one white, one pink. Sigmund stirred, and I imagined them –

'That's my two lovelies,' says Norman, as though intercepting the vision. 'Sociable is putting it mildly.'

'Can I help you with anything, Norman?' I asked quickly.

'No, mate, just you relax. Abbie is just finishing off her TV rehearsal in the kitchen, bless her. She'll be along with the rest of the or doovers in half a tick. I'm off for some more of these charcoal pellets; the gals'll keep you on the straight and narrow in the interim, won't you, gorgeouses?'

'TV rehearsal?' I said. 'I didn't know Abbie was involved in television.'

'She isn't,' said Norman. Then added, loyally, 'But she will be, if there's any justice in the world!'

The twins snorted.

'Food's her thing,' says Rose.

'There's nothing she doesn't know about food,' adds Blanche. 'Food allergies, the origins of food, the sociology of food, food and music, the nutritional value of food, how to cook food, when and how to re-use the leftovers, storage of food, how to tell if something's edible or non-edible –'

'And she's an expert on food symbolism,' says Rose.

166

I wasn't entirely sure what food symbolism might be, but I nodded knowingly.

'Food and love, food and the post-war generation, food and cutlery,' continues Blanche.

'Food and discipline,' adds Rose.

'Food and God,' counters Blanche.

A pause.

Then Rose blurts, 'Only she's never really made it.'

There's another pause, and then Blanche adds, 'Never will.'

Food and failure, then.

'Well, Buck. What's your real name, then?' asked Blanche, or was it Rose, when Norman had disappeared from view. Not a great start.

'Buck de Savile *is* my real name,' I insisted. I'd have to think on my feet here.

'Pull the other one,' said Rose, or was it Blanche. They were nothing if not direct.

'My father was French,' I lied. 'That's where the *de* comes from. It's what's called an aristocratic prefix, I'll have you know. *Voulez-vous coucher avec moi ce soir*, et cetera.' They giggled. So they liked the idea, too. 'And the Buck is short for Buckingham.'

'There was a young Frenchman called Buckingham,' began one of them.

'Who always kissed girls before –' giggled the other.

'I've seen you both,' I intercepted. 'In the hypermarket in Judlow.'

'Saturday job,' the Roseblanches said in unison, and sniggered some more.

'But you didn't notice me,' I said ruefully, teasingly. Flirtatiously. They laughed.

'We're the living dead in there,' said Rose.

'Yeah,' agreed Blanche. 'If God himself walked in, we'd just treat him like any other customer.'

'I'd prob'ly ask him if he wanted extra carriers,' laughed Rose.

'I wouldn't even notice if he signed his cheque GOD in big letters,' added Blanche, enjoying the fantasy. 'Or if he didn't pay for his shopping at all but just wheeled his trolley right through the checkout area, past the redemption desk, and out into the car-park.'

'And then flew up into the air with it.'

'To His celestial home beyond the clouds,' finished Rose.

They certainly had a vivid imagination.

Then the conversation moved on to wildlife.

'I'm just a glorified plumber with a stash of drugs,' I told them, when they begged me for details about which was the cutest fluffy animal I'd ever cured of cancer. Norman was under a similar illusion about my veterinary knowledge; he'd been going on about the stuffed-animal collection again, and had insisted that I take a look at it this afternoon. Frankly, I had other things on my mind.

'We had a hamster called Mohammed,' Rose was telling me.

Uh-o, I thought.

'He used to run about loose in our bedroom,' sighed Rose.

And together: 'He was so sweet!'

'He'd sit on your shoulder, and stuff his cute little cheeks with sunflower seeds,' remembered Rose.

'They'd be so bulging that sometimes he got overloaded and keeled over like a little wheelbarrow,' added Blanche.

'Then Dad trod on him by accident,' said Rose.

There was a brief pause as they exchanged a glance, recalling their shared mini-moment of tragedy.

'But we're going to get another one,' offered Blanche. 'A female, because we want babies.'

Disaster ahoy!

'But we'll need a male, too,' suggested Rose.

'You'd better watch out or you'll create a plague of them. One day soon there'll be more hamsters in the world than humans.'

Their faces went suddenly serious.

'It might just be a blip, like they say,' I said, to break the sudden silence that had fallen. The subject of extinction was quickly turning from an obsession into a taboo. I'd heard a stammering psychologist on the radio saying that since the b-b-b-b-bomb, we were going through a d-d-d-d-denial phase. 'You never know,' I added weakly.

The signs were indicating the opposite, though, and we all knew it. Funnily enough, the less people suddenly talked about it, the more it began to hit home that we might actually die out.

'It's because we're badly designed,' said Rose ruefully.

'Especially us,' offered Blanche, exchanging a secret look with her sister. For some reason, they both glanced down at their shoes. They were wearing oddly shaped trainers that looked familiar, though I couldn't place them.

'Two friends of ours have tried committing suicide over it,' offered Rose.

'And everyone's having sex like crazy,' mused Blanche, giving me a sly look.

'Is that an offer?' I asked, flashing them a smile.

'Might be,' they said together.

Which I took as a yes.

During the course of the meal, despite my promise to myself to avoid fluffy-animal fans, I found myself charmed by the twins' unity as sisters, their team-spiritedness, the way they took it in turns to speak, the way they held my attention like something in a pair of pincers. I noticed, too, their habit of biting their rather narrow lower lip and letting their round, quite deep-set eyes go slightly out of focus. I observed their innocence, their gaucheness, their fun-loving turn of mind, which I guessed – rightly, as it turned out – was the outward manifestation of a fun-loving turn of body. The smell of their flesh, which I now began to detect beneath the protective layers of cheap perfume, was unusual, almost feral, and marvellously tantalising. I had to admit that by the time we'd finished the meal, I was completely under their extraordinary spell.

I have had cause to ask myself since then, in my more

philosophical moods: Was it because I was two men, Bobby Sullivan and Buck de Savile, that I was so inevitably drawn to two women? What if it had only been one girl? Would I have felt the same way about her?

Does one feel differently about broken scissors? Were lives revolutionised by the first photocopiers?

Buy the sausage and onion lattice pie, get the coleslaw free.

'Delicious, Abbie,' I told their mum, when I finally pushed away my plate. 'Mouth-watering, unusual, and satisfying. And very attractively presented.' I winked at the girls. I was talking about the food, but I meant them, and they knew it. 'I'm sure you noticed that I took double helpings of everything,' I added.

They giggled.

'And now,' said Norman firmly, steering me indoors, 'you're coming with me. I'm luring you up to the loft for an hour to inspect Abbie's stuffed menagerie. There are some beasts up there that are sorely in need of a professional assessment, mate,' he informed me, as I followed him upstairs, resigned to my fate.

As it turned out, the Victorian stuffed-animal collection in the attic turned out to contain some interesting stuff, including a corgi named Suet – obviously someone's pet, because taxidermically speaking it wasn't a great specimen – a few birds, all rather greasy but worth a bit if you sold them in the right place, i.e. some kind of fayre – and a weird primate, strangely humanoid and dressed in red velvet pantaloons. The brass plate underneath was labelled 'The Gentleman Monkey'. If that was its species name, it was a new one on me, I thought – but then it's all too easy to forget that there are more than two hundred and fifty species of primate, other than us. I must admit, though, that I shuddered when I looked at it. It was the clothes that did it. I couldn't help remembering Giselle, in her little pink frock and her nappy, and Mrs Mann, and her threat to –

'Abbie says they're worthless,' Norman was telling me. 'She

called the Antiques Hotline, and now she wants me to bin the lot.' He patted a stuffed wombat on the head absent-mindedly. It was wearing a frock-coat. 'That's the danger of your loft refurbishment. Bugger of a house, if you'll pardon my franglais. Jellyfish in the larder, salt all over the flag-stones, and there's sweet FA you can do, cos of the blinking listed building malarkey. Thank God for charity shops, say I. A bit of recycling doesn't go amiss, eh, Buck? Or maybe we could flog 'em at a car-boot sale. There's a big Firework Night do at the community centre looming on the horizon; we could do with some funds for a few bits and bobs.'

I was staring at the primate. No; it was nothing like Giselle. There were similarities with the macaque family – the shortness of the tail, the humanoid expression of the face – but it didn't fit into any of the categories I'd seen. And Christ knows, back in Tooting Bec I'd seen quite a few. I'm not a specialist by any means, but I knew enough to recognise that this was an unusual specimen. It had ape-like characteristics, a strangely human-looking head, and was stuffed in an upright posture – a posture which the angle of its pelvic girdle indicated wasn't a mere whim of the taxidermist, but the creature's natural stance. I was immediately fascinated. It appeared to be more of an ape than a monkey, but there was a tail sticking out of its pantaloons like a question mark. It didn't make sense. And its glass eyes were blue; an unlikely colour, and also over-large, I reckoned, for any of the primates.

'Keep it,' I told Norman. 'I've got a hunch that it's rare.'

'Can't,' he replied. 'Boss's orders. Everything's got to go.'

'I'll take it back to my place, then,' I told him. I'd taken a liking to the thing. There was something familiar about its features that I couldn't place.

'Abbie says it looks like her grandmother,' said Norman, reading my thoughts. 'Gives her the creeps.' I peered at the creature again. Now that he said it, you could even see something of Abbie in it, when you looked. The odd pelvis, and the deep-set eyes. I laughed.

'Not flattering,' I said. 'Best get her Gentleman friend out of the house, then, mate.'

Norman helped me load the monkey on to the passenger seat of the Nuance, and I took him home. I tried him in various rooms, then finally opted for the bathroom. I hung a towel off him. His arm was crooked in just the right position.

It was almost as though he had actually been stuffed with that in mind.

CHAPTER 17

A COMING OF AGE

Higgins feeds me throu the bars.

Let me out, I wispas. I wil do anything.

Cant he sez. Wer on the SEA. Nower to go. NOWER. Exept DIE in the wavs.

Then I wil throw myself out and DIE, I sez. I dont care.

(Here another stain obliterates a few lines of the text.)

– stil in darkness. The giraf cums on in TANGEER. And the turtels and the wulvs and the smaller creechers. Higgins feeds them. They grunt and they howl. Thats wy its DARK, to mak them sleep mor. Lordnum for all of us.

Im sleepin all the tyme. Sleepin away my lyfe. DREEM sumtymes that sumwun wil cum and SAVE me.

But fat chance of THAT.

I did my best to forget what had happened at the Travelling Fair of Danger and Delight, and I swore Tommy Boggs to secrecy. But the Contortionist began to haunt my dreams, and barely a night passed without some terrible visitation from her or the Man-Eating Wart-hog. In one dream, she was slitting open her belly to reveal writhing tadpoles. In another, Parson Phelps was nailed to the cross, and she and the Wart-hog were lapping up his blood. In another, she was an Angel again, but when she spread her wings, they were no more than dusty, battered old cobwebs.

It was perhaps in an effort to banish such dreams from my thoughts that I ventured to take part in the Thistle-Pulling

Contest for the first time. Perhaps I hoped that the experience would purge me. Or make me a man. After all, my fifteenth birthday having passed, I was now eligible for manhood – defined by Thunder Spit as showing the ability to skewer oneself alive on thistles without complaint.

'Now you're to start on a count of three!' yells Farmer Harcourt. 'You're to grab 'em with your right hand, and pull 'em by the root, and may the best man win!'

The villagers cheer. Down by the gushing Flid, beneath the scraggy junipers, a little Boggs boy, Tommy's youngest brother, takes a straw and blows a live frog into a balloon until it pops. The Thistle-Pulling Contest might easily be defined as a pagan ritual, but Parson Phelps has nevertheless always given it his blessing, for it tallies well with his 'Marble Friday' principles of self-denial and sought-after hardship. And as his sermon this morning reminded us, the thistle is part of the glorious function of Nature, designed by God to serve man in a myriad ways. 'Just as birdsong is God's way of making music for us, and the herring gull is there to serve us as a warning not to ill-treat our children, and sardines are there to remind us of the loaves and fishes, and the horse He provided for us to ride as transport, and the sheep for wool, so the thistle' – here he gave one of his famous four-second pauses – 'the thistle is there to remind us that there is pain in His glory as well as delight.'

Thunder Spit has been holding Thistle Day, in the same scrubby field by the Flid, 'since the beginning of time', according to Mr Clegg, who was eighty-three. His own great-grandfather was a champion, in the days when, according to nostalgic memory, the thorns were the size of bodkins, and the plants themselves grew to five feet.

Everybody is here; old Mr Clegg and his entire family – four generations, all with the same rolling seaman's walk, the squint-eyed Lumpeys, Mrs Sequin with her hat made of felt and papier mâché, the silent Peat-Hoves, the literal-minded Balls, the crabby Bark twins, the stubborn Tobashes, and the exaggerating Morpitons, with their dancing eyes.

And I, the freak, the foundling, the cuckoo, whose sphincter is being cruelly tortured by Mildred at the very thought of grasping these brutal weeds that jut like threatening weapons before me. A pang of envy overcomes me as I spot Tommy on the far side of the field, rubbing his hands together as if they were a pair of tools.

'One, two, three, GO!' yells Farmer Harcourt, and the agony begins.

'Get on with it, Tobias!' yells Parson Phelps from the hawthorn hedge. 'You owe it to your Saviour!' As usual, it isn't quite clear whether he is referring to himself or to the Lord. Dutifully, I flail about, praying that the world's first thornless thistle will suddenly appear before me. Beside me, young Charlie Peat-Hove, bloodstained and tearful, has already pulled his first thistle. Parson Phelps' voice is thundering at me now.

'Shut your eyes, son, and God will be with you! He will preserve you from all pain if you only have faith!'

I shut my eyes, and think of the Lord, who resembles the portrait in my Noah's Ark picture; a gentle-faced, Roman-nosed gent with a long white beard and a toga-like cassock flowing down. A man in the clouds. And close my fist around the thistle's stalk.

'OUCH!' It was like being stapled through with steel bolts.

'Go on!' shouts Parson Phelps again. 'Have courage! Think of Christ and His crown of thorns!'

'AAAGH!' I wail, and pull another one. Is it faith in the Lord, or the desire to please my father, that triumphs at this point? Either way, the thistle pulled, and my hand gushing bright blood, I can stand it no more, and withdraw from the game. Parson Phelps arrives and mops busily at my bleeding hand, applying camomile nipple-cream in silence. The words milksop, sissy and coward are not uttered, but they hang in the air between us as we witness Thunder Spit's bravest toiling amid the whirling thistledown to prove their manhood.

'Perhaps next year, I will be a man?' I offer. But my father sighs; I have let him down.

Within half an hour, Farmer Harcourt's thistle field was plucked clean as a chicken. The contest was won by Tommy, who had by now started as an apprentice to his father in the forge, and who had calluses on his hands as tough as bull-hide. He had become a hero; that night, the mountain of dead thistles was dragged down to the beach and set alight to cook the feast of clams and lobsters and sardines; as the great bonfire took light, illuminating the grey sand and grey bleached rock with an orange glow, I prayed that next year I, too, would pass the test of manhood.

That night I dreamed of her again – more vividly than ever. She was standing on top of a burning pyre of dead thistles, her face calm. Out of the smoke, she rose like a phoenix or an Angel. Her great wings flapped as she flew off into the night.

Despite my failure to become a man at the Thistle-Pulling Contest, I think of that time as my coming of age. It was also more, and worse. It was a fall from grace. I have always thought that it's in the nature of childhood to misunderstand. To witness adult behaviour and, because there is no reference in the child-world, to invent a story around that thing which turns out to be a completely garbled and inaccurate concoction. But I was no longer a child. I was a fifteen-year-old who stared, and wondered, and made assumptions, and who signally failed to do the one thing he should have done, which would have possibly saved him so much grief. I did not insist on knowing.

In short, I was a coward. And I was a coward because I feared the truth. And this, as you will see, dear reader, has been my story. A fear, a lack of courage, because of a further fear, that the thing itself, the truth, will be so unacceptable that –

'That what?' she asked me, years later, as we stared into our favourite rockpool.

'That I will be rejected. And that you will not love me. That no one will.'

My dream was prophetic. It was a windy Friday after the Thistle Contest. Tommy Boggs and I were returning from the harbour, where we'd been helping with the lobster pots. It was my task to tie their claws together once we had heaved them from the pots, and then hurl them into the lobster bins to take to Judlow. I kept getting pinched. Tommy, being stronger, had the job of ripping the seaweed from the pots and flinging the pots into the boats. When we had finished, Mr Tobash handed me and Tommy each a bunch of sardines on a string, flipping and flashing in the sun. Clutching them like heavy jewellery, we headed home through the buffeting wind: I to the Parsonage, to cook the sardines for our tea, and Tommy to the forge, where his father was teaching him how to make fancy whorled doorknobs to sell in Judlow. St Nicholas's Church had just come into view, and it was as we were rounding the corner by the gnarled chestnut tree, where Tommy's path diverged from mine, that we saw Parson Phelps standing in the graveyard with a stranger.

Tommy and I stopped in our tracks and stared. The smell of fresh fish. The lash of the wind.

You couldn't see her properly. She seemed to be a tiny woman – so small I thought at first that she was a child – wrapped in a hooded cloak that flapped wildly. They stood a foot or so apart from one another next to a thick tombstone, my father stooping slightly to catch her words, but clutching his hands behind his back in a nervous mannerism that I recognised. It was apparent immediately that they were engaged in an intense and heated discussion.

Tommy now gestured to me to creep towards the low hedge that separated us from the graveyard; we crouched against the briars, near a blackbird's nest with four blue eggs in it. Suddenly Tommy grabbed my shoulder and pulled me down.

'Shhhh!' he said. 'Listen!'

My father had begun shouting, and gesticulating furiously as he did so. As the words flew, I strained to catch them.

'Foulness'. 'Evil'. 'Slander'. 'Whore'. I recoiled. How could this unknown woman have so induced his wrath? 'Devil himself'. 'Dare you'. 'God's name'. Then he shook his fist in her face. Surely he could not be about to attack her? I flinched.

177

Then suddenly, perhaps recognising how close he had come to violence, he stopped. His arms hung loose by his sides, and his shoulders slumped in a dismal triangle.

'Look!' said Tommy. 'She's reaching in her cloak!'

I squinted. 'She's giving him something.'

'What is it?' asked Tommy, peering, too.

'Looks like a bottle. Or a jar of some sort.'

Whatever it was, it appeared to be heavy and unwieldy, and after lifting it to his face for inspection, she stood it on the tombstone. As he stared at it, his upper body still in the same sad posture of defeat, the woman reached in the folds of her cloak again, brought out a white rectangle of paper, and thrust it in his hand.

'An envelope,' breathed Tommy. 'She's giving him a letter.'

Without taking his eyes from the jar, my father took the envelope and shoved it deep into the pocket of his frock-coat.

We could see even from this distance that his face was unnaturally pale.

Then he said something to her, and lifted the jar from the tombstone. Holding it in outstretched hands, as though it might explode, he turned, and walked stiffly into the church. The woman stayed outside. She had her back to us now, a huddled figure amid the gravestones. She didn't move, but just stood there as the daffodils bounced wildly about her feet. After a few minutes, my father emerged from the church. He no longer had the jar. He walked like a frail ghost. Mechanically, he pulled something from his waistcoat.

'Money!' exclaimed Tommy. 'He's counting out notes, look!' And so he was. On and on, until a whole wad of money – where did this come from? From his own savings? From the church's funds? – had passed from his left hand to his right. He said something to the woman, who held out her hand, and he gave her the wad.

Then, suddenly, my father had sparked back into life and was shouting once more. 'Ever again', I heard. 'Wrath of the Almighty'. Then, 'Forbid you, ever'. The other words were indistinct but their despair and rage carried over to us, and we were afraid. Even Tommy looked suddenly smaller and quite white. The blackbird came back and hopped around her nest. Taking my eyes off my father, I stared at the perfect symmetry of her four blue eggs, and my tapeworm Mildred writhed within me. I do not know how long I stared at these eggs; a minute or an hour. When I lifted my eyes again, my father had turned on his heel, and was disappearing into the church. The woman was stuffing the wad of money into the folds of her cloak. Then turning suddenly, she was walking down the path towards the church gate.

It was then that Tommy and I saw her face and gasped.

I swear to this day, and Tommy swears, too, that it was the expression we recognised, rather than the face itself.

She swept past us and was gone.

We stayed there in silence for a while.

'I'll come and see you tomorrow,' said Tommy finally. 'I'm on my way to the forge, and Dad'll beat me if I'm late. You be all right?'

'I'll be all right,' I lied. I was half-crying by now. Somehow I managed to stagger home, and began to gut and fry the sardines. Father still didn't return, so I put the fish aside and made my way to the church, to find him on his knees, sobbing before the altar.

'Father –'

He swung round, his moon-face streaked with tears. 'Go home!' he shouted. 'Go home now, and lock yourself in your bedroom! Read from Genesis, and do not come down until I return and call you!'

'Father – who was that woman?'

'You saw her?' he whispered. His face was waxy pale.

'I saw you argue with her.'

'And what else?' he mustered. The tears had suddenly dried, giving way to a hardness I had not seen before.

'Nothing else,' I lied. 'I was just passing. I went home. Then I sat and waited for you, because I had prepared four sardines

179

for our supper, God's own fish, but when you didn't come, I came looking for you. The sardines are burnt now, father. They are now far from triumphant.'

'The sardines be damned, Tobias!' Parson Phelps was suddenly quivering all over. 'Go home now and pray.'

I turned and left. I had no courage. My spine ached.

At home, I prayed more fervently than I had ever done. Life had changed shape. My hands shook. I opened my Bible at the Book of Genesis.

'*The earth was without form, and void, and darkness was on the face of the deep,*' I read. '*And God said let there be a firmament in the midst of the waters.*' Yes. That is how it had been, in the Beginning. I could picture it happening quite clearly. Who could not, when they read these words? My eyes swam down the page. '*And the earth brought forth grass, herb yielding seed after its kind, and tree bearing fruit, wherein is the seed thereof, after its kind.*' I looked at the gourds I had collected from the plant that grew on my mother's grave. I kept them in my bedroom, in a wooden bowl. This year the fruits had not been green and stippled, as my mother's original gourd had been, nor yellow and frilled, as last year's had appeared; they were orange and warty, with little black flecks. I shivered.

'*And God created the great sea-monsters, and every living creature that moveth, which the waters brought forth abundantly, after their kinds, and every winged fowl after its kind: and God saw that it was good . . . And the Lord formed man of the dust of the ground and breathed into his nostrils the breath of life; and man became a living soul . . . And the Lord God caused a deep sleep to fall upon the man, and he slept; and He took one of his ribs, and closed up the flesh instead thereof; and the rib, which the Lord God had taken from the man, made He a woman, and brought her unto the man . . .*'

Bone of my bones, and flesh of my flesh.

For hours, I listened for the return of my father, and then, after the front door had slammed, to his mutterings and wailings emanating from downstairs. And then, for the first time in my life, I heard my father curse – 'Buggeration and double damnation!' – and then weep. Finally, I fell asleep.

In the morning, slumped in Parson Phelps' chair, was a man I did not recognise. His hair had turned completely white. His skin had washed to the grey of a weak autumn sky. For a dreadful, lurching moment I thought he was dead.

He seemed to sense me in the room, then, because he opened his eyes. When he saw me standing there, he groaned and covered his face with his hands.

'Father?'

Slowly, he lowered his hands and looked at me with an expression of hatred, pity and horror.

'Yesterday,' said the Parson, his voice struggling, 'I met a witch.'

'A real witch, Father?' I whispered.

'As real as you or I.' He gazed at me for a minute, then averted his eyes from my face.

I felt myself flush. Yes; I had recognised her. From my dreams, and my vision during the Great Flood, and from the Tent of Miracles. And Tommy had, too.

She was the Contortionist.

When a leaf dies, its colour changes so gradually from green to brown, its skin shrivels so imperceptibly, and yet with such purpose, that its final dropping from the tree is more a blessing then a sadness. But to observe this process speeded up, and not in a leaf but in a human – ah. There is a pitiful sight, and one I now witnessed day by day as my Father lost his faith. His voice was increasingly bereft of conviction when he said his prayers, and those passages of the Bible which had once been of the most comfort to him now seemed to be the source of some bitter irony. Every day was now Marble Friday, and I winced as I watched him stuffing the glass balls in his shoes with such a look of grim determination as to make you weep. One morning I even spotted him put itching-powder made from rosehip seeds down his own shirt. In his madness he refused to speak of the Contortionist, and every time I opened my mouth to ask a question he would put up his hand to stop me, with an expression on his face so tragic that I had not the heart to pursue my enquiries.

Not the heart, nor the courage, either. For where might my questions lead?

As Parson Phelps turned his broad back on God, his congregation, once solidly packed into St Nicholas's Church, began to thin out. As the weeks went by, his sermons became more and more haunted and rambling.

He talked of the sin of cities, and of corruption so thick you could scrape it off the walls. He said the Bible was a lie.

'Throw each of you your own so-called holy book into the deep, and see its pages disintegrate and fall away,' he hurled at what remained of his congregation one Sunday, namely Mrs Harcourt, Mrs Sequin, Dr Baldicoot, Mr Tobash and myself. 'And if there is a God, let Him work a holy miracle to save His word.'

'The Contortionist has done something to your father,' Tommy said, when I reported this to him. 'She's poisoned him. I reckon she's made him give her all his money, and then drink what was in that jar, and it's a witch's brew that's sent him mad.'

Tommy and I stared at each other.

'It's not our fault,' said Tommy, but his voice was shaking.

That night I dreamed of her again. This time she was slitting her own belly with a knife, and tadpoles were slithering out, surrounded by horrible clots of frogspawn. I touched my own skin, and screamed. I, too, was jelly.

'Something came to me in my sleep,' my father announced to me the next morning. I shuddered; had she crept into his dreams, too? But no. 'When you are seventeen you will go to Hunchburgh,' he announced, 'and become a servant of the Lord.'

God – or what was left of Him – had spoken.

And that was that.

Trapp sez we hav past Cape Horn.

Wer is Cape Horn, I sez. I do not no the shape of the Globe, and all its Places. I have no LERNIN.

He dus not tell me, so I do not discuver wer Cape Horn is. I hav been SEESICKE all nite and all day.

The Queen wants Trapp to bring bak animals for her stuffd colecshun, Rogers sez. I nows this much by now. The Animal Kingdom, its calld. He gets the animals from other zoos, African zoos, Indian zoos, zoos everywer. The hole of Empyre. Brings them bak alive, to London, that's the PLAN. There a man calld SKRAPY will keep them in the ZOO, kill them wun by wun and stuff them. Sooveneer for her Majisty. But they must be kept wel. Nice fur, nice fevvers, no bad spessymens. She wonts kwality.

I am giving you a job, soon, Trapp sez wun Day. A very important job. Wen we get to Moroco.

Wots that I sez. I am SLEEPIN all the Tyme in my cage,. It is the onlie way not to run MADDE. Ther is a DWORF GIRAF arrived next to me, maks fartin noisis in the NITE. Ther is a walrus and an antylope and a big Beaver. Al of them so RARE, says Rogers, that they is practicly the LAST IN THE WURLD.

I dont think I wonts a job, but I sez to TRAPP, wot job? from my CAGE.

Lookin after a certin GENTLEMAN, Trapp sez. You wil LIKE HIM. He is verie Hansum, verie HUMAN.

And he larfs and larfs.

CHAPTER 18

ADIEU

Last night Violet had found herself on a beach of grey rocks and grey quicksand. She was walking and sinking at the same time. The more she tried to struggle, the quicker and more greedily the quicksand gulped her down. Then it changed to soup; a thick, greenish primordial soup, writhing and lukewarm; she slapped into creatures with dark, flapping wings, horned elbows, jutting teeth, razor-edged beaks, gruesome tusks, metallic scales, prehensile talons of rusted iron. Metal-riveted sea-monsters and fowl of the air whirled in the viscous firmament, brandishing curved claws, cruet sets, flippers and dinner forks. They pinioned her to a waterlogged commode, where they bit, and pecked, and clawed, seasoning her with cloves and cayenne pepper, and ripping out the guts from her abdomen like visceral spaghetti. And she watched, helpless, pinned to her useless piece of furniture, as a stream of jeering animals paraded before her, yelping and baying and yowling for her blood. An eye for an eye! A tooth for a tooth! A rump for a rump!

And then she awoke, screaming, in a soggy pool of her own menstrual blood.

She shudders now at the recollection of her dream, and shivers in the cold breeze. All that pain! And now more!

'So not *au revoir*, Miss Scrapie,' says Cabillaud finally, when Violet has finished recounting her carnivore's nightmare.

'No, not *au revoir*.' Both of them, involuntarily, shiver, as the word hangs, unspoken, in the October air outside 14 Madagascar Street.

Then falls.

'*Adieu.*'

The yellow-painted cart is almost fully loaded. As Violet watches the frozen kangaroo carcass being slowly winched aloft and placed precariously on the top of the meat pile, she inhales deeply to smother a sob. In all, some forty-odd skinned creatures from Trapp's *Ark* are to accompany the Belgian chef as he leaves 14 Madagascar Street for the last time. Violet will not be sorry to see them go, but the departure of Monsieur Cabillaud is another matter. More personal. Less clear-cut. Messier. Sadder.

'All ready, zen, to go.' The Belgian bows stiffly, and takes Violet's hand, whereon he plants a chilly kiss. Their eyes slide away from each other. Cabillaud vaults atop his stack of frozen carcasses, making a niche for himself within the natural *chaise-longue* created by a half-zebra, its exposed rib-cage glistening with ice. Around them, pale and twinkling, stand the frozen statues of hippo, mongoose and chameleon, wombat and jackal, hammer-headed shark and tiger. Violet Scrapie's uncooked-pastry skin pales further, and she feels a lump forming in her throat. She gulps painfully. Her coming of age, she acknowledges, had been a bitter conflict. A clash of wills and minds, as experienced in families, that had evolved, inevitably, into a broader argument, such as lovers might have, provoking wider disagreements, as enacted by politicians and ideologues, and thence to a huge full-blown opposition of belief systems such as in war. The two sides solidly intractable. But one with a definite edge, formed by her higher social status and class, her position as the man's employer, and her sudden, newfound crisis of conscience. Everything has its price. And I am paying it now, Violet reflects as she watches Cabillaud now, settling himself into his icy seat. The price of principle. And the price of pride.

Violet has heard a rumour, via the next-door scullery maid, his one-time mistress (she of the stuck-pig episode), that Cabillaud's monstrous ambition has secured him a prestigious post in the Palace kitchens. As Cabillaud's cart, pulled by two shire horses, creaks off down the road, Violet is aware of the lump in her throat expanding, as though a walnut is growing within it at great speed, against her better judgement. She swallows with difficulty, but the walnut will not budge. If Cabillaud sheds tears, it is in secret, and they freeze on his face as the yellow-painted cart trundles towards Buckingham Palace with its ghoulish load.

The meeting of the Vegetarian Society in that dusty hall in Oxford Street, and in particular the words of Mr Henry Salt, following hard on the heels of her mother's poisoning, have continued to prey on the distraught conscience of Violet Scrapie – day and night, with a cruelty and relentlessness that beggars belief. Witness her soup dream. Cabillaud's departure, Violet realises, watching as he turns to a speck that vanishes around the corner of Madagascar Street, has done little to alleviate the unspeakable burden of her guilt.

The dream comes back to her again, and she shudders. Then turns, waddles back inside the house, and slams the door in her wake.

A moment later she is seated at her kitchen table, her big shoulders heaving, the tears running freely. Feeling more alone than she has ever felt in her entire life.

Alone? Wait! For is that not the corgi Suet, snoring beneath the table? And is a certain ghostly presence also discernible? Over there, by the door to the larder? Could it possibly be, gentle reader, that the cloud of flickering ectoplasm that is forming on the fourth shelf of the dresser is the Laudanum Empress herself, metamorphosed into phantom form?

'Still wallowing in self-pity, then, Vile?' murmurs a familiar voice.

Violet sits up rigid in her chair and listens intently. Suet stops snoring, pricks up his ears and begins to whimper.

'Mother?' ventures Violet through her tears. 'Is that you?'

'Gone, but still with us!' whispers the petticoated Empress, quoting the epitaph from her own gravestone.

'Mother?' falters Violet. She was so sure that she heard something!

'You wouldn't believe what I can see from here!' the Lauda-num Empress is saying. 'A huge grocery store, Vile. Motorised vehicles driving into its great maw, and emerging with improb-able merchandise, wrapped in a substance known as cellophane. A National Lottery. Shoes with wheels, like ice skates. The young ruling the world!'

'Pardon, Mother?' whispers Violet. She can make out indi-vidual words, but they do not seem to cohere. Vehicles? Cello-phane? Wheeled shoes? She must be having another nightmare. Violet's meaty shoulders slump once more.

'Vile! I'm talking to you!'

But Violet is oblivious. It is all a ghastly dream, induced by guilt! The Empress sighs with frustration. What can one do to nudge her out of this decline? 'And did I ever tell you about the workings of a high-speed food-warmer called the microwave oven?' she offers.

But wild horses cannot drag Violet Scrapie from the misery that is rightly hers. At least, not yet. In her lifetime, Violet Scrapie calculates, she has not only killed her own mother, but cooked and eaten four thousand chickens, twenty cows, nine hundred sheep, a thousand fish, and three thousand sea crustacea. And what of the incalculable? All those creatures from the Zoo and from Trapp's *Ark*, all those jettisoned carcasses from her father's workshop – how do you begin to assess quantities as vast as those? Mammals, fish, reptiles, birds, insects – where, oh where, can one even begin? All that meat. All that blood. All that murder. And for what?

FOR WHAT?

Violet shudders again, and blows her nose loudly into a large lace handkerchief.

'I will atone for all those lives!' Violet snuffles, her eyes red with weeping. 'I will atone for them, in the only way I know how!'

'Ow-ow-ow!' echoes Suet from beneath the table.

'Pure melodrama,' snorts the Laudanum Empress, and floats off.

CHAPTER 19

2005: THE MATING
RITUAL

The Thistle Festival was the second-biggest community event in
the Thunder Spit calendar, after the Guy Fawkes Heritage Party
in November, Norman told me. And when I arrived there that
Saturday afternoon I realised he wasn't bullshitting. '*Le tout*
Thunder Spit,' as Norman called the clientele of the Stoned
Crow, was represented. Scattered about the famous Thistle
Field I spotted all the blokes from the pub, Jimmy Clegg,
Ron Harcourt, Jack and Ken Morpiton, Charlie Peat-Hove,
Billy Tobash, and a whole gaggle of wives, kids, mobile phones,
dogs and mountain bikes. The Festival was jointly sponsored
by the Baldicoot Medical Centre and the *Hunchburgh Echo*,
and sure enough, the local nobs were there, too: I spotted
Sir Terence Baldicoot mingling among the *hoi polloi* – I'd put
his daughter's Indonesian iguana out of its misery – and the
MP Bruce Yarble. He'd called me out to Judlow once to
bandage his racehorse, and now here he was in a tweed
cap, strutting about giving the *Who's Who* types little salutes
of recognition. Mrs Sequin and Abbie Ball had hired a marquee
for pizzas and chicken nuggets, and Mrs Firth had organised
a crèche and video room for the kiddies. I wandered through
the gathering crowds. Someone had lit a wall of joss-sticks
to counter the reek of dead fish from the River Flid, and
their incense wafted across the field, mingling with the odours
of popcorn, crushed grass and car-grease, giving the whole
event a real buzz of community. I get sentimental about things
like that.

'Not bad, eh,' agreed Ron Harcourt, when I commented on the size of the thistles. 'Thank God for phosphates.'

'Ron managed to wangle two grants for this field, didn't you, you cunning bastard,' said Billy Clegg, appearing beside me and thrusting a can of Guatemalan lager at me. 'A Euro grant not to plant genetic aubergines on it, and a Nature Council one, to stop the thistles becoming endangered weeds.'

'Nice work if you can get it,' said Norman, emerging from the Portaloo behind us.

'Bugger off,' said Ron Harcourt, and fired his stun-gun for the start of the game.

'Hey!' yelled Norman, wrestling with his machine. 'Wait for me, guys!'

Within seconds, the air was filled with the roar of a hundred strimmers. The men charged up and down the field with their excitable appliances – state-of-the-art, in Norman's case – thistledown flying all over the place, little thistle-thorns whizzing through the air at hectic speed. The women, standing in rows by the thorn hedge, jeered and whooped and blew the men kisses, swigging Buck's Fizz out of plastic cups.

Then I spotted the twins.

They were jumping up and down by the electricity generator. 'Get a move on, Dad!' they were yelling. You couldn't call them beautiful, I thought, in any classical sense. Their eyes were too close together, and they had Abbie's slightly bony, tilted pelvis – but nevertheless there was something about the two of them that drove Sigmund wild. I wasn't the only bloke looking in their direction. They must give off some undetectable animal scent, I thought. A sort of musk. Watching them, my resolve kept stiffening. Then they looked up and saw me, too, and smiled invitingly. Hey, Buck, I thought. Now's your moment, mate. I was just wandering nonchalantly over in their direction when Mrs Clegg tapped me on the shoulder.

'About my foal,' she said. Talk about bad timing, missis, I thought.

When I'd countered all her accusations, her son crashed into me with three pints of beer and in the imbroglio I lost sight of Rose and Blanche. Then a huge cheer went up: the last thistle had been mown down.

'And the judges have decided,' farted a megaphoned voice across the field, 'that the winner of the year's strimmer event, and therefore this year's Thistle Champion, is Mr Tom Boggs!'

There was another huge cheer, and some honking of car-horns. Tom Boggs stood on the podium and waved, then burst open a bottle of champagne, slewing everyone near him with froth. I recognised him; he was the young bloke who ran the Texaco garage. The field was suddenly swarming with people carrying candy-floss and talking into their mobiles. After wandering about trying to catch sight of the girls again, I finally gave up and retreated to the beer tent.

'It's a cheap way of getting my field mown,' Harcourt confided. He'd been getting quietly sozzled all afternoon. 'My dad did the same thing. And his dad before him. That's tradition for you.'

'That Tom Boggs' great-great grandfather was a champion, too,' mused Billy Tobash. 'Back in the old days. It runs in his family.'

Ken Peat-Hove said nothing, as usual, but spat on the floor. It could've meant anything. On the way back, I had to stop off at Ned Morpiton's farm, to see to some poisoned Lord Chief Justices, and give his new BSE-free moo-cows the once-over; by the time I drove up the high street, and turned into Crawpy Street, it was evening. I kept thinking about Rose and Blanche Ball. The look they'd given me.

Then I caught my breath. Christ! There they were, just standing there! In the street. The two of them, at the bus stop, right opposite my front door!

Hey! *Yes!*

It was a chilly evening, for spring; they were standing in the bus shelter smoking, and kicking at old blobs of dried-up chewing-gum with their elasticated trainers. Like they were waiting for a bus, but for me, too. Whichever came first.

190

I drove up slowly.

'Like a kerb-crawler,' they said to me later.

'Where are you going?' asked Rose, as my window wound down.

'Wherever you're going,' I told them. I gave them my sexy grin.

'What are we waiting for then?' asked Blanche. 'Let's go to a club.'

They were dressed in black, with fake jewels twinkling, and wearing the bold red lipstick, dramatic eye-shadow and vicious nail-extensions that I soon learned were their night-wear hall-mark. They were temptation incarnate. I opened the doors of the Nuance for them, and gave them one of my Elvis looks, which they missed because they were too busy settling themselves on the back seat, where they sank fragrantly into the soft leather. I say fragrantly, but actually they'd overdone the perfume a bit and once we were on the road I had to keep the window open to prevent myself from asphyxiating. Like good girls, they'd stubbed out their fags first.

'We saw you at the Thistle Festival,' said Rose.

'In the old days, it was like an initiation ceremony,' said Blanche.

'To prove you were a man,' said Rose.

'You want proof, girls,' I said, glancing at them in the mirror, 'I'll give you proof.'

I thought that was quite a witty thing to say.

On the journey to Hunchburgh we talked about their geneal-ogy module, and their mum's loopy idea about some television producer called Oscar or Jack arriving on her doorstep. Then they wanted me to explain how birds digest hard seeds, and why there were so many pet monkeys and apes in the cities, but hardly any in the country.

'It's a fashion thing, I reckon,' I told them. 'I used to get loads of them in my surgery back in Tooting Bec.'

'You had a surgery in Tooting Bec? In London?'

'Yup.'

'Why did you leave?'

Bugger, I thought, remembering Giselle the macaque and Mrs Mann.

'Well?'

'Because I had a sixth sense that, if I came to Thunder Spit, I might meet the two most desirable girls in the whole country.'

They liked that, and giggled.

'And you know something?' I said. 'My sixth sense wasn't wrong.'

They were good dancers. They were exhibitionists. There are plenty of starers in Hunchburgh. Male and female: people who prefer to watch, and comment. As they whirled about under the big glitter-ball, and waggled their peachy arses, I felt special. Special, that everyone was staring, the blokes with admiration and lust, the girls with criticism and envy. The twins were dancing for me, and I felt like a million Euros.

Later, I said, 'Come to my place.'

'Both of us?' suggested Rose, running her red nails up my right thigh.

'Together?' whispered Blanche, nibbling at the lobe of my left ear.

'Both of you,' I said. 'Together.'

Because as well as feeling a million Euros, I felt twelve metres tall and three metres wide.

And Sigmund felt thirty-five centimetres long.

CHAPTER 20

FAREWELL!

I felt small and alone. It was October on our herring-shaped peninsula, and the freezing air crackled with salt. Under a thin sun, slate roofs shone bright with hoar-frost, and the silhouettes of trees stood bare and stark against the churning seascape. Never had Thunder Spit looked colder, or bleaker, and in my heart, a part of me was glad to leave.

'God has cursed you!' Parson Phelps called after me as the silent Mr Peat-Hove flicked his whip and my horse and cart trundled off along the slippery shingle path. 'You can never atone! Begone! Abandon yourself to that cursed metropolis, where the corruption is so thick that you can scrape it off the walls!'

My father appeared to have forgotten that it was his own idea – and God's – that I should go to Hunchburgh in the first place. There was no pleasing him, I thought dismally, as my father's ranting died in the distance. I pulled my wool hat down over my ears, and shivered. In my hand, I clasped the linen bag that contained my most treasured possessions: my Bible, Herman's *Crustacea* and Hanker's *World History*, four dried gourds from my mother's grave, the whelk shell Tommy Boggs had given me as a leaving present, a fish-knife from his mother, and my mermaid's purse.

'Goodbye, dear Father,' I whispered under my breath, as the gnarled trees of the peninsula gave way to mainland shrubs.

My new life had begun.

*   *   *

What I knew of cities amounted to what my father had chosen to relay to me, namely, that they are dens of vice; that they are crawling with women of ill-repute who are receptacles for foulness, and bear infants unblessed by God; that there is neither neighbourly nor brotherly love; that there are beggars in the street with suppurating sores that can never be healed.

My train from Judlow arrived in Hunchburgh, and tipped me out on to thronged streets, where I saw at once what my father had failed to tell me: that there were more people in the world than I had ever imagined. It was market day, and the centre of the city was bustling; a million chattering voices filled the air; the cries of the stall-holders, the shrieking laughter of women, the plaintive whimpers of beggar children thrusting out grubby palms for halfpennies. I wandered through the market, past coffee-stalls and mountains of oysters, butchers' carts and fruit-stalls. The place was buzzing and teeming with humanity – and yet these folk represented just a tiny fraction of the human population of the world! I suddenly felt small and insignificant, and invisible, as I wandered the cobbled streets in search of the Seminary. Nobody stared at me in the way they did in Thunder Spit and Judlow, or laughed at my gait; they were too busy, I soon realised, just going about their business. I saw a man with a painted face, juggling apples, and spotted a young urchin, a pickpocket, jostling the crowd who watched. By the wall of a church, I also spied a huddle of women guzzling gin and showing their bloomers to whomsoever cared to look; heeding my father's warnings, I buttoned my frock-coat tighter and hastened my step, my head whirling with light and sound. O strange and bright and frightening new world! Yet my heart lifted in hope. For here, surely, I could begin life anew!

I found the Seminary near the heart of the city, a red-brick rectangle, curlicued at the corners, and ringed with threatening holly trees, their glinting leaf-spikes flashing in the autumn sun like knives. When I saw the grandeur of the building and its big black shiny doors, I understood why my father had once dreamed that I should come here. For who could attack God, when He was housed in such a formidable fortress? After the chaos of the market, I entered the building with relief, and made my way along echoing tiled corridors to the Abbot's office. I knocked hesitantly on his door.

'Come in,' called a loud, fruity voice. I entered. The room was lined with books and smelt of tobacco.

He was a big red-faced man, with a handshake that nearly lifted me from the ground.

'Welcome to the Seminary, Tobias,' he said. 'Your fame goes before you.'

I quailed. What had he heard? Had my father written to him, telling him I was cursed by the Devil? I would not have been surprised.

But my fame turned out to be of a more quotidian nature, and relayed to the Abbot by Mrs Tobash's cousin, a former Thunder Spitter who was now married to his own cousin's niece. 'They tell me,' said the Abbot, 'that you've been reading aloud in church in Thunder Spit since you were five years old, and can do tongue-twisters like the Devil himself!'

I breathed a sigh of relief, and smiled. 'It's true,' I said.

'Well?' he said, folding his arms.

'Miss Mosh mashes some mish-mash,' I ventured, and he applauded.

'Betty Botter bought some butter,' I went on. 'But, she said, this butter's bitter! If I put it in my batter, it'll make my batter bitter! So Betty Botter bought a bit of better butter and she put it in her batter and it made her batter better!'

'You'll go far,' pronounced the Abbot, slapping a meaty hand on his tattered Bible. 'Now, I've found just the landlady for you. Her name is Mrs Fooney and she is a fine woman, with a very large – er, a large heart,' he said, indicating the curve of a female bosom. I blushed. 'In the meantime, let me introduce you to your fellow students.'

The students were at luncheon, and the refectory echoed with the voices of five dozen noisy conversations. The Abbot led me to a table.

'This is Farthingale,' he said, indicating a weasel-faced youth who was shovelling boiled beans into his mouth with great speed. Farthingale looked up from his plate.

'And, Farthingale, this is Tobias Phelps,' said the Abbot. 'I want you to take him under your wing. He is the son of a parson who attended this very seminary many years ago. Also has a knack with tongue-twisters. Did Betty Botter for me in my office. Most impressive.'

Farthingale gave me what looked more like a smirk than a welcoming smile, and exchanged a glance with a fellow student sitting next to him. 'Pleased to make your acquaintance, Betty,' he said. 'Serve yourself to beans.' And he jerked his head in the direction of a metal pot.

'That's the stuff!' said the Abbot, and slapped Farthingale on the back with a hearty laugh. Then he turned to leave, clasping his Bible in his hand like a brick he was going to plant somewhere. 'Come to my office after lunch, Phelps,' he said. 'Farthingale will make the rest of the introductions.'

'Well, Betty,' said Farthingale, when the Abbot was out of sight. 'Impressed the Abbot already, have we? There's a good boy. Come and meet the new student, Popple,' he said to his neighbour, a podgy lad with crooked teeth. 'His name's Betty Botter.'

And so it was that Betty became my nickname – or rather one of them. My fellow seminarians had smelt meat. During the course of that meal, during which I made the acquaintances of Popple, Ganney, Hicks, McGrath and other seminarians, I was offered further appellations: Fartybockers, and Hobble-de-Hoy among them. I chewed on my beans, and said as little as possible. I had entered this building full of hope – but now, with a lurching feeling of recognition, I recalled my lonely days at school, when I was taunted by the other boys, or played alone in the playground.

'So what brings you here, Betty?' asked Ganney.

'The Church is my vocation,' I mumbled fearfully.

They all laughed like drains at that. By the end of the meal,

Farthingale, Popple, and Ganney had elected themselves my persecutors.

'They're just boisterous,' the Abbot said airily, drumming his big sausagey fingers on his Bible. I had returned to his office after luncheon, and recounted some of the conversation. 'I'm afraid that if you view the Church as your true vocation, you're an exception here,' he explained. I was taken aback by the somewhat breezy manner in which he announced this news. 'Most of the fellows here are either younger sons, failures in other professions, or otherwise here against their will. That's the truth of the matter.' Then he sat back, and made a thick, blunt steeple of his hands. I wondered whether the same applied to him.

'As a matter of fact it does,' he said, reading my thoughts. 'I'd like to have been a builder, but it would have been over everyone's dead body.' He stopped and chuckled. 'So here I am, constructing souls instead. And doing repairs.'

I hung my head, and tried to stifle my tears. 'Look, son, let me tell you something,' he said, when he saw my distress, taking my hand in his large benign paw. 'This is a dying profession. I fear the Church is headed for extinction. And Darwinism hasn't helped. All this stuff about being descended from monkeys and apes has turned people away. In a hundred years' time, this seminary will be gone, and your little church in Thunder Spit will be but an empty shell.'

I said nothing; I just sat there, miserable beyond words.

'But maybe you are different, Phelps,' he said kindly. 'If you have faith, then it's a good thing. Keep a hold of it. Just see Farthingale and his chums as a challenge God has given you,' he proposed. 'You must remember about turning the other cheek, son.'

'Yes, Abbot, I will.'

'And another thing.'

'Yes, sir?'

'I have the impression that you carry a burden, Phelps. Am

197

I correct? You don't walk straight, and you appear to stoop. Your shoes, if I may say so, look like a couple of pancakes.'

I explained to him about my deformities of the foot, and the fact that I had been a foundling, and that my spine had been mutilated when I was a mere babe.

He appeared sympathetic, in his rough and ready way, but had a warning for me.

'You have suffered Tobias, I grant you that. But the way out of this suffering, son, is to witness for yourself how others suffer more, and to help them. If you're serious about this as a vocation – God help you – you'll need to get stuck in. Understand?'

'Yes, sir.'

'So go out there, Tobias, and visit the slums, of which there are many. Go to Mickle Street, and Petersgate, and Upper Hayside, and bring succour and help and faith to the needy of the parish, and thereby forget your own troubles. That's my advice to you. Now go and settle in at Mrs Fooney's, and come to me if you have any problems.'

Although it was by no means what I had expected of my first encounter with my new vocation, I decided to put my worries to one side, and take up the Abbot's advice. If he gave me little solid comfort, at least I found it elsewhere. Mrs Fooney's lodging-house was next to the Seminary, and as soon as I crossed her threshold, I felt at home.

'Come in, young gentleman!' said Mrs Fooney. 'Welcome! Wipe your feet on the mat and let me make you a cup of tea!' Mrs Fooney was as big-breasted as the Abbot had indicated, and also as warm-hearted. Indeed, they are characteristics that have always gone together, in my limited experience of women. You cannot have the one without the other. Needless to say, Mrs Fooney reminded me very much of my own mother, and even offered me barley flip-cakes.

I also met her granddaughter, Tillie, a charming, ringleted, cheeky child of seven who immediately settled herself on my lap and took my hand in hers.

'You're very hairy,' she remarked, stroking my wrist. Suddenly she pulled her hand away. 'Ugh! He's got a flea!'

'Shush, Tillie!' Mrs Fooney rebuked her. 'We all have fleas, child. Even men of God!'

Between them, Mrs Fooney and Tillie lifted my spirits immeasurably. Tillie helped me to arrange my possessions on the mantelpiece in my room, and I let her hold my whelk shell while I read to her from the Bible.

So began my new life.

I am proud to say that I was good at my work; I already knew most of the Bible by heart, and the Abbot praised my diligence and the quality of my fledgling sermons. My first sermon, which concerned fossils, was a treatise condemning Darwinism – a subject close to my heart. He heralded it as a work of genius. I argued, just as Parson Phelps had taught me, that God had planted the fossils in the earth to muddle geologists into believing that the world was much older than it was, and tricked Darwin into developing a fantastical theory about man descending from monkeys and apes.

Towards the end of my sermon, I held up the fossil I had brought with me from home.

'This is God's joke,' I concluded. 'And a fine one it is, too!'

Needless to say, my presentation provoked much derision from my fellow students. However, I persisted with my studies, applying myself with fervour to my library books, thus earning myself another nickname; the Bookworm. In private moments of loneliness, the needs of my male object became ever fiercer, and I spent much time fighting my own bestial urges.

It was then that I thought of my father and his marbles: would that, perhaps, bring me some respite? I bought a bag of these glass balls from a pedlar, and put them in my shoes.

After half an hour, I realised that Parson Phelps must have been mad for longer than I'd thought.

I gave the marbles to Tillie, who thanked me most prettily.

Then she floored me with a strange query, which unsettled me for weeks.

'Mr Phelps, who made God?'

She had arranged her marbles on a plate, and was now stringing beads. The question hit me like a slap, for it was the very same one I had asked my father, when I was her age. I recalled the reply he had given me then.

I cleared my throat. 'God is self-made. Like a self-made man, but God.'

'What d'you mean, self-made?' asked Tillie, her eyes squinting in puzzlement. 'Nothing can *make itself*, Mr Phelps. That would be a very silly idea, I think!'

I considered this for a moment.

'It requires a leap of faith,' I told her finally. 'It requires believing in what you don't understand. It requires believing that everything is connected, like your beads are connected, but with an invisible string.' Tillie looked puzzled. 'A gourd plant sprouted on my mother's grave the year after she died,' I went on. 'And every year since, the gourds it sprouts have been of a different shape, colour and texture. Look,' I said, and took her to the mantelpiece, where I had arranged my dried gourds. 'This was the first one that grew.' I pointed to the green, stippled fruit, now somewhat shrunk from its original size. 'And the next year, this one came from its seed.' I pointed to the gourd with the orange frill and yellow blotches.

'And then this one?' asked Tillie, picking up last year's gourd, which was green and yellow, and striped.

'That's right,' I said. 'See? It looks nothing like it, but this is the next generation.' And then from the seed of the stripy one, came this one,' I said, handing her the gourd I had picked just before I left Thunder Spit. It was knobbled and almost mauve in colour. 'Can you explain that?' I asked.

'No,' said Tillie. 'But there must be a reason.'

'There is. But only God knows it. All we know,' I told her, the thought striking me as I said it, 'is that they are related to each other, as surely as an island is related to the shore. Look deep enough, and you will see that, below the level of the sea, the land is joined.'

I thought of Thunder Spit. I thought of the Flood, which had turned our herring-shaped peninsula into an island. And I thought of my father's words in the church, just before we fell into the water and I saw my vision of the Contortionist. He had quoted John Donne's poem to me, which I quoted to Tillie now.

'"No man is an island,"' I told her, '"entire of itself. But a piece of the continent, a part of the main!"'

The tears came into my eyes most unaccountably as I said these words, and Tillie put her little arm around my shoulders.

'Let's play marbles, Mr Phelps,' she offered gently.

And so we did.

When not occupied with my studies, I haunted the slums. I had taken the Abbot's advice about avoiding self-pity and bringing help to others, and within a few weeks of my arrival in Hunchburgh, I had thrown myself with conviction into my task as a saver of souls and a champion of the Bible. I found Parson Phelps' voice emerging from my larynx as I preached. I trod the bumpy streets with a stride that mimicked his, and grew increasingly confident in my manly gait, thanks, in part, to the well-fitting shoes Mr Hewitt had so skilfully cobbled for me. Slowly I learned to live without my father's words and presence; I recreated him inside me instead. I had no choice; he returned my letters unopened. Turning the other cheek, I continued to send them, in the hope that charity, if nothing else, would prevail.

The misery and poverty of the slums had at first made me gasp: whole families of up to twelve children shoved together in stinking rooms, without enough to eat, and dragon-sized rats constantly on the rampage. I saw many children die, or become orphans. I wondered, in my darker moments, what relief I could possibly bring into this despair, with nothing but my prayer-book and my humble bag of medicines. But lo and

201

behold, my deformities worked in my favour: one woman, Mrs Jeyes, said to me that clapping eyes on a sight as pitiful as me put her own troubles into perspective. I did not know whether to be hurt or grateful.

There was one particular hovel, on Mickle Street, that I visited more often than most, as its need was the greatest; indeed, no other slum dwelling that I knew seemed to match its squalor and decrepitude. I was often to be found there.

'Like a fly to dung,' commented Farthingale, my harshest critic, when he saw me one morning preparing my medicine bag and my Bible for my next visit to Mickle Street.

'He's got a whore down there,' speculated Ganney.

I turned the other cheek so many times with my fellow seminarians, I sometimes became dizzy with it. But I ignored their taunts, and continued my regular visits to Mickle Street, for here dwelled a family by the name of Cove, who seemed to be in permanent need of my attentions. The elder Mr Cove, a former seaman with a pitted face and beery breath, had recently developed an ulceration on his leg, and because he was unable to afford the doctor, I took it upon myself, as my Christian duty, to see to him as best I could. It was in this unlikely setting, and quite unexpectedly, that during one of my visits, I had an encounter with physical temptation that was to create both excitement and turmoil within me, in equal measure.

The object of my desire was a thing of great lewdness.

I didn't even know its name, at first.

'I stole it off a cargo ship,' confided the little Cove boy, a little lad of seven with an elfin face and knickerbockered legs as skinny as a sparrow's.

I had arrived to change the dressings on the ulcerous shin of Grandfather Cove to find the whole family staring and sniffing at a curious object on their table. It was yellow, and about eight inches long, and in circumference, about the same thickness as an engorged male object. As soon as I saw it, I blushed a fierce red, and I felt the base of my spine tingle at the site of my ancient mutilation.

'They was hanging in huge bunches,' whispered the boy, recounting what he had witnessed in the ship's hold, his voice reduced to an awed whisper. 'From hooks. Some bunches was yellow,' he said, his eyes flaring wide with excitement. 'But some was green!'

No one approached the table.

'I went to grab one,' said the boy. The Coves were all listening intently, although I was sure it was not the first time he had recounted his tale. 'But then I saw there was this giant hairy spider guarding them.'

He indicated its size by making a hoop of his thin arms. Bigger than a plate. I knew the wonders of God's earth to be manifold, and some of them even beyond the scope of the redoubtable Hanker's *World History*, but I was beginning to suspect that the boy was telling an untruth. 'So I goes on peering round the place till I sees another bunch, that don't have a spider,' the boy continued. 'And I grab it like this with my bare hands.' He showed me his hands. They were bony and grubby. I nodded to acknowledge his bravery. 'I just took the one. I could've taken more.'

The boy looked suddenly anxious.

'You did right, son,' said his mother. She had a flat face, like a plaice. 'We don't know as it's not poison.'

The thing was dark yellow, and blotchy, and as I have already indicated, obscene in shape. But as I stepped further into the room, I was struck by a sublime and mesmerising fragrance, which pulled me towards it like a helpless magnet.

'Have you ever in your life seen such an ungodly-looking specimen?' the ulcerous Mr Cove asked me, eyeing it worriedly. 'Can the Lord ever have given His holy blessing to it?' He was looking to me for God's answer, and I searched my heart to find the reply that Parson Phelps might give, but my thoughts were in turmoil. I did not know what to make of this thing, but I knew that I desired it more fiercely than I had ever desired anything.

'Beauty is in the eye of the beholder,' I said at last, dredging up something my mother always used to say to me when she caught me gazing miserably at my reflection in the hall mirror. I inhaled deeply, and with every second that ticked by on the ancient grandfather clock in the corner of the room, I succumbed still further to the fruit's exotic lure.

'The boy swears it's edible, but we're not so sure,' said Mrs Cove. 'You'll need to peel off its jacket first!'

She was not to know it, but I was by now so overwhelmed by a desire to eat the thing and to possess it for ever, that I could barely prevent myself from leaping forward and grabbing it.

'I'll try it, if you like,' I offered. I was trembling with a wild urge to cram the whole thing into my mouth. 'I'll just take a bite, and tell you if it's all right.' Cautiously, I removed its yellow skin, and bared its white flesh.

I had intended to take a small bite only, but a sudden and unnatural greed overwhelmed me. My shameful urge at that moment was simply to stuff the whole thing in, but I managed, with extreme difficulty, to restrain myself. Instead I merely took a large bite, which broke the fruit in half. I closed my eyes and ate, transported into Heaven. When I opened them again, the whole of the Cove family was gawping at me. They must have been surprised at how much I had bitten off. The adults said nothing, but the boy let out an indignant, 'Hey!'

It was the best thing I had ever tasted; better, even, than the toffee apple Tommy had stolen for me at the Travelling Fair of Danger and Delight. And as I chewed on it, savouring it, I knew that I must have it again. As its glorious taste spread across my tongue, I even contemplated cheating the Cove family, by twisting my face into an expression of disgust and telling them I thought the thing was poison. Anything to keep the whole fruit for myself! But in the end, God's stern leadership prevailed, and I reluctantly quelled my more selfish desires. I told them, 'It's good.' Then added, weakly hoping it might yet repel them, 'though not to everyone's taste, I imagine.' Reluctantly, I held out the half-fruit to the Cove boy, who sniffed it, then took a bite. He chewed slowly, and a smile spread.

Guiltily, I cornered him on the way out, and slipped him a coin.

'There are more pennies where that came from,' I said, 'if you can get hold of a whole bunch of those things.'

The boy grinned at me, showing broken teeth.

'And mind the giant spider!' I called after him, as he ran off to the harbour.

My new-found passion for bananas – a passion so extreme as to be almost uncontrollable – provided me with inspiration and comfort in my moments of darkness. The Cove boy brought me several bunches of the fruit, which I cloistered in my wardrobe, and I repaid him generously with all the money I could spare from my ever-dwindling supply. Occasionally I worried about the single-mindedness of my diet, and forced myself to eat a little bread or fish to supplement it, but both my palate and my tapeworm recoiled increasingly from such fare, and I returned to the comfort offered by the noble fruit.

Comfort I was coming to need more and more. For events at home had taken a sudden downward turn.

This is Dr Baldicoot's letter. I have it still.

Dear Tobias,

It is with a heavy heart that I write to tell you of your father's removal to the Sanatorium for the Spiritually Disturbed at Fishforth, where he declares he will not see you. It grieves me to tell you this, but it is for the best, I am sure. He is there among men who are similarly distressed by the issue of man's creation, and has learned to knit. If he were in his right mind he would convey his kind regards, for I know he loves you. It was he who fought for your life when you were a baby, though I personally would have given up, if you will pardon my being so blunt.

Yours sincerely,

Will Baldicoot.

PS. The Parsonage is now inhabited by a temporary parson by the name of Gudderwort, of whom none of us is fond, as he has tried to ban our Thistle-Pulling Contest, which he says is paganism. All of Thunder Spit wishes you well in your studies, and awaits your return as Parson, for we are a flock with no shepherd!

PPS. A few ounces of good tobacco would not go amiss, on your next visit.

'Welcome home, my little friend!'

Tommy squeezed me tight against his huge muscled torso, so hard I feared he might crack my ribs, for he did not know his own strength. I hugged him back. How I had missed him! I had arranged a week's compassionate leave from the Seminary, and travelled to Thunder Spit to settle Parson Phelps' affairs. Tommy was a father now; he had a bonny child, a boy, by his wife Jessie. 'We've called him Nicholas,' said Tommy. 'After the church.'

Although she was now a grown woman, I remembered Jessie from childhood days; the little Jessie Tobash who had once upset me by calling me Prune-Face – a cruelty about which she was most red-faced and apologetic as she welcomed me into her kitchen and laid a place for me at table.

'She's expecting another,' Tommy told me proudly, patting her rump as if she were a horse. Jessie served us sardine pie and sloeberry wine, and I gave them a present of a small bunch of bananas, at which they marvelled.

I begged for news of Thunder Spit, and they furnished me with a brisk account of how Ron Harcourt had lost five of his cows, and Tommy's brother Joe had run away to sea, and Mrs Firth's idiot cousin Joan had got her senses back for a week and then lost them again, and the new parson, Gudderwort, had banned the Thistle-Pulling Contest, as Dr Baldicoot's letter had said, prompting the whole village to boycott the church.

'And Hunchburgh?' Jessie begged. 'Tell us all about your life in Hunchburgh!' So as they savoured their bananas, I told them about the Seminary, and about the weasel-faced Farthingale and his henchmen Ganney and Popple, my trio of persecutors. And I told them about my visits to the poor and needy, and about

206

the breezy nonchalance of the Abbot who ran the Seminary, and about Tillie and Mrs Fooney, and the Cove family and my discovery of the banana.

Then I came to the letter I had received from Dr Baldicoot. When I told them its contents, Tommy confirmed that Parson Phelps had indeed gone quite mad.

'Jessie was there, at his last service. 'She saw him.'

'Yes,' said Jessie, sitting down heavily at the table next to us. 'He didn't read aloud from the Bible,' she said, 'but from other books.'

'What books?' I asked.

'Hanker's *World History* was one,' said Jessie, untying her hair and letting it fall across her shoulders. I would one day like a wife who would do that, I thought. But I am Prune-Face. Fartybockers. Hobble-de-Hoy. The Bookworm. Only a blind woman would ever want me as a husband!

'And the Origin of Something,' said Tommy, interrupting my reverie. 'That selfsame book he was always preaching against before.'

'The *Origin of Species*,' I murmured. 'By Charles Darwin.'

'That's the one,' confirmed Jessie. 'We didn't understand a word of it. It was all science and nonsense to us, about the fins of fish transforming into arms and legs. It quite turned my stomach to hear it. And then he tore up his Bible.'

I felt the blood fade from my face. Oh, my poor beloved father! I hated Mr Charles Darwin at that moment, stranger to me though he was, for putting Parson Phelps through this agony. Parson Phelps, and all the others, too! For he was not alone in his suffering, if Dr Baldicoot's letter was to be believed. Had the letter not implied that there was an entire sanatorium in Fishforth, chock-a-block with befuddled souls such as my father's? And that the blame lay entirely at Mr Charles Darwin's feet? I pictured the Bible pages fluttering to the church floor, just as the pages of Mr Darwin's book had once done, at a happier epoch in our lives.

'Then he swore foul oaths at us,' Jessie continued, putting her hand on mine gently. 'And then he called us all sea-slugs and barbarians. And he called you, Tobias, a –'

'Never mind,' interrupted Tommy. 'He is mad.' In the silence that followed, a flea hopped off my wrist and on to the chequered tablecloth. Jessie squashed it with her nail, and continued: 'And then Mrs Sequin got up to leave, and we all followed her. Only Dr Baldicoot stayed.'

'And then?'

'And then the next day, Dr Baldicoot took him away to Fishforth. He was clutching an envelope, but he took nothing else with him, not even a bag of clothes. He left it all behind.' She patted my hand, and passed me a white handkerchief that smelt of fish. I took it, and blew my nose fiercely.

I wondered about the envelope. Could it be the same one that the Contortionist had thrust at him when she gave him the jar? I shuddered.

When I visited Dr Baldicoot the following day, he told me that his diagnosis of a tumour of the brain remained a possibility. Such an affliction, he said, would undoubtedly account for the Parson's odd behaviour over the last few years, and his painful rejection of me.

'Fate is cruel,' he said, knocking out the dead seaweed tobacco from his pipe and filling it, with barely disguised rapture, with the tobacco I had brought him from Hunchburgh. Lighting it with his tinderbox, a cloud of smoke, pungent as a burning haystack, was soon trailing upwards, spreading to fill the whole room.

'Yes!' he exclaimed, sinking back in his chair and savouring the smoke.

A jealous God, my father had said. The smell of Dr Baldicoot's burning tobacco made me dizzy, and I was suddenly filled with an immeasurable sadness, not only that my father might die, but that our relationship should be so soured by principles I could not understand.

'One day,' I coughed through Dr Baldicoot's smokescreen, 'I shall bring him home.'

208

'I hope that you one day shall,' he replied, laying down his stinking pipe on his desk. 'But for now, I fear he still has no wish to see you. He has developed what I consider to be an unhealthy obsession with your origins.'

'Of what nature?'

But Dr Baldicoot began to fiddle furiously with a sheaf of pipe-cleaners, and would not speak.

The new Parson, Gudderwort, was dry and gaunt and ascetic, with a high, domed forehead, and skin like parchment. He poured out acidic seaweed tea, and I poured out some of my woes to him, but I fear they fell on stony ground. My father had left a legacy of mistrust in Thunder Spit, Gudderwort informed me somewhat accusingly.

'After he'd torn up his Bible in the church, nobody was keen to return,' he said bitterly. He seemed to lay the blame for this on me. Or so I felt.

'Shall we pray?' he suggested, in his mealy-mouthed way, when we had finished our tea.

So we knelt down together on the uncomfortable flag-stoned kitchen floor (Where was the embroidered pew-cushion my father had always used, his one concession to luxury?) and Gudderwort pressed his dry palms and skeletal fingers together, and we prayed for the safety of my father's diseased soul, and my forgiveness of him. And I prayed, secretly, that Dr Baldicoot was not lying to me about the cause of my father's madness in order to make me feel better. Uncharitably, I also prayed that Gudderwort would get water on the knee.

Just as I was leaving, Gudderwort called out to me. He was carrying something in both hands.

'Your father left this,' he said drily. 'Mrs Firth suggested that I not bother you with it, once she saw what it was, but I have no use for it, and it appears to be a personal object.'

And he thrust it towards me.

I felt a lurch of vertigo. The room seemed to contract, and then expand.

The jar.

'So here you are,' prompted Gudderwort irritably, waiting. My hands felt jelly-like as I took the jar from him. Its thick glass was cold, and heavy.

'I found it in the vestry,' said Gudderwort, guessing my thoughts. 'Hidden away beneath his spare cassock.'

I gulped and trembled, summoning the courage to investigate what the jar contained. When I did, I had to squint. It was full of a dark liquid. A dark liquid, with something floating in it. I felt both sick and baffled in equal measure.

'Do you know what it is?' I asked Gudderwort. My voice cracked as I spoke. There was a pause before Gudderwort replied. His parchment lip creased with disapproval and distaste.

'An umbilical cord,' he said finally, depositing the words as if they were small turds. He clearly wanted to be rid of me, and even more, it.

'A what?' I blurted.

'An umbilical cord, according to Mrs Firth,' he said. Mrs Firth was his housekeeper. He was still unable to hide the deep disgust in his voice. What foul parish had he landed himself in, he must be thinking. What bad luck to be obliged thus to mop up the mess of another parson's spiritual crisis!

I raised the jar to my eyes: and sure enough, behind the swirling blur of dark pickle, there lurked a whitish thing.

Suddenly I found myself laughing aloud. But there was hysteria in that laugh.

'Shall I see you to the door?' said Gudderwort with finality. 'I think it best that you be on your way.' Like father like son, he was no doubt thinking. Lunatics both.

I wrapped the jar in a crumpled old fish-paper and took my leave.

Back at the forge I told Tommy what had happened. I showed him the jar, and together we peered at it.

'Mrs Firth told Gudderwort it was an umbilical cord,' I said. Tommy grunted. 'Not poison, then,' he said. 'Let's ask Jessie.'

She'd borne a babe. She would know. Jessie lifted Nicholas from her hip and plonked him on the floor, then wiped her hands on her apron, and peered into the jar.

After a while, she said, 'Yes, I think she's right. An umbilical cord.'

Tommy and I stared at each other. It made no sense. But then, my father had gone mad. Perhaps it made sense to a madman.

As I shook his hand in farewell, the jar wrapped in fish-paper and tucked beneath my arm, Tommy smiled at me stiffly, and slapped my back.

'We didn't half get scared, eh?' he said. 'Over something as small and silly as that?' But his voice lacked its usual hearty conviction, and his words did nothing to quell the anxiety in my heart, or the sudden distress in my sphincter. Until this visit to Thunder Spit, I suddenly realised, the parasite Mildred had been leaving me increasingly in peace. But now she was back with a vengeance. Something was wrong. Just as a strip of seaweed can detect oncoming rain, so my tapeworm could sense ill. I'll say that to her credit.

In the meantime, a question of a practical nature occupied me: should I bury the cord, or burn it? Or just leave it as it was, floating in the jar? The pickled human flesh was, after all, my only heritage, that I knew of. I was faced with a dilemma, though not one of the kind that I was used to grappling with in the Seminary. Fundamental questions there concerned such things as whether or not Adam possessed a navel. Not: What does one do with an anonymous umbilical cord, when it is presented to you in a jar, as your sole heritage?

No two omphalic issues could be further apart.

I sat in the coach on the way back, with my boxes in the luggage rack and the jar clasped to my breast. I pictured the tiny strip of flesh within, that had once connected a baby to its mother.

What baby, to what mother?

Why had the Contortionist sold my father the jar?

And why had he kept it?

Did I, even then, suspect the answer to these questions, and deny them to myself?

I was in a woeful state by the time I returned to my lodgings, where Mrs Fooney, remarking that I looked pale, fussed over me with hot-water bottles and cups of tea, and home-made muffins, while Tillie put my whelk shell to her ear, and listened to the sea, and chatted over her dolls on the kitchen floor. But after a while I could bear this scene of domestic contentment no longer; hot tears welled in my eyes, and excusing myself, I tore myself away, clutching my jar to my bosom.

For several days, I shut myself in my room, afflicted by a deep and unfathomable depression of the spirits, staring at the jar, and the jar staring at me. It was a wonder the glass hadn't cracked on the journey from Thunder Spit, or leaked. The pickle was murky-looking; the cord was barely discernible inside: a bulbous, tapering thing, floating in suspension. There was a residue at the bottom, black and gritty-looking. The disintegrated placenta, perhaps? I wondered. I did not know. I was no more familiar with women's bodies, and their workings, than with the geography of the Planet Mars. I should have thrown it out, then and there, perhaps.

But I did not; I kept it there on my mantelpiece, as if it was the only thing I had left in the world.

I am all filld up with a medicin calld lordnum. We hav been at Sea five or six munths, acordin to Higgins. The Arke is getin crowded, and the more crowded it gets, the mor lordnum we gets. Ther is very few cagis left emptie. Howlin and screemin and fartin all nite. Higgins and Steed and Bowker playin cards all day. Trapp drinkin his CLARIT and talkin about the Queen's Collekshun, and his Slave-tradin days.

And how wot we need is a NEW WURLD, wer no-wun will

hav to WURK. On and on he goes, about this idea. His Uther Biznis, he corls it.

Then we reech the shors of MOROKO.

Oi, Deerie. Redy to sher yor HOME with a nice GENTLE-MAN? Trapp sez to me, twurlin his MUSTARSH.

CHAPTER 21

METAMORPHOSIS

There's no smoke without fire, is there? That's what they say about rumour. It can begin anywhere there's a tinderbox and a match, or lightning. There is no telling where the flames will spread, or where the smoke will drift.

The latest rumour doing the rounds of London Society is this: that Miss Violet Scrapie, said to be the anonymous joint author of Monsieur Cabillaud's controversial book *Cuisine Zoologique: une philosophie de la viande*, published last week to general bemusement, has become a militant vegetarian!

What's more, the rumour is true.

Mr Henry Salt, who had last seen Miss Violet Scrapie heading determinedly away from the assembled throng of non-carnivores muttering something about her need for a pork chop, had been pleasantly shocked to witness her presence at the November meeting of the Vegetarian Society, an occasion that featured an edifying speech by a guest vegan – a former abattoir-owner – and a display of etchings depicting the horrors of vivisection.

At the end of the meeting, Violet Scrapie, her face creased with anxiety and excitement in equal measure, approached the podium bearing a covered silver platter, and made her announcement.

'My name is Violet Scrapie, and I am writing a book of vegetarian cookery, with which I dare to rival the achievement of Mrs Beeton herself!'

There! Done it! She bit her lip and stared down bashfully at her domed dish.

The audience, who had heard the rumours of Violet's conversion, gasped and exchanged whispers of amazement at the young woman's intriguing combination of modesty, presumption and passion. Suet, unaware of the impression his mistress was making, was scrutinising the poster display. It featured ghastly representations of dogs like himself in cages, and prompted him to recall once again the worst moments of his puppy-hood. His mouth went dry with fear, and he began to pant, his tongue lolling out like a slice of ham.

'Now try this, Mr Salt,' Violet was urging the President, whipping the cover off the platter to reveal an unusual but strangely elegant display of *amuse-gueules* featuring creamed asparagus, celeriac mousse, jellied mushrooms and devilled grapes, garnished with zest of orange, angelica and fern leaves. 'My own recipes!'

The vegetarians gawped at the audacity of her vision, then began to whisper animatedly in little huddles. Their conclusion: Farewell, perhaps, boiled turnips! Let Mr Salt decide our fate!

Mr Salt, no culinary ignoramus himself, tasted. His first mouthful told him that Miss Scrapie had a fluency with garlic. His second, that she had an innate understanding of the wayward vagaries of paprika. His third, that she had expertly married the demands of texture and taste, form and content, raw and cooked. He swallowed, and spoke.

'I declare this young woman a genius.'

When the roars of approval died down, Miss Scrapie, perspiring somewhat from the strain of the occasion and blushing from the roots of her hair, but proud of the impact she had made, announced, 'I shall be inventing and compiling a collection of vegetarian dishes, as mouth-watering as can be imagined.' Mr Salt smiled in benign approval. 'May I beg you for your support in this endeavour?'

The platter was passed round, and within moments, Violet's offerings had been snaffled up.

'You try to stop us!' yelled a woman encouragingly.

Never had herbs of the field tasted so good. It was a moment, they all agreed later, of supreme civilisation.

With one voice, the thin campaigners cheered in approval.

'Hurrah for Miss Violet Scrapie!' proclaimed Mr Salt.

Violet smiled, the first smile of genuine happiness she had been able to muster in recent weeks, and *The Fleshless Cook* was born.

Violet Scrapie, a woman with a mission.

Three hundred miles north from this happy metropolitan scene of conviction, picture another landscape; the landscape of loss. The Fishforth Sanatorium for the Spiritually Disturbed stands high on a hill overlooking the North Sea, the shore on which the Vikings once landed. The Sanatorium, tall and stark and built of grey stone, is perched on the edge of a precipice, as though in sympathy with the mental state of its inmates. Herring gulls and guillemots, oblivious to the symbolic disjunction between land and water, belief and chaos, wheel in the sky overhead, jostled by the sharp salt wind, and screech their hoarse and plaintive cries. Ink-blue, the sea rolls far below, its surface dashed with the startling white of horses' tails on the wave-crests. The looming shadows of giant squid, patrolling the coast, lurk ten fathoms deep beneath in an unknown world.

On the precipice, in a window in the high central tower of the Fishforth Sanatorium, a light burns. Here, in the drawing room, the firelight dancing behind him in the wide grate, the fragrance of cedar-wood filling the high-ceilinged room, Parson Phelps sits alone with his knitting. The wool he knits is dark red, the colour of Christ's blood. The tightly upholstered chair upon which he is seated has an antimacassar to counter hair-grease, and padded wings to protect its occupier's head from evil thoughts and cold draughts. A book, a torn and bedraggled copy of the *Origin of Species*, balances precariously on his once plump, now bony knees. Inside it rests the envelope he brought with him from Thunder Spit when Dr Baldicoot took him away. The envelope

216

contains a crumpled old letter, on onion-skin parchment, and is covered in splattery stains. A useful bookmark.

'She sells sea-shells on the seashore,' mumbles Parson Phelps, slurring on the words whilst recovering a slipped stitch. Knitting does not come easily to him. Nor do tongue-twisters. Tobias used to recite tongue-twisters, he recalls. The Parson winces in pain at the memory of his son. 'Miss Mosh mashes some mish-mash,' he mouths sadly, winding some more red wool around his bony finger. 'Betty Botter bought some butter!' A tear falls.

Despite its forbidding exterior, Fishforth is a far cry from Bedlam. All the inmates here are thoughtful and courteous. Their voices, which once thundered from the pulpit in the confident fortissimo of righteous conviction, are now soft and hoarse with bewilderment, murmuring only the husks of discourse. The gentlemen's table-manners are impeccable, and such homely gestures as the placing of knives and forks, the breaking of bread, or the smoothing of a table-napkin, are performed with simplicity and grace. After lunch, they read poetry or discuss the religious and social issues of the day, while those who are inclined to pray do so in the privacy of the small chapel in the upper half of the tower. Paying homage to God is neither encouraged nor frowned on here, for Fishforth is an enlightened establishment, which sees the dilemma of its inmates as a passing phase, a rite of passage on the journey towards a fuller spiritual maturity. The beliefs of men like Parson Phelps have been shattered by Darwinism – but should their life's work be set at nought as a result? And cannot shattered objects be re-assembled in different ways, like fragments of stained glass in a church, to form a new holy picture: another facet of truth's kaleidoscope? Why, surely they can! As a result of this generous approach, most clergymen recover within a few months of rest, and return to their parishes with a deeper conviction of the Bible's wisdom, or a broader understanding of creation.

'All depending,' says the Principal, a former inmate himself, 'on whether you choose to cling to the solid rock of your already

217

established belief, or to take that leap of imagination and faith that will hurl you into an abyss of chaos and wonder.' Of those who leap, he preached gravely, some crash upon the stony ground of atheism, while others float or even fly.

He personally had stayed on his rock.

While waiting to make his choice of direction, Parson Phelps found himself reasonably content. If you have to be in turmoil, let it be among like-minded men.

'See it as a stage in your spiritual development,' said the Principal. Obediently, Parson Phelps had tried to see it that way. He'd floated weightlessly, as though emptied, through the thinly furnished rooms, and the hallways where bales of wool were stacked. The Sanatorium ran a small cottage industry of carding, spinning, and dyeing; the institution received no payment, but inmates were permitted, in exchange for work, to use the wool for their personal and recreational purposes. Parson Phelps was not the only clergyman here who had decided to seize on this opportunity. He had fond memories of Mrs Phelps knitting. He could picture her now, sitting on a hard chair in the flag-stoned kitchen, knitting a jersey for Tobias in one of the boy's favourite colours, either mauve or green. Tobias, who as a child had seemed such a blessing, such a prodigy! Who had spoken in the tongues of angels until the age of five, and had then astonished them all suddenly with his pure, clear speech! Oh, Tobias! God help you now, in your cruel catastrophe!

And Parson Phelps remembered God, too – God, who had worked His great needles slowly, as he listened patiently, like a second wife, to the Parson's long, baggy prayers. Long ago. It is now two years since the marriage of their true minds began to go awry, and since that time, Parson Phelps has not directed a single word in God's direction.

'There was a jar –' Parson Phelps had said, when Dr Baldicoot first brought him here.

'Shhh, rest now,' they told him.

'I lied to Tobias.'

'Tobias?'

'My son. Or rather –'

'Your son must look after himself. All shall be well. Concentrate on your own needs, Parson Phelps. You have been shepherd to a flock for too long. Now it is time to be a sheep for a while.'

'Baa,' said a young clergyman all the way from Basingstoke, whose head was a gleaming ball of silver-blond hair that fitted him like a cap.

'Baa baa black sheep,' sang his bearded friend. They were making a cat's cradle together, in purple wool.

'A woman came to see me,' insisted Parson Phelps. 'She was from the Travelling Fair of Danger and Delight. She had a jar, and she gave me this letter, too.' He held out a crumpled sheaf of onion-skin pages, and thrust them beneath the Principal's nose. 'She said she was his – Mrs Phelps and I –' A pause. The Parson cast his eyes to the ground, and flicked at a stray piece of yellow fluff with his slippered toe.

'Yes?'

Parson Phelps lowered his voice. 'There was an adder in my knickerbockers as a child. I had to strangle it, and –'

'I see.' This was said very gently. 'You must be tired from your journey.'

'So when Tobias arrived –' Parson Phelps persisted, crumpling the letter back into his pocket.

'Arrived?'

'In the church. By the altar. I thought he was a piglet.'

'A piglet?'

'Yes. A young swine. He bit me.'

'Ah.'

'But it seemed like a miracle, because of all the feathers.'

'Feathers?'

'From the pillow.'

'The pillow?'

'He tore it, and the feathers flew out.'

'Ah. I see. Pillow-feathers.'

'Yes. We thought he was a gift from Heaven.'

219

'All children are gifts from Heaven.'

'Not this one,' said Parson Phelps, suddenly vehement. 'He is from Hell!'

'Let me show you to your quarters.'

'Baa,' said the blond-headed young clergyman. 'Welcome to the flock.'

He and his friend inverted their hands, and a replica of the Clifton Suspension Bridge was revealed.

'Isambard Kingdom Brunel,' said the blond clergyman. 'The greatest engineer who ever lived.'

'Apart from God,' murmured the Principal.

Parson Phelps said, 'I paid the woman for the jar, and then I paid her some more so that she would go, and never come back.'

'Baa,' said the dark-haired clergyman.

'Lunch is served at twelve, and tea at five. As you see, our main window in here is south-facing, so we have the benefit of a sea view, and plenty of sunlight.'

This was true. During the daytime, the sun's brilliant rays pierced the windows, creating haloes of dust on the furniture, and causing the dark wood table to gleam, Parson Phelps now noted, like the carapace of a great mystical beetle.

'God loves the beetle,' he said, staring at the table. 'That's why He made so many.'

'"*And the earth was without form and void*,"' intoned the bearded clergyman, '"*and darkness was on the face of the deep*."'

'I had to pay her,' said Parson Phelps. 'Otherwise she'd have told him who his father was.'

'"*Our Father which art in Heaven*,"' droned the blond-haired clergyman, doing something complicated and unsuccessful with the tangle of his fingers.

Parson Phelps asked in a croak, 'Did I do wrong?'

'*Thy Isambard Kingdom come*,' said the bearded clergyman. '*Thy Isambard rum-te-tum*.'

'God will forgive you. You are a lost sheep in distress.'

'Baa-aa,' bleated the blond and the bearded clergymen in unison, untangling the purple Clifton Suspension Bridge.

Charles Darwin had a lot to answer for.

Now, alone, Parson Phelps adjusts his needles and his ball of wool, and commences another row of knitting, but after three stitches, he stops. He can't see for tears. He sniffs a long, shuddering sniff, then wipes his eyes with his ball of blood-red wool. Snatching up his crumpled letter, he rises from his chair, and his knitting falls to the floor. The ball rolls to the other side of the room, dividing the floor with a thin line of red. Parson Phelps stands still for a while. Then he carefully steps over the line, and walks to the darkened window.

Below: the ocean. Huge. Chaotic. Dark as ink. He pictures the slashing rain on the glassy waves, and the *Ark* bobbing. A toy of wood and string.

Clutching the Frozen Woman's crumpled letter in his hand, he stares out into the void, and into the darkness on the face of the deep.

Then, just as we reechis the shors of MOROCKO, I falls ill.

Very ill. Fever.

The Arke rolls and rolls on the wavs, and I thinke: I am in a dreem. I hav been so SIK wiv this Fever that I dont no wen the Ark stops, or wen the GENTLEMAN cums. Just wak up wun mornin or afternoon or wotever, an smel the harber, stil in darknis, and he is ther. I tuches him and I SCREEMS, an he SCREEMS too. I shufles to the other side of the cage.

Storm in the nite. Arke rockin in the dok like its goin to sinke. Giraf forls over an dyes. Rogers sicke like a dog, serv him rite. TRAPP nower to be seene.

Me and him is thrown agenst eech uther. He stil hasnt sed a wurd. But in the storm, suden, we is flung together and he puts his arms round me, stil dusnt sa a wurd. And nor dus I. He just holds me and I feel his HART beeting, beeting, against MY OWN HART.

221

CHAPTER 22

BESTIAL URGES

I could feel a heart beating on either side of me, as we lay in bed. And my own heart a piggy-in-the-middle.

'Polygamy's a natural instinct,' murmured Rose, breaking the silence with a yawn of Sunday-morning contentment.

'A bestial urge,' mumbled Blanche, reaching for the heritage chart on the bedside table. They'd start conversations like that, sometimes halfway through. Like they'd done the first half in silence.

'Look, Buck, we're nearly done,' said Rose, thrusting the chart at me.

'We worked on it last night,' said Blanche, 'while you were down the Crow with Dad.'

I looked. It was impressive. They'd added some heraldic shields with fleurs-de-lis and lions rampant round the edge since I last saw it, and felt-tipped in the structure of the tree; just the names were missing.

'Hope it's all worth it,' I said. I had my doubts. The more I heard about this Dr Bugrov, the less I liked the sound of him. He'd managed to convince the girls that the American heritage craze, where the newly retired come over in coaches to bore you with their roots, was also going to take a grip on our own dying nation, and make them rich. Though how they'd managed to wangle a grant to research their own family tree was beyond me. Oh well. Maybe he was right. There were certainly a lot of foreign film crews about the place, recording poignant documentaries about the end of an era, like they did in Hong Kong, before it was handed back to China. Voyeurs, I thought. Parasites.

'Look, Mum's mother was a Clegg,' said Rose, shoving a computer printout at me.

'And her mother was a Tobash,' put in Blanche, accordioning it out in front of me. They could be a couple of trainspotters, with a map of a gigantic and rather tedious railway junction.

'And before that, there were Boggses on her father's side, and Morpitons on the mother's.'

'So we're incredibly interbred,' they said together, and made a face.

'Practically a species in your own right, then,' I said. They seemed to like this idea, and did some giggling.

'Just one generation to go,' commented Blanche, yawning.

'God, I feel sick,' said Rose.

'Me, too,' said Blanche.

'Must be those Victorian veggie things Mum cooked,' says Rose, yawning. 'From that recipe book she found in the attic. *The Fleshless Cook*. Puke City.'

'But who's to say when you stop?' I asked, peering at their genealogy chart. 'Surely a family tree can go on for ever?'

'The module only requires five generations,' said Rose firmly, yawning again.

'Then we get our diploma,' said Blanche, yawning, too. Yawning's infectious; suddenly I had to do it, too. I snuggled down under the duvet. Idly, Sigmund stirred. I ran my foot up Roseblanche's shin. Ugh; it was all stubbly. I tried Blancherose's: likewise. Sigmund shrank back. It hadn't been like that in the beginning.

'We haven't shaved lately,' they said together.

'We've been feeling too lazy,' said Rose. 'In fact, we're going to spend the whole day in bed.'

'Because we feel ready to throw up,' finished Blanche.

'You certainly know how to turn a guy on,' I said.

What was it about women? This was a question that was aired from time to time in the Stoned Crow, but no one seemed to have

223

the answer. Charlie Peat-Hove thought it was purely hormonal. Ron Harcourt said it was their mothers' fault. Tony Morpiton said it was to do with the nature of society. But I reckoned they just evolved that way.

'Your turn to make the coffee, Buck!' said Rose, jabbing me in the ribs.

'It's always my turn.'

'Hey, he's observant!' they giggled.

'Except this morning, we don't feel like coffee,' announced Rose.

'We feel like Ovaltine.'

Roseblanche, Blancherose, my Balls and chain, I thought, as I heaved myself out of bed, and headed downstairs to do their bidding.

'Chop chop!' they yelled after me.

'Your whim is my command!' I yelled back. I'd heard it somewhere.

Believe it or not, it had only been a month since they moved in. It had certainly been a novelty in the beginning. I suppose that's the nature of novelties. I hadn't been involved in anything polygamous before. I'd always associated it with baboons and sheiks.

After the nightclub in Hunchburgh, they'd stayed the night at my place. And the next night, and the next. The beauty of it, but the trouble, too, was that there were two of them, and only one of me. I'd always been in charge of things in bed, with other women. But I wasn't, with these two. It wasn't just our limbs that got entangled; it was our roles as well. It was quite a thrill, at first, being outnumbered and manhandled like that. I was the luckiest bloke in the world, I kept telling myself. Not everyone could have hacked it; there was stamina required, after all. I was doing the work of two men, let's face it. At weekends they'd wear me out, so that sometimes, come Sunday night, Sigmund would go on strike. Then they'd insist, and pummel away at me and cajole me with licking and whispers and I felt like their sex object, being pushed and shoved about according to their whims. Afterwards, I'd lie between them and listen to their stereo breathing. But it wasn't just sex they dominated. They kept making bilateral rulings about everything we did. Whose decision was it, that they'd move in with me? Not mine.

You went and asked the father's permission, in the old days.

'I would like to ask you for your daughter's hand in marriage, sir,' you'd say.

Those days are gone.

'Bog off,' was Norman's reaction when I announced that his daughters and I were all three planning to live together on a semi-permanent basis. 'That's what they call it in advertising,' he said, noticing my puzzled look. 'Buy one, get one free. Good thinking, Batman! I'll buy you an emperor-sized bed. There's a flat-pack model down at B and Q. Sorted!'

'Now we'll all be able to breathe,' sighed Abbie happily. It wasn't that it hadn't been a joy having the twins at home all these years, she explained; it was just that with the Pepto-Bismol addict in the lounge all the time nowadays, the place was feeling a bit crowded. 'Plus – don't laugh – I feel ready to spread my wings a bit, TV career-wise!'

We didn't laugh. It was sad.

'Time they flew the nest, anyway, I reckon, if the truth be told,' said Norman. 'No offence, Buck, but we'd been scratching our heads a bit over their future. We reckoned they'd be on the shelf for ever, what with the curtains coming down on Britain, and all the young blokes buggering off like rats leaving the proverbial.'

All had gone well to begin with, I reflected, as I hunted for the Ovaltine and microwaved the milk for the two-headed monster upstairs. It's every bloke's dream, I reminded myself, to have two nubile women squirming all over him like a couple of audacious eels. 'So don't knock it, mate!' I murmured aloud, as I fumbled about with mugs and artificial sweeteners.

Then I stopped. 'Come on, Buck!' I urged myself. 'Get a grip! Isn't it obvious that you're living in paradise?'

I plinked two sweeteners into each mug of Ovaltine.

I realised early on – within a couple of days – that the girls had their eccentricities, but I coped. While I went about my veterinary practice, which consisted mainly of vaccinating cows against BSE and grappling with a dispute over Mrs Clegg's foal, which she claimed had been driven insane by the hallucinogen I'd administered, the twins had been working on their genealogy chart with disconcerting zeal, using the St Nicholas's Church marriage register for what they called empirical data. They'd spent hours poring over it, and copying out entries, and computerising tables. As for their obsession with unwanted body hair – they'd been great leg-shavers in the early days, both of them – it hadn't bothered me unduly. Quite the opposite, in fact, I thought now, ruefully. Call me old-fashioned, but who wants to be scratched all over by stubble, or have his girlfriends look like a couple of dykes? And their phobia about showing their feet – well, Sigmund and I actually found it quite sexy that their feet were a no-go area, and that they insisted on keeping their socks on during –

'The joy of socks,' I called it. They'd made a face, like it wasn't the first time someone had made that quip. Like it was the hundredth, in fact. I'll admit that it did bother me that they'd been round the block somewhat. The twins exchanged one of their secret looks whenever their genealogy teacher, Dr Bugrov, cropped up in conversation, and I got wolf-whistled in the pub, when the word spread that we were a threesome. Ron Harcourt made a 'Rather you than me' sort of face, and Jimmy Clegg winked at me, and Keith Hewitt made the double thumbs-up sign, and Tom Morpiton asked me rather pointedly how I was bearing up.

One night I went out with a spray-can, and attacked the graffiti on the harbour wall. It made me feel gallant, to insert that word NOT, in between the ARE and the SLAGS.

The microwave pinged at the same time as the doorbell rang. It was Abbie, laden with boxes from the Old Parsonage, which she thrust at me with finality. 'If they're moving in with you, they might as well make a thorough job of it,' she announced, taking off her coat and beginning to sort through some of the paraphernalia she'd brought: an array of Barbie dolls, sheets, quilts, thermoses, aspirin, and articles of feminine hygiene. When I saw the economy boxes of tampons, my heart sank; female plumbing always makes me squirm. It's all those rogue hormones.

'By the way, Buck,' said Abbie, smoothing the pristine cuffs of her baby-blue seersucker blouse, 'there's something for you in that box of magazines over there; I thought it might be of interest. I found it stashed away in a corner of that old Victorian wardrobe, the one that had the stuffed animals in.'

I looked at the cardboard box she'd indicated: it was full of women's magazines. I pulled one out; it was covered in headlines about human freaks. MY MUM STOLE MY HUSBAND – AND THEN MY CHILDREN! THIS MAN WAS PREVIOUSLY A WOMAN – TWICE! I PAID MY TEACHER FOR SEX – IN CHEWING GUM! I was getting quite sucked into one of the articles – about a beautiful woman whose plastic surgeon had accidentally amputated both her ears – when Abbie interrupted me.

'There it is,' she said, pointing to the box. It was a yellow, tattered old notebook, bound together with string. 'I thought you might be interested, it seems to be zoological.'

Reluctantly, I abandoned the article about the woman who'd lost her ears (she married the surgeon who did it), and blew some dust off the notebook. The title was hand-written, in faded ink. *A NEW THEORY OF EVOLUTION*, BY DR IVANHOE SCRAPIE. The date at the bottom was obliterated by a smear of what looked like blood.

While Abbie bustled about re-arranging the furniture and running her finger along the mantelpiece to check for dust, I flicked through the treatise. I'm not much of a reader, but there were some pictures in it that caught my attention. They were quite amateurishly done, but I recognised the ink sketches none the less; they were of mammal bones and the skulls of what were undoubtedly primates.

227

'Interesting?' asked Abbie. 'The Empress suggested it would be up your street.'

'Yes. Thanks.' I continued leafing through. It was the ink sketch of the monkey that made me stop and stare.

'Christ Almighty!'

'Buck?' called Abbie faintly from the other room. 'With you in a mo!'

'It's nothing,' I murmured.

But it wasn't nothing. The sketch wasn't just any monkey. It was my towel-holder. No mistaking it. Only in the picture, he was minus the blue glass eyes and complete with male genitalia. The same humanoid stance, caused by the unusual slant of the pelvic girdle. The same fragile-looking ears, the same hair distribution, the same –

Below it, Dr Ivanhoe Scrapie had written: '*The Gentleman Monkey, last remaining specimen of its species, captured in Mogador in 1843, and transferred from the Jardins Zoologique de Mogador to Britain in the zoological research vessel, the* Ark, *in 1845.*'

Well, I'll be buggered, I thought.

'Buck, where d'you want these pillow-cases?' called Abbie. But I didn't answer. By now I was riveted. I kept reading. And I kept turning back to the page with the monkey picture. I barely noticed Abbie leaving, and the twins had to shriek at me for their Ovaltine.

While they lay in bed all day, sleeping or working on their chart, I sat downstairs on the settee, poring over Dr Ivanhoe Scrapie's document. The ink was faded in a lot of places, and barely legible, but by the end of the day, I'd read the whole seventy pages. It was clearly written by a madman. Its main thesis – an absurdly childish and unscientific conjecture concerning the monkey that had turned up in the Balls' attic – appeared to be inspired by jealousy of Charles Darwin. I reckoned that the author, Dr Ivanhoe Scrapie, probably *had* been a taxidermist of some sort, as he claimed. There was no question that he had a sound grasp of taxonomy, and if the specimens in the Balls' attic were his own work, he was clearly an expert. But like many taxidermists, he appeared to be a failed zoologist, and very keen to make his own impact in zoological circles.

It was entertaining stuff, in its way. Complete rubbish, of course.

The thesis itself could be dismissed. But the sketch of the monkey got my brain racing. My appetite was whetted. I needed to know more about this creature. Urgently. Because if Scrapie's claims that the monkey was extinct were true then it might well be worth a lot of money.

A *lot* of money.

I couldn't get the thought out of my mind all day, and it was still rattling about in my head when I strolled into the pub that night.

Norman Ball saluted me as I entered.

'Hail the conquering hero, mate! What d'you make of the news? You must be getting pretty excited, with two of them on your hands.' He gave a big wink.

'What news?'

'You haven't heard?' laughed Ron Tobash.

'It's been on all the news bulletins since five o'clock,' said Tony Mulvey.

'What has? Spit it out!'

'There's a woman in Glasgow who says she's pregnant,' announced Norman triumphantly, handing me a beer. 'Cheers, mate!'

It took me a while to absorb this. 'What, naturally? Not from the Egg Bank, before the bomb?'

'No. It's too recent for that.' His eyes were bright with excitement. 'See for yourself, mate.' And he flicked on the news.

The TV news confirmed what the blokes said about the woman in Glasgow. But went further. The number of pregnant women had now risen from one to –

'*Seven thousand*? What, just in a couple of hours?' shouted Ron Harcourt. We all gawped at the screen.

'Nice ONE!' exclaimed Norman. 'Quite a turn-up for the

books, eh? I always said the British were survivors!' He pulled out a tissue from the pocket of his cardigan, and unashamedly wiped away a tear. 'The miracle of life, Buck! Just think! We'll be hearing the pitter-patter of tiny feet again!'

The programme on the news channel showed a map of Britain. Concentric circles were emanating from Glasgow, where the first pregnancy had been reported; it seemed that subsequent reports of pregnancy were coming from areas to the north, south, east and west of the city.

'Look!' cried Ron Harcourt, pointing at the animated graphic. 'It's reached past Hunchburgh! Yo!'

Various scientists, church leaders, and politicians were discussing the reports excitedly. It was a rebirth, they agreed. A triumph. We could begin to plan for the future again.

'We always maintained that it was just a blip,' said a politician smugly.

Only one man – a washed-out-looking academic type with a stammer – was expressing doubts.

'Where's the p-p-p-p-proof?' he kept saying. 'Do we have one case that's actually corroborated by m-m-m-m-medical evidence?' I'd heard him before on the radio. He was some kind of psychologist.

'Seven thousand home pregnancy-testing kits can't be wrong!' said a woman.

'C-c-c-c-can't they?' mustered the weedy man. 'And do we know that they all took home p-p-p-p-pregnancy tests? I don't think we d-d-d-do. We are t-t-t-t-talking about seven thousand w-w-w-w-women. I don't think there are that many p-p-p-p-pregnancy t-t-t-t-testing k-k-k-k-k-kits in the c-c-c-c-country!'

'Shame on you!' yelled Norman, red in the face with indignation.

The studio audience and the Stoned Crow all agreed with him. There were boos, and calls of 'Get him off the show!' and 'How dare he!'.

'The last thing we need is more gloom and doom,' agreed the

religious man. 'I say we fall on our knees and give thanks unto the Lord for this, folks!'

But the weedy psychologist was quite pathetically persistent. 'I don't like to put a d-d-d-d-damper on the euphoria that's sweeping the n-n-n-n-n-nation. Believe me. I want my wife to have a b-b-b-b-b-baby as much as the next m-m-m-m-man. But we should bear in mind that these k-k-k-k-kits are easily tampered with. And that there's a very b-b-b-b-big reward being offered here.'

'Get him off!' yelled Tony Morpiton.

'There may be some w-w-w-w-wishful thinking going on,' he was saying, but his stammers were being drowned out by a chorus of boos.

'What a d-d-d-d-dog-in-the-manger!' said Billy Clegg indignantly. 'He's suggesting that they're inventing their p-p-p-p-p-pregnancies just for the money!'

Everyone laughed.

'But you must admit it *is* pretty odd,' I said. 'Everyone suddenly getting p-p-p-p-pregnant all at once.'

'It's not everybody,' said Norman. 'Just look at the m-m-m-m-map!' It's Glasgow! It's starting in G-G-G-G-Glasgow, and spreading outwards. Anyway, it's no odder than conceptions just stopping with the M-M-M-M-Millennium.'

I had to admit he had a point.

'Rule Britannia!' shouted Norman. And began to sing. Soon we had all joined in. It made you feel quite patriotic, the whole thing. Blokes together.

'Rule Britannia, Britannia rules the waves!' we sang, lurching about, our arms around one another's shoulders. 'B-B-B-B-B-Britons never never never shall be slaves!'

It was that night, when I staggered home from the Crow, that the twins broke their news to me. They were sitting up in bed surrounded by party balloons, drinking more Ovaltine through novelty straws.

'Buck, we're pregnant.'

'Congratulations, girls,' I said. They were kidding, of course.

231

They'd seen the news, and they were trying it on. But I felt myself going faint.

'And am I the lucky father?' I tried to keep my voice steady, but what with all the beer and the nationalistic emotions sloshing about inside me, it came out slurred. They sucked on their straws, then looked at me solemnly.

'Yes,' they said together. 'You are.'

'We're going to be rich!' said Blanche.

'I need to sit down for a minute,' I said. And fell into blackness.

CHAPTER 23

THE JAR

It is true that in nurturing me from boyhood to manhood, Parson Phelps had prepared me to follow in his footsteps. Had he and Mrs Phelps not raised me as their son, Heaven knows what path I might have followed. Would I ever have ceased to scramble on all fours? Would I ever have learned to speak?

Yet the expression 'a self-made man' came to my mind with increasing frequency as my stay in Hunchburgh drew to a close. For what had I been, these past three years, but a young man, forced by circumstance, into the process of making of himself what he could? Like the whaling-ship that Tommy Boggs and I had once unleashed from its moorings, I was now a vessel voyaging alone. I had left the captain on the shore. And I had finally (if I may be pardoned the pursuit of this nautical metaphor) landed on an even keel. Or so I thought.

But how quickly and suddenly can a storm break, and fortune change! In my case, it took no more than a few seconds.

It was the winter of 1864, and I was about to become ordained. The ceremony was to be the crowning moment of my two years' stay in Hunchburgh, and as a gift to myself, I had indulged in purchasing from little Jimmy Cove a bunch of eight green bananas, which were just ripening nicely in my wardrobe. I planned to eat them, one by one, after my ordination ceremony, which was the following morning at eleven o'clock, presided over by the Abbot and the Bishop. I was looking forward to both events – though I am ashamed to say that I was by now so in thrall to the banana that the prospect of eating some more of the fruit appeared even more exciting to me than my elevation to the status of Parson.

'Hey, Betty!' yelled Farthingale across the refectory table at me that morning.

I looked up and saw his weasel face.

'We're holding a party in your rooms tonight!' he said. It was a Seminary tradition, he told me, that a sort of 'stag-night' is always held for those students about to enter the Church. My heart sank, for now I understood what all the recent whisperings in corridors had been about. Mrs Fooney was away in Wales with Tillie visiting her cousin, and would not be back for a week; my fellow theologians had clearly discovered this.

'Happy, Fartybockers, that your lodgings have been chosen?' Farthingale asked, smirking. 'Quite an honour for you, eh? And if you're a good boy, you'll even be invited!'

'So what d'you say, Hobble-de-Hoy?' asked Ganney menacingly, joining Farthingale with his plate of soup. I turned the other cheek.

'Hey, listen, everybody!' yelled Popple, standing on the table. 'Fartybockers is inviting us all to a party in his rooms tonight! Meet at Mrs Fooney's lodging-house at eight o'clock sharp!'

At eight, as threatened, my unwelcome guests began arriving, and within half an hour, my two small rooms were swarming with fellow theologians. Soon the place was crammed to bursting; students from other disciplines had caught wind of the party, and before I knew it, five students of botany, a geology student, and several medical scholars who had just finished their final exams decided to turn up, with more hangers-on in tow. The rooms were filled with the pungent haze of tobacco smoke, and I began to feel ill. Soon the party had no choice but to implode, or to spill over into Mrs Fooney's own private quarters. The former not being an option, the latter course was taken, and I was horrified to see my beloved landlady's neatly arranged belongings being scattered to the floor, and the contents of Tillie's toy-box investigated.

A group of young men were soon playing with the marbles I had given her, and peeking beneath the petticoats of her china dolls. I was horrified, and from time to time tried to stammer my objections, but to no avail.

'Enjoy yourself for once, Fartybockers!' jeered Farthingale.

'Unless, of course, you would rather celebrate with your whore on Mickle Street,' added Ganney, swigging at a bottle of rum.

'Hey, look at this!' yelled a student from my bedroom. And he emerged bearing the trophy of my cherished bunch of bananas – the very bananas I had been saving to celebrate tomorrow's ordination.

'Bananas!' cried Ganney. 'I tasted one once! Capital! Share them out, everybody!'

I groaned, and could only watch as my prized fruit was torn from Ganney's hands amid big beefy roars of delight. The revellers made quick work of the fruit, and soon there was nothing left of my bunch of bananas but the scattered skins on Mrs Fooney's floor.

'Hurrah for Parson Fartybockers!' yelled out Higgs through a mouthful as he thumped me on the back. 'Most excellent bananas!' A morsel flew out of his mouth and landed on my waistcoat, and I was filled with melancholy. 'Have a drink, sir!'

At this, a bony-kneed boy of about twenty, already quite drunk, had the bright idea of standing on my mantelpiece, which was wide enough to take three men, and proposing further toasts to us all, in honour of our forthcoming ordinations.

Some of my ornaments had to be displaced for this purpose, and I watched nervously as Farthingale swept my whelk shell to the floor, and Ganney fingered the fish-gutting knife that Tommy's mother had given me. My Bible, likewise, was removed, and my mermaid's purse, and my copy of Hanker's *World History*, and Herman's *Crustacea*; my dried gourds were all shoved unceremoniously to one side. My eyes were on my jar;

I did not wish to draw attention to it, but was concerned for its safety. I watched worriedly as Farthingale slid it over to the far end of the mantelpiece, and Ganney gave him a leg-up. But as soon as he was up there, Farthingale must have spotted that my focus was on the jar, for it immediately became a topic of interest.

'What's in here, Phelps?' he asked, picking it up.

I said nothing, but my heart yawned in fear.

'A secret?' asked Farthingale. He could spot any sign of weakness at a thousand paces.

'Yes, tell us what you keep in it!' demanded Popple. 'Is it rum?'

It was he who had once referred to me, because of my cordial respect for the Abbot, (forgive me, reader, for repeating his crude words) as an 'arse-licker'.

'Or pickled herrings?' asked Farthingale. He knew I came from a fishing village. I was dragged over to explain.

'How about the toast?' I managed weakly, but Popple had set his heart on my explaining what was in the jar.

'It's nothing,' I said. 'Just something my father left me.'

But Popple was infuriatingly insistent. I racked my brains for a lie, but untruth does not come naturally to me, having been punished for it so consistently when I was a child, so I could think of nothing.

'Well?' Farthingale was demanding. 'What's the big secret? Is it edible?'

'No!' I cried, shocked. God forbid that they should eat human flesh!

'Animal, vegetable or mineral?' called another student.

'It's animal,' I managed weakly. I just wanted them to stop talking about it. So I blurted, 'It's an umbilical cord. I have reason to believe,' I faltered, 'that it once joined me to my mother.'

At this, the room burst out into a cacophony of jeering, laughing, baying, hoots and whistles, as the jar and its by now distraught and miserable owner both became the focus of their mirth and derision.

'Hand it over here!' called Farthingale, egging them all on. 'Let's have a proper look.'

'Yes, go on,' said Popple. 'Kinnon's a student of medicine. He can give you an opinion as to the health of this intriguing object.'

'There's nothing to see,' I cried. 'Nothing!' This was true enough; the liquid in the jar had reacted to the heat of my fireplace by becoming even murkier than on the day I received it from Thunder Spit. The cord was just a fuzzy blur.

But Kinnon, the young medical student, was adamant that he must inspect the thing, as he was currently most interested in obstetrics and gynaecology (here he winked at his fellow students), and he would hand it back to me as soon as he had had a peek-a-squeak at the object in question.

'Please, I beg you, be careful!' I cried, as my jar – suddenly incalculably precious to me – was handed down from the mantelpiece. I watched it being passed across everyone's heads to Kinnon, who was over by the door next to another student smoking a pipe.

'There may be a risk of fire!' I murmured, feeling faint. Then I sank into a chair and said a silent prayer. Kinnon squinted into the jar.

'May I open it?' he asked, finally beginning to wrestle with the seal.

'Yes!' urged Farthingale. 'Let's all have a look!'

'No, I beg you not to!' I blurted, suddenly gripped by an inexplicable panic. My spine bristled. 'It is an heirloom,' I added weakly.

At this, the whole room fell about laughing again, and the women squealed with derision. One of them, I noticed, had her skirt hitched up high above her waist, and two drunken students were snapping at the elastic of her bloomers. I shot up from my chair and thrust my way through the throng as best I could to grab the jar back. This was going too far. With a sudden force of will, and an unaccustomed courage, I reached across to snatch it, but by now Farthingale had grabbed the jar from

237

the medical student and was holding it high above his head. I could see the sediment in the bottom swirling up, hiding the white organ completely from view.

Farthingale was now standing on the table. 'Shall I open it, everyone?' he yelled.

'Yes!' Many of the students, I now realised, were quite drunk, and I saw that the woman with the bloomers had now reached inside the trousers of one of the men and was fishing about inside. He was groaning.

'No!' I called pathetically, and lurched forward to snatch the jar. I managed to grasp it with one hand, but at that moment I trod on something slippery – doubtless a banana skin – and lost my grip. Farthingale pulled backwards and in the ensuing flurry of hands, the jar went flying through the air.

And smashed, horribly, and suddenly, at Kinnon's feet.

Pandemonium!

A horrendous, pungent stench rose up from the puddle on the floor, and the room exploded into immediate panic as everyone flung their hands to their faces, choking.

'Quick! Get out!' shrieked Popple through the coughing. 'Open the door, before we all suffocate!'

'Fetch water!' Ganney's voice choked. 'Dilute it!'

There was a great rowdy and chaotic surge for the door, and more slipping on banana skins, as screaming, shouting, coughing people, their eyes and noses running, tried to escape the fumes, but I just stood there, my eyes smarting from chemicals and tears, staring at the shattered fragments of glass and at my umbilical cord there on the floor. I groaned.

Kinnon, the medical student, was holding his nose and had crouched down to peer at it. Together, coughing, we stared at the thing.

'A strange mother you must have had, Mr Phelps,' he spluttered, 'to play a trick on you like that.'

'Trick?' I asked shakily. 'How is this a trick?' I felt very faint.

'All right, lad?' enquired Kinnon. 'Shall we get out of here?'

But I couldn't answer just then. Kinnon wiped his mouth and nose with the back of his sleeve and coughed some more.

Finally, 'How's it a trick?' I faltered. My voice was like that of the dying Mrs Phelps. Suddenly I had a vision of her blackened lung on the white sheet. She had thought it was her soul. 'How's it a trick?' I repeated.

We gazed at the thing together as the formaldehyde vapour steamed off it. Kinnon looked at me. 'Because that's no umbilical cord,' he said at last.

'What is it, then?' I managed queasily. I was still choking on the fumes that rose from it.

I need not have asked him, though, for anyone looking at it could have told me.

Help me, God.

'Steady on,' coughed Kinnon. 'She was probably just having a joke.' The base of my spine tingled in a violent, ghastly recognition: I reached across Kinnon and was violently sick into his lap.

Of the fifteen theological students due to be ordained the next morning, one was missing from the ceremonies. For I had fled.

The thing I had seen was a tail.

Wot I beg you to UNDERSTAND, Parson Phelps, the Contortionist wrote, *is that the Cercumstancis woz most partikular.*

CHAPTER 24

A PREGNANT PAUSE

The circumstances were unprecedented; unique, even. That was the world's verdict. Britain, as a nation, had entered a nine-month period of insanity. The first trimester was a shaky time, during which many marriages dissolved amid mutual recriminations.

'It's a war of the sexes,' declared Norman. He was right; the situation was serious. Not least because –

No; wait. I'm telling this all arse about face.

The night the twins made their pregnancy announcement – along with five million other women – I was so battered by alcohol and shock that I'd passed out, unable to digest the news. The next morning, I didn't have to: the nation had regurgitated it on my behalf. It turned out that the whole thing was an out-of-season April Fool's joke. Or, as Ron Harcourt put it, 'A load of hormonally induced female gobshite.'

Within twenty-four hours of the first scare in Glasgow, it had emerged that what we were witnessing was not a sudden wave of fertility emanating from Glasgow, but a sudden wave of mass hysteria, prompted by greed, prompted in turn by the five-million Euro Fertility Reward. The stammering psychologist had been right after all. Not a single pregnancy was real. They were all either deliberate hoaxes, or cases of delusion. And that was official. So official, that the Prime Minister said it three times in the House of Commons. 'Official, official, official.'

'Never in history,' jeered the Leader of the Opposition, 'has a government – or the media in its response – been so disastrously

hoodwinked! The words *headless* and *chickens* spring to mind!'
You couldn't help agreeing. A domino effect set off by one
woman, a certain Mrs Belinda Gillie, was to blame for the
epidemic of delusion and trickery. Her pregnancy – the first
case to be reported – had been a deliberate fake. Mrs Gillie
had persuaded her husband – a doctor – to falsify two tests.
She'd wanted the money from the reward.

'She was so insistent,' pleaded the shamefaced Dr Gillie on
television. 'I just wanted to make her happy.' He paused, desperate. 'You do things like that sometimes, to please someone.'

'Even if you know it's wrong?' jabbed in the reporter.

Dr Gillie hung his head. 'Well, sometimes, yes.'

When the news of Mrs Gillie's 'pregnancy' had spread,
first by word-of-mouth, then by rumour and local radio,
then nationally – other women had latched on to the idea,
subconsciously. All the pregnancies were either copycat hoaxes,
or the result of a contagious mass hysteria whose epicentre
was Glasgow. Everyone had been out for the Reward, was the
analysis. Mass hysteria was common among women in times
of crisis – varieties of Münchhausen's syndrome in particular.
It was practically *de rigueur*. It was a wonder, some speculated,
that it hadn't happened before.

'Still pregnant?' I asked the twins, after we'd switched off the
TV the next morning. They were looking pale and worried.

'Yes,' they insisted indignantly. 'Theirs may be fakes, but ours
are real.' Their voices, I noticed, were quite shaky.

'Well, there's a deadline on this one,' I said. 'Shall we lay
bets?'

They scowled at me, and I left for Clegg's farm. When I came
back that evening, they were still huddled together in bed in
their yellow dressing-gowns, whispering conspiratorially. There
was a special programme on TV about it that night; a national
poll had shown that, despite the quite incontrovertible medical
proof that the pregnancies were fake, 60 per cent of the women
who had claimed to be pregnant at the beginning of the scare
hung on to their delusion.

And therein lay a social problem, the TV experts said, on a massive scale. You couldn't get hold of a pregnancy-testing kit for love nor money, and all ultrasound scans were booked six months ahead. With delusional chaos – either euphoric or depressive – among the female population, male morale was hitting hitherto unplumbed depths. Primate sales had slumped since the mass hysteria struck, according to *Pets Today*, and many apes and monkeys – once beloved child-substitutes – were being found abandoned, now that their surrogate mothers were convinced they were expecting the real thing. In London, they'd set up a refuge for orphaned primates. That's where I'll go, I thought, if it all gets too much up here. Back to the jungle. The threat of Mrs Mann's litigation seemed more distant than ever now; she'd be pregnant with the rest of them.

The weeks passed, and sociologists and social psychologists from all over the globe flocked to Britain with their camcorders and their questionnaires to chart the progress of the new 'British disease'. A whole new industry seemed to spring from nowhere: suddenly there were phone-ins, ante-natal classes, public debates, pram sales, crisis-counselling services, baby books, hypnotherapy, aromatherapy, reflexology, foot massage, divorce negotiation, suicide counselling, and cuddly toys on every street corner. In the Stoned Crow, opinion was divided about how to handle the phenomenon of the mass hysteria. Keith Eaves, the weedy stammering psychologist who had been booed off the television on what became known as the Night of Madness, was now revered as an icon of common sense, and was appearing at charity events, photo opportunities and garden centres up and down the country. When he confessed to having considered abandoning his wife and emigrating to Finland at the beginning of the crisis, he was guaranteed instant hero status and offered his own TV show – *Breakthrough* – as counsellor to the nation. We watched *Breakthrough* regularly in the Crow.

'There are three natural responses to any p-p-p-p-predicament of this n-n-n-nature,' declared Dr Keith Eaves. 'F-f-f-f-ight, f-f-f-f-flight, c-c-c-c-ollusion, or n-n-n-n-non-reaction.'

'That's four,' I said.

'I reckon it's kinder to go along with it,' said Norman. He and Abbie had taken the line – right from the beginning – that it would be unfair to burst the twins' bubble. I disagreed; I thought it should be popped right away – if only I could pop it. I was a fighter.

'Of these responses,' Dr Eaves told us, 'c-c-c-c-ollusion is the most dangerous.'

'Hear that, Norman?' I said.

'Well, I happen to know that my wife *really is* pregnant,' said Ken Morpiton, addressing the TV indignantly. 'So what d'you say to that, Dr Eaves?' We all exchanged a look. Ken was nuts.

'I'm buggering off to my mum's for a few weeks,' confessed Ned Peat-Hove, taking the flight path. 'I can't stand it any more. All the nest-building that's going on. The wife's bought a buggy, and she's knitting like crazy.'

We all agreed – apart from Ken Morpiton – that it was exploitative of the babywear manufacturers to flood the market with all this baby paraphernalia that was going to be unusable. It'd all have to be exported to the Third World, like all that frozen beef a few years back.

'It's greed that started it,' said Billy Clegg. We all – apart from Morpiton – agreed.

'Subconscious, of course,' I added. 'We're dealing with severe delusion here.'

Ron Harcourt favoured the non-reactive approach, which Dr Eaves reckoned was the best way of dealing with the pregnancy delusion; neither confirm nor deny the fantasy. Not difficult, in his case. His Filipina, whom he'd ordered from a catalogue in the days when it was believed foreign women could be fertile in this country, was one of the few wives in Thunder Spit who wasn't claiming to be pregnant. That was because she refused to have sex with Ron any more. He wouldn't tell her he loved her. She couldn't live without love. It had been a bad transaction. She was going back to the Philippines; she

243

was fed up with him. She'd rather live in poverty with a real man, she said.

'Well, what if they really *do* have babies?' persisted Morpiton, shouting over the television. 'What if the doctors' pregnancy tests are wrong?' I exchanged a glance with Ron. Morpiton spotted it, and swung round to poke me in the chest accusingly. 'OK, Buck, so when did your two girlfriends last have a period?'

This was true; the monster pack of tampons Abbie had brought remained untouched.

'At least we won't be suffering any more of that PMT malarkey,' mused Billy Clegg. 'But it's funny, the way they all reckon they're due nine months to the day after the Reward was announced.'

Norman agreed that we were talking loony tunes. That five-million yo-yo Reward had certainly had an impact on the nation's psycho-wotsit. 'If you'll pardon my German.'

Not least in my own ménage. To celebrate the five million Euros – ten million, they reckoned, if they gave birth simultaneously – Roseblanche stole my credit card and went on a spree. Their bogus hormones had turned them into a couple of decorating maniacs, who felt the need to give my rented cottage a complete overhaul: Venetian blinds and a cloggy ochre paint-job in the downstairs loo, too close to shit-colour for comfort, peach and cranberry marble effect in the porch, reminiscent of dog-spleen, a Jackson Bollocky sort of wallpaper in the kitchen, three-piece suites with tassels and framed prints of arty-looking turnips bunging up the lounge. All my virtual Elvis concert tapes were relegated to the garage. As lust triangles go, it was expensive: within a month, they'd run me up a huge overdraft. Abbie, who took the collusion approach to their fake pregnancies, was the high priestess of taste, master-minding the whole operation from the John Lewis catalogue and cooking for the giant freezer she insisted I buy for her gals, to make honest women of them. The labour-saving device stood out in the garage, waiting to be fed with little cling-filmed dishes like a hungry gourmet animal. Meanwhile Norman would call round every day with his toolbox, exhorting me to call him Mr Fixit, and nailing me ever more securely into my coffin of domesticity. By the end of the second trimester, Thunder Spit was awash with waddling women padded with wind, cushions, or genuine fat. Rose and Blanche, who had opted for genuine fat, had swelled to such a size that they could barely squeeze through the doors; the way they shared the weight of their phantom pregnancies, it was like a triplet had joined them. They were still attractive, but only in the way that a sculpture fashioned out of pure lard might be. Like all the other hysterics in the town, they were enjoying their mock fecundity, and flaunting it. They'd all get together in a gaggle for the swimaerobics classes at the leisure centre, then converge on Pizza Hut, which had a special 'Eating for two' discount on pizzas.

'We were born to breed,' said Rose, as she and Blanche returned from their ante-natal session at the Baldicoot Medical Centre. There was another place that had cashed in on the crisis; it had bought St Nicholas's Church and converted it into a surgery, where it ran both pregnancy classes *and* a Denial Group.

'We want to start up a whole tribe,' explained Blanche.

'It's a primal urge,' said Rose authoritatively.

'Since the time of Noah,' added Blanche.

A primal urge which had soon rendered us flat broke. As we neared the second trimester of delusion, Rose and Blanche kept buying things we didn't need; endless electrical appliances – toasters, ghetto-blasters, bottle-warmers – for which Norman, the great colluder, had to come in and make a little shelf. 'I warned you,' he'd say cheerily, dusting down a high-chair or an ancient plastic bath-toy. 'Double trouble!' Then he'd leave.

The twins' bellies grew and grew, and eventually I was forced to vacate the emperor-sized bed for fear of being squashed to death in my sleep. I set up on the sofa-bed in the surgery, where the smell of praxin gave me queasy dreams – dreams in which the macaque Giselle would jabber at me, or whimper, or howl. Was her sudden re-appearance trying to tell me something? It was she, after all, and the terrible Mann woman, who had been the trigger for my arrival in Thunder Spit – a place of refuge, I reflected, which had quickly become a trap. I tried to analyse it. I pictured Giselle with her little upturned face and her hairy legs and her pink frock, but it still didn't dawn on me.

'A lot of m-m-m-m-men have been having anxiety d-d-d-d-dreams as we enter the f-f-final stages of the delusionary ph-ph-ph-phase,' warned Dr Keith Eaves on *Breakthrough*. 'Now I'm going to ask you to look at the c-c-c-c-components of your d-d-d-d-dreams carefully, and try to make c-c-c-c-connections. It might well be the k-k-k-key to the future well-being of your r-r-relationship.'

Time passed; the lambing season turned to the cat-flu season and then the abandoned-dog season; as we entered the third trimester, I dreamed about Giselle with increasing frequency, and tried to make sense of it, as Dr Eaves had suggested, but was still none the wiser. Then, when I was shaving one morning and reaching for the towel, I suddenly made the connection.

Giselle – monkeys – Eureka!

Monkeys!

My towel-holder! The Gentleman Monkey! Dr Ivanhoe Scrapie's manuscript! The sketch!

Money! How could I have been such a moron all this time?

Thank you, Dr Keith Eaves!

The Gentleman Monkey had become so much a part of the household furniture that I barely noticed him any more; he had become reduced to pure function. With all the upheaval over the pregnancy hysteria, I'd put Dr Ivanhoe Scrapie's treatise to one side. Abbie had given it to me the very day the news had broken about that Gillie woman in Glasgow. I'd been meaning to do something about it and then –

Christ. In all the madness about the twins being pregnant, I'd just forgotten about it. Now, I cursed myself for letting it slip to the back of my mind. Hadn't I decided that this monkey might be valuable? Where had I put the treatise? Christ knew. I turned the house upside-down looking for it, then discovered that the twins had shoved it under the kitchen sink, along with my animal-anatomy books and the bleach. I re-read it. It looked like this bloke really believed what he was saying. Just like Rose and Blanche really believed what they were saying. Not hoaxing: pure delusion. But the sketch of the Gentleman Monkey, and the claim that it was extinct – that was still exciting, as a prospect. A financial prospect. And a good reason to pack my blue suede shoes and hit the road.

As their due date approached, I noticed with some satisfaction that the twins were finally beginning to fret about money. Perhaps it was about to dawn on them that they might *not* be about to get the Reward. They even began work on the genealogy chart again – a project they'd abandoned as soon as they were up the imaginary spout. It was the morning they presented me with their four-point financial plan scrawled in lipstick on a sheet of greaseproof paper that I decided that now was as good a time as any to bugger off back to London, take a break from country life, and research the Gentleman Monkey. I'd trawled the Internet for more information, but despite endless E-mails from enthusiastic primate-watchers, I'd been unable to locate anyone who knew about a creature of that name. There's nothing like doing something in person.
I re-read the twins' list of objectives and sighed.

1. Get genealogy diploma and sell roots charts to Americans.
2. Apply for another grant increase from Dr Bugrov.
3. Flog all our old junk at the car-boot sale.
4. Give birth, and win ten million Euros! Hurray!

'I'm thinking of going down to London,' I said.
'Fine by us,' said Rose, holding up a little knitted jump-suit.
'Where are you going exactly?' asked Blanche, putting the finishing touches to a mobile of dangling pastel bunny rabbits and bulbous butterflies.

'To the Natural History Museum,' I said. 'To discover the origins of our increasingly fascinating towel-holder.'

They looked at each other then, and made a face.

'Funny, we've just been talking about that old thing,' said Rose, sniggering. '*Vis-à-vis* our financial plan.'

But she wouldn't tell me what was funny. I went upstairs and packed my things.

'Well, come straight back,' they called after me as I left. 'We're due the day after tomorrow!'

Along with twenty million other women, I thought, chucking the keys to my Nuance in the air like they do in films, but failing to catch them.

I left with the sound of their stereo laughter ringing in my ears.

CHAPTER 25

ON THE THRESHOLD OF
THE FUTURE

Nature red in tooth and claw: who has not witnessed its very particular horrors? Who has not observed Mr Jaws the Beetle crunching up poor Mr Bobby Centipede alive, or Mrs Itsy-Bitsy Spider cannibalising her husband only seconds after congress, or Mr Moggy Cat (Here, Pussy, here Pussikins!) torturing and disembowelling the innocent rodent, Miss Squeaky Shrew? Call it bad design if you will, but this is life!

So the idea of a natural carnivore such as *Homo sapiens* reverting to the allegedly herbivorous diet of his most ancient, primitive ancestors, on the grounds of 'humanity', is no more and no less than an absurd and sentimental whim. And worse, an argument without logic! Take it to its obvious conclusion, Mademoiselle Scrapie, *ma petite chérie*, and you will discover yourself not stepping into your vegetable patch for fear of crushing a garden slug, and holding your breath, for fear of inhaling an innocent germ! If Mr Darwin is right, then surely, the more we evolve, the more frequent, demanding, wide-ranging and imaginative should our visits to the butcher's be! *This* is civilisation!

So run the thoughts of Monsieur Cabillaud, the Belgian chef, as he stirs his pot of guinea-pig broth for Her Majesty's luncheon. Yet he is grateful, paradoxically enough, for the illogical argument and sentimental whim that led Miss Violet Scrapie to lose her wits and boot him out of Madagascar Street. For what turn of events could have engendered a happier outcome?

Being head chef at Buckingham Palace is not to be sneezed

249

at. Jacques-Yves Cabillaud does not sneeze. He breathes in the sweetly scented air of simmered guinea-pig and freedom. Freedom to, and freedom from! What can be more sublime a thing than to have risen in a few short months through the ranks of Her Majesty's servants, and now to be master of the best kitchen in the land, at a time when one of the greatest ever of Victoria's famous feasts is *en pleine préparation*. Never more so than today. The Banquet approaches, and the Palace kitchen plays host to an odoriferous whirlwind of activity: filleting, sizzling, chopping, basting, kneading, and whisking in readiness for the event, which is, dear reader, none other than the Celebration of Evolution Banquet!

Long live Charles Darwin, guest of honour and excuse for all this kerfuffle!

Cabillaud smiles to himself. Will Mr Darwin recall him now? Will the great zoologist in whose honour the Banquet is being held, recognise in the rounded, confident form of the Queen's head chef the vestiges of the seasick but ambitious young cook who once travelled with him on the *Beagle*? Unlikely, but tantalisingly possible. Darwin, after all, is an expert on the subject of evolution. And what is Cabillaud's life-history, if not a dramatic example of personal transformation over time? What indeed is Cabillaud, dare he suggest it himself, if not a shining example of Nature's quest for – and attainment of – perfection?

''Ere. Take zis.' Shoving his wooden spatula at a callow *sous-sous-sous-chef*, Jacques-Yves Cabillaud points the minion in the direction of the steaming broth, and begins to pace the kitchen, reviewing for the umpteenth time his plans for the Banquet. There is to be a meringue castle, the preparation of which requires fifty dozen eggs. There are to be a thousand jellied eels. A tub of mongoose pâté. Five thousand oysters. Poached desert weasel. A whole field's-worth of strawberries, to be glazed and placed inside individual puff-pastry moulds. Grilled dolphin. The biggest fruit salad ever made in the civilised world. Jackal mousse *à la triomphe*. Kebabbed cat. Fifteen hundred individualised *amuse-gueules* featuring zebra mince and *coulis de tomates*.

Not to mention the Time-Bomb. The magnificent casing of which is being steered into position as we speak.

'A bit to ze left!' orders Cabillaud, rubbing his hands in anticipation.

'Yes, sir!'

'Now to ze right a little!'

'No sooner said than done, sir!'

'And now you will PUSH!'

The hefty *sous-chef* heaves with his bristling fore-arms, and the giant clam shell – measuring a good fifteen feet across – wobbles dangerously, then topples into its pre-ordained horizontal atop the specially designed trolley. Jacques-Yves Cabillaud surveys the clam, a big rocky bowl of calcium deposits, with the critical eye of a connoisseur. It is rumoured that this clam once housed a pearl, a pearl so extraordinary that it has been squirrelled away to a secret pearl room, to which only the Royal Hippo has the key. But Cabillaud doesn't give a hoot about the pearl. It is the shell that is his concern – and its safe arrangement on the trolley.

Why, dear reader?

Because it is to become part of his greatest work of culinary art to date – a work so ambitious that it will eclipse even the glory of his published tome, *Cuisine Zoologique: une philosophie de la viande*, that's why!

The bristle-armed *sous-chef* now stands back, sweating, and awaits further instructions from his master.

'Now you will scrub it clean until it is gleaming!' commands Cabillaud, patting its bumpy surface. 'Until I can see my own face in it!'

'Yes, sir!'

Everything about the Time-Bomb must be perfect. Including its delicate mechanics. When Cabillaud had first heard of the extraordinary Mechanical Millipede, he sent out search parties to locate its engineer, an acknowledged genius.

251

''E must 'elp me,' Cabillaud insisted. ''E will understand. Only ze best minds in ze 'ole country can do justice to my *idée*.'

It was in this spirit of culinary idealism that the engineer, Mr Hillber, of the Travelling Fair of Danger and Delight, was eventually tracked down, lured away from his regular work in exchange for a fat fee, installed in the servants' quarters, and roped into Cabillaud's grand plan. A major ingredient of which – the giant clam – now stands before Cabillaud, its rocky exterior about to receive the scrubbing of its life, its delicately coloured inner shell hidden, but gleaming with promise. The promise of secrets. The promise of a surprise within a surprise within a surprise.

'What's for pudding?' Cabillaud used to ask his mother as a boy.

'Wait-and-see pudding,' the reply always came.

Amid the clatter of pots and pans, and the hiss of fragrant steam, Cabillaud is once again eyeing the clam critically. It suddenly reminds him of his unhappy days of seasickness and seaweed aboard the *Beagle*, and he shudders.

'All zis seaweed must vanish completely!' he commands. 'If zer is one sing I 'ate and detest, it is ze seaweed!'

'Yes, sir!'

Kashoum, kashoum, kashoum, goes the wire brush, as scraps of stinking weed, along with rotting mussels, limpets and barnacles fall to the floor. Kashoum, kashoum.

Yes: the Time-Bomb requires extraordinary levels of commitment, negotiation, inspiration, technique, fervour, and plain honest elbow-grease. Pistons have been discussed at length, ink diagrams sketched on linen tablecloths, pros and cons weighed, decisions reached, abandoned, and resurrected; promises made and reneged upon; plans hatched and scuppered; hair torn out, nails bitten, brandy drunk, sleep lost, and floors angrily spat upon. *Vive la création*!

'Ah, my dear Hillber!' calls Cabillaud, spotting the Mechanical Millipede engineer. Hillber – so small and wiry he might almost be fabricated from a coat-hanger – skips past a row of pastry-makers in a cloud of flour, and comes to shake Cabillaud's hand warmly. Then he gestures to introduce his companion, also emerging from the flour: he is a sharp and frostbitten-looking man sporting a bow tie.

'Mr Edward Ironside. I believe you have met in the past. He arrived this morning.'

'Welcome, my dear friend!' says Cabillaud, smiling in recognition. It has been many years since they last met, at Dr Scrapie's, when Ironside was a mere stripling, an apprentice taxidermist. It was he who supervised the Arctic iceberg and its safe arrival in the Scrapie ice-house, and now his expertise in the dual disciplines of freezing and taxidermy make him an invaluable member of the team.

'Excellent,' says Cabillaud, shaking Ironside's freezing hand.

'Shall we zen begin? We 'ave ze problem of ze breathing to discuss.'

'And the woman?' asks Ironside. 'The artiste? Has she been informed of our requirements?'

'Yes, indeed,' confirms Hillber. 'She volunteered herself – begged, even – to be a part of it. She has asked me to report that she is honoured to do anything we require.' He pauses, then lowers his voice to an excited whisper. 'Anything, *within or even beyond* reason!'

'*Merveilleux,*' beams Cabillaud, gratified but not surprised at the reaction of the artiste concerned. Who would not give their eye teeth to be a part of his great creation?

'Shall we proceed, zen, gentlemen?' Cabillaud motions them towards a table upon which sketches and diagrams of the Time-Bomb and its audacious contents are pinned. Within minutes, they are deep in discussion, and Hillber is sketching furiously.

'A system of holes?' he suggests.

'Or a periscope solution?' wonders Ironside.

'Perhaps a hosepipe?' offers Cabillaud.

'Or,' ventures Hillber, 'more daring but more aesthetically discreet – a miniature inflatable balloon?'

'Why yes!' The man is indeed a genius!

Kashoum, kashoum, kashoum.

'Zer! Over zer!' yells Cabillaud, glancing up from Hillber's latest drawing and pointing to a barnacle half-concealed beneath the ridged lip of the clam.

The *sous-sous-sous-chef* looks up anxiously from his brushing. 'Yes, sir.'

Kashoum, kashoum, kashoum.

Is it not something, to be master of one's own kitchen, the best kitchen in the whole of Britain?

A something which Cabillaud, who once served seaweed gratin with human vomit in it aboard the *Beagle*, is entitled to celebrate.

And celebrate he will!

Kashoum, kashoum, kashoum.

Jusswannabe
Yurteddyber
Puddachaynarannamahnekkah an leedmi anywayah . . .

Blaggerfield, Norton's Krig, Wipperby. The Nuance purred its way down the motorway, and I yodelled along with Elvis. But it wasn't long before the sound of my own voice began to grate on me, and my singing turned to yawning, and then silence. Outside the car, the green grew greyer, the skyscrapers taller as I journeyed south. It had been almost a year since I'd left London, I realised with a jolt. Christ. For the first time in ages I thought of the surgery in Tooting Bec, and then I suddenly remembered Mr Mann, and the thousand Euros, and Giselle in her little pink frock. And Holly and the body-bag and the letter. And the phrase 'Would not hesitate'. I shuddered. Odd, that I should have left because of a monkey, and was now returning because of another one.

I glanced at the photo of the Gentleman Monkey that I'd perched on the dashboard. I'd thought of taking him with me to London, to show him to an expert at the Museum in person – but then dismissed the idea. He was too bulky. And possibly – exciting thought, this – far too valuable. So I'd borrowed the twins' polaroid camera and taken a few shots. They hadn't come out very well, but I was in a hurry. This was the best one, but it still didn't do him justice. The ruffed shirt and the red pantaloons didn't help; they were the kind of clothes an organ-grinder's monkey might wear. They demeaned him, somehow. I say 'him', but it still wasn't clear to me whether the creature had been male or female. He was dressed in male clothes, but the genitals had been completely done away with. Although Scrapie's treatise claimed the creature was male, you had to take anything he said with a shovelful of salt. A madman with a vision is a dangerous thing. I thought about his bizarre hypothesis: *A New Theory of Evolution,* he'd called it. Nothing if not grandiose. Maybe the idea didn't seem so crazy at the time, I thought: the Victorians didn't know about DNA. And it was another century or so before blokes like Dawkins and Gould evolved.

Looking at the photos now, that feeling of excitement I'd had when I first saw the monkey started rummaging away again. He really was some specimen. I realised that I was curious about this weird, almost human creature in a way I hadn't been since I was a kid, when I unearthed three-quarters of a desiccated fox in the garden, and kept rat spleens in the fridge.

At midday I stopped for lunch at a service station at Grommet Hill. While I was waiting for my order, I spread out the photographs in front of me and inspected them one by one. I also had my eye on the waitress; it wasn't often these days that you spotted a young woman who wasn't sporting the obligatory pregnant belly. She wore a badge on her tit that said I'M PAULA, HOW CAN I HELP YOU? When she came back to my table with my chicken and chips, plus side-salad, I peered at her chest closely.

'Sorry,' I said, when she showed signs of embarrassment. 'I'm dyslexic.'

'It says "I'm Paula, how can I help you?",' she said.

'By getting me a Coke, Paula, my darling,' I told her. And gave her my Elvis look, the one that's designed to make them melt with desire. But she hadn't noticed my curled lip; she was looking at the photographs.

'Aaaw, isn't he sweet,' she said, in a gooey voice. 'I do love children. I've got a chimp. How old is he? Have you had him long?'

Christ, I thought, snatching up the pictures. The whole nation is insane.

'He's dead,' I snapped.

A tear instantly welled in her eye. 'Oh, I am so sorry!' she said, touching my arm. 'How did you – lose him?'

'I killed him,' I said, remembering Giselle. 'I'm allowed to. I'm a vet.'

That sent her packing.

Betty Botter bought some butter . . .

Before I left the north by steam train I said a prayer on the platform: Please God, make this a wild goose chase. As we chugged and stopped at every small town on the way to London, I cheered myself up as best I could with my tongue-twisters, and read the names of the towns we stopped at: Snail's Rump, Hinkley Firth, Knaveswood-under-Gab, Blaggerfield. By the time we reached Grommet Hill, my mind was awash with a flotsam of Viking balderdash.

An elbow kept jamming into my ribs; it belonged to a woman who was knitting a strange pair of leggings for her son. She told me he was a member of a dance troupe. The front gusset was the size of a horse's nosebag.

'He's quite a man,' she said, reading my thoughts, and burst out laughing.

I laughed with her for politeness's sake, but my laughter was hollow. If a male object is all it takes, I thought, then I am human, too.

256

'What makes a man, in your opinion, madam?' I asked her suddenly.

'That he's a civilised gent is all I ask,' she said, her face looking suddenly weary. 'That he says his pleases and his thank-yous, and if the need arises, he would lay down his life to protect another.'

I scratched my flea-bites for a while, lost in thought.

When I had told Kinnon my story two nights earlier, he had diagnosed madness, and administered first Epsom salts, then castor oil, then laudanum. Now, as the steam train chugged though the flatlands of Northumberland on its journey south, I could feel all three remedies beginning to wear off, and my heart began to shrink in cowardly trepidation.

Norton's Krig, Wipperby, Brill. The trees grew taller, the landscape lusher as we journeyed south. We stopped for half an hour at Nobb-on-Humber, where the sun came out and threw a shaft of sudden wonder into the carriage, and the knitting-woman offered me a bite of her chicken leg. Politely, I said no. I was weak with hunger, I told her, but had to starve today on account of my tapeworm. It was at that point that she spotted my fake dog-collar beneath my scarf, and apologised for her crudeness *vis-á-vis* the mentioning of her son's 'thingummyjig'.

'Not at all, madam,' I said, in my parson's voice. 'A mother's pride is a blessed thing.'

'He's doing *Swan Lake* at the Royal Ballet,' she said, relieved that I had not taken offence. One plain, one pearl. 'He's not a swan, he's one of them other birds.'

A crake? A cormorant? A herring gull? I wondered, remembering the sea-birds wheeling in the skies of Thunder Spit, and Jared, my carrier pigeon, now asleep in his cage, covered with a cloth. I would sooner place my faith in a humble bird than in the Penny Post.

Fib's Wash, Crowtherly, Axelhaunch. I slept fitfully and awoke half-crazed, remembering my dread quest.

'Are you all right, dear?' the woman asked me suddenly, near Gladmouth, jamming her elbow in my ribs as she jerked at her skein. 'You're trembling.'

257

I said nothing, but pulled my coat tighter around me, like a shell.

London at last: at St Pancras Station, the train disgorged me and I stood on the platform, fingering my whelk on its string. It was indeed soothing, I reflected, to carry the ocean round one's neck at all times. Tommy must have known, when he gave it to me, how much I would miss the sound of crashing waves. I will go nowhere now, I thought, without my precious whelk.

I put it to my ear. Slosh, slosh.

But after a minute standing there on the platform I gave up, and nestled the shell back in the warmth of my greatcoat next to my crucifix rum-flask.

The platform was noisy. My heart was skinned.

'You must forget this nonsense,' Kinnon had insisted, pouring me more castor oil. After my jar had smashed, he had taken me back to his lodgings, and I had shown him the evidence of my feet.

Never, I thought, as we gazed at them together, had they looked hairier or more deformed. 'You need rest, and sleep,' prescribed Kinnon.

He was wrong. I had learned my lesson. What I needed was the truth.

I can't, I protested to myself.

But I will, said the creature within.

I left Jared with the pigeon man at St Pancras, saying I would return in a week to send my letter back north.

In Paddington, I found a boarding-house; the woman who ran it obviously had a sixth sense about her lodgers' finances, because she warned me she'd always need the money in advance. The place was dismal and filthy – a far cry from my cosy bachelor rooms back in Hunchburgh, where Mrs Fooney's motherly warmth permeated the kitchen along with the smell of baking bread and poppyseed.

I slept with cotton wool in one ear and my whelk pressed

against the other. The next morning I found a tick on my shin. I burnt it, but its jaws remained in my flesh.

'And no more screaming in your sleep!' the landlady commanded the next morning, ignoring my mention of the parasite. Unlike the pillow-chested Mrs Fooney, her bodiced torso was as flat and hard-looking as a beetle's carapace, and her eyes were small green marbles of mistrust. 'This isn't Bedlam.'

It was some other little Hell, though. I paid the woman for another night, and she put a mark in her ledger. I knew for a fact that I wasn't the only screamer. Parson Phelps always used to tell me that London was a place where young men from the provinces quickly go insane.

'Or a place they flee to once their madness is a fact,' he'd add darkly.

I found a little coffee gazebo in Regent's Park where I sat, absorbing it all: the deals struck, the philanthropy, the pimping, the Empire-boasting. In the end, homesick for the ocean, I wandered to the docks, but this wasn't water as I knew it. I had seen many a ship out at sea, her sails bloated with wind, but what I saw here were stranded sea-creatures, their great hulls cracked with sunlight, their souls trapped by gang-planks and wheelbarrows and ropes.

As I left my lodging-house the next morning, a fellow lodger joined me; he introduced himself as Hikes. Together we strolled to my coffee gazebo in Regent's Park, and there he listened to my tourist's tales.

'You're nervous,' he said, eyeing me up.

'It's nothing,' I said.

'Here.' He proffered me some brandy in a hip-flask – little knowing what I carried in my hollow crucifix. 'Drink this,' he said. 'Then do what you really came here to do.'

'And you?' I asked.

'I bought an hour's worth of fat whore and gambled the rest.'

We sipped our coffee.

'I'm going to find a man,' I blurted at last, smashing my

cup down on to the saucer and spilling half my coffee in my jitteriness. He raised an eyebrow. 'And I am going to make him tell me the truth.'

'Go on,' said Hikes, shoving his liquor-flask under my nose. 'Get that inside you.'

'I'm normally teetotal,' I lied. But I took it from him and swallowed a large gulp of brandy and it glowed in my upper body like religion.

'The truth about what?' Hikes called after me as I left.

In Portobello Road I stopped and made some purchases: a waistcoat, a pair of scissors, a needle and thread, a small revolver. I mended the waistcoat, and slipped the gun into its pocket. Then I headed for the centre of the city.

That bit of London near the Museum has always been Hell, parking-wise. I'd forgotten that. It was pissing with rain; I eventually found a space in a nine-Euros-a-day multi-storey, then bought a paper and stopped for coffee in a gloomy little roadside caff called The Gazebo. The waiter who brought me my *cappuccino* slopped it into the saucer and didn't apologise; he was wearing a Walkman. My paper reported that hoax calls to the ambulance service had risen by 50 per cent, as the phantom pregnancies reached their barren and inevitable conclusions. In most cases, according to the report, it was an accumulation of wind, and the women felt physically much better once they had released it. Pity the ozone layer, I thought. In the distance I could hear the sirens.

'Intense depression is bound to ensue,' it quoted the ubiquitous Dr Keith Eaves, now the undisputed therapist to the nation's buffeted psyche, 'as we all undergo a period of mourning for what never was.' They'd cleaned up his stammer for him in print. 'In *Swan Lake*, the swan flutters before it dies. What we are witnessing here, in a final act of yearning, disappointment and acceptance, is the dying dance of *Homo Britannicus*.'

You had to hand it to him; he had a way with words.

The article also made the point that the inevitable anti-climax of the largest attack of mass hysteria on record was causing chaos on a practical level, and genuine emergency cases were being forced to wait up to 47 per cent longer than stipulated by their health charter. Some poor sods had even died as a result, I read. Now there was going to be a one-hundred-Euro fine for every hoax call. Enter a small industry in the form of cowboy midwives offering phoney services for bogus events. I thought of Rose and Blanche, with their Ovaltine and their novelty straws and their pathetic industriousness, sighed, and shoved my cup and saucer to one side. The coffee was pure swill.

I left.

In the underground walkway, I fought my way through crowds of Saturday shoppers, street hawkers, homeless and sightseers. I followed the signs like an obedient tourist, climbed a flight of pissy-smelling concrete stairs, and emerged in the open air, next to a life-sized fibreglass triceratops guarding the Museum.

Pray God this is a wild goose chase, I murmured as I approached the vast building. As I entered the arched portals and stepped into the gloom, I thought of Jonah. The Museum's belly was filled with footsteps and echoes and whispers. I looked above me. The cornices crawled with ornamental tiles, and the stained-glass windows refracted and smithereened their colours, stippling the varnished walls with haphazard designs; it was not a whale, I realised, but an Aladdin's cave, monstrous in its grandiosity, not a surface left undecorated. I know what Parson Phelps would have said. He had always hated a decorated surface. Something about the Devil finding work for idle hands. Something about the worship of graven images. He would have made the sign of the cross.

I reached inside my greatcoat, where my hand brushed against the crucifix and the whelk. Still there.

261

HER MAJESTY'S ANIMAL KINGDOM, said the copper-plate writing on the notice before me. EXHIBITS ON LOAN FROM HER MAJESTY THE QUEEN'S COLLECTION. Following the direction of the sign's pointing finger, I walked nervously into the gloom, my footsteps echoing on the ceramic tiles.

I could feel the eyes before I saw them. They stared from all directions, baleful and disturbing. My spine was bristling, and I felt my heartbeat betray my fear. And then I saw the beasts, and a chill ran through me.

They stood in stiff rows, staring at me from plinths and pedestals.

'Good God!' I breathed. I closed my eyes for a second, hoping that when I opened them again, the vision would have disappeared. But it had not.

The creatures were all wearing clothes.

A giraffe in a long tent-like dress with a fleur-de-lis design towered above me. A lion in pantaloons and braces, wearing a top hat, crouched next to it, ready to pounce. A wildebeest in a white nightgown and matching nightcap stood fixing me with its glare, its hooves clasped in a position reminiscent of prayer. What frozen forest of horror had I entered? Feathers gleamed beneath frilled shirts and frock-coats; fur was flattened beneath petticoats and pinafore dresses. An ostrich wore a frilled hat, like the one Mrs Sequin used to wear to church. A cow sported spectacles. A raccoon in a cassock wielded a walking-stick. The human eyes stared, both knowing and blank.

'A travesty,' I murmured, half-choking with horror. 'A travesty of Nature!'

Scrabbling in my knapsack for my pen and notebook, I copied down the name of the taxidermist from a plinth – Dr Ivanhoe Scrapie – and fled from the Museum like a bat out of Hell.

Christ, what a whopper of a building; big enough, I reckoned, to house umpteen wide-bodied aircraft if the need arose. After queuing up for ages, I had to pay nine Euros fifty to get in, though I noticed that, with a family ticket, it would have been a lot cheaper. The place resounded with the echoes of a million children oohing and aahing in the shadow of a huge brontosaurus skeleton. I hadn't been to the Natural History Museum since I was a kid. I was in for a shock. No stuffed animals, for a start. Apart from the brontosaurus skeleton, it was all acrylic reconstructions and interactive hands-on stuff. A group of schoolkids suddenly poured in and started yelling obscenities. To my left, an ineffectual-looking bloke in a mauve tracksuit put up a hand and called, 'Yo, kids! Let's have a bit of shush, please!'

They ignored him, and carried on yelling and kicking their Coke cans about, and making silly faces. He was their teacher.

The primates were upstairs, in an exhibition all about the evolution of man.

In 14 Madagascar Street, Belgravia, Violet Scrapie is dressing for dinner, and picturing the capture of a whale by harpoon. She has recently seen an Italian *gravura* of such a scene, in which the artist, Rafael Ortona, disturbingly managed to show in the creature's wildly swivelling eye all the agony and indignity of the blubber being stripped from its still-living flesh. In her imagination, she colours in the heart-breaking detail that Signor Ortona has delicately omitted from his *gravura*, yet so vividly evoked: the sea heaves red with blood, while beneath the water-line, the smaller fragments of blubber and flesh float down into the depths.

Nature, like Violet Scrapie, loathes the sight of wasted protein: these fragments will feed whole armies of sea-life. She sees the great sea-cucumber, a living ocean turd, laying claim. She observes the wily scissoring of the lobster's claws as it snatches a hunk of blubber from a passing quillsnapper. And the thuggish gang of sharks attacking the carcass and stripping whole sections of it to the bone as the skeleton is hauled off. Violet knows,

263

having read it in one of her father's zoological treatises, that depending on the swiftness of the action, and the temperature of the surrounding waters, the creature will emit vast quantities of steam from its flesh. Yes, steam. This is the effect of the heart's great pounding motion as the mammal enters into a state of shock, pain and fright.

Imagine!

Imagine, too, how the blood then boils. How the flesh itself is heated, and the bones cook. And how the whole brute edifice is transmogrified into a grotesquely floating stew, a loose scaffolding of hot bones dragged through the choppy waves to Hunchburgh, where it is dismantled much as a ship itself can be dismantled in a shipyard, and the merchants dispatch its cleaned components – ribs, jawbone, tailbone, skull, in tiny quantities relative to the whale's size, to the haberdashers and hosiers and couturiers of the Nation.

It is said that the bodices and hats and fashion accessories of Queen Victoria contain so much whalebone that two skeletons'-worth have not been enough to feed her rapacious wardrobe.

Violet bends asthmatically for the corset, reflecting with some resentment on the Royal Hippo's hosiery supplies. No stingy annual clothes allowance for *her!*

(Should whalebone be boycotted? she wonders suddenly. Why, surely it should!)

The contrast, Violet reflects, is stark: Victoria – wife, Queen, Ruler of Empire, owner of two skeletons worth of whalebone, and mother to a whole litter of blue-blooded royal babes. Violet Scrapie, distressed spinster. Violet Scrapie, daughter of the eminent Dr Scrapie, stuffer of animals By Her Majesty's Appointment. Violet Scrapie, prisoner in her own home:

> *A violet by a mossy bank,*
> *Half hidden from the eye,*
> *Fair as a star*
> *When only one is shining in the sky.*

Huh. *When only one.* And when there are more? Eh, Mr Wordsworth? Ugly as a blasted moon.

On a more positive note, Violet's mission, *The Fleshless Cook*, has been progressing in leaps and bounds. Only this morning, she has taken pride in the preparation of a hearty chestnut soup containing both cinnamon and parsley. Furthermore, she has finished making her last batch of walnut ketchup, invented asparagus and lemon pudding, made a dozen pastry ramekins, fried two giant Jerusalem artichokes for tomorrow's dinner, and perfected a recipe for baked Spanish onions which makes Mrs Beeton's version look laughably naive, and indeed almost inedible. All seventeen stone and five pounds of flesh that is Violet Scrapie stands now in the bedroom in her vast bloomers, staring down at the complex structure that lies at her feet. The Royal Hippo and I have little in common, she reflects: just womanhood, Dr Ivanhoe Scrapie, and whalebone. Or to be more precise, the miracle of soft engineering that is the corset.

Like a clockwork ectoskeletal creature of the deep, Violet now begins the task of assembling the shell of wire and padded whalebone around her stupendous body. First she heaves the heavy black sheath up to her gigantic hips, then twists it so that it lies symmetrically around her pelvis. There are wire hooks that must be aligned, and made to cling together like wrung hands. To do this, she must first draw in her breath and lift her rib-cage so that her waist is elongated, insofar as is possible, a celebration of cause and effect, soon to be reined in by structure. Each breast is the size of a human baby. They quiver and shake, setting up a rolling judder across the great vista of her belly, as – whup! – she hauls up and clasps together, at waist-level, the two sides of the encasing pod.

What are the alternatives? Bamboo? she wonders, exasperated at the effort of it all. Or wire?

'Fasting,' whispers a ghostly matriarchal voice. 'The answer, Vile, is to consume less food.'

'Bugger off, Mother,' mutters Violet, wrenching her carapace into position and tugging at the cords.

265

Three floors below, a small man with an odd gait and unusual shoes is peering at the numbers on the doors. He, too, has little in common with Queen Victoria, apart from his diminutive stature. Like the head of our great British Empire, he measures five foot two, but there any resemblance to the reigning monarch ends abruptly, would you not agree, gentle reader? After all, Queen Victoria does not have a mutilated coccyx, nor does she wear orthopaedic shoes, or a phoney dog-collar, or house a temperamental tapeworm, or harbour fleas; nor does she have the organs known, in polite society, as a male object and related accoutrements (cock and balls to you), and nor does she urgently need to discover the truth of her origins – because Queen Victoria has a family tree that stretches back centuries, adorned with heraldic plates of Huguenot shields and Plantagenet memorabilia, Battenburg gewgaws and Tudor roses, and Tobias Phelps (for it is he) has nothing but the evidence of his own deformity, and a piece of pickled human flesh, re-bottled for him in Hunchburgh by a medical student named Kinnon.

To read the brass-plated numbers on the doors, he has to squint.

Number two.

His deep-set eyes are wild, haunted.

Number four.

His face is thin-lipped, wrinkled, sad.

Number six.

He is mumbling feverishly to himself. A sharp ear might make out the words to a tongue-twister about a woman called Betty Botter buying some butter but finding it bitter and not being able to put it in her batter.

Number eight.

He clasps his frock-coat about him tightly.

Number ten.

He fingers a whelk shell.

Number twelve.

'Pray God this is a wild goose chase,' he murmurs.

Number fourteen.

266

Home of Dr Ivanhoe Scrapie.

Tobias Phelps mounts the steps, and performs a sudden upward leap to ring the bell.

Ding, dong!

Suet, prone on Violet's eiderdown, lifts his head and yaps feebly at the doorbell. He has not been himself at all lately; his vegetarian diet has weakened him immeasurably.

'Oh, botheration!' mutters Violet Scrapie. She's still struggling with her corset, and wondering about whalebone.

Suet yaps.

The bell rings again. Ignoring its insistent jangle in the hope that her father will remember it is Mrs Jiggers' day off and answer it himself, Violet abandons her buttoning and lacing in order to fix her late mother's jet choker around her neck. Despite the jeweller's recent adjustments, it's still a fraction too tight, as though the Laudanum Empress is trying, by whatever means she can, to throttle her disappointing daughter from beyond the grave. Which indeed she is.

'Please, Mother,' croaks Violet, who has lately become increasingly aware of her ghostly presence in the house. 'A little less pressure!'

And the choker's grip is instantly relaxed.

'Chop, chop!' the phantom is bossing. 'Answer the bloody door, child! The future depends on it!'

'Did you say something, Mother?'

The doorbell rings again, wildly this time. Violet Scrapie shuffles over to the window, irritated by the noise, her white cotton bloomers swishing about her puckered thighs, and peers down on to the street, where a sulphurous yellow glow leaks from the gas lamps across the slush. A small figure directly below her, on the front doorstep, is hopping about in wide pantaloons. Taxidermy, like chess, attracts a strange breed of men, she reflects. Not artists, not scientists, neither fish nor fowl nor duck-billed platypus. Often, Violet has noticed, they have some kind of deficiency, physical or moral, which they must feel can be remedied by stuffing straw and sawdust into cured skin,

267

and sipping Amontillado sherry at meetings of the Zoological Society.

Could the stranger be one such specimen?

No. He could not.

She realises this instantly, as the man looks up at her, and their eyes lock.

What round eyes he has, she notices. And what thin lips! Now where has she seen that face before? A peculiar and not unpleasant sensation – one Violet has seldom felt before, and certainly never with such exquisite intensity – insinuates its way into the most private interstices of her corset.

She knows this man.

She knows him!

'We have cause for celebration!' murmurs the Laudanum Empress, observing her daughter, and interpreting the delicate feelings playing across her face as only a dead mother can.

'A distressed spinster no longer, perhaps?' she shouts.

'Mother?' breathes Violet. 'Are you there? Did you speak?'

'A distressed spinster no longer, perhaps, I said!' yells the phantom. But Violet hears nothing but a buzz as she sinks heavily on her bed, suddenly aware that she is still in a state of undress. Her whalebone creaks, as the feeling she cannot identify creeps its way further into her –

Her loins, reader. Not to beat about the bush.

Should she go downstairs, and find out who he is? And why that face looks so familiar?

'Not yet,' Violet murmurs, putting her hand to her breast to calm the pounding of her heart. 'Clothes first.'

And she begins to rummage in her wardrobe, in search of her best red frock.

I have since asked myself: is love an instinct, or something learned? Is it part of Nature itself, or a reaction that comes from the way in which we are nurtured? What makes one man seek out the familiar, while another will travel the world in search of an exotic mate? What propels us? I do not have the answers. All I know is that I looked up at her, and our eyes locked.

That she was clad in nothing but a corset.

And that she was magnificent.

And that my heart shrieked within me, and that my tapeworm twisted my guts into a cruel knot of longing and delight and fear.

Yes, gentle reader: we met in the most particular of circumstances.

The cercumstancis woz most partikuler.

The nite of the storm, she wrote, *wen he took me in his arms, I did not no WOT he wos, or WHO. It woz the next day, or the next, that Higgins came and litte a candel, and I saw the Creetcha for the furst tyme.*

Meet a GENTLEMAN, sez Higgins. And larfs.

Remember, Parson PHELPS, I had no book lernin, and no understandin of SYENSE, and at that time I nowd nuthin of MISTER DARWIN'S BELEEFS.

All I nowd, woz that I had ikkstreemlie bad LUKKE in LUVVE.

CHAPTER 26

DARWIN'S PARADOX

I was still reeling from the sight of the magnificent corseted woman – reality or apparition of my crazed mental state, I knew not which – when the door of 14 Madagascar Street opened abruptly, and I found myself face to face with a thin, grey-bearded, grumpy-looking gent whose mouth appeared to be bristling with pins. In his right hand, he was wielding a hoof.

'Dr Scrapie?' I stammered.

'Yes?' With a gesture of disgust, he spat out his pins into his hand and settled his eyes on me, where they blazed uncomfortably. The shirt beneath his frock-coat was splattered with what might have been cochineal, or blood. A hole gaped in the sleeve of his jacket. 'Well, young man? What is it?'

'May I come in, sir?'

'What for?' he barked. 'I'm busy. State the nature of your business, sir, or bugger off.'

My heart began to thump crazily under my ribs. I must persevere, I thought. I have come this far. What I have started, I will finish. Betty Botter bought some butter. Peter Piper picked a peck. Axelhaunch. Fib's Wash. Blaggerfield.

'Well?'

'I would like to request you, sir –' I begin, trying to effect an entry. But he blocks my path.

'Yes?'

'– And as a matter of fact require you –' (Courage, Tobias!)

'Yes?' He was scowling at me now.

270

'– And furthermore demand you, sir –' (Yes!)

'What, dammit?'

'Humbly, sir, to –'

'To what? Get on with it, fellow!' His voice has growling thunder in it.

Three words left. Grasp those thistles, Tobias, and prove you are a man!

'Examine my body. Sir.'

Silence. He's looking at me as if I'm mad.

'I'm not a bloody physician,' he spits finally. 'I am a taxidermist. I stuff and mount animals. Whoever directed you here is an imbecile. Now bugger off.'

'Please, sir. Please!' I am wedging my way in now, and reaching in my pocket. 'There is something only you can answer.'

'I said NO!' he shouted. 'Now bugger off! I'm in the middle of stuffing –' He stops.

I'm pointing my revolver at him. My hand is shaking. Dr Scrapie freezes.

I can hear how thin and desperate my voice sounds. Like a tin whistle.

I say, 'You will do it, sir, or I shall blow your head off, and then my own!'

Yes: a man at last!

None of the plastic replicas of primates or the hologram exhibits resembled my towel-holder in any way. There was an interactive CD ROM, though. I scrolled through, beginning to feel that my visit here was already a waste of time. I'd been through all my old veterinary books, and even rung a friend who specialised in primates. He'd never heard of the Gentleman Monkey, and when I described my towel-holder, he drew a blank. The CD ROM display repeated a lot of the stuff I'd already come across in the virtual library that I'd accessed from Thunder Spit: how the monkey differs from the ape in crucial ways such as DNA structure, teeth, skull size, and skeletally, in particular with regard to the tail. There are only three living exceptions to this rule: Kitchener's Ape, which has a cingulum on its molar teeth, more in keeping with the monkey family, the Yeoman Baboon, whose skull is closer to the fossilised humanoid Neanderthal than an ape as such, and the extinct Ape of Mogador.

Mogador rang a bell. Wasn't Mogador mentioned in Scrapie's treatise?

'My God,' says Dr Scrapie, a minute later when Tobias Phelps has bashfully undressed. A brief glimpse of Tobias Phelps' anatomy would be enough to tell any zoologist that they had something remarkable on their hands. As Scrapie's expert eyes take in the sight of the creature before him, he stifles a gasp.

'Extraordinary,' he murmurs.

The hand-like feet.

The abundance of orange body hair, peppered with animal fleas.

The mutilated coccyx.

'And then there's that,' says Tobias Phelps, pointing to the jar.

Scrapie peers at its contents, and soon his pulse is racing furiously.

'Am I the first to –?' he asks Tobias Phelps in a haunted whisper.

'Apart from Dr Baldicoot, when I was a baby. And my mother, but she is dead.' Tobias Phelps is silent for a moment, and then confesses, 'I rarely have occasion to be entirely naked, sir. Even when alone.' Scrapie raises his eyebrows. 'My upbringing, you know,' Tobias Phelps whispers sadly. 'My parents – discouraged nakedness.'

Scrapie's heart does a complicated somersault.

'Yes,' he says, clearing his throat. 'I quite understand. Now lie down, please,' he instructs the young man. The phrase 'on a plate', keeps running through his head. Meanwhile Tobias

Phelps, for his part, cannot help noticing that the taxidermist's manner has altogether altered, in the direction of sudden, extreme interest.

'Now,' announces Scrapie, forcing his mouth into a smile. 'My dear young man. I need to investigate you further.'

I keyed in 'Ape of Mogador', and waited for further details. As the computer was running the search, I looked about: the schoolkids were flowing up the stairs like an anti-gravitational pancake mix. Everything echoed. I didn't like this place. It gave me the creeps.

Just then there was a muted beep, and some text came up on the screen: in pink, on a yellow background, with an insistent techno-beat of music behind it. I began to read.

The Ape of Mogador: Also known – erroneously, because of its misleading tail – as the Gentleman Monkey.

Jesus Christ. And there was more.

As I read on, I began to feel sick with excitement.

Peter Piper picked a peck of pickled pepper, I said to myself as Dr Scrapie took out a small roll of measuring tape and encircled my skull with it. Miss Mosh mashes some mish-mash, I thought, as he shone a little torch into my eye. Minewort, lungwort, I thought, as he peered first into one ear, and then the other. Gudderwort. The arid Gudderwort. I can see his face. I can see his face and the distaste on it as he hands me the jar. And other faces, too: the Mulveys, the Cleggses and the Balls and the Tobashes. Tommy Boggs' wife was a Tobash. Jessie, who had called me Prune-Face. Jessie's belly, rounded with child.

The girl in my rooms, her hand down a student's trousers, fishing about for his –

The woman I had glimpsed in the upper window, beneath whose corset –

The jar that contained my –

273

'Now breathe in slowly,' Scrapie is saying; he has a cold stethoscope to my chest. Can he hear how fast my heart is pounding?

From this angle, with his flowing white hair, grizzled beard, and authoritarian expression, Dr Scrapie resembles God; the same God whose beard dissolved into the white storm-clouds of the Great Flood in the Noah's Ark picture on my bedroom wall at home. Have I not come to the expert of experts? The man who single-handedly peopled the Queen's ghastly Animal Kingdom Collection with its human-eyed bestiary?

His eyes are all fired up with a strange gleam, and it dawns on me that I will have no more need of my revolver. I have his attention.

'*Sir* Ivanhoe,' I hear him murmur.

'I beg your pardon?'

'Nothing,' he replies quickly. 'I am just trying to think how I can –' There is a long pause as he appears to search the recesses of his memory for the right word. 'Help you,' he says finally.

Now he is questioning me intensively, scribbling notes as he does so, and I am suddenly telling him everything. About being a foundling, discovered by the altar of St Nicholas's Church in Thunder Spit, the day after the Travelling Fair of Danger and Delight left Judlow, with a ghastly mutilation to my lower spine which had nearly killed me. About the way the animals of Thunder Spit growled at me, and how I was rejected by humans, too. About the Contortionist at the Travelling Fair, who had handed my father the jar containing the –

'The object in question,' I falter. Scrapie's eyebrows shoot up.

'Aha,' he says. 'Now we are getting somewhere.'

But he does not say where. Instead, he questions me in detail about what he calls my 'well-spokenness'. This prompts me to impress him further with a few tongue-twisters, and I recount how I used to read long passages from the Bible in church.

'Speech came to me late,' I tell him, 'prompted by the sight of a cake on my fifth birthday.' This seems to stir even more excitement in him.

'And before that? How did you communicate?'

'In squeaks and grunts, as far as I am aware,' I told him. 'They said it was a miracle.'

'A case of nurture overcoming nature, perhaps?' mutters Scrapie, almost to himself. And then, addressing me: 'In what manner were you raised?'

'In a Christian manner, sir,' I tell him. 'Cleanliness, reading, self-improvement and piety were encouraged. Indulgences of the flesh, nakedness and childish play were not. A traditional English upbringing, sir.'

He questions me further, and I find myself telling him more: about how I believed the jar to contain an umbilical cord, until it had smashed, and about how Kinnon had put me right. About how, when I had told Kinnon my fears, he had assured me I was mad. About how I had insisted on knowing the truth. About how he had advised me to come to London, and search out an expert.

'You could not have come to a better place, young man,' murmurs Scrapie reassuringly, as he begins to carry out a series of quick sketches of me in his notebook. 'You can trust me implicitly.'

This is a profound relief.

'And you say your foster-father will not see you?' Scrapie asked when I had finished telling him about Parson Phelps' removal to the Fishforth Sanatorium for the Spiritually Disturbed.

'That is so, sir.' I hung my head.

'I am – sorry to hear that,' he said thoughtfully. 'And nobody has any idea that you are here in this house? With me?'

'No, sir. Why should they?'

'No reason at all. Indeed not. My poor young man. No relatives? No friends? You are here completely – alone?'

It seemed important to him, though I could not see why.

'Completely alone,' I confirmed. Although I did not like

this lonely thought, Dr Scrapie seemed to find it particularly appealing; he started rubbing his hands as if I were a warm hearth.

Finally he blurted excitedly, 'You looked familiar to me, young man, as soon as I saw you.'

I was surprised.

'Are there others like me, then? I asked, filled with a sudden tremulous hope.

'In a manner of speaking, yes,' said Scrapie. 'Or at least there were. What I mean is, I have seen a creature that resembles you. Resembles you so closely, and according to my records so accurately, anatomically speaking –'

He went over to his desk and pulled out a notebook full of measurements and sketches. Then he said, 'Have you heard of a creature called the Gentleman Monkey? An extinct primate, from Morocco?'

'No.' I said. Why was my heart suddenly plummeting downwards like a leaden fishing weight?

'That is the creature you resemble, young man.'

I pressed the key to call the picture up from the CD ROM, and watched the 3-D image emerge. It was an artist's impression, and was accompanied by an etching of the creature, made in 1843 by a wildlife artist who had visited the last remaining specimen in the Jardin Zoologique in Mogador, Morocco. I gasped when I saw it. It showed the monkey standing with its hands on its hips, in a defiant and disconcertingly human posture, behind the bars of a large cage.

'It's him!' I shouted. 'It's bloody-well him!'

'*Lang*uage!' said the man in the mauve tracksuit. The pancake mixture had finished its progress up the stairs, and was now slurping Coke from cans and mock karate-kicking each other with feet clad in blocky trainers. 'There's kids about,' the teacher went on. 'If you can't keep your mouth clean you shouldn't be here in school hours.'

276

'Sorry,' I lied, desperate to get rid of him. He was glaring at me now like I was some kind of paedophile. When he finally shuffled off, trailing his charges behind him like a pedagogical jellyfish, I turned my attention to the text that accompanied the etching. The Gentleman Monkey was an unusual specimen, and had baffled naturalists at the time. Strikingly humanoid, with a larger brain than man's, and a fun-loving temperament.

Polygamous by nature.

That word 'polygamous' got me thinking. It was then that some phrases from Dr Ivanhoe Scrapie's eccentric treatise came floating back into my head, and my brain began to whirr.

'So this – Gentleman Monkey,' I croaked finally, gulping at air. 'What is it, exactly?'

'Was,' Dr Scrapie corrected me. 'It is no more. It was an interesting species of monkey; not so much a monkey, in fact, as a tailed ape. Anyway, highly intelligent, and strikingly human in appearance. Polygamous by nature, and a fructivore, but in other respects remarkably similar in many ways to the human. Child-like but courteous by nature; that's why they called him the Gentleman, I suppose. And probably also why he became extinct,' he added thoughtfully.

I was having trouble breathing by now. 'And what happened to it?'

'The last remaining member of its race is now housed in Buckingham Palace,' said Scrapie. 'I stuffed him and he became a towel-holder for the ladies' powder room in the banqueting suite. That's where he is now.'

If only I had heeded Kinnon's advice, accepted his diagnosis of madness, and remained in Hunchburgh! I would be ordained by now! I would be Parson Phelps the Second, preaching my anti-Darwinian sermon loud and clear from the pulpit!

I pictured the creature's skin being removed from its body,

277

and filled with sawdust, then dressed in human clothes, like the creatures I had seen at the Museum.

'And the – carcass?' I mustered finally, following the ghastly thought through to its conclusion.

'You'd rather not know about that, young man,' said Scrapie, looking suddenly tired and slightly throttled. 'Suffice it to say that it was highly toxic. It contained poison.'

'Poison?'

'So it would appear. Not something I discovered till – later,' said Scrapie. 'When I had cause to investigate the creature's remains.'

'You mean the monkey was poisonous by nature, or it had *been* poisoned?'

'It had been poisoned,' he said slowly. 'With praxin.'

'But why? Where? Who did it?' I felt my sanity slipping away as I spoke.

'Nobody knows,' sighed Scrapie. 'But I have my suspicions.'

The last of this species of ape, according to the interactive CD ROM display, had been purchased by the entrepreneur Horace Trapp from a Moroccan menagerie for Queen Victoria's collection and shipped over to Britain, but it had died in mysterious circumstances on the voyage back to London, following a mutiny on board Trapp's vessel, the *Ark*. The creature had later been stuffed by the Taxidermist Royal, Dr Ivanhoe Scrapie, as part of Queen Victoria's Animal Kingdom Collection, most of which was housed in the Museum. But the Queen had so taken a liking to the primates that she decreed they should grace the rooms of Buckingham Palace, which was where the ape was dispatched, once stuffed, sometime in the 1850s. But in 1864, to the dismay of later generations of evolutionary scientists specialising in primates, the stuffed creature was stolen from Buckingham Palace. And never traced.

It was there, as I flicked through the interactive zoology encyclopaedia, that I realised. The Gentleman Monkey in my bathroom was the only known specimen in the whole world of this breed of extinct primate. The only remaining evidence that such a creature had ever existed. There was no mention of its having been stolen in Scrapie's treatise. Could he perhaps have written it before the creature had disappeared from the Palace? And if he had not been lying about the rarity and the final extinction of the species – was it (I got all choked up at the thought), was it possible that the rest of his extraordinary document was also true?

That word 'polygamous' kept haunting me.

Yes: I'd definitely have to think about this.

'We found the Gentleman Monkey dead on the *Ark*,' said Scrapie, after he had finished telling me what he knew about Horace Trapp's career, first as a slave-trader, then as an animal-collector for the Queen. 'Along with all the other creatures. Over a thousand of them. Most of them half torn to bits. Nature's cruel, you know, young man,' he said, eyeing me in a strange way. 'But there wasn't a mark on the monkey. It was the praxin that killed him. It must have been injected.'

I winced.

'We found Trapp's head, too,' Scrapie continued, going slightly pale. He paused for a moment and re-filled his pen with ink. He did it slowly, applying great concentration to the task. 'Not a pretty sight,' he said finally.

'When was this?' I asked. 'When did Trapp's *Ark* arrive in London?'

'1845, the same year Violet was born,' said Scrapie. 'It was found floating on the Channel, and hauled in.'

'Violet?'

'My youngest daughter.' I remembered the face of a woman in the window. So this was Violet Scrapie. I felt my heart shift, and desolation sweep through me like a cold wind. 'It was a bloody nuisance,' Scrapie was saying. 'Had to ship an iceberg over to deal with it. Trapp's *Ark* kept me busy for fifteen years.'

I gulped.

'1845 was the year of my birth,' I told him. 'As far as it is known.'

Scrapie picked up his notebook again, and began to scribble furiously.

I had dismissed the assertions in Scrapie's treatise as nonsense; the ravings of a demented man.

But –

Hope gobbled at my innards, and my brain raced. I found myself actually having to grab hold of a fibreglass gibbon to keep my balance. The kids had moved off, but their voices wafted up from the hall below, a faint echo buzzing in my head.

What I was thinking was that, by a quirk of fate – that chance meeting in the pub with Norman Ball? Or was it even earlier, when the threatened litigation over Giselle catapulted me north? Or did it date back to my childhood wish to work with animals? In any case, by some quirk of fate, some kind of extraordinary missing link had fallen into my lap.

The de Savile Theory of Evolution, they would rename it. I would insist on it. I'd hold the Gentleman Monkey hostage, if necessary, until it was official. You try stopping me.

I'd be given a Euro Award.

Then I started thinking about the other stuff in the document, and my stomach heaved. There were implications. Phelps, the man was called. Tobias Phelps. I didn't recognise the name from the twins' family tree. But they hadn't finished it.

I was hallucinating now, surely. I had never seen their feet. They didn't have tails, that was for sure. But it was still possible – was it not? That –

No. I was going mad. It was impossible.

'Impossible!' I said.

Scrapie said, 'So you know, since you have become aware of

280

Mr Darwin's theories, that we are all descended from the humble primate?' He spoke slowly, as if I were suddenly a child, or a creature not too quick on the uptake. Perhaps he was right. '*All* of us,' he said. 'Even Her Majesty Queen Victoria.'

No, I thought. It wasn't like that. *The earth was without form and void, and darkness was upon the face of the deep.*

'Human beings stand at the top of Darwin's ladder of nature, you know, Mr Phelps. Of all the species of primate, we are the most evolved.'

Blasphemy!

'Have you ever seen a fossil, Mr Phelps?'

'I have. My father used to say that they were God's jokes,' I told him. My voice sounded weak and thin.

'Jokes?'

'God moves in a mysterious way,' I said, scraping about in my memory for the comfort of my fledgling sermon on God and the fossils. 'Fossils are clearly the Lord's doing, and evidence of His grand design.'

But my heart wouldn't stop pounding; I felt that I might explode and scatter, like a distraught firework.

'Well, according to Darwin and others,' said Scrapie, 'they are evidence of a distant past, of which we are the biological inheritors. Have you heard of natural selection, young man?'

'Yes,' I said. 'It is Darwin's theory. I have studied his book, and his profane ideas.'

'Natural selection,' said Scrapie, brushing my remarks aside, 'is Nature's way of making advancements. From simple to complex, from complex to even more complex, until you reach man. Darwin says that we must not, however, forget the principle of correlation, by which many strange deviations of structure are tied together, so that a change in one part often leads to other changes of a *quite unexpected nature.*'

Scrapie stopped in his tracks and steered me towards a *chaise-longue.*

'Sit down here,' he said. Obeying him, I found myself face

281

to face with the male object and related accoutrements of a stuffed horse.

'A fine specimen, your horse,' I mustered politely. Miss Mosh mashes some mish-mash. The creature looked nothing like the horses back in Thunder Spit.

'Well, it would be an odd specimen, if it were a horse,' says Scrapie. 'Actually, it's a mule. An ass. A hybrid.'

'A hybrid? A sort of cross?'

Mildred doesn't like this idea one little bit, and wrenches violently at my long-suffering sphincter.

'Exactly. Father a stallion, mother a donkey. Or occasionally vice versa. They are always sterile,' continued Dr Scrapie slowly, keeping his eyes levelled on my face. 'They are sterile,' he said, 'because Nature doesn't like breeding across species. Yet – *paradoxically* – it has always happened. In the case of the mule, it has been virtually an institution. Most examples occur in the world of botany, but there are plenty of zoological examples as well. More than you'd think. Wallabies and kangaroos. Crocodiles and alligators. Lions and tigers, even. And then there are historical cases, or should I say mythological ones, though where mythology ends and history begins we can only guess at.'

'Cases such as, sir?' I falter faintly.

'Such as the Minotaur, the Centaur, the mermaid; Pegasus, the winged horse. Medusa, the snake-headed woman. The Devil is half goat, is he not? And then of course there's the Angel.'

Blasphemy and more blasphemy!

'I cannot agree with that, sir,' I retort, my cheeks burning. 'The Angel is a creature of Heaven.' But then I feel my face slacken, and I reach for my whelk. For I know, suddenly, and with a force that sets Mildred attacking my innards, that if a creature of Heaven is possible, then so is a beast from Hell.

'So how –? What –?' I stammered.

'Darwin,' said Scrapie, 'asked the following question: "*If the cross offspring of any two races of birds or animals be interbred, will the progeny keep as constant, as that of any established*

breed; or will it tend to return in appearance to either parent?"
I'll say this much for Darwin: he's asked some sensible questions.
But he doesn't have all the answers. Not by a long chalk.'

I am perched stiffly now on the edge of the *chaise-longue*.

'And – do you have answers, sir?'

'I think your existence upon this earth is beginning to provide
me with some,' he replied. He sat still for a while, lost in thought.
'A form of natural selection,' he finally murmured to himself.
'An evolutionary tangent. A new branch of the family. Or an
old one.' Then he jumped up and began to pace the room. I
could see his mind was tumbling in all directions. 'Yes; very
possibly an old one. Humans are evolved from other primates.
Apes. Monkeys, too, but further back. But what if –?' He paused,
then began to drum his fingers on a table.

'Hypothesis,' he said, his eyes dancing with excitement.
'Hypothesis. A human mates with another species of primate.
On board Trapp's *Ark*, let's say. Mates, let us speculate, for
the purposes of argument, with *the Gentleman Monkey*. And
creates a new breed of human-like primate. You, Mr Phelps!'

I was winded by the very absurdity of the suggestion, but
there was no stopping Scrapie by now. He was leaping up
and down.

'Yes, you!' he yelled, slapping me hard on the back. 'Raising
the intriguing scientific question: Can the unaccountable leaps
and bounds of our evolutionary path be explained by the
occasional injection of the blood of other species into the
veins of some creatures? Could the mouse have emerged from
the elephant, or vice versa, by an incredible act of sexual union?
Which occasionally bore fruit?'

I gulped.

Scrapie said that a man called Mendel had bred peas that told
such a story. The botanical examples were all about us. I thought
of the gourd plant on my mother's grave. Had it been trying to
tell me something, after all?

'Yes!' Scrapie was almost shouting. 'There's not enough time,
you see, for everything to have happened! To get from a fish to

an amphibian to a man takes longer than it should. It doesn't work on paper. So there have to be sudden changes, not just gradual ones. And you are the answer!'

My head was thudding, and the air about me seemed suddenly strangely dappled, as though my vision were disintegrating. 'I still don't understand.'

'Two different species, breeding, Mr Phelps! Imagine such a thing! Not possible now, to create a new species, out of two. But *was once*, maybe. Why on earth not? So imagine this, as the answer to Darwin's time-paradox: that man didn't evolve slowly from a gorilla or a chimpanzee. He appeared suddenly, like Adam and Eve in the Bible. Just one. A freak cross-breed. From two completely different – and perhaps incompatible – species. Two species that would perhaps otherwise not have *survived*! That would have *died out*! Two wrongs, therefore, Mr Phelps, making a right! You are living proof that it's possible.'

One of the briefest, but also the most potentially historic conversations on the theory of evolutionary science, had just taken place.

'*I'm all shook up!*' I sang. '*Oooh!*'
Pedal to the metal. Go, cats, go.
This was the biz.
And I was the King.

So, I thought miserably, Genesis *was* a lie. And evolution *was* a fact. But its mechanics – its mechanics were not quite as Mr Darwin thought. It had progressed at times in great magical leaps. And I was proof of it. A mutant, an aberration, a misbegot. One year a green and stippled gourd. The next a yellow, blotchy one. The following year an orange fruit, with warts. The year after that, a mauve one with stripes. The year after that, a green one again, but with warts, or stripes, or mottled patches. A bit of this, a bit of that. Fling it in the primordial soup pot and await

God knows what! The world looked different, all of a sudden. It had transformed itself, before my eyes, from an ordered place, a hierarchy created by God, into a floating Darwinian whore-house. There reigned a new, chaotic higgledy-piggledyness that defied belief and astonished the heavens. And I, Tobias Phelps, was part of this crazy hotchpotch of nature called evolution, a dangerous and wild and virtually unexplored new territory of understanding. But was I a victim or a pioneer?

Was I one of God's jokes, or the butt of it?

I hung my head in an unfathomable mixture of pride and shame.

Scrapie was fingering a syringe now, and giving me a strange look.

'Have you ever had laudanum?' he asked.

'Yes. Kinnon gave me some before I left Hunchburgh. To calm my nerves.'

'He did well. I would now like to give you some more. I shall administer it by injection; it'll act faster and more effectively that way. Now roll up your sleeve for me.'

Betty Botter bought some butter, I murmured to myself as the needle entered my vein and he squeezed. But, she said, this butter's bitter. Scrapie had been right; I began to feel both relaxed and dizzy immediately.

'How tall are you, Mr Phelps?' he is asking.

'Five feet two,' I reply, sinking back on to the *chaise-longue*.

'That's right. Make yourself comfortable. And your waist measures – approximately?'

'I have no idea, sir,' I murmured, feeling drowsy.

'Will you permit me then,' he asked, 'to measure you again?'

'With a view to what, Dr Scrapie?' I moaned.

But before I could hear his answer, I had succumbed to blackness.

I sped through the streets of Thunder Spit, went the wrong way round the one-way system, got flashed at by the speed-sensitive road-sign on the high street, and swerved to a halt at my front door. I thumped my way in; in the hallway I stumbled heavily and crashed over a double buggy; an ancient vehicle of steel and nylon, parked there like a tangle of dead crickets.

The twins were sitting in the kitchen knitting.

'Hi, gorgeous,' said Rose, not looking up.

'Been missing you,' lied Blanche.

Something was up. I could tell.

'How's tricks, girls?' I asked, trying to stay cool.

'We've finished the family tree, look,' said Rose, shoving a big chart at me with phoney-looking heraldic shields decorating the margins.

'We're descended from a parson,' boasted Blanche.

'Parson Phelps?' I asked. I could feel myself going white.

'Yeah, how did you know that?' But not waiting for my answer she went on, 'He used to live in Mum and Dad's house. The Old Parsonage.'

'According to the church records.'

'Quite a coincidence, eh?'

So they *were* descended from the man Scrapie mentioned in his treatise. The man who according to him, was –

'Mum said she could've told us that ages ago, but it would've been against Dr Bugrov's genealogy rules,' says Rose.

'It's cheating to get anything by oral history,' explains Blanche. 'You have to have the paperwork to back it up, or the Americans complain.'

I didn't have all day. 'Let me see that thing,' I said, grabbing it. I still felt uneasy, like there was something they weren't telling me. The huge sheet of card wobbled as I snatched it.

'Hey!'

'What are you doing?'

'Looking for Tobias Phelps,' I answered.

'He was our great-great-great-great-grandfather,' says Rose, pointing to a name near the very apex of the tree. 'See? Five generations back.'

Christ Almighty.

286

'Let me see your feet,' I demanded.

'No,' they said together firmly. 'No way.'

'Why not?'

'Because we think we're about to go into labour,' said Rose swiftly.

'Any minute now,' threatened Blanche.

'Along with twenty million other women,' I said impatiently, my mind still racing. 'Did you know they're slapping hundred-Euro fines on hoaxers?'

'We're not hoaxers!' shrieked Rose and Blanche after me, as I rushed upstairs towards the bathroom, two steps at a time. To hell with their feet, I thought. Let's get this monkey loaded in the car first. They were still yelling after me. Abuse, it sounded like.

But I wasn't listening. My mind was on the Gent.

In his workshop, the cage assembled and the padlock checked, Dr Scrapie sits in silence, drinking brandy, his brain racing faster than it has done in years. What he has seen is strange and not strange. Bizarre and yet obvious. Unthinkable, yet perfectly possible. Darwin did it. He made that leap of imagination. He made that crude and unwholesome and shocking yet brilliantly true connection. It is the connection a virgin bride makes on her wedding night. After the chintz and flowers and confetti-showers, after the dancing and the music and the merriment, after the well-wishing and the lace-handkerchief-waving and the cooing of doves, there is a moment when she comes face to face with a man's prick.

It is that sort of blunt information that Scrapie feels he has met in the case of Tobias Phelps.

But he cannot, should not, ought not, shall not and *will not* – God help him – make the same mistake twice, he thinks, his mind on the *Origin of Species*. Another opportunity will not pass him by. And this one has been handed him on a plate. As though by God himself!

Tobias Phelps will be the making of him!

It was then, as I sank into darkness, and all hope died within me, that my madness began. I let it happen. Where else could I flee?

I learned afterwards that my insanity involved neither ranting nor raving: just a terrible, introspective silence broken only by rasping groans and the occasional weak utterance of names such as Tommy, Father, Mrs Fooney, and Gudderwort.

All I knew at the time was the feel of her gentle hand on my brow. And the sound of her murmuring softly as she fed me the strangest food I had ever tasted.

Her. She.

In my miasmic half-sleep, I see the beach again, and I see myself as a young child, clambering among the rocks on all fours, and climbing the little gnarled trees of Thunder Spit, and my parents begging me to stop. I see Parson Phelps guiding my hand as he teaches me to write with a goose-feather quill, and I see me and Tommy Boggs playing in the sand-dunes, burying each other among the spiky sand-grass. I see myself at fifteen, watching with Tommy as the Contortionist argues with my father in the graveyard, and her handing him a jar, and him returning with thunder in his face and stuffing money into her hand. I see him in the church, the ripped pages of Darwin's book fluttering wildly down from his pulpit. I see the import of my holy vision, and then I see the smashing of the jar. I see my tail, and Kinnon picking it up for me with his handkerchief, and thrusting it back at me to keep. I recall my hasty visit to Fishforth for the purchase of Jared, the carrier pigeon, and then the train journey to London. The Museum with its dreadful knickerbockered creatures and their blue glass eyes. The boarding-house, the visit to Portobello Road and finally the trip to Madagascar Street. And in a ghastly caricature of consciousness that feels like half-dream, half-death, I pick along the shoreline of my past and I see my father, knitting in the Sanatorium. I see him knitting a scarf so long it could span the world. And I see Tommy in his forge, with his simple life and his bouncing babies, and the seashore, and the Thistle-Pulling Contest. How memory changes things: I see it now touched by my own nostalgia, transformed from a scene of ritual humiliation into an idyllic rural tableau, the cheering, yelling faces of the Balls and the Cleggses and the Peat-Hoves awakening in me a cruel longing for home. I see the Man-Eating Wart-hog.

I awake to find myself in a bed, with her warm hand again on my brow. I open my eyes. She is clad in a huge red dress, with small beads that glitter in the light of the chandelier.

'My name is Violet Scrapie,' she tells me.

She is magnificent. I find tears welling in my eyes. I do not know why. I would like to tell her how marvellous I think she is, but all that emerges is a hopeless groan.

She blushes a deep and fetching pink, and offers me a spoonful of something sweet-smelling, glutinous and green.

'Delicious,' I murmur, still half-choked with a feeling I cannot name. 'What is it?'

'Nettle preserve,' she murmurs, spooning more in. 'With caramelised beetroot. My own recipe.'

'Miss Mosh mashes some mish-mash,' I murmur.

Through my drugged haze, I feel the power of her.

Bom, bom, bom.

The sound of my heart. Its pounding suddenly fills the room.

What a woman! Her hand on my brow reminds me of home. Sometimes, floating far above me, I see her face. She doesn't speak, or if she does, I have gone deaf.

The days pass. I am a man, I am a man, I am a man, I say over and over again to myself.

I awoke screaming.

She held me in her arms. And I sobbed.

'Oh Miss Scrapie, help me, help me!'

She stroked my head, and pulled me closer to her chest. Made calming noises. Felt my forehead.

'All shall be well,' she murmured.

'No!' I groaned. 'It can never be!'

Nor could it. For I had realised in that moment, just as my manhood had been denied me, that this was the very moment that God had chosen to subject my soul to a torment more terrible, even, than the one to which I had just been subjected. I had fallen, madly and passionately, in love. The situation was utterly, utterly beyond hope.

Much later, I awoke again and heard her voice, a voice that made my heart veer about like a loose cannon, asking me sharply, 'Who is Mildred?'

'My tapeworm,' I confessed. 'Could I trouble you, my dear Miss Scrapie, for a banana?'

I pounded up the stairs two at a time. I'd thought it all through. This was a raid. I was bundling him in the car and taking him straight back to London pronto. I'd hold a press conference. That's what you do, isn't it, when you've made a discovery. I'd take the twins with me. Hold them hostage if need be. Force them to show their feet. Reveal the contents of Scrapie's treatise. Wheel out the family tree. And be declared the discoverer of a hitherto undreamed-of missing link.

A-be-bop-a-loo-bop, a-bop-bam-boo!

I burst into the bathroom, and there was Norman sitting on the toilet with his pants round his ankles, reading a DIY magazine called *An Englishman's Home*.

'Just performing a *mea culpa*,' he explained, folding his mag. 'Forgot to lock. Good article in here on all the child-proof gizmos on the market. Fancy a trip to B and Q next Saturday? We could get this place fixed up for you in two shakes of a lamb's whatsit, with the power screwdriver.'

I didn't say anything. I couldn't speak.

Norman reached for the toilet roll and measured out five sheets. He was staring at me, puzzled. My face must have shown something of my dismay, because he said, 'Sorry, mate.

But a man's gotta do what a man's gotta do, eh, Buck? I'll be through in a tick.'

'No,' I croaked. 'It's not that.'

It was the Gentleman Monkey. He had vanished.

CHAPTER 27

IN WHICH TOBIAS
PHELPS ATTEMPTS A
CONFESSION

They cald me the FROZEN WOMAN later, wen I came to the Workhous, run by that Fat BASTARD wot threw me out, but it wasn't in the SEA that I freezed, it was befor, wen I lernd wot TRAPP woz plannin for me and my Gentleman FREND. Wen I diskovers wot his Uther Biznis is. Its Higgins wot tells me. Sez it like a JOKE and LARFS and LARFS.

I dusn't beleev it at furst, and then I duz.

It's then I no it is TYME TO LEEV.

We must ESKAPE, I tells him, strokin His FUR. Wen I tels him about Trapp's Uther Biznis, wot hes plannin for our CHILD, he dusnt say nuthin, just givs me a LOOK. As tho hes sayin: so this is CIVILIZASHUN, eh?

We felt the STORM cumin, and that's wen we dus it. Higgins is REECHIN in for our plates of slop, and I distraks him, and my GENTLEMAN FREND filchis the KEES from his pockit, and it's dun in a flash.

We opens the CAGES, kwik as we can, bifor BOWKER and STEED and TRAPP cums down, and OUT they rushis, FRANTIK and PANIKING.

God! PANDYMONIUM, in ther. They attaks the slop-bin furst, the LYON and the ELIFANT gobbles neerly evrythin up, then the JAKALS and the RINOSSERUS chargis in, and the smorler BEESTS is grabbin wot they can from the floor, and FITIN over skraps. The doors of the CAGIS clangin and clangin.

The STORM is ragin now, and the creechers we has releesd

is yelpin and howlin and screemin, and wunce the SLOP is gon, the FITING bitween them gets more and more vylent, and thers NO stoppin it. Nacheral instinkts is takin over. HOWLS, YELLS, SCREECHIN. Eetin eech other ALIVE, sum of them. The ARKE is rockin, rockin on the WAVs, and then I heer a clatter from ABUV, and it is the sound of TRAPP.

BLOOD everywer. Fur, fevvers, scales.

Then, clatter clatter, down the sters. Then I sees him. TRAPP. Furie on his FACE. And feer.

He is sterin at me and my Gentleman FREND, and my Gentleman frend is sterin bak.

In His hand, TRAPP has sumthin GLINTIN and SHARP.

In the days that followed my arrival in Madagascar Street, Dr Scrapie took yet more detailed measurements of me, some of a most intimate nature, and launched himself into a spate of feverish scientific activity in his basement workshop, from which the sound of his own laughter, his shouting or his impressively loud farts would emanate at intervals. I felt almost flattered that so much bustle and excitement on the part of the eminent taxidermist was on account of me. Dr Scrapie informed me that he was working on a treatise entitled *A New Theory of Evolution*, about my 'unusual origins'. He swore me to secrecy on this subject, and instructed me not to leave the house on any account, unless accompanied either by himself or his daughter.

'You must speak to nobody about my hypothesis,' he warned, 'until I have finished my treatise, and have occasion to present you to Mr Darwin himself.'

'Not even Miss Scrapie?' I asked him, feeling my spine tingle in trepidation. Had he already told her the truth himself? Although I had seen no hint of it in her behaviour towards me, which remained both charming and courteous, I could not be sure.

'Most certainly not,' he replied. He cannot have guessed that a huge warm wave of relief swept through me when he gave me the blessed confirmation, that Miss Scrapie was ignorant of my secret. Although I knew that it was only a matter of time before my lowly status on the evolutionary ladder was revealed, I wished to savour every moment of my new friend's most delightful company before she learned the truth. For what chance would I have then, of my growing interest in her ever being returned?

'How can I ever thank you for your kindness to me, Miss Scrapie?' I asked her one morning, as I sampled some more of the delicacies she referred to as *Cuisine Biologique*. Miss Scrapie looked surprised.

'The pleasure is all mine,' she assured me. 'Here, try this,' she offered, preparing to post a piece of pickled fungus into my mouth. I parted my lips, and she popped it in. 'I have taken great pleasure in nursing you, Mr Phelps, as you are a most useful guinea-pig for my recipes!'

I smiled. This was true; I ate everything she offered me with enormous relish, and was feeling healthier and in better spirits by the day as a result.

'But I hope it is not *only* my appetite that appeals to you, Miss Scrapie,' I ventured, and she blushed, and I blushed, too, causing her to blush even more, and her blushes in turn increasing my own still further, until soon we were both as fiery-faced as a couple of red-hot pokers.

Miss Scrapie and I had by now exchanged stories about our childhoods; she, too, had been lonely. All the more so, when she had parted company on ideological grounds with a man – a certain Monsieur Cabillaud – who had been more of a father to her than Dr Scrapie himself.

'All those years when he was stuffing the creatures from Trapp's *Ark*' (I winced at the mention of this vessel) 'I was in the kitchen with Cabillaud, cooking the carcasses,' she said wistfully. 'He taught me everything I know.'

I sympathised. 'I, too, am estranged from a loved one. When Mr Darwin published the *Origin of Species*, my father went insane.'

Miss Scrapie gasped. 'No! Did he really? Why so did *my* father!'

And she told me how Dr Scrapie had entered a monumental sulk and taken to his workshop with a bottle of rum, and stayed there for a week. In turn I recounted to her the story of Parson Phelps' public shredding of Darwin's tome, in full view of his congregation in the church, and his subsequent removal to the Sanatorium for the Spiritually Disturbed. Omitting, I must confess, the part about the jar and its contents.

'You must write to Parson Phelps,' she urged. 'He would surely not wish to be estranged from you for ever.'

'And you?' I asked. 'Will you be reconciled to your Monsieur Cabillaud?'

She shook her head slowly. 'I do not know,' she said, 'but I shall see him soon at a banquet.' All of a sudden she was looking anxious, and twisting away at the cloth of her voluminous skirt. I knew how she must feel.

'Fear not, Miss Scrapie,' I said softly. I put my hand upon hers. And she did not resist me, reader, or pull away. Was I right to draw hope from that?

I must tell her, I thought. But my cowardice stopped me.

The next day I begged Violet for writing paper on which to pen Parson Phelps a letter. For what had I to lose, that had not already been lost? What could I do, but appeal to his sense of justice? He was a fair man.

'*Should the sins of the mothers and the fathers be visited upon their children?*' I wrote. '*Surely not, dear Parson Phelps! If there is one thing you have taught me, sir, it is that God is just!*' Although I was personally beginning to question this. What was 'just' about the pickle He had landed me in? '*All I desire is that we shall be reconciled again,*' I ended my letter. '*If you cannot love me as your foster-child, then love me as one of God's creatures!*

'*Your loving son, Tobias Phelps.*'

Miss Scrapie, ignorant of the contents of my missive but pleased that I had followed her advice to attempt a reconciliation, accompanied me, with the ailing and now skeletal Suet, to St Pancras, where my carrier pigeon Jared was housed. I personally attached the tiny envelope containing the tightly folded letter to his ringed ankle. He fluttered out of his cage, disoriented for a moment by the cornices of the station, but he soon found a skylight, and as we watched him take wing northwards, I said a small and hopeful prayer.

With Dr Scrapie so preoccupied with his *New Theory of Evolution*, of which the Gentleman Monkey and my own self formed the unique basis, Miss Scrapie and I had been thrown together more and more. Thrown? Or dare I venture to say that it was by choice that we found ourselves in one another's company for the greater part of each day?

It was the following morning, emboldened by the fact that she had once again allowed my hand to rest upon hers, that I decided to summon the courage to confess to her the full truth. I trembled as I spoke.

'There is something I should like you to know,' I began. 'Concerning my origins.'

Did I imagine it, or did a ghostly figure appear briefly at my side as I said these words? Something in petticoats? I blinked. A trick of the light. She had gone. Violet looked up from her ledger, in which she was noting my comments about her latest recipe, swede regale ('Most delicious,' had been my verdict), and smiled.

'Your origins, Mr Phelps? You mean Thunder Spit, and Parson Phelps, and your late foster-mother? I thought we had told each other everything, Mr Phelps!' She smiled coquettishly. 'Or is there a shameful secret?'

My heart began pounding with slow and heavy thuds. But I could not stop now. I cleared my throat.

'Well, in a manner of speaking, there is, actually,' I began. Miss Scrapie's fine eyebrows arched questioningly. But then, observing my intense discomfort, her expression softened into pity and concern, and she held up a hand, gesturing me to halt my words.

'Please, Mr Phelps.' she begged. 'I would hate you to distress yourself over something that is after all a private matter.'

'No,' I blurted. 'I must tell you, Miss Scrapie. 'At the Travelling Fair of Danger and Delight, I saw a Contortionist, and she –'

Violet took my hand – so hairy it looked suddenly, next to her smooth padded flesh, as fine as uncooked pastry! – and held it tightly.

'Mr Phelps, you have turned quite pale!' she said. I swallowed, and breathed in deeply, willing myself to continue. My voice was cracked and thin.

'I have reason to suspect that this Contortionist was really my true mother.'

'A Contortionist?' Violet enquired, smiling. She did not withdraw her hand, but continued to clasp mine firmly. (So far, so promising!) 'A Contortionist! How – unusual!'

'There is more,' I said. 'More, that is even more unusual.'

I paused, then whispered, 'Concerning my true father. I have reason to believe, Miss Scrapie, unlikely though it may sound, and perhaps somewhat shocking to your delicate ears, that my true father was a –'

'Yes?'

I hung my head. 'Please, Miss Scrapie, will you be so good as to furnish me with a pen, ink and paper, that I may write it down for you? For I fear that I cannot bring myself to say it.'

'Why certainly, Mr Phelps,' she said, eyeing me in a puzzled fashion, then waddling over to the writing desk. She returned with the writing implements, and handed them to me in silence. She watched me with concern as I began to write my secret shame with a slow and trembling hand. But I had barely started when a violent clatter of shoes upon the stairway broke my flow and Dr Scrapie burst into the room. Instinctively, I crumpled up the half-completed confession and shoved it into Violet's hand, and she in turn stuffed it into a fold of her dress like a guilty child.

'I have an idea, Mr Phelps!' Scrapie was shouting excitedly. 'Would you do us all the honour of attending the Celebration of Evolution Banquet on Saturday?'

'The what?' I mumbled. 'Am I to understand –'

'You see,' he interrupted me, 'I would very much like to present you to Mr Darwin, before –' He paused for a moment, and shifted on his feet. 'Before you have to leave us,' he said finally. 'The Banquet will be the perfect opportunity!'

Before you have to leave us? I had not thought of leaving. Violet and I exchanged a glance of incomprehension. Dr Scrapie had been behaving rather strangely of late.

'I am in your hands, Dr Scrapie,' I replied courteously.

He seemed to like this idea.

'In my hands!' he beamed. 'Yes! Most excellent! Then I shall lend you one of my old dinner suits, and you will join us!'

Violet was smiling, and thrusting my piece of paper further into the folds of her dress.

'Us?' I asked, exchanging a glance with Miss Scrapie. 'Do I infer, therefore, Dr Scrapie, that your charming daughter will be among the guests?' I mustered, trying to hide my blushes.

'Who?' he asked. Then the penny dropped. 'Oh, you mean *Vile*. Yes, of course,' he replied, looking distracted. 'Violet always tags along to these things, don't you? Though she's not much of a dancer.' Violet, who had not missed the import of my question, was smothering a little embarrassed giggle.

'Then I will be even more delighted to attend,' I told him, attempting, but failing, to suppress the smile that was spreading across my face. I was to attend a banquet at the Palace, in the company of Miss Scrapie! I was so delighted at this prospect that for a moment I forgot that I had just handed her the beginnings of my hideous confession. My admiration of the taxidermist's daughter was surely by now as plain as the day, but Dr Scrapie seemed quite oblivious.

'Then come with me at once,' he commanded, striding out of the room. As I began to follow, I saw Violet smoothing out the piece of paper I had shoved at her, and reading it. Remembering what I had begun to write, my heart began to thud once more.

'Come on, Phelps!' Scrapie was calling me impatiently from the corridor. 'Let's get you fixed up with some clothes.'

298

I turned to Violet. She was looking at me with obvious consternation.

'Your revelation is indeed most unusual,' she whispered. 'What a singularly strange mixture you carry in your blood, Mr Phelps! Your mother a Contortionist, and your father a monk!'

A monk?

'No!' I blurted. 'Not a monk! I didn't finish writing it! Not a monk, a –'

'*Come on*, Phelps!' yelled Scrapie.

Fate had intervened. I shook my head and fled.

A firework suddenly went off in the sky above me, and I realised it was Bonfire Night.

'Where the fuck's the monkey?' I yelled at the twins, storming down the stairs.

'Gone,' said Rose, patting her huge belly. 'Ouch! I felt a twinge.'

'Me, too,' said Blanche. 'We're definitely going into labour.'

'Yeah, we felt a bit funny earlier,' said Rose.

'Like a dam about to burst,' explained Blanche.

'For Christ's sake,' I told them, wondering how many other blokes up and down the country were going through this very scenario. It was nine months to the day since the Government had announced the Fertility Reward. Coincidence, or what? 'You've probably just got flatulence or indigestion,' I told them. There are limits to a bloke's patience, I was thinking. 'Listen, I've just been up there, and there's no sign of the –'

'We've never been surer of anything,' warned Rose.

'Never,' agreed Blanche.

'Bollocks!' I said. 'Have you seen the news? The whole country's full of phoney emergencies. The ambulance service is going bananas. Just tell me where you put the monkey. It's urgent.'

I'd realised, of course, as I drove up the motorway, that

my discovery of the monkey carried the most extraordinary implications. I'd somehow always known that I deserved more in life than just being a vet. And here it was. Or here, all of a sudden, it was not.

'So? Where is it?'

'We sold it,' said Rose, smiling. 'At the car-boot sale.'

'The *what*?'

'Thought you'd be pleased,' offered Blanche.

'*Pleased*?' I yelled. 'Did you say *pleased*?' I felt so angry at their stupidity that I wanted to kick something to death. But I just groaned instead.

'Well, why not?' pouted Rose. 'You're always going on at us about paying our way. We made a list of ways to make some money. *Number three. Flog all our old junk at the car-boot sale.* Don't think we've just been sitting on our arses while you were in London.'

'We showed you our financial plan, Buck,' Blanche reproached me. 'So don't pretend you can't remember. We got quite a bit of money for it, in the end.'

'Twenty-five Euros,' boasted Blanche.

Keep calm, Buck. Just get the facts. I cleared my throat, and tied to sound mature. 'Who d'you sell it to?' Silence. Well, fuck that approach then. I'll start yelling. 'Come on! Where the fuck is it?'

'Slow down, Buck.'

'I said where the fuck is it? I've got to get it back!'

'Why?' they asked together.

'Because it's valuable,' I said. My hands kept making fists of themselves. The desire to kill and smash was almost overwhelming.

They looked chastened.

'What, worth more than twenty-five Euros?' questioned Rose.

'Worth millions, you fucking idiots.' My voice snagged on tears of rage.

There was a short silence. They hadn't seen me like this before.

Then Rose blurted: 'We sold it to Harry Gawvey.'

'He lives on Ladder Hill.'

'But he won't be there now.'

'He'll be over at the community centre. Dad's been helping him with the Heritage Firework Party.'

'Which is due to begin any minute,' said Norman. His weight made each stair creak as he descended, zipping up his fly. 'Fancy coming along, mate? You're a party animal. The Stoned Crow will be there *en masse* – hey! Whoah! No big hurry, mate!'

I'd snatched up the keys to my Nuance and rushed out.

CHAPTER 28

THE CELEBRATION OF EVOLUTION BANQUET

If you are not familiar with Buckingham Palace, now is perhaps a good moment to contemplate its inner ballroom. It is situated in the West Wing, and occupies the same size, approximately, as Thunder Spit: four acres. How I would have loved to see the Barks and the Tobashes, the Peat-Hoves and the Mulveys and the Boggses watching me arrive at its grandiose portals in a hansom cab! And enter its arched galleries with Miss Violet Scrapie on my arm! But then, as the footman took our cloaks, and ushered us towards the centre of the Banquet, I wondered suddenly what Parson Phelps would make of it all. The thought of him sent a bleak shudder through me. Will Jared have arrived at Fishforth by now, I wondered, accepting a glass of chilled champagne and an unusual-looking sweetmeat which sent Mildred into instant convulsions. Will the Parson be reading my letter at this very moment, I mused, as Miss Scrapie, clad in a great meringue soufflé of a garment which suited her so well it looked as though it had grown out of her, like the wings from a butterfly, grabbed my hand (Oh joy!) and, catching me in the majestic tumble of her skirts (Oh further joy!), swept me along in the direction of the buffet.

Will I ever have the pleasure, I wondered, of addressing her as Violet?

I gasped at the scene that streaked past me as she dragged me in her wake, thinking: What a fabulous beast is man! Chandeliers probably do not come much more elaborate than this! Curtains probably do not come in much redder a velvet, or

302

heavier, or more strangulated with gold silken cords than these! Ballgowns surely do not come so ponderous, or so fabulous, or so mesmerising!

'Look!' whispers Miss Scrapie in my ear. 'Over there! The Royal Hippo!'

And there she is, by the potted palm, Queen Victoria herself, a dumpy little madam, no taller than myself, in her widow's black garb, scowling a petulant fat-faced scowl, and surrounded by fawning courtiers and admirers – Dr Scrapie now suddenly among them, and barging his way to the fore.

'Old hypocrite,' murmurs my paramour, watching her father perform an elaborate and dangerously low bow, then unfold himself to kiss the Monarch's black-gloved hand.

'And look,' she says, pointing in the direction of the buffet table. 'Cabillaud has surpassed himself!' She says this with pride, but a hint of sadness.

A marvellous, glistening quilt of food is spread before us, on a white-clothed table which runs the whole length of the ballroom; guests, armed with china plates, are tucking in to pale jellied eels, glistening prawns, huge tureens of chilled turtle soup, tubs of pink paste, little pastry cases filled with odd-smelling chopped meats, mounds of Turkish Delight and other exotic *bonbons;* waiters are milling about bearing great platters of oysters with wedges of lemon and lime, huge blancmange desserts and nougat cake heaped with chocolate cream. On a small pedestal stands a great wobbling white jelly topped with a splash of fragrant strawberry sauce, surrounded by tiny dishes of liquorice and sherbet. Beneath it, upon the floor, stands an enamel bathtub containing a fruit salad; a waiter is ladling out raspberries, melon, blackberries and – my mouth waters as I spot the first slice – banana into little dishes, and adorning them with grated chocolate and swirls of cream.

Impressive.

So impressive, indeed, that suddenly Miss Scrapie is deserting me to congratulate the chef.

'Monsieur Cabillaud!' she cries, rushing headlong into the outspread arms of a small tubby man in a tall white hat.

'*Ma petite chérie! Ma petite Violette!*' he responds, pressing her to his bosom.

Oh, what it must be, to be reunited with a loved one! What would I not give to be so embraced by dear Parson Phelps!

Assaulted by my own sudden feelings of longing, I averted my eyes from the touching scene taking place before me. But it was an error to do so, for when I looked up again, having contemplated my shoes for the space of perhaps one minute, I saw that Miss Scrapie and the chef had vanished in the throng. The sudden loss of Miss Scrapie left me feeling horribly alone and ill-at-ease. I had been obliged to dress for tonight's occasion in a cast-off old dinner suit of Dr Scrapie's which was far too big, and which, thanks to the well-intentioned but ultimately unhelpful adjustments made by a certain Mrs Jiggers, hung off me in a way that Miss Scrapie could surely not find attractive.

'Stay where you are!' ordered Scrapie, suddenly re-appearing and grabbing my arm with force. 'Do not move. I'm going to find Mr Darwin, and bring him here, and we will tell him of your origins!' He was clasping *A New Theory of Evolution* to his breast, and his eyes were darting eagerly about the room in search of the great man. 'My dear, dear young specimen!' he choked, still clasping my arm tightly. I winced in pain. 'I must confess I was growing almost fond of you!'

Specimen? I felt foolish, and uneasy, as though an important fact hung just beyond my grasp.

'Stay right here by this pillar,' ordered Scrapie again, more bluntly this time. 'Don't move a bloody inch.'

So I stood there obediently, thinking of my sudden 'specimen-hood', and my imminent meeting with Mr Darwin, the man whom Parson Phelps blamed for the decline of Christianity itself. In short, the man responsible for a multiplicity of woes.

I very much hoped he would not expect my gratitude for the fine mess he had landed me in, I thought, as the band struck up a waltz.

*   *   *

The speakers in the community centre were blaring out some dated old techno rubbish. The place was teeming with people. The Cleggs, the Peat-Hoves, the Mulveys, the Tobashes. Harcourt, his grumpy Filipina swaying on his arm, grabbed me by the arm and thrust a foaming beer at me.

'Get that down you,' he said. There were plastic tables along each wall, with a mass of paper plates and decorated serviettes, bearing sausages on sticks, various dips, blobs of cheese, and an array of pizzas. Some meringue pavlovas were de-frosting at the back. I swigged my beer, my eyes still scanning the room for Gawvey. I'd had the foresight to stop off at the cashpoint in the high street on my way, and I had a hundred yos in my pocket to buy the monkey back. I'd offer him more, though, if he wanted it. I could get an overdraft, if the need arose. I reckoned it was worth going up to a thousand, without arousing his suspicions. After all, it was a family heirloom.

The music had changed to the Hokey Cokey, and a great human caterpillar was forming. I barged past.

'Where's Gawvey?' I shouted. 'I've got to find him!'

'Outside,' said Boggs. 'Easy does it, mate. He's doing the bonfire.'

Just then a tinkling burst of music cascaded down from a shiny orchestra perched on a balcony, and couples began to glide to the dance-floor. Soon the whole space was packed. As the dancers whizzed about me in a human hurricane of sequins and perfume and chinking medallions, my eyes scoured the ballroom once again for Miss Scrapie. But there was no sign of her in the crowd. Had I lost her for the whole evening? Perhaps for ever? Pondering this ghastly thought, a sadness and fear overwhelmed me. I thrust my hands deep into my pockets, and invoked Betty Botter, until a sudden instinct told me to ignore my promise to Dr Scrapie, and seek shelter from the crowd. To this end I found myself shuffling, half-tripping on my over-long trousers, and with some difficulty arriving at a small table beside a huge marble fountain. And here I sat, fingering my crucifix, doing my best to become invisible, and attempting, with the help of a glass of port proffered me by a waiter, to pick up my flagging spirits, and to ignore the distinct feeling of unease emanating from my lower spine.

Then the quadrille came to a sudden halt and the clocks chimed eight. A hush fell, and a tail-coated Master of Royal Ceremonies struck a huge gong with a padded stick, signalling to the assembled ladies and gentlemen that it was time for the celebrations to begin in earnest.

'My Lords, Ladies and Gentlemen! Please raise your glasses to Her Majesty the Queen!'

The Monarch smooths her black skirts and purses her lips as we raise our glasses and ask God to bless her. The gong sounds again, and the Master of Royal Ceremonies gives further utterance.

'And to Mr Charles Darwin!'

The small bearded man next to Queen Victoria performs a neat little bow, as we salute him. 'To Mr Charles Darwin!' When he unbends himself, I notice that he has a twinkle in his eye.

'Now stand back, please, Ladies and Gentlemen, for the revelation of our gastronomic centrepiece this evening, the Evolutionary Time-Bomb, a masterpiece of cuisine designed and constructed by Her Majesty's head chef, Monsieur Jacques-Yves Cabillaud!'

There is a rustling of gowns and a clapping of hands as the crowd pulls back from a central area hitherto hidden from view by dancing bodies, hanging curtains and swathes of flowers. At first, the area is so huge and so grey it has the appearance of a wall – but suddenly, the eye adjusts and a new perspective is revealed: the thing we see before us, seated within an enormous clam shell, is nothing more and nothing less than an entire roast elephant!

'Good grief!' mutters a brigadier, an expression of surprise which is echoed, in various forms, throughout the hall, in a sudden windy rustle of words.

'Her name was Mona,' whispers a man who has appeared at my side out of the blue. 'She's from the Zoological Gardens. They slit her throat last Thursday, and it took a week for her to die. Have you heard the rumour that Monsieur Cabillaud used to be her keeper at the Zoo?'

A shudder goes through me as I stare across the room at Cabillaud, who has suddenly materialised next to his gruesome exhibit and is bowing deeply to the assembled throng. Now he takes a huge sword and places it, with an obsequious bow, in the hand of the dumpy little woman Miss Scrapie refers to as the Royal Hippo.

'If it please Your Majesty,' he says. He's all red in the face with pride. 'Would you graciously do us all ze great honour of making ze first incision into ze Time-Bomb?'

A murmur of appreciation rises from the ladies and gentle-men as the little monarch obliges by taking hold of the scimitar. I stand on tiptoe to watch her; as she takes a grip on the weapon, I see her mouth twisting into what might be a smile, or a pang of indigestion, I cannot be sure which. Then I spot Dr Scrapie stepping forward to help her.

'If I may be of assistance, Your Majesty,' he murmurs, stand-ing behind her and encircling her with his arms. 'And if you will excuse the necessary intimacy . . .' Delicately, he places his own hands upon hers, and helps her to lift the heavy scimitar.

A burst of cheering and hand-clapping as Dr Scrapie helps the Queen make a deep cut into the huge creature's rubbery flesh.

'Raise your glasses again,' intones the Master of Royal Ceremonies, 'to Her Majesty the Queen!'

As we wish the Monarch a long life and good health, and the orchestra strikes up 'Rule Britannia', Scrapie and the Monarch are busy cutting a huge slit down the front of the elephant's chest. The grey flesh divides like a pair of thick felt curtains and –

Whispers. Genteel murmurings. Hushed gasps.

Out tumbles a lumpy waterfall of pungent mushrooms and garlic-ball stuffing. A gurgle of steaming liquid and more mushrooms follow, all captured in the huge natural tureen of the giant clam beneath.

Delighted screams. Whoops. Cat-calls.

For there, revealed inside the elephant's cavernous interior – Yes! It's true! – amid a mass of foliage that resembles parsley, there appears to be an entire zebra!

A massive cheer erupts spontaneously from the crowd.

'Bravo!' shrieks a woman next to me, whipping up a strong-ish wind with the excited flapping of her lace fan. And then a further and even more frenzied cheer emerges as seconds later, Queen Victoria, warming to her task, once again wields the scimitar, with Scrapie's help, and makes a deft incision in the zebra's exposed belly to reveal, among the baked apples and glazed onions, its skin criss-crossed with diamonds of cloves and apricots, a gigantic roast hog!

Astonishing!

We can hardly believe what we are seeing. But then – No! Surely not!

'Good Lord!' exclaims the fan-flapping woman next to me. 'I don't believe it!'

'Look!' yells a military gent, his medals crashing together as he jiggles with excitement. 'She's cutting again!

The Royal Hippo, who has warmed to her task enough to spurn Dr Scrapie's renewed offer of help, is indeed wielding the scimitar a third time. With a swift and expert lunge, impressive from a woman so small and stiffly padded, she stabs the hog, whose skin splits neatly along a stitched seam to reveal a cavity from which –

My God! From the heart of the Time-Bomb, a live woman is stepping out!

A dropped fan. Gasps and applause from the men. Excited screams from the ladies.

And a groan from me, followed swiftly by a ghastly surge of nausea.

308

For this is not just any woman.

It is a woman in a tutu and little ballet shoes.

It is the human herring gull, Contortionist Extraordinaire of the Travelling Fair of Danger and Delight –

My mother.

Ding, dong! chimes the Balls' doorbell.

The future is calling.

'Damn and blast!' says Abbie, under her breath. She's been rushed off her feet all day, and has only just finished her cookery rehearsal – a full ten minutes behind schedule.

'Hold on a second!' she calls, as she wipes the flour off her hands and glances at the Apfelkuchen. They're browning nicely in the oven. And the coffee's just on. She'd been planning to put her feet up.

'I'm sorry to trouble you,' says the young leather-jacketed stranger. He has a small gold earring in one ear, and is carrying a clip-board. He's waving a set of car keys at her apologetically. 'But my car's broken down, and my mobile phone's –'

'On the blink,' falters Abbie, suddenly feeling rather sick as a feeling of *déjà vu* engulfs her.

'Yes,' says the man, flashing her a handsome smile. 'How did you guess? Look, I'm sorry to ask you this, but –'

'Of course you can call the AA,' says Abbie. 'And perhaps while you're waiting, I might tempt you with some of my Apfelkuchen and a cup of nice fresh coffee?'

You could say that Abbie Ball has been blessed with a form of second sight, for is this not her dream coming true?

'May I ask you your name?' she falters, pouring a china cup of Colombian Special Blend.

'Of course,' says the stranger, whipping out a business card. 'Sorry, I should have – Anyway . . . Pleased to meet you.'

Abbie takes his business card with a trembling hand and reads.

OSCAR JACK.

ERA PRODUCTIONS.
At last!

The Apfelkuchen are going down a treat.

'Can I offer you a fifth?' Abbie asks, five minutes later, after she has completed her tour of the kitchen for Oscar, and he has settled himself on the settee in the living room with the air of a man who is no longer the slightest bit worried about his seized-up car or his broken mobile.

'Abbie,' he begins. He has a soft, cultured voice, but there's excitement in it. Genuine excitement. 'May I call you Abbie?' She swallows hard, and nods vigorously.

'I couldn't help noticing – well, your extraordinary poise. It struck me immediately – the minute I clapped eyes on you – that you have a certain *je-ne-sais-quoi*, and that – well.' He lowered his voice. 'This is rare, this is extremely rare, I don't want you to think that this is the kind of thing that happens every day, in fact, never before in my whole television career –'

'Yes?'

'Spit it out, then,' says the Laudanum Empress from Norman's armchair. She is darning one of her cobwebby old stockings.

'Well, Abbie,' says Oscar Jack, oblivious to the interruption, 'some people are simply what we call "television naturals," and –'

It always happens, doesn't it? Something. A crack of thunder. The ping of the microwave. An urgent call of nature.

Or the ring of the telephone.

'Excuse me, just one moment,' says Abbie. Her heart is pounding in a way it hasn't done since she met Norman for the first time twenty years ago, in the park. She'd been sitting by the sandpit babysitting her friend's little girl, and he'd rammed her in the bum with his nephew's remotely controlled racing car. 'It's probably your AA man.'

Abbie picks up the phone, and instantly turns as white as self-raising flour.

'Mum, it's us. You've got to come now. *Now*.'

310

'What's happening?' she whispers shakily.

'We've just gone into labour, Mum!' shrieks a twin. 'And Buck's buggered off!'

'Are you *sure*, Roseblanche?' asks Abbie nervously, cupping her hand over the receiver so that Oscar Jack can't hear. 'I mean there have been an awful lot of false alarms . . .' she whispers.

'Please, Mum!' shriek the voices in unison. '*You've got to believe us!*'

What mother can resist a cry of help from her baby?

The unfairness of it! Dilemma city. The recipe for disaster, thinks Abbie, drifting into a shocked reverie as Oscar Jack tucks into another Apfelkuchen. Cruel-world stew:

Take several ounces of extreme bad luck, and spike with a measure of ill-timing. Add a pinch of malevolence and stir up well with the base ingredient of injustice. Throw in some intolerance and bitterness. Pour on heavy dollops of meanness, spite and pessimism, and refrigerate until an uneasy chill is achieved. Dose in individual portions with a dash of bile and garnish with shite. Note: the result is addictive.

So much blood has drained from Abbie's face that Oscar Jack is thinking she'll need a lot of panstick when the time comes.

'Bugger,' she mutters finally.

'Language!' trills the Empress gleefully.

'Is there anything I –' begins Oscar Jack.

'Mum!' yells Roseblanche down the phone.

'Yes?' manages Abbie, faintly, her eyes on Oscar Jack's well-shaven, innocent face. He's already punched her name and address into his personal organiser. If only –

'I can't come now! My television producer's arrived! Just call an ambulance!' she hisses weakly into the receiver.

'We did!' shrieks Roseblanche. 'They don't believe us! They

311

think it's a hoax! They say they're getting three a night like this! We're nearly ready to push! Mum, help!'

Abbie groans. 'I'm on my way,' she sighs, and slams down the receiver.

The Contortionist, having made several curtsies to the crowd, is now scampering balletically atop the elephant's head and beginning, amid enthusiastic applause, to tie herself into a human knot.

Meanwhile below, at ground-level, a regiment of *sous-chefs* are busy attacking the Time-Bomb with carving-knives, cutting slices of elephant, zebra, and hog meat and placing it on the platters held by the *sous-sous-chefs*, who are in turn handing them to the *sous-sous-sous-chefs* for the addition of garnish. Minions further down in the kitchen hierarchy mill about, proffering plates of food to guests, who comment delightedly upon the unusual taste and texture of the meats.

The Time-Bomb, Cabillaud reflects, has certainly been the crowning triumph of his whole glittering career, the pinnacle of his own personal evolution. Even Violet, now a militant vegan, has mustered the *politesse* to congratulate him on it, despite her opposition to all forms of cruelty.

'May I present you with my book?' Cabillaud now enquires of Violet, thrusting a first-edition copy of *Cuisine Zoologique: une philosophie de la viande* into her hand. She is looking quite magnificent, he notes. Extraordinarily well, and happy. There is beauty in ugliness after all. The dress she is wearing suits her. She seems distracted, though. Her eyes keep scanning the room, as though she is looking for someone.

Which she is. And now, finally, Violet has spotted him. He's over at the buffet table, where he is serving himself to a generous portion of fruit salad. Tobias's gaze, she notices, is firmly resting upon the little ballerina-woman who recently emerged from Cabillaud's Time-Bomb. The woman, having untangled herself from her scorpion position atop the elephant's

312

head, has now leaped off it and is pirouetting across the room at great speed in the direction of the ladies' powder room. Violet watches as, just as suddenly, Tobias abandons his fruit salad and strides across to follow the little ballerina.

'Violette?' Cabillaud is saying. 'You will accept a copy of my *oeuvre*?'

'Oh,' says Violet distractedly. She has lost sight of Tobias and the ballerina (surely he could not have followed her into the ladies' powder room?), and turns her attention reluctantly back to the chef. 'Thank you, Monsieur Cabillaud.' Despite the nature of its contents, she feels the need to accept the book with grace. Such is compromise.

'I am working on a plant version of my own,' she offers.

'Ze foliage?'

'Yes. I am planning to call it *The Fleshless Cook*.' Cabillaud raises an eyebrow.

'One day, my dear, you will learn that ze human being is not designed to eat plant life alone.'

Violet smiles. 'I survive very well,' she tells him.

'May I interrupt?' asks a small, bearded, twinkle-eyed man who has been hovering at the edge of their conversation.

Violet and Cabillaud exchange a glance.

'Please do, Mr Darwin,' says Violet. At last, an expert witness in their ideological dispute! 'We would be most grateful, Mr Darwin, for your opinion on the matter, wouldn't we, Monsieur Cabillaud?'

'Of course! And very honoured! Please allow me, Monsieur, to present to you Miss Scrapie.'

'Charmed to meet you, Miss Scrapie,' begins Mr Darwin. 'I am acquainted with your father. Now the human body originally evolved, as we know, from the primate. Primates are largely fructivorous, although there are exceptions. However, if we study the evolutionary path of man, we will discover hints that his descendence from several species of *ape*, descended in turn from a branch of the *monkey* family, involved an adaptation of the alimentary canal which –'

313

'Mr Darwin!' interrupts Dr Ivanhoe Scrapie, yelling from across the room, and fumbling his way through a mêlée of sparkling ballgowns. 'Mr Darwin! I have finally found you! You must come with me immediately, and see an extraordinary specimen. A walking, talking, human-monkey hybrid, here in this very room!'

Charles Darwin bursts out laughing. 'This is indeed an exceptionally entertaining banquet,' he smiles. And then, lowering his voice, to address Violet, 'And not at all what one would have expected from Her Majesty.'

'It is true!' yells Dr Scrapie, his faced flushed. 'And the creature's father is in the ladies' powder room to prove it! The Gentleman Monkey! I stuffed him myself!'

Violet, feeling something curdle violently within her, and recognising there is a strong risk that she will faint, collapses with a padded thud on a stiff little seat and begins flapping her fan furiously. A human-monkey hybrid? What is her father talking about? He couldn't possibly be referring to – her breath catches in her throat.

'*My father was a monk*.' Violet releases a quiet moan as Dr Scrapie and Mr Darwin continue their conversation. '*I didn't finish writing it*,' he had said.

'A monkey? Excellent!' Mr Darwin is exclaiming. 'I do approve of your sense of humour, my dear Scrapie! Lead me to this alleged specimen at once!'

As Violet fans herself with such force that she risks mimicking the un-aerodynamic bumble-bee and taking flight, Charles Darwin's laughter is overheard by a group of military gents and their wives, who, somewhat affected by champagne, repeat the joke and join in the laughter, which thereby becomes so amplified that the curiosity of others is aroused, and the joke is passed on, and more people are attracted to the steadily growing throng, until a huge gaggle of laughing banqueteers has encircled the two scientists. Violet, pale beneath her face-powder, and still seated near the heart of the kerfuffle, has the presence of mind to keep listening to her father's urgent and

314

garbled speech to Mr Darwin, the content of which is causing her increasing unease.

'His name is Tobias Phelps,' continues Scrapie excitedly. As the import of her father's words dawns on Violet, she groans, then freezes, immobilised with shock. She has not felt such a churning confusion of emotions since the death of the Laudanum Empress. Her father is tugging at Darwin's sleeve.

'He is a creature aged some twenty years,' her father is telling Darwin. 'Nurtured as a man, and with quite remarkable – really *most astonishing* – success. What I am planning to do, Mr Darwin, once you have inspected him for yourself and verified my findings' – Violet leans forward, straining to listen – 'is to keep him captive for a few days, so that other zoologists may have a chance to view him while he is still alive' – Violet gasps, and clutches her hand over her mouth – 'then kill and stuff him myself, and present him thus to the Zoological Society.'

Keep him captive? Kill and stuff him?

Violet feels suddenly quite monstrously sick. She drops her fan to the floor with a clatter and clutches her chair, her knuckles whitening with the pressure of grasping on. It's as much as she can do to prevent herself from keeling over. So that is what Tobias was trying to tell her that day! That is why he was so upset, and why he had insisted on writing it down on that piece of paper. Not monk, but *monkey*! The Gentleman Monkey!

'Oh no!' she groans, remembering with sudden clarity the braising process, and the shrimp sauce that had accompanied the dish that killed the Laudanum Empress.

'I ate him!' she whispers to herself, appalled. 'I ate his father! I am a cannibal!'

'Come along, then, Mr Darwin!' Scrapie is saying. 'I left him standing over by that pillar. Let's go and meet him!' Another huge smile spreads across the face of Charles Darwin, and the naturalist once again throws back his head and laughs uproariously, shaking little fragments of food from his beard as he does so.

'I should have thought to come in fancy-dress myself,' he chortles good-humouredly. 'Dressed as a gorilla. I believe one can hire such a costume. Would that not have been more apt, for such an occasion, Dr Scrapie? Might the' – he lowers his voice conspiratorially – '*Royal Hippopotamus*, as you call her, have been amused?'

But Dr Scrapie is not laughing. He is looking strangulated instead. His face is almost blue. He is still clutching Mr Darwin's sleeve, and now starts tugging it again with urgency.

'There is no time to lose,' Violet murmurs to herself, gulping back her urge to vomit and smoothing the cream crêpe of her billowing skirts.

'But he is the answer to your paradox, sir!' Scrapie is insisting to Mr Darwin, who is by now laughing so heartily that he appears at serious risk of choking. 'I swear, sir, that this is not a joke!'

Darwin laughs some more. 'I do not possess a paradox,' he replies.

'Well, you do now!' explodes Scrapie, wrenching the man by the arm and frog-marching him across the ballroom. The bevy of interested spectators follows chattering and giggling in their wake. What an unexpectedly entertaining occasion this is turning out to be! As they move off, Violet bites her lip, her mind racing.

'Push!' Abbie is yelling at the twins.

'I warned you,' says the Laudanum Empress, hovering by the loo. She did no such thing, but Abbie is in no state to argue. When Abbie had made the call to the Baldicoot Medical Centre, she'd been referred to the Ambulance Service, which had refused point blank to send an emergency vehicle.

'But this is real!' Abbie had screamed.

'That's what they all say, love,' said the duty nurse wearily.

'We'll pay the fine – we don't care!' shrieked the twins.

'Sorry, love,' said the duty nurse, when Abbie relayed this. 'The fact is, all the ambulances are out. They're calling it the Day of Madness.'

'Well fuck you, then!' shrieked Abbie, distraught. What was happening to her? She'd never uttered a swear-word before in her life, until today. And now two (there was a 'bugger', earlier) in front of Oscar Jack! Could she be developing Tourette's syndrome? Good thing Oscar's here, though, she realises suddenly. Because there's no sign of Norman, or of that wastrel Buck. He's off on some wild monkey chase, apparently.

'Bless you!' she sobs at Oscar Jack. The television producer has grabbed the twins' camcorder, perched it on the kitchen table and left it running; no slouch he, when it comes to capturing a potential exclusive. In addition, he's rolled up the sleeves of his leather jacket and is now doing sterling work with towels and bottles of Perrier.

'AAAGH!' yell the twins again.

Wow. If this is another of those bogus ones, thinks Oscar Jack, then it's frighteningly realistic.

When I saw the Contortionist leap off the elephant's head and pirouette across the room, I knew I must confront her.

Following her with difficulty across the banqueting hall, tripping over the legs of my trousers and bumping into dinner guests with plates piled high with meat, I reached a corridor which led to a parlour which led to a door which swung shut in my face. LADIES' POWDER ROOM, it said.

I hesitated for a moment, and then entered.

And came face to face with my father, the Gentleman Monkey.

I stopped in my tracks and caught my breath. And stared. He was holding a towel of purple and yellow. His eyes were a bright and unnatural blue. His fur was a rusty orange-red – the same colour and the same coarse texture as my own hair. Like me, he had a thick down on his arms. He was a little shorter than me. His expression was one of great nobility and poise. He had a short tail, which emerged from a slit in his red pantaloons and curled upwards behind him like a question mark.

The Contortionist was standing in front of him, gazing into his blue and strangely human eyes. She was oblivious to my presence; for a while, we both stood there staring at the monkey, each lost in his own thoughts. Finally I cleared my throat.

'Excuse me, madam?' I said.

She jumped, and turned to look at me. She seemed to be crying; the frills of her little ballet tutu were trembling.

'Madam, I believe you are my mother.'

She stared at me. She said nothing. She just stared.

'And this – gentleman – is my father,' I ventured. 'Am I right?'

'Lawks a mercy,' she said, sucking in her breath. 'Fancy meeting you here.'

She bit her lip. I held out my hand, and she took it. We shook hands formally.

'Madam, I think you owe me an explanation,' I mustered.

'S'pose I do, Tobias,' she said, sighing. 'S'pose I do.'

'You – know my name?'

'Yes.'

She told me everything. Horace Trapp had kidnapped her, and kept her in a cage on his *Ark*.

'It was an old slave-trader,' she said. 'Cos that's what he used to do. Travelled between London and Africa and Georgia, selling slaves. But then he had a shipload die on him, and there was a big scandal in London. So he switched to animals instead, got this caper going for Queen Victoria. The Animal Kingdom Collection.'

I nodded. This much tallied with what Dr Scrapie had told me.

'But I finds out he has some other business. And that's why

318

I'm in the cage with – this dear gentleman,' she said. Her voice softened, and she took the monkey's hand in hers as she spoke. It was an oddly moving sight.

'Other business?' I asked. 'What sort of other business?'

But she ignored me; she appeared to be speaking almost from a trance. 'It's Higgins tells me what Trapp's planning. Trapp never bothers to tell me himself, does he? There I was then, having this idea that I was just there to keep the gentleman company, like a playmate for him. But he's soon a lot more than that to me.'

I blushed, as the little woman continued the extraordinary tale of my genesis.

'I discovers I'm up the spout, around the same time as I discovers that this is what Trapp was wanting all along. *That* was his other business.'

'He *wanted* you and the – gentleman here – to . . . ?'

I was unable to find the words to complete my question.

'Yes. Higgins tells me he was hoping to breed from us.'

'*Hoping* to breed? *Hoping* to? Why?' I felt sick.

'Slaves,' she said. A chill ran through me. 'He had this theory. After the scandal over his dead slaves, and the campaign to have the trade abolished, he'd been hatching this plan to mate a human with a monkey, to get an offspring. To breed a new kind of slave, that's not completely human. "A race of natural inferiors", he calls it. If you're not strictly speaking a man, see,' she said, 'you haven't got no rights like men does.'

I gasped.

'But why?' I asked.

'Profit,' murmured my new-found mother. 'He was after making a profit. He'd seen the slave trade coming to an end. He reckoned the problem all along with the human slaves was that they'd end up with the same rights as other folk. The only way to ever get that kind of cheap labour again without a big hoo-ha was to create –'

'I see,' I said.

'Yes. But he hadn't bargained on my gentleman friend.'

We both looked at him, with a mixture of pity and awe.

'Anyway, when I finds this out, that that's what he's planning, that's when I know we has to escape, even if it means –'

She hung her head.

'They all died,' she said bluntly. 'It happened the night the storm was brewing. When Steed comes to give us our slop, I distract him with a few little favours while my gentleman friend sneaks the key to our cage from his pocket. When they've gone back up to their cabins, we opened all the animals' cages to take attention away from us, and they all shot out and started rioting, and ripping each other to pieces.' She paused, and squinted painfully at the memory. 'It was a nightmare. They was all killing each other and my gentleman friend, when he sees Trapp come towards us, he pounces on him, and grabs him by the throat, all ready to kill him, and I'm screaming at him to do it, to strangle him, but Trapp's got a syringe in his hand and as soon as the needle goes in, my gentleman friend just falls to the floor stone dead.' Her eyes fill suddenly with tears.

'So it was Trapp who killed him? With the syringe?'

'Yes.' She looks up at me, and the tears fall. She makes no attempt to wipe them away. 'He died trying to save my life, Tobias. And yours. I couldn't stop him.' She is sobbing now. 'I saw him die.'

Tentatively, I put my arm around her, and hand her my handkerchief. She grabs it and blows her nose furiously.

'He loved life so much,' she's whispering through her tears. 'He was so funny, so clever, so innocent. So good-hearted. He was all instinct. I realised as soon as I saw him in the light of day that he wasn't a man. I never pretended he was.' She strokes his arm. 'He was more than a man.' She pauses. 'And he was better than a man.' The tears begin again. 'He laid down his life for us, Tobias,' she wails. 'He wasn't called a gentleman for nothing.'

I swallow painfully. 'And then?' I whisper.

'When I sees he's dead,' she sniffs, 'that's when I jumps ship. I have no idea where we are. Could be in the Caribbean, for all I know. In fact it's the English Channel. We must've been on our way back. Anyway, I swims till I'm half-drowned. I'm just wearing my tutu. Bloody cold, it was. Near froze, but I'm a strong swimmer. Then I gets caught in a fishing net, and pulled along. Must've been dragged aboard with all the fish, cos when I wakes up, I'm on a fishing boat, stinking. The next thing I know, I'm in London bloody docks, of all places. Went straight to the workhouse. I got there, and gave birth to you.'

I felt myself swaying on my feet.

The Contortionist laughed suddenly. 'Silly of me, but when I saw your tail, I still got the shock of my life.'

'What is zis, Violette?' asks Cabillaud, reappearing before her with the fan she has dropped, and flapping it to cool her. 'You are not well, *ma chérie*?'

He has seen this look before. Years ago, on his own face, when he gazed in the mirror aboard the *Beagle*, and thought of his sweetheart Saskia.

'No. I am suddenly most terribly unwell!' croaks Violet, still clutching her chair. 'You must help me, Monsieur Cabillaud! My father is planning to kill and stuff the man I – the gentleman I –'

'Love,' finishes Cabillaud. He knows. It is written all over her face. 'You must escape wiz 'im, zen,' he suggests.

'How?' wails Violet, kneading her pudgy hands together in distress.

'I will open ze kitchen doors for you, *ma chérie*! Now go and get 'im! Quick!'

Violet, her heart beating like a war-drum in her heaving bosom, scans the room; the two scientists and their accompanying mob of laughing guests have finished their search of the northern corner of the ballroom, and are now heading west in the direction of another marble pillar.

'I told him to bloody-well stay put!' she hears her father

shrieking as he strides through the dancing throng, still frog-marching Darwin with him.

'This is a most amusing game of hide-and-seek, is it not?' laughs Mr Darwin good-naturedly. He had not wished, initially, to attend the Banquet, bad health and a hermit-like disposition combining to make him shun most public occasions – but he has been pleasantly surprised by this evening's turn of events.

'Hey! Has anyone seen a monkey-man?' yells Scrapie. And the mob takes up the cry.

Lifting up the billowing swathes of her skirts, Violet rises from her chair and hurtles off in the direction of the ladies' powder room like a human torpedo.

My mother had left me speechless.

'He's the only reason I come here to do this banquet job,' she said, still stroking the Gentleman Monkey's hairy arm. 'I heard he was here. Friend of mine, Nancy, I told her all about him and me. Her man Frank, he's a Palace footman. She says to me she's sure my gentleman's here, from what Frank's said. That settles it. When Hillber talks to me about the Time-Bomb, I says yes. I'd've done anything to see him again, one last time.'

The tears were running freely down her cheeks, leaving grey tracks. I, too, brushed away a tear as the Contortionist continued her story.

'So you were born in the workhouse. When they saw you, with your tail, and your monkey feet, they said I'd mated with the Devil, and they chucked me out. I came straight to the Fairground. I knew there was a way of making money, and we did – hand over fist. You were called the Devil-Child of Greenwich. It's the workhouse people in Greenwich, what gives me the idea to call you that.'

Devil-Child? I was far from keen on the sound of this, but I held my tongue. Instead I asked, 'And then what happened? How did I lose my tail?'

'Well, I kept you in a cage –'

'A cage?' I interrupted. 'You kept me in *a cage*?' I remembered my vision during the Flood: I had seen a cot with golden bars, guarded by a beast.

'I was working, wasn't I?' she said. 'I didn't have the choice. I had to do this contortionism thing: human knots and all that. Mr Hillber wasn't just going to pay me for existing, was he? But you wouldn't suckle from anyone else, so he had to keep me. Anyway, your cage is right next to the Man-Eating Wart-hog's.' I had a sudden memory of the creature; its orange-ochre eyes, with their vertical slits; its vile carbuncles. I shivered.

'Well, it's thanks to him you lost it. He's a tricky customer. He's hungry one day, or playful. You tail is sticking through his bars. So he –'

She stops. Looks embarrassed. Ashamed. Then drops her voice.

'He bites it off.'

My God. Again I remembered my vision in the church during the Flood. Suddenly it all made sense. The Angel. The creature. The blood. The screaming, shrill and hoarse.

'I remember it,' I said. She had been the Angel.

'But he didn't like the taste,' she said, giving a little bitter laugh. 'He spat it out. We tried to sew it back on, but it was no use, so I stuck it in an old jar of pickle.'

She paused, and began to stroke my father's furry cheek wistfully. For my own part, I was having trouble taking all this in. All my life I had wondered about my origins. But now – it was as if a dam had burst, and the answers to all my questions were all gushing out at once. I was left reeling.

'After you'd lost your tail,' my mother continued, 'you were doing badly. You had a fever, and I knew that unless you saw a doctor, you was going to die. Mr Hillber said you'd have to go. You were no use to him without a tail, and to be honest, I knew that if you were to stand a chance, I'd have to –' She stopped again, clearly distressed.

'Abandon me,' I finished.

'Yes. That's about the size of it.' Her voice was a mere croak, lost in the increasingly wild noises coming from the banqueting hall. She wasn't looking at me when she spoke. She was looking at the creature. Staring into his blue glass eyes, as though she could read the past in them.

'The circumstances was most particular,' she murmured.

'I am sure they were,' I whispered. I felt a lump in my throat.

'So I left you in little church, in a village near Judlow. Thunder Spit, it was called. I kept your little tail as a sort of memento,' she said softly. 'To remind me of you, and of my gentleman friend, and what happened between us.'

'How did you know about Parson Phelps?'

'I didn't, when I left you. I had no idea. I just reckoned a church was as likely a place as – well, you know. Charity, and all that. And I wasn't wrong, was I?'

'No, I said, remembering Parson Phelps' story of finding me beneath the altar of St Nicholas's Church the day after the Fair left Judlow, and his piglet story.

Wrong animal, I thought.

'Parson Phelps saved my life, then,' I murmured.

'Yes. Parson Phelps,' she said. 'Though I doesn't find out his name till later. I asked about you every time the Fair came to Judlow. Asked a few questions, you know. Looked out for you. Didn't even know if you'd survived or not, but thought you would have. You were a tough little bugger. Then I meet a man who I service once a year at the Fair, a bit of money on the side, turns out he's a cobbler from Thunder Spit.'

'Mr Hewitt?'

'Dunno. I don't do names. Names is extra. They want me to use a name, they pay. Your Grace costs more. Any kids there with funny-shaped feet, I asked him. Great big fat man, smelt of leather. Just the Phelps boy, he says. The Parson's son. Tobias. I don't do names, but I remembered those two, Parson Phelps. And Tobias. Wrote them down, after. The cobbler docks me sixpence for jabbering while he was at it, and spoiling his peace and quiet, but after that I knew you were alive.'

She turned to look at me, and I saw that the tears were once more trickling down her face, leaving little painted rivulets on her cheeks. She looked suddenly old.

'I saw you,' I stammered. 'At the Travelling Fair of Danger and Delight. I saw you doing your act.'

'And I saw you, too,' she said slowly. She held out her arms to me, and we clasped each other tight. She was sobbing into my shoulder now. 'And I saw the fear on your face. It nearly killed me, that.' I fought back my own tears now.

'But then, the next year,' she's sobbing, 'some bloke in Hunchburgh attacks me when I'm doing my sherry-glass act, and I need some money bad. I tied myself in a knot, got all twisted up, couldn't work. Hillber refused to pay me. So when we goes on to Judlow, I goes to the Parson with the jar. And a letter, telling him the story.' She looked up at me then, and I saw that there was a small glimmer of pride on her face. 'I wrote it myself,' she said. 'I learned writing when I was a girl.'

But I pulled back from her. 'You blackmailed him with this jar, and your letter?' I asked, looking into her tear-stained face. Her eyes dropped, and would no longer meet mine.

'Call it what you like. He paid me all he had to get rid of me. He made me promise I'd never approach you, or tell you about the tail.'

'So he *knew all along* that my father was a –' I couldn't quite say it. 'Gentleman?' That sounded much better.

'From that day, yes. I told him. He wouldn't have believed me, he said, if it hadn't been for some book by a man called –'

'Darwin? *Origin of Species?*'

'Some such. He kept talking about it, said it was beginning to make sense. Anyway, after a while I think he sees I might be telling the truth. Either way, he curses me, and wants me gone for ever.'

No wonder her visit had put the seal on my poor father's madness: shortly after the *Origin of Species* had rocked the Christian world, Parson Phelps had had his own, personal version of the crisis. I could imagine his distress on discovering that he had taken a half-monkey to his bosom all these years. He, who had so railed against the very idea of our origins being anything other than stated in the Bible! If you know of anything crueller than that, gentle reader, I would like to hear about it.

'And then?' I asked.

'I went to see a quack, and he fixed me up, so I could do my contortions again. Forgot you existed,' she said. She was still looking at the floor. 'Or tried to.'

'How do I know you're not lying?' I asked her, weakly, in a sudden, last-minute attempt to make myself believe the whole thing was falsehood. I was suddenly aware of a terrible commotion outside in the ballroom.

'You don't,' she was saying. 'I *might* be lying. Perhaps I wishes I was. But I bet you've got a scar at the base of your spine. And a couple of strangely shaped feet stuffed into those fancy shoes of yours.'

I could not deny it.

So here I was, at last, in the company of my two long-lost natural parents. Was that not something? I looked at my father. Despite being a towel-holder, he looked smart, I thought, in his ruffed shirt and his red pantaloons. There was nobility in the way he stood. And why not? He had after all died in an act of bravery, attempting to save the lives of a woman and her unborn child. His wife. That's what she was, though no priest had married them. Suddenly I was caught unawares by a great shudder of pride. It gave me a fierce urge to take the towel away from my father; it demeaned him, to stand there before us like a servant. Or a slave, I thought with a sudden chill, thinking of the fate Trapp had planned for me and my eventual siblings.

Then the Contortionist did a strange thing, which touched me deeply. She leaned forward, put her arms around him, and kissed the Gentleman Monkey on the lips.

'It was love,' she said, slowly. 'True love. Between me and

326

him.' She kissed him again. 'Can you understand that? Can you forgive me?'

At this, an extraordinary feeling of calm and of well-being and of Godliness swept over me. It came from nowhere, and filled my heart to bursting.

'There is nothing to forgive,' I said.

Just then a meringue-clad figure shot in from nowhere and grabbed me. She squashed me against her marvellous pastry bosom and squeezed me until I could hardly breathe.

I was choking in the beery fug of the community centre. I had to get some air. The heat of the bonfire blasted me in the face as I stepped out of the double doors.

'Welcome!' yelled a voice at me. It was Gawvey, his arms loaded with logs. Sparks were flying all around us, and I caught the unmistakable smell of burnt hair.

'Hey, that monkey you bought off the twins!' I yelled. 'I want to buy it back!' And I reached in my pocket and thrust the hundred yo-yos at him.

Gawvey straightened himself up and laughed. 'Tempting, mate,' he said.

The Hokey Cokey ended and a stream of people began to emerge from the community centre, their faces flushed with alcohol and merriment.

'Well?'

'Sure,' he said, jerking his head in the direction of the bonfire. 'If you can get him down from there, me old cock.'

I looked up. Through the smoke and the swirling fragments of ash, I could see the Guy standing on the pinnacle of the bonfire, his tail curled behind him like a jaunty question mark. His whole head was lapped by a halo of blue flames, and the towel he was holding in his crooked arm had transformed into a sheet of fire. I groaned. Then yelled at him.

'Christ! You can't do that!'

'Why not?' asked Gawvey, laughing. 'He's only an old

monkey, mate. Terrible old specimen, according to the Antiques Hotline. Hasn't even got a dick.'

'But you can't burn him!'

'Sure I can mate,' he said. 'Hey, who rattled your cage? Get yourself a beer and calm down, Bucko. Bloody original idea, if you ask me. Beats an old stuffed-clothes-and-a-mask job hands down.'

'But he's not a monkey,' I wailed, watching the halo of fire curl around the creature's head. I could feel water on my face. I brushed it with my hand, and realised I was crying. 'He's – he's a – a sub-human! He's almost a man!'

Gawvey laughed and laughed.

'That's why he's called a Guy, mate,' he said.

'Come on,' said Norman gently, taking my elbow and leading me away. 'Big boys don't cry.'

And he handed me a paper napkin decorated with Mickey Mice.

Violet and I kissed.

'Bless you both,' said the Contortionist, her arm around the Gentleman Monkey. 'You must take love where you can find it, and enjoy it while you can. I did, and I've no regrets.'

'May I present my mother?' I said to Violet. 'And' – I hesitated to call her this, but she had no other name that I knew of – 'Mother – Mother – this is Miss Scrapie.'

'Pleased, I'm sure,' said the Contortionist.

'Delighted to make your acquaintance, madam,' said Violet, curtseying prettily.

'I can see you're a fine young woman,' said my mother. 'My son's in good hands. You take good care of him, Miss Scrapie. I can see you love him, and that he loves you.' Violet and I glanced surreptitiously at one another and blushed deeply. 'But I must leave you now,' she continued, hitching up her tutu and adjusting her little stockings. 'I've got my scorpion act to do before they dance the polka.' And she was gone.

328

After a short silence, during which neither of us knew where to look, Violet cleared her throat. 'They're searching for you,' she whispered. 'We don't have much time. We must escape.'

I was puzzled. 'Who is searching? Why?'

She did not answer my question immediately. Instead she looked me in the face and said slowly and delicately, 'Mr Phelps, I am – *aware* – of your true origins.'

Oh God. My heart plummeted to the floor, and Mildred twisted within me.

'And?' I was quivering. 'Do you –?'

'Of course!' She cried. 'I love you all the more!'

I flung my arms about her marvellous bulk, and held her tight, and for a moment our two hearts seemed to beat as one. Then I noticed she was crying.

'I, too, have a confession to make, Tobias,' Violet sniffed. She looked into my face. 'I – ate your father's flesh.'

I felt myself going pale, and swallowed hard. Then I remembered. Something Scrapie had mentioned. 'Was that – *Cuisine Zoologique?*'

'Yes. I didn't know, Tobias!' she sobbed. 'I had no idea who he was!'

'Of course not,' I soothed her.

'It poisoned my mother,' she was saying. 'And Father and I were both nearly killed, too. His flesh contained –'

'Praxin,' I finished. 'Yes, I know. Trapp injected him when he and my mother attempted to escape from the *Ark*.'

'Can you forgive me?' she begged, clutching at my hands.

'Of course!' I assured her, clasping her hands in mine. 'You were an innocent!'

We kissed.

'Whatever I have learned here in London, Violet, in my heart, I am a man,' I whispered. 'I was born a half-breed, and I do not deny it. In fact I can say now, after all that I have learned tonight, that I am proud of my uniqueness. But monkey though I am, I was raised to be a man, Violet, and above all else, I should like one day to prove it to you.'

Violet blushed, and whispered, 'My monkey-man, Tobias! I love you no matter what!'

Outside, a single silver firework exploded.

A burst of music awakened us from the tender reverie that followed.

'We must go,' Violet said, glancing nervously about her.

'Why?'

'My father,' she said.

'What about him?'

She said bleakly, 'He plans to stuff you.'

A cold wave of nausea rushed through me. I also felt instantly foolish for not suspecting. But proud, too; Parson Phelps had always told me to think the best of people. Those measurements – of course!

Only men have rights.

'Quick!' said Violet, blowing her nose and getting creakingly to her feet. 'We must leave this place!'

Peering out from behind the door of the ladies' powder room, we saw a curious procession of ladies and gentlemen gyrating around the ballroom, in the wake of Charles Darwin and Dr Ivanhoe Scrapie.

'Find the Phelps creature!' Scrapie was yelling. 'Grab him, quick, and pin him to the floor!'

'AAAGH!' yell the twins in unison. The last bottle of Perrier slithers from Oscar Jack's hand and smashes. Abbie screams. Rose and Blanche lie prone on the emperor-sized bed, their four legs aloft.

It's real!

'Push!'

'I can see the crowns!' yells Abbie. 'Push again!'

'AAGH!' yells Rose.

'OUCH!' shrieks Blanche.

'YEEEEH!' they scream together. And one, two, out they come.

'My God!' breathes Oscar Jack. Although he has been moved to tears by the historic event he is witnessing – none other than the rebirth of *Homo Britannicus* – he has nevertheless maintained enough of his cool professionalism to check that the Camcorder is still running. For which footage he will surely clock up a Bafta nomination in days to come.

But what's going on now? Why are Rose and Blanche still screaming?

'AAAGH!'

Screams that are fierce enough to drown out the lusty cries of the two babies flailing about unheeded on the bed.

'Push again!' yells Abbie.

Three! No! My God! Four!

Two sets of twins!

'Hey!' murmurs a panting Rose, staring down at the writhing beasts. 'A whole litter!'

'We did it!' groans Blanche, choking and laughing at the same time.

Together, the four adults peer at the four babies.

'Look!' gasps Abbie. 'I can't believe it!'

They look. There are the family feet – more like hands, really. The deep, close-set eyes. The copious down of red hair.

But – down there – my GOD!

'Do you see what I see?' falters Abbie. They stare. Exchange glances. And stare again. Yes. They do.

'Throwbacks, surely,' murmurs Oscar Jack.

Violet lunged behind a pillar, and dragged me with her in the direction of the Contortionist, who had emerged from the ladies' powder room to resume her duties as artiste. As my mother scaled the carcass of the elephant and stood on its still-steaming skull juggling peaches, it was easy enough to gain a moment's anonymity in which to return to the ladies' powder room and steal the gentleman monkey. A ghostly petticoated figure who had materialised at Violet's side ('My late mother,' she explained hurriedly) advised us to keep a cool head.

'Just brazen it out,' she advised, 'and they'll never notice. He just looks like a rather hirsute guest with bad dress sense who is a bit the worse for wear.' She had a point. 'Come on, Fatty,' commanded the phantom, giving Violet a shove. 'Get a move on.'

So Violet and I took one hairy arm apiece, and hauled my father, still attached to his wooden plinth, out of the ladies' powder room.

In the ballroom, the Contortionist was still giving the show her all. Letting out a high screech, she leaped around atop the head of the elephant, executed a sudden somersault in the air, and then proceeded to dance a wild and dangerous-looking jig in her little ballet shoes, pitter-patter, all the while maintaining her scream and hurling strawberries from a panier upon the heads of the throng below.

As far as distractions go, I had not seen better. With the room now raining strawberries, and the women beginning to scream as their ballgowns became increasingly spattered with red juice, as though a terrible bloodbath was occurring in their midst, we had enough cover to haul the Gentleman Monkey across the back of the crowd and through the door which Cabillaud held open for us, and to escape through the Palace kitchens.

'Zis way!' the chef yelled, indicating that we should follow him past the ranks of steaming pots and pans, and the flurries of chefs and the little clouds of icing sugar. Violet and I were both panting and dishevelled. I kept tripping on my over-long trousers, and Violet's hair had become unpinned and had tumbled across her face. Her meringue dress was clearly not designed as a garment in which to race, but somehow we managed to stagger to the back door of the kitchens, whence we escaped into the night.

'I wish you all ze best!' Cabillaud called after us, as we hailed a hansom cab and bundled the Gentleman Monkey inside with us. 'Do not forget zat you av ze blessing of Jacques-Yves Cabillaud!'

As the cab jerked into motion, I took Violet's hand in mine.

'If I am Adam,' I asked her, 'will you be my Eve?'

'Yes,' she breathed. 'Yes, my dearest Tobias! I will! I will! I will!'

Norman was still helping me blow my nose on the Mickey Mouse napkin when his mobile phone rang. He stuffed a finger in one ear and retreated to a corner.

'WHAT?' he shouted after listening for a minute. 'No! Say it again, clearly ... No. Abbie! You're kidding me! Abbie! Tell me you're bloody kidding me!' He began to jump about. Then he looked up in my direction, grinning his head off and signalling at the phone with his free hand. Finally he said, 'Right, I'm telling him now. Be over in a tic,' snapped the phone shut, and shoved it in his pocket.

'You'd better sit down a minute, mate,' he called across. His voice was breathless with emotional exertion. ''Cos you're about to receive the shock of your life.'

'I thought I just had,' I muttered. I didn't like the look of this. My priceless Gentleman Monkey had just gone up in smoke. Wasn't that enough for one evening? For a whole lifetime?

'What is it?' I asked, approaching him warily.

'Congratulations and celebrations!' yelled Norman. Then his face crumpled and he burst into tears. I handed him the Mickey Mouse napkin. Too much beer, I thought, as he grabbed me in a big bear-hug. That's his problem. 'I don't bloody believe it!' he whispered, and squeezed me tighter.

'Come on, Norman!' I muttered, trying to shake him off. But he was attached to me like a heavy rucksack. 'Are you going to tell me or not?'

'You're a father of four, mate! And I'm a bloody grandad! I kid you not!'

333

And with that he fell away from me, reeling with it.

I don't really know what I felt. Shock does the strangest things to a bloke. Look at me. I'm just standing there. Not moving. Covered in soot. My eyes are smarting. Must be from all the smoke. I'm rigid. Rooted to the spot, like I've been stuffed.

My head began to throb. The King was dead, I thought. Long live the –

The what?

'Come on!' I yelled at Norman. Swinging into action, I grabbed him by the scruff, dragged him out to the car-park, shoved him in the Nuance and drove home like a bat out of Hell.

'Bastard,' said the twins in unison, when they saw me. But their faces were flushed with joy.

'Come on, now, girls,' said Abbie. 'He is their father, after all. If it hadn't been for his, er – *input* –'

But I wasn't listening. I was looking at my babies. There they lay, on the bed, in four pillow-cases. I felt inexplicably humbled. And surprised. I hadn't seen a baby since the Millennium. But I didn't recall them looking anything like this.

'Strange but true,' murmured Norman.

And it was. Because the new *Homo Britannicus* did not take the form of four little Buck de Saviles, spiritual grand-children of Elvis Presley, as I might have wished. Nor, as one might have expected, did it take the form of four miniature Roseblanches.

I caught a sudden whiff of mothballs, and turned to see the sour-faced woman in petticoats I'd met once before. She smirked. 'Two miniature Violets, and two miniature Tobiases,' she pronounced. 'With more than a hint of towel-holder.'

'Champagne corks'll be popping tonight, eh, Buck?' said Norman, wiping away more tears and slapping Abbie triumphantly on the bottom.

'Ouch!' she squealed, and looked nervously across at a man

334

with a leather jacket and an earring, who was inexplicably filming the scene with the Camcorder.

'Time for a feed,' said Rose, lifting a baby out of its pillowcase and nestling it against her left breast. It found the nipple and began to suck.

'Come on then, coochie-coochie coo,' murmured Blanche, doing the same.

'Pass us another one, Mum,' said Rose.

'And me,' said Blanche.

'Four boobs, four babies,' they said together, and giggled.

Abbie obliged, and there they were, Rose and Blanche, on the emperor-sized bed, with the babies clamped to their breasts. I felt tears of joy streaming down my face as I watched my offspring clinging tightly to their mothers with their perfect little hand-like feet. And as they suckled, their four little tails, curled like question marks, twitched in happiness.

'This is the future,' said the ghostly voice of the Laudanum Empress. 'Do your best to deserve it.'

EPILOGUE

Violet and I went to Fishforth by steam train. Nobb-on-Humber, Fib's Wash, Coleman's Haunch, Maggsdale, South Brill: as I gazed through the glass at the landscape I was returning to, my heart swelled with joy. In Fishforth, Violet and I climbed the hill to the Sanatorium. Seagulls and cormorants swung through the sky and a fresh wind, a sea wind, blew about our ears.

The fortress of the Sanatorium loomed above us; we craned our necks. And there he was at the window of a high, lonely tower, staring out like the Lady of Shalott. It was as though he had been waiting there, all this time, for our arrival.

We waved frantically. Then he seemed to see us. And instantly vanished.

'I'm going up!' I called after him.

'Wait! I am sure he's coming down!' said Violet, and we rushed through the gate and up the spiral stairway. In my desperation to reach him, I quickly removed my shoes, and scrambled up the stairs on all fours, two and three and four at a time, to greet him.

'I am Darwin's paradox,' I called up to him, as I saw him descending the stairs.

And he smiled down at me.

'Or God's joke,' he croaked.

We met halfway. And there, on the landing, we came face to face. We stood there for a long time. His moon-face had thinned, and what remained of his hair was straggled and white.

336

'I was wrong,' he said.

But I said nothing. I was too choked to speak. Instead, I flung myself into his arms, and he held me tight.

'"No man is an island,"' he said finally. '"But a piece of the continent, a part of the main."'

He loved Violet instantly. Not least when I reported to him that it was thanks to her that I was free of Mildred.

'How?' he enquired, flabbergasted. 'Your mother did everything to rid you of that worm! Everything in her power!'

'Mildred never existed,' Violet announced. It was her discovery – one of which she was justly proud. When I had finally told her in detail of the bodily symptoms induced by my shameful inhabitant, her eyes had narrowed and she had looked at me assessingly.

'And how long is it since your tapeworm has bothered you?' she asked.

'Since I met you,' I told her, only realising it as I said it, 'she has left me, mercifully, in peace. Apart from at the Banquet, when I ate something that looked like –'

'Meat,' finished Violet. 'Or fish.' She laughed. 'Mildred will bother you no more,' she said with certainty. 'I have discovered that the Gentleman Monkey was a species that consumed nothing but fruit, vegetables and nuts. Anything else disagreed with him, and made his gut snarl up. You've inherited his alimentary system; that's my guess. You've been on the wrong diet all these years, Tobias.'

Could it really have been that simple?

Parson Phelps was much impressed by this news. 'If only dear Mrs Phelps could be alive to hear it!' he said, and wiped a tear from his eye, then put down the yellow jerkin he was knitting, and blessed us both on the spot.

We travelled home together, all three of us, by coach, with the bulky parcel that contained my natural father.

As we left the mainland shrubs of Judlow behind us and

caught our first glimpse of the herring-shaped peninsula that was my home, my heart soared.

'See, Violet, how it is in the shape of a fish?' I said. 'Its tail nailed to the mainland, and its head straining out to sea?'

'It is just as I imagined it,' she said, breathing in the salt air. And squeezed my hand.

The arid Gudderwort, hearing of our decision to return, had already left the Parsonage, grumpily, abandoning any show of Christian goodwill. I pushed open the oak door, still warped from the Flood, and stepped into our kitchen. The flag-stones still twinkled with salt. I was glad to see that some things did not change.

While Parson Phelps went to tend Mrs Phelps' grave, I unwrapped the Gentleman Monkey and dusted him down, while Violet ironed his shirt and pantaloons. Once we had stood him by the hearth, and I had polished his eyes, he looked well, I fancied, and in better spirits than before. Violet hung a tea-cloth in the crook of his arm. It gave him a homely look.

When Parson Phelps returned and saw him standing there, he was almost shy. He stood in the doorway with his hoe and trowel, blushing.

'Please, Father,' I said. 'Come and meet him. He will not bite you.'

Finally, tentatively, Parson Phelps stepped forward on the flag-stones, reached out, and took the Gentleman Monkey's hairy hand in his.

'I am pleased to meet you, sir,' he said formally. Then cleared his throat. 'I have spent many hours thinking about you, in the Sanatorium. And I can now declare that, although I maligned you in my heart, for which I beg your forgiveness, it is now a great honour to welcome you at last' – here he choked back tears – 'as a part of my family.'

Violet and I cheered.

As for Dr Ivanhoe Scrapie, he never recovered from the night of the Banquet. My disappearance, along with that of Violet

338

and the Gentleman Monkey – coupled with Scrapie's public humiliation at the hands of Mr Darwin – gave him an emotional shock so potent that he entered a brief phase of madness, followed swiftly by death. We read his obituary in the *Thunderer*. 'Scientist, craftsman, thinker, and immortaliser of beasts', the paper called him.

Three months later, some of his favourite works of taxidermy, accompanied by the petticoated ghost of the Laudanum Empress, arrived in a huge sealed wardrobe from London. Opening its creaking door, Violet and I found an ostrich in a nightdress; a kangaroo wearing pantaloons; a wombat in breeches, and various smaller mammals, in children's knickerbocker outfits. And the loyal corgi, Suet. He was the last animal Scrapie had stuffed, the Empress informed us as she dusted down her petticoats.

'How did he die?' wailed Violet.

'You killed him,' said the Laudanum Empress bluntly. 'With your silly vegetarian thing. He died on the night of the Banquet.'

Violet cried bitterly upon learning this. She needed no further prompting from her gruesome mother to blame herself for his death.

'Dog cannot live on veg alone,' she sobbed as she stroked Suet's stuffed and emaciated body, the husk of the dog that had been. A lesson had been learned.

'Rest in peace, dear Suet,' whispered Violet, kissing the corgi and returning him gently to the wardrobe.

The Empress snorted contemptuously, then began inspecting the kitchen. 'I recognise this house,' she said, peering into the gloom of the fireplace. 'It's the Old Parsonage in Thunder Spit, is it not? Look at the state of it!' she said, kicking a flag-stone with her lace-up boot, and dislodging a little puff of sea-salt. 'Believe me, in a hundred and fifty years you won't know it's the same place! There'll be a telephone over there, and these two walls will have been knocked through, and the TV room will be just –'

But Violet had taken hold of her mother's arm and was steering her firmly back in the direction of the wardrobe.

'And you can be laid to rest, too, now, Mother,' she declared, pushing her in and closing the doors firmly. 'Go and haunt someone else,' she said. And locked the door.

'All right, I will!' came the muffled voice of the phantom from within her mothbally prison. We never saw her again.

As Violet promised, the tapeworm Mildred has troubled me no more. While I have returned to the natural diet of my forefathers: fruit, vegetables, and the occasional insect, Violet's book, *The Fleshless Cook*, has been heralded by the Vegetarian Society and the *Times* newspaper as a masterpiece of its genre, and a worthy riposte to Cabillaud's *Cuisine Zoologique: une philosophie de la viande*, which proved to be a flash in the gastronomic pan.

'And I was so sure,' I told Violet, 'that my mother was trying to tell me something with those gourds on her grave!' I had told her about the foul purgative I had once made from them, to banish Mildred.

'Perhaps she *was* trying to tell you something,' murmured Violet. 'But not what you thought. Look.' She was pointing at a new fruit swelling at the base of a big yellow gourd flower. 'What colour did you say the first one was?'

'The one I planted when she was dying? Green. Green and sort of stippled.'

'Well, look at this.' I peered through the thick bristle-backed leaves and saw a small green fruit swelling.

'It's the same,' I said. Eight years and eight generations had passed.

'A throwback,' she murmured.

'Well, if it's a message, it's making no sense to me,' I confessed. 'Let us hope that the future may unravel its mystery.'

Parson Phelps went back to preaching, but it was a new message that he delivered from the pulpit.

'My son had a tapeworm called Mildred,' began his first sermon. 'We were convinced she existed, and did all we could to banish her. And then the day came when we discovered she was a mere chimera, and we were delighted, but there was sadness, too, because when you house a belief, a belief so real that it feels like a being, and you discover that it was a mere product of your own desires and thoughts, then there is loss.'

He looked about the congregation. They were hanging on his every word.

'God is like that tapeworm,' he said. Faces began to frown in puzzlement, and there was the sound of indrawn breath. 'An invisible presence, which we attribute to one thing. And then we discover He is the product of something else. Our hopes. Our fears. Our natural desire for order in the world. But I ask you this: Does the knowledge that He does not exist make Him any less necessary to our lives? Should we not be permitted to imagine Him? And for that figment of imagination to be so real that it becomes tantamount to fact? And then – simply – is?'

The congregation, intrigued by the parson's new-found understanding of the meaning of life, and relieved to be rid of the excruciating and po-faced Gudderwort, came flooding back, and in St Nicholas's Church, all the old familiar faces are there: the Morpitons, the Tobashes, the Peat-Hoves, the Barks, the Balls, the Harcourts. Parson Phelps' sermons are passionate in a way they never were before.

Now he visits the spiritually disturbed clergy of the Sanatorium in Fishforth once a week, and shares his new beliefs with them, bringing them succour in their distress. And every Sunday, St Nicholas's Church, which languished rudderless for so long, is full to bursting with worshippers who come from as far away as Hunchburgh just to hear him preach. In his sermons, Father doesn't mention God by name: just the wonder of things, and the glory. And as I sit in the front pew with Violet, her hand in mine, my mind wanders to the ocean, my old childhood toy-box full of miracles. The mackerel flashing and jumping in the sunlight; the herring gulls wheeling in the sky. And there I see a Nature that is neither good nor bad, but its own pure self.

Reader, I married her.

After the ceremony in St Nicholas's Church, which still bore the watermark from the Great Flood, I took Violet to the beach, and to my favourite rockpool, and there we lay on the barnacled rock and stared into the water. We saw baby quillsnappers, and anemones, and shrimps, and whelks. 'God's doodlings,' Parson Phelps used to call them. To think, that such humble creatures are our origins. And that with every tide, and every lapping of time's wave, everything changes, and our world wakes afresh, and all is new again. New and brave, and peopled with miracles.

Miracles. We had never imagined that we could produce offspring of our own, after what Dr Scrapie had said about the nature of the hybrid, but in this, as in many things, he was wrong. I am delighted to report that a happy event is on the horizon. Violet is now in what is termed a delicate condition.

'I feel that it will be a girl,' she said smilingly, as she told me the news. 'We will have a daughter, Tobias.' And I thought of little Tillie and felt glad.

So in our attic bedroom, Violet and I lie together on the big wrought-iron bed, and await the evolution of events.

On the mantelpiece sit the eight generations of gourd, and my whelk shell, and my fossil, and my fish-knife, and the jar that still contains my amputated tail. Above us, on the wall, hangs the picture of Noah's Ark: God above, in a silver Heaven, with His great beard dissolving into the clouds of the flood-waters. Noah and his family on the deck. The beasts below, from mighty elephant down to humble ant.

And I think: We will call our daughter Tillie, and I will tell her the story of the *Ark*. But it will be a different story from the one Parson Phelps told me when I looked at this picture as a boy.

342

The story I will tell my daughter begins with the ocean. Huge. Ink-dark beneath a black sky. And a vessel, bobbing on the waters. A toy of wood and string.

But in this story, the *Ark* has no cages and no captain.

And there is land on the horizon. Look. A vast, bare continent, beneath a rainbow.

'That continent is the future, Tillie,' I will tell her. 'It is waiting for us. We are its creatures.'

And a boundless hope floods my heart.

ACKNOWLEDGEMENTS

While writing this novel, I drew great inspiration from Edmund Gosse's *Father and Son*, and Keith Thomas's *Man and the Natural World*. I am also grateful to Nick Baker, Viv Black, Chris Brandon-Jones, Valerie Jensen, Martin Lloyd-Elliott and Nick Royle for reading and commenting on the manuscript at different stages. But my deepest thanks go to my friend Polly Coles and my partner Michel Coleman, who have been supportive and generous beyond words.